33204

Critical acclaim for the n

D0196453

TRAN

"Displays McIntyre at he~

—*Library ~~~~~~~*

"*Transition* is a must for those who enjoy scientific extrapolation and interesting people."

—*Locus*

"A fine novel of adventure."

—Greg Bear

METAPHASE

"With this third novel, *Starfarers* clearly becomes the most important series in science fiction . . . the most exciting and satisfying science fiction I have read this year."

—*Ursula K. Le Guin*

DREAMSNAKE

"[*Dreamsnake*] is filled with scenes as suspenseful as anyone could wish . . . but most of all it addresses the humanity of all of us."

—*The Seattle Times*

"[*Dreamsnake*] is an exciting future-dream with real characters, a believable mythos and, what's more important, an excellent, readable story."

—Frank Herbert, author of the *Dune* series

Agora Books
228 - 7 Avenue S.W., Calgary, Alberta, Canada T2P 0W8
403-234-1449

Bantam Books by
Vonda N. McIntyre

The Starfarers Series

STARFARERS
TRANSITION
METAPHASE
NAUTILUS

DREAMSNAKE

And coming in November in hardcover

STAR WARS®: THE CRYSTAL STAR

METAPHASE

Vonda N.
McIntyre

 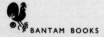 BANTAM BOOKS
NEW YORK TORONTO LONDON SYDNEY AUCKLAND

METAPHASE

A Bantam Spectra Book / September 1992
Bantam reissue edition / October 1994

SPECTRA and the portrayal of a boxed "s" are trademarks of Bantam
Books, a division of Bantam Doubleday Dell Publishing Group, Inc.

All rights reserved.
Copyright © 1992 by Vonda N. McIntyre.
Cover art copyright © 1992 by Michael Herring.
No part of this book may be reproduced or transmitted in any form or by any
means, electronic or mechanical, including photocopying, recording, or by
any information storage and retrieval system, without permission in writing
from the publisher. For information address: Bantam Books.

If you purchased this book without a cover you should be aware that this
book is stolen property. It was reported as "unsold and destroyed" to
the publisher, and neither the author nor the publisher has received any
payment for this "stripped book."

ISBN 0-553-29223-4

Published simultaneously in the United States and Canada

Bantam Books are published by Bantam Books, a division of Bantam Double-
day Dell Publishing Group, Inc. Its trademark, consisting of the words
"Bantam Books" and the portrayal of a rooster, is Registered in U.S. Patent
and Trademark Office and in other countries. Marca Registrada. Bantam
Books, 1540 Broadway, New York, NY 10036.

PRINTED IN THE UNITED STATES OF AMERICA

OPM   0 9 8 7 6 5 4 3 2

DEDICATION

To the folks in the Wallingford-Wilmot Library and the Fremont Library who let me move in on them, laptop computer and all, fleeing the marsians who decided that right next to my office was a good place to build ufo hangars.

For ten months.

ACKNOWLEDGMENTS

MANY THANKS,

To the people who helped me get *Starfarer* right: Kristi
N. Austin, John H. Chalmers, John Cramer, Howard L.
Davidson, Jane E. Hawkins, Marilyn J. Holt, Nancy
Horn, Ursula K. Le Guin, Debbie Notkin, Paul Preuss,
Kate Schaefer, Carol Severance, and Jon Singer;

To Gerard K. O'Neill and the Space Studies Institute for
the work on which the campus is based;

AND, OF COURSE,

To the Starfarers Fan Club.

PARTICULAR THANKS,

To Teresa Meikle and Charles E. Griswold, whose
Natural History article on *Stegodyphus* spawned (as it
were) the squidmoths.

—VNM

METAPHASE

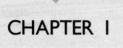

CHAPTER 1

J.D. SAUVAGE, THE ALIEN CONTACT SPECIAL-
ist, picked her way across the rough surface of a rocky planetoid.

A gossamer thread, shining blue-
white in the actinic glare of the star Sirius, stretched across the stone beneath
her feet. She followed it. A coarser line,
her lifeline, unreeled behind her.

The planetoid was more or less
spherical, so small that its pitted and
scarred surface curved sharply away to
nearby horizons. At first glance, it
looked like a barren, airless asteroid,
weathered by primordial meteors; after
a first glance, it would be easily over-

looked. J.D. and her colleagues in the alien contact department almost *had* overlooked it.

The silken strand thickened, branched, and intertwined, gradually forming a lacy gauze. Not wanting to damage the fabric, J.D. followed it without stepping on it, as if she were walking beside a stream. This stream flowed upward, climbing a steep escarpment. J.D. climbed with it, moving easily.

The low gravity was far higher than a natural rock this size would create. The least of the small world's anomalies, the gravity hinted at a complex interior, perhaps even a core of matter collapsed to neutronium.

The planetoid repaid a second glance. Great masses of webbing filled a dozen of its largest craters. J.D. was walking on an extraordinary asteroid. The worldlet was the starship of alien beings.

Iridescent fibers wove together, forming a solid ribbon that led through a cleft in the escarpment. J.D. stepped cautiously onto the fabric. It gave slightly, a springy carpet over solid rock.

The band of silk guided her to the edge of one of the web-filled craters. Somewhere within it, the alien beings waited.

The message from the squidmoths had been brief and direct.

"You will be welcomed."

J.D. scrambled up the last steep slope to the edge of the crater. Her destination lay below.

The silken pathway blended into a convoluted surface, filling the wide, deep crater. Valleys and ridges rumpled the webbing, and half a dozen trails twisted into it from where she stood. To proceed, she would have to walk off the edge of the crater and let the web alone support her weight.

She hesitated, listening and hoping for another message from the squidmoths.

"I'm here," she said softly. Her spacesuit radio transmitted her voice.

In the silence, waiting for a reply, she knelt down and slid her hand across the smooth webbing. The faint *shussh* of her touch transmitted itself through her glove. She wished she could feel the silk with bare fingers, but the atmosphere was far too thin for her to remove her suit.

A single filament, darker silver than the rest, crossed the surface and disappeared along one of the trails.

J.D. rose, lifting the thread, holding it carefully across her palm. Starlight spun along its length.

She slid one foot gingerly forward. The floor yielded, then tightened, bouncing gently in the low gravity. She felt like a skater crossing ice so thin it flexed beneath her. She feared her touch would rip the silk; she feared a dark tear would open beneath her, and she would fall fifty meters to the bottom.

Most of all, she feared that her presence would cause the structure to self-destruct. She had watched Tau Ceti's alien museum destroy itself rather than admit human beings. Rather than admit her.

But the squidmoths had invited her. The thread in her hand acknowledged her existence.

J.D. moved farther onto the silk, following the thread into the labyrinth. Her boots left no marks.

The path dipped into a meandering valley. J.D. descended through a cleft of delicate cascades. The fluttery fabric responded to her footsteps, trembling, vibrating. The cascades closed together overhead, and she found herself walking upon one horizontal sheet, and beneath another, past and through translucent tissue-thin layers like huge fallen parachutes that filtered harsh starlight. The membranes formed tunnels and chambers; cables and strands connected the membranes. The sheets rippled silently as she passed.

If a suspension bridge and a Gothic cathedral had interbred, this construction might be their offspring.

Without the filament, she would have no idea which way to go. If it broke, only her lifeline would lead her out.

Silvery-gray illumination surrounded her, suffusing the space with a luminous glow. The spun silk carried the light within its strands.

Deep within the crater, she paused at the top of a slope that plunged into light. Afraid she would slip, fall, and slide sprawling to—wherever the hillside led—she wrapped her fingers around a supporting strand and tested its strength. It gave, then contracted, as if to embrace her hand. Like the floor, the fiber was elastic and strong. She reached for another strand, an arm's length farther on, and ventured deeper into the web.

"No more communication yet," J.D. said, though her colleagues in the alien contact department and everyone back on board *Starfarer* could see and hear all that she was witness to.

Don't say things just because you're nervous, she told herself firmly. You're supposed to be the professional, bravely facing the unknown.

Some professional: you've only been certain for a week that your profession really exists.

She did not feel brave. Being watched and recorded only made it worse.

J.D. concentrated on climbing down the smooth silken slope. Even in the low gravity, it was painstaking work. Her metabolic enhancer kicked in, flooding her body with extra adrenaline and inducing extra adenosine triphosphate. Not for the first time since the expedition started, she was glad she had decided to maintain the artificial gland. When she left the divers and the orcas, the long days of swimming naked in cold salt water, she had assumed she would not need to enhance her metabolism anymore.

Thirty meters down, the slope curved to a nearly horizontal level and she could again walk upright on its springy inner surface. Sweat beaded on her forehead. The spacesuit's systems evaporated the sweat away.

Within the webbing, thick silk strands glowed brightly, filling the corridor with a soft pink light that imitated some other star than Sirius. J.D. knew, by inference, that the squidmoths had not evolved beneath this star. Other than that, she knew very little about them. They were intelligent beings, reticent. They drifted through the galaxy in their small massive starships, ignored and apparently despised by the interstellar civilization.

Maybe they're outcasts, just like us, J.D. thought.

The squidmoths had, at least, invited humans to visit them. The rest of interstellar civilization had ordered *Starfarer* to return to Earth, so human beings could spend the next five hundred years growing up.

This they had declined to do. In response, in retaliation, the cosmic string by which *Starfarer* traveled had begun to withdraw. If *Starfarer* stayed in any one place too long, it would be stranded there forever.

The passage curved and branched. The guide thread passed into the central tube. J.D. followed it. Behind her, her safety line snaked along the floor and pressed against the convex wall. The line creased the silk, an anomalous, coarse dark strand.

J.D. thought she saw the guide thread move. She hurried forward, but the tunnel's curve straightened and she saw nothing but the guide thread lying motionless on the floor, disappearing into the tunnel's next descent.

But her spacesuit replayed for her what she had seen. The thread *had* moved.

She stopped and leaned sideways, pressing her helmet against the tunnel wall. Could she hear a faint scuffling, or was it her imagination? Replayed and amplified, the phantom sound vanished into background noise.

Increasing her pace, she tried to catch up to whatever was laying the guide thread. But the delicate strand grew even thinner, dangerously thin, as if it were being stretched as it was created. J.D. slowed down, afraid she would cause the thread to break.

She rounded a curve and confronted a complete constriction of the passageway. She stopped. The end of the guide thread lay in a tangle at her feet.

"Damn," J.D. muttered.

She asked for a visual display of the radar traces of the tunnels around her. Her suit obeyed. Up until a few minutes ago, this tunnel had continued, leading deeper into the web.

"Victoria?" J.D. said.

"I'm here." Victoria spoke softly into her ear through her suit radio. "Shall I follow you in?" Victoria was J.D.'s backup; she waited outside the *Chi*, the explorer spacecraft, at the home end of J.D.'s lifeline.

"Not yet. There's no threat of danger." Disappointed and confused, J.D. smiled sadly. "Maybe I just misunderstood what I was supposed to do." Recently they had misunderstood, and been misunderstood, more often than not.

"J.D.!" Zev exclaimed.

The backward-watching recorder, a little tiny machine that clung between J.D.'s shoulder blades, flashed an image to the *Chi* and to J.D.'s display.

Zev whistled a sharp warning in true speech, the language of the orcas and the divers. The shrill sound raised the hair on the back of J.D.'s neck. She spun around.

The tunnel was slowly constricting. She took one step toward it.

Outside the translucent wall of the tunnel, creatures moved.

J.D. stopped, her heart pounding. She glanced at the LTM display in her helmet, but the recorders saw the creatures no more clearly than she did.

Around her, vague shapes made deliberate motions. Legs or feelers or tools pressed the tunnel inward, cinching it with a narrow band that grew progressively smaller.

The tunnel puckered, lifting her lifeline and the guide thread off the floor till they hung in the air, drooping from the closed sphincter.

"J.D., get out of there!" Victoria said.

She was trapped in a silken cocoon, a twist of the tunnel.

"No," she said. "Not yet. Victoria, Zev, I'm all right."

She was frightened, but she calmed herself and slowed her thudding heartbeat. The creatures that had immobilized her came no closer.

"I'm coming in after you," Victoria said.

"No. Stay there."

"But—"

J.D. pressed her hands against the wall. It yielded. Unlike the floor of the chambers higher up, it remained supple. The constricting band stretched. Thinking about what this must look like to all her colleagues, J.D. blushed and released the band. She dreaded hearing Stephen Thomas make one of his offhand, off-color remarks.

But when he remained silent, it troubled her even more. He had been silent a lot, since Feral's death.

"I think I could force my way out," J.D. said to Victoria. "In either direction. But I'm not quite ready to try. I don't think I'm in any danger—"

"You're in the middle of the world's biggest spiderweb, that's all! And the spiders are closing in!"

"I don't feel like a fly just yet. It wouldn't make sense. You'd get awfully hungry, orbiting Sirius and waiting for dinner to come along, what—? Once every million years?"

"Especially if you cultivated a reputation for not being interesting to visit," Satoshi said.

"Satoshi's right. And Europa said the—" It occurred to her suddenly that her hosts had not referred to themselves as "squidmoths." Europa, representing the interstellar civilization, had done so, but she had spoken of them with contempt. For all J.D. knew, "squidmoth" was civilization's version of an ethnic slur. She decided not to repeat it. "She said the beings here wouldn't talk to us—she didn't say they were dangerous."

"Quite true," Victoria said dryly. "But she was wrong about them talking to us, eh?"

"Um, yes." The alien human was wrong about a lot of things, J.D. thought, but she felt, stubbornly, that she should wait and see what happened.

"I don't want you to compromise your safety," Victoria said.

J.D. chuckled. "But Victoria . . . this is my job."

A hissing sound, a classic raspberry, interrupted her. At first she was embarrassed, then startled.

Oh, *no,* she thought. A leak in my suit—?

Instead of fading out, the noise of the raspberry increased.

The suit ought to seal—! J.D. thought.

"Behind you again," Victoria said again, more calmly this time.

More creatures surrounded the other end of the bubble where she was trapped. They loosened the constricting band. J.D. could not be sure, but she believed their shapes were different from the creatures who had trapped her. The sphincter had relaxed enough to let gas spurt into J.D.'s cocoon.

She giggled, involuntarily.

"What?" Victoria said.

"Nothing," J.D. said quickly. The first image to come to her mind was hardly something she wanted to admit to her colleagues, to the records *Starfarer*'s control computer was making, and by way of Arachne, to history. The image was far too undignified.

For once, Stephen Thomas was giving some thought to propriety, for he remained silent too.

J.D.'s giggling fit vanished.

"It's an airlock!" she said. "I'm in an airlock!"

"Could be . . ." Victoria said.

"It makes sense—Satoshi, you *said* this place must have a reservoir of oxygen and nitrogen. I just found the reservoir."

"The craters do show a lot of outgassing," Satoshi said. "Enough to give the asteroid a very thin atmosphere. Nothing like Europa's ship."

Europa's starship, similar in size and gravity to the starship of the squidmoths, had looked like a miniature Earth: land masses, surface water, a normal atmosphere, plants and animals and topography.

The tunnel before J.D. relaxed, opened, and smoothed. The forward constriction disappeared; beyond the translucent wall, the creatures receded and vanished. The constriction behind her remained tight.

J.D. waited, hoping the alien beings would communicate with her. Her suit radio received only silence.

But at her feet, a second guide thread took up where the first had ended. The second thread was darker and thicker, like a strand of glossy black hair.

J.D. followed the thread deeper into the tunnel.

The soft silk floor silenced J.D.'s footsteps, but she clapped her gloved hands together and heard the dull *thunk*. The spun walls absorbed and deadened the sound, but it *was* a sound. Earlier, she had been in vacuum; now she was in air. She linked briefly with one of the LTM transmissions and read the analysis: Majority gas nitrogen. Minority gas oxygen, a couple of percentage points higher than on Earth. Trace gases: carbon dioxide, ozone, hydrogen sulfide, a spectrum of hydrocarbons and fluorocarbons.

"If you took your helmet off, you could breathe," Victoria said. "Not that I'm suggesting it."

J.D. glanced over the trace gases again. "I wonder if all this stuff is meant to make me feel at home?"

The air on Europa's ship had been crystalline and pure. Earth, as Satoshi had said, before the Industrial Revolution. Earth, from the time of Europa's birth, nearly four millennia ago. Europa and Androgeos had been rescued from Knossos, after the eruption of Santorini on Thera. They had been saved to welcome human beings to the interstellar civilization.

Some welcome, J.D. thought.

The air in the squidmoths' ship was closer to the air of Earth in the present day, pollution and all.

Or maybe, she thought, the beings who live here just like it that way.

"I wouldn't want to strike a match here."

J.D. pressed further and deeper into the webbing. She wondered if the silk could burn. She hoped not. The high concentration of oxygen would feed a fire into a rage.

As far as she knew, nothing she carried with her could produce an open flame, or even a spark. She was glad the *Chi* had landed at a good distance. Suppose it had come too close, and the heat of its engines had set the complex structure on fire? That would have been worse than back in the Tau Ceti system, watching the alien museum collapse. Worse, because alien people lived here. A fire would kill intelligent creatures, the only members of interstellar civilization to welcome human beings.

J.D. continued onward. When the guide thread quivered, when she thought she heard the scrabble and scuffle of small feet on the silken floor, she forced herself to maintain her deliberate pace. Whatever or whoever she was following, she did not want to scare it again.

Why are the squidmoths taking the risk of welcoming us? J.D. asked herself. We're outcasts, and our invitation to interstellar space has been withdrawn. Europa fled so she and Androgeos wouldn't be cut off along with us. The same thing might happen to the squidmoths.

Europa had spoken of the squidmoths with contempt and dismissal. Were they so isolated, so lonely, that they would take such a risk just to talk?

The light grew brighter, and the tunnel surface more convoluted, with strands and sheets of silk stretching and overlapping in all directions.

The tunnel abruptly ended, several meters up the side of a huge chamber. J.D. stood at the top of the slope, gazing out at a visual cacophony of glowing lines and overlapping, curving, rippled membranes. She felt as if she had walked into a sculpture made of light.

The light-bearing cables focused here. The silk carried the light of Sirius from the surface of the planetoid to the center of the web, softening its harshness while its brilliance remained, shedding a bit of its energy burden on its way into the depths. J.D. had reached a focus of the illumination.

"This is amazing." Satoshi's voice was soft, but excited. He was a geographer: his work involved mathematical analyses of the interaction of people with the environments they created for themselves. J.D. suspected that Satoshi would be studying alien beings who created every detail of their surroundings.

The slope was steeper than the previous descents. J.D. climbed down the soft rumpled silk. The guide thread disappeared into the most concentrated light.

J.D. steadied herself, grasping a glowing, wrist-thick strand. Her suit registered warmth, but her glove protected her from the sensation. This was like swimming with the orcas in a wet suit: removed, alienated.

Interleaved silk curtains curved around the concentration of light. J.D. moved carefully between the soft, bright sheets of fabric, hoping she was not entering a maze. The mazes of Europa and Androgeos had been quite enough.

The guide thread led her in a switchback pattern of arcs: between two curtains, to the edge of one, around the edge, along the next closest arc to the center. The lifeline unreeled behind her, creasing the end of each successive curtain.

J.D. rounded a final curtain and stepped out into an irregular area formed by the overlapping draperies.

A tiny creature, trailing a glossy black thread, riffled across the floor and vanished beneath a sheer membrane. The membrane fluttered, then smoothed itself against a massive form.

J.D. saw the squidmoth.

"My god," Satoshi said, in amazement.

Victoria's response was feeling, rather than words: a deep, astonished joy flowed from Victoria, through Arachne, to touch J.D.'s internal link.

"J.D., it's wonderful!" Zev said.

Stephen Thomas said nothing.

Strangely enough, J.D. had no doubt that she had come into the presence of one of the intelligent beings who inhabited this starship. Back on Europa's ship, in familiar, Earthlike surroundings, J.D. had wondered if she should try to converse with everything: the ground cover that surrounded the landing platform, the aurochs that had chased her up a hillside, the meerkats who had watched her flee. When she finally encountered Europa and Androgeos, who were very nearly ordinary human beings, she was shocked beyond words.

"Hello," J.D. said to the squidmoth. She stopped, and waited.

The squidmoth said nothing.

It lay in the focus of the light-conducting curtains, bathed in a bright and gentle illumination. Light that would have driven off an ordinary ocean creature heightened the vivid peacock iridescence of its skin. And yet its shape did hint at an origin in the sea.

The alien's body was at least three meters long, and probably much bigger. It lay cushioned and cradled and partly concealed within and beneath the folded layers of silken web. Its glossy, leathery body flattened at each side into membraneous fins, where the guide-thread creature had vanished. The edges of the fins rippled gently, exposing feathery undersides and delicate jointed appendages. Vestigial legs? Gills, and legs that would be functional in very low gravity, or underwater? J.D. resisted making assumptions. The squidmoth did not look like it walked anywhere, ever, for its fluted lower body disappeared into the wrinkled floor. It looked like it had grown from the chamber, as if it were the intricate exposed root of some life form even larger and more complicated.

J.D. took a step toward it, cautious, moving slowly, keeping her hands in plain view.

She wondered if the being even understood hands. The squidmoth itself had tentacles, a number of short, thick ones and three long, slender ones. The long tentacles lay in a coiled and tangled mass before the being. A creature the size of J.D.'s hand scuttled down the curtain beside the squidmoth. Scaled skirts hid its legs; its carapace bore an explosion of feathery plates.

The end of one of the squidmoth's long tentacles writhed free, rising like a snake, probing the air. The tentacle caressed and guided the creature toward a large silken pouch that lay crumpled on the floor. Finally, the creature burrowed beneath the edge of the pouch, and inside.

"Thank you for the invitation to visit you," J.D. said.

The skin above the squidmoth's tentacles shifted and wrinkled. The leathery, peacock-blue skin split—J.D. started—and opened. A narrow flap of skin wrinkled upward, and the squidmoth gazed out at her through a row of glittery, faceted eyes. The wrinkled skin circled the bulge above the being's tentacles. J.D. tried not to assign familiar body parts to a creature built on a completely different body plan from any she was familiar with. For all she knew, she was approaching the being from behind, the tentacles were its feet, the vestigial, segmented legs were its hands, and the eyes sparkling at her from beneath the mobile brow were sensors of smell or hearing or some sense she did not even possess.

But she found it *very* hard not to think of the bulge as the squidmoth's head, the tentacles as its organs of manipulation.

Slow down, she told herself; she was giddy with joy and apprehension. Hold on. Remember how embarrassed you were, when you were a kid and you finally looked up horseshoe crabs in the field guide: the long pointy thing was the tail, not its sensors or its whiskers.

J.D. took another hesitant step toward the alien being.

"Hello," she said again.

A voice transmission whispered into J.D.'s suit radio.

"Do not fear me," said the same flat voice that had invited *Starfarer* to visit it.

"I don't," J.D. said. "Yes, I do. A little. Can you hear me?" She was broadcasting through her suit radio, but broadcasting might not be necessary if the squidmoth could hear her through her spacesuit.

Do squids have ears? she asked herself. She had no idea; even if they did, that would not mean the alien being followed any similar specifications.

"My vibratory sense responds to very low frequencies."

"Then you don't hear me—but you receive my radio transmissions."

"I receive your transmissions."

J.D. moved a few steps closer to the squidmoth, fascinated. She wanted to ask a hundred questions at once. Remembering how disinclined Europa and Androgeos had been to answer any questions at all, she decided to take things slowly.

She understood the "squid" part of the being's name, but not why Europa had called the being a squidmoth. Moth, because of its vestigial legs? Then why not form the second part of its name from some sea-living arthropod, a crab or a shrimp or a lobster?

The being's eyelid opened widest in the direction facing J.D. Beneath it, several small round faceted eyes peered steadily at her. More of its eyes—J.D. could not help but think of them as eyes—glittered through the half-closed edges of the eyelid. J.D. deliberately moved to the side as she approached the being. Instead of shifting its position, the squidmoth rippled its eyelid open farther toward the back of its head. It must have vision in a complete circle.

"How do you communicate with other sq—" J.D. caught herself in time—"with others of your kind?"

"I communicate with all intelligences as I communicate with you."

Its tentacles moved. The row of short tentacles quivered, and their tips oscillated in a wave that began at one side before it ended on the other, so that two different waves moved along its shorter proboscises. The squidmoth looked like it had a thick, rubbery mustache.

The tips of the three long tentacles rose like the heads of snakes. One moved absently to the pouch on the floor, guiding a small silk-spinning creature across its surface to lay new threads in a bright pattern.

J.D. was nearly ten meters from the squidmoth. Its tentacles shifted and untangled, coiled and writhed.

She thought she had stopped well out of its reach.

She was wrong.

The tentacles whipped toward her. J.D. gasped and jumped back, surprised and frightened. The tentacles stopped short. They were not yet fully extended; they could reach her. Trembling, J.D. forced herself to stand still.

A month ago, a week ago, she would have been surprised, but she would not have been scared. Meeting Europa and Androgeos had profoundly changed J.D.'s assumptions about what the citizens of an interstellar civilization would be like.

Did you expect them to be perfect? she asked herself, with a tinge of sarcasm. She answered her own question: Yes. I did.

She took a deep breath and moved a step closer to the squidmoth.

"I'm sorry," she said. "You frightened me."

The ends of the tentacles rose, weaving like mesmerized cobras. J.D. held her ground. The tentacles bore no obvious sensory organs: no eyes or orifices, no hands or fingers. Instead, the tips looked soft, furry, feathery, cloaked in a corona of iridescent purple fur.

Sensory cilia? J.D. wondered.

"I frightened you by moving toward you."

The squidmoth's voice remained flat, expressionless, and uninflected.

"You frightened me by moving without warning me," she said, treating its statement as a question. "You frightened me by coming so close, so fast."

The tentacles drew back.

Great, J.D. thought. Now I've offended it.

"You prefer more distance."

"I prefer more warning. What do your tentacles do?"

"They touch."

"My hands do that for me." She extended her arms, spreading her gloved fingers.

"I know that."

"Do you know everything about us?" She could not help but think, What's the point of my coming here, what's the point of the deep space expedition, if Civilization already knows more than they ever wanted to know about us?

J.D. had spent her adult life preparing to be the first human to meet aliens. But she was not the first. Europa and Androgeos had preceded her, by thirty-seven hundred years, and that distressed her more than she wanted to admit.

"No, but I want to," the squidmoth said.

J.D. smiled. She still had some knowledge to offer the alien being.

"We're even, then."

"You want to know everything about you."

"That, too. But I meant I'd like to know everything about you."

She hesitated, wondering how forthright she could be in what she said. In all the years she had thought about making contact with an alien intelligence, she had never thought that the first time she stepped into a room with it, it would be able to converse in English. Back on board *Starfarer,* J.D. kept programs and diagrams, introductions to humans based on physics, on math, on biology, on art. She had thought about communicating with a being that conversed by color, by smell. Her colleagues had done similar work, even before she joined the department a few weeks back, experimenting and speculating on the difficulties of communication. Some people believed alien beings would be so different from humans that they would never be able to communicate at all.

She could speak with the being, but she might not always understand it. They could easily misinterpret each other.

"Androgeos said you were . . . reclusive."

"Androgeos never visited me," the squidmoth said.

Lacking the clue of voice inflection, J.D. could not tell whether the squidmoth spoke with regret, with relief, or to offer a neutral point of information.

J.D. felt very calm. Her rush of fear had subsided, leaving enough adrenaline behind to make her hyperaware, sensitive, as if all her nerves extended beyond her skin.

"I'm very grateful for your invitation, and very glad

to visit you," J.D. said. "We haven't made proper introductions. My name is J.D. Sauvage."

"I have no verbal name," the squidmoth said.

"Call it Nemo!" Zev's voice whispered in her ear.

"Shh, Zev!" Victoria said.

"Tell me what that meant," the squidmoth said.

"One of my colleagues suggested that I give you—
that I offer you a name," J.D. said. "The name of a
famous fictional character."

"I will be Nemo," the squidmoth said.

"I'm glad to meet you, Nemo," J.D. said. "May I
come closer?"

In response, the squidmoth drew its long tentacles
toward itself. They twisted and tangled, their tips coming together and parting. J.D. followed, till she was
barely two strides away. Even this close, she could see
no reason for comparing the alien being to a moth. Up
close, it did not look all that much like a squid.

It was exquisitely, strangely beautiful. Bits of every
iridescent color flecked its peacock skin. Its slender
jointed legs splayed out into tiny pointed feet, alter-
nately concealed and exposed by the rippling gills.

For all her resolution, J.D. had begun to analyze the
being in familiar terms.

"I would like to touch you," the squidmoth said. Its
long tentacles, untangling themselves smoothly, coiled
before it, their tips waving as if in a gentle breeze. Its
mustache of short proboscises continued to ripple.

Again, J.D. hesitated, and she realized just how
deeply the alien humans' duplicity had changed her.

Dammit, she said to herself, you may not be able to
trust everybody out here completely; you may not be
able to be as open as you'd hoped. But you *cannot* be
afraid all the time.

"Very well," she said coolly.

The being extended one long tentacle toward her.
The tip hesitated at her foot, then curved over her toes
and down around her instep, meeting the floor where
her boot sank into the thick soft silk. A second tentacle
moved toward her, arching up till it reached the level of

her face. The fine hair of the tip brushed her helmet, with a sound as soft as dust.

"This is not your body."

"It's my space suit," J.D. said. "It carries my air."

"You may breathe this air."

"I know. But the suit also protects me from unfamiliar infections—and protects you from contamination."

"Nothing here will infect you."

"Androgeos said the same thing—but he wouldn't tell me how he was so sure. You'll forgive my fears, I hope. I trusted Androgeos, but my encounter with him was . . . unfortunate, in many ways." Androgeos had tried to steal Victoria's new work on cosmic string. He had tried to take away all Earth had to offer to claim respect within the interstellar community.

"Androgeos is young, and zealous."

"Young! He's thirty-seven hundred years old!"

The squidmoth's tentacle brushed back and forth across J.D.'s faceplate. The pattern of the rippling of its proboscises had changed: from a single wave-form, moving regularly across its mustache, to a double pattern, two waves starting one at each side, clashing in the middle, adding to each other, canceling.

Could I have perturbed it? J.D. wondered. But the question of contamination must be the first one everybody wants the answer to, and the first question these people must have solved. They've been interacting with each other for millennia.

Maybe I made it mad because I don't want to put my life completely in its hands.

"Androgeos is young," the squidmoth said again.

J.D. wondered if she heard a tinge of amusement or irony in its voice. Surely not; it was her imagination.

Strangely enough, Androgeos *had* struck her as young. He was physically young, while Europa had chosen a more mature physical presence.

"Androgeos *acts* young sometimes," J.D. said.

"We have nothing to fear from each other's symbiotic microbes," the squidmoth said, and waited.

J.D. hesitated. The potential danger was very low.

She and Nemo were products of completely different evolutionary backgrounds. It would make more sense to worry about catching Dutch Elm disease from a tree.

J.D. reached for the seal on her helmet.

"J.D.—" Victoria said, and then fell silent.

J.D. had walked out onto Europa's planetoid, unprotected. She had hesitated then, too, but she had made the decision to trust the alien humans. In several respects, Europa and Androgeos were not trustworthy at all. But when they assured J.D. she was in no danger of catching, or transmitting, a human or environmental pathogen, they had told her the truth. They had probably eliminated every disease in their environment; they were probably in more danger from *Starfarer* than *Starfarer* was from them. And all Stephen Thomas's tests had come out negative.

It would make no sense at all, besides, to throw Earth a lifeline in the form of cosmic string, and then wage biological war on whoever responded. The interstellar community had been keeping an eye on the solar system for generations; if they had wanted to eliminate humanity they could have done it long since, easily, without ever being detected.

The only difference between walking unprotected onto Europa's planetoid and taking off her spacesuit in the squidmoth's presence was that here, her surroundings were strange, and there, they had been familiar. And, perhaps, that then she had not known what her hosts would look like, and now, she was in the presence of a supremely alien being.

Her only reason to refuse was fear: xenophobia.

Recognizing such a reaction troubled J.D. deeply.

Too many bad alien-invasion movies, she said to herself, and then, Bad joke.

She unfastened her helmet. She took it off.

She drew a deep breath.

J.D. started to cough. The air was pungent, musty, reeking of hydrocarbons. It stung her eyes. She breathed shallowly, tempted to seal herself back up with her own clean air supply. The high oxygen content of Nemo's atmosphere made her giddy.

Once she got used to it, it was about the same as back home in one of the more polluted regions. Spending so much time in the wilderness had spoiled her and weakened her resistance to fouled air.

J.D. unfastened her suit and climbed out of it. She put it carefully on the floor. The LTMs clambered around so they could still see and record her actions. She hoped their resolution was insufficient to capture the trembling of her hands.

Nemo's voice, tinny and indistinct, droned from the helmet. In order to converse, J.D. would either have to wear the helmet without the suit, which struck her as ridiculous, or communicate with Nemo through her direct link. Ordinarily she used the direct link only to communicate with Arachne.

J.D. reached out, cautiously, tentatively, into her link. She could talk with her colleagues via the direct electronic transmission, if she wished, but she usually did not do so. Like many people, she found it discomforting. She did not like the sensation of other people's voices in her head. It took a considerable effort of will to overcome her reluctance and speak directly to Nemo.

"Can you hear me?" she asked.

"I can hear you." Nemo's voice whispered in her mind.

The tentacles of the squidmoth hovered nearby, raising and lowering themselves from the silken floor, twisting and turning as they waited. J.D. faced the squidmoth, moved a step closer, and held out one hand.

The tentacle brushed her palm lightly with its tip. The sensory hairs, soft as fur, quivered against her skin.

J.D. closed her hand gently around the tip of the tentacle. Its motion stilled. Nemo waited, saying nothing. She opened her hand.

The tentacle moved up her arm, curling around her wrist like a snake. Its skin, beyond the fur, felt like suede. Its warmth surprised her. The squidmoth must have a body temperature well above hers, if its appendages felt so warm to the touch. She had unconsciously expected the slick wet coldness of a real squid, the sharp pull of predatory suckers.

Nemo touched her sleeve, exploring it, probing beneath the cuff.

"This is clothing," J.D. said, touching her shirt, her pants. "It's the custom of human beings to wear it most of the time."

Maybe I should strip down, J.D. thought, but I'm not quite ready for that yet.

Nemo touched her palm, her sleeve, her palm again, testing the differences between skin and fabric.

The tip of one tentacle brushed her throat, her lips. She closed her eyes. Fur caressed her eyelids. A second tentacle curled around her waist, gently embracing her. The tip probed at her, tracing the texture of her shirt, touching each button, following the curve of her heavy breasts and coiling softly down her arm. The third tentacle wound around her leg, then its tip traveled up her spine, touching the bump of each vertebra through her shirt.

She opened her eyes. Her lashes brushed against the sensory cilia.

"You detect sensations with these hairs," Nemo said.

"No." She smiled. The squidmoth was trying to make the same kinds of assumptions about her that she was making about it. "That is, I can feel your tentacle, but my eyelashes are for protecting my eyes. Um—do you call this a tentacle?" She brushed her fingers across the soft peacock skin.

"In English, I call it a tentacle."

This time J.D. thought she heard a flash of humor in Nemo's voice. Again, she told herself she must be imagining it.

"I meant, is 'tentacle' an accurate translation of what you call it in your language? What *do* you call it in your language?"

"I have no language."

"I don't understand," J.D. said.

"Our communication does not consist of sounds."

"I know, you told me: you use transmissions. But what do you transmit? Words? Visual images? Sensations?"

"A surface of meaning and perception."

J.D. frowned. "A neural visual image?"

"Position, and change of position, within a multidimensional surface of meaning, intensity, rapport between the speakers."

"Multidimensional? More than three dimensions?"

"Many more."

J.D. tried to imagine a more-than-three-dimensional surface; she tried to imagine being shown a more-than-three-dimensional surface in her mind. An acquaintance of hers claimed to be able to imagine rotating a sphere around a plane, but she had never been able to explain to J.D. how to do it.

"It sounds beautiful," J.D. said.

The squidmoth tentacles twined and curled before her; their tips touched her cheek, her breast, her hand.

"It is beautiful," it said.

"Do you have art forms associated with your communication? The way humans have singing and stories and poetry?"

"It is an art form in itself, whenever a talented one extends the limits and forms new regions and new shapes."

"May I . . . Will you show it to me?"

Without warning, a flash of perception tantalized her brain. She heard sugar dissolving, smelled the pink clouds of a brilliant sunset, sensed the position of a billion raindrops like muscle fibers. She saw a melody of Nemo's vision. Each sensation had its own particular place, its own connections with all the others. More information poured into her. But her internal link acted like the narrow end of a funnel. Nemo's transmission filled the funnel to the brim, and spilled out into nothingness.

J.D. gasped acrid air. She sneezed, and began to cough. Nemo's transmission faded away, and J.D. found herself sitting sprawled on the floor. She buried her nose in the crook of her elbow, breathing through the fabric of her shirt, forcing herself to take shallow breaths, until her coughing stopped. She wiped her teary eyes.

Nemo lay placidly before her, short tentacles ruffling slightly, long tentacles guiding a frilled, wormy little creature as it spun silver thread in concentric circles.

The radio in her helmet rumbled with a faint hollow sound. J.D. sent an "I'm okay" message back to Victoria and the *Chi.* The rumbling ceased. J.D. pulled herself together and sat crosslegged near Nemo.

"I didn't understand what you sent me," J.D. said to Nemo. "But you're right, it *was* beautiful."

"You cannot absorb enough information to gather the complete communication surface," Nemo said.

"Internal links aren't one of our natural senses," J.D. said sadly. "They're pretty limited."

"It is too bad," Nemo said.

"But any of us can use them to talk to you," J.D. said quickly. "And my colleagues would like to meet you. Would that be possible?"

"I want to become acquainted with one human being, first," Nemo said. "I want my attendants to become familiar with you."

"Your . . . attendants?"

Nemo's fragile legs drummed on the floor. J.D. felt the vibration, and heard a faint thrumming.

She heard the same sound she had heard farther out in the webbing, tiny feet scratching against soft silk. Several small creatures scuttled from beneath the curtains, moving on many legs, and another slithered down a steep slope. They gathered around Nemo, crawling up the iridescent skin. Their dull colors changed and brightened. Like chameleons, they blended into their background. If she watched carefully she could make out their shapes, malleable and indistinct, reaching out with long pincered fingers to groom Nemo's skin. One clambered up the feathery gill-leg, and vanished beneath the fluted fin.

"The attendants are not used to the presence of other beings."

"Oh," J.D. said. She did her best to be diplomatic. "How long will it take?" She wondered if she would get a useful answer; she did not even know if Nemo reckoned time in long spans, or short ones.

"I don't know, I've never received a guest before," Nemo said.

"Never?"

"We're solitary beings," Nemo said.

"Does it—does it bother you to have me in your crater?"

"I enjoy unique experiences." Nemo guided the circling creature around the edge of the disk of silk.

"Would you like to visit *Starfarer?* I don't know if you're mobile or not—" And I have no idea what you might be sensitive about, either, she thought, doubting the brilliance of her spontaneous suggestion. I only know that human beings are most sensitive about what's hardest, or impossible, to change. "You—you or any of your people—would be welcome on board *Starfarer,* if you cared to visit."

The squidmoth's mustache ruffled, from left to right, then back again.

"You inhabit the inside of *Starfarer,"* Nemo said.

"Yes."

"I wouldn't fit inside *Starfarer,"* Nemo said.

"Oh." She glanced at Nemo's iridescent back, the tail section disappearing into the floor. "How much of you is out of sight?" Anything that could fit inside the crater would fit inside *Starfarer,* though the logistics could be difficult.

"You see all of me."

"I don't understand," J.D. said.

Nemo's long tentacles touched the silk, the walls.

"All you see is me," the squidmoth said.

"The whole crater?"

"Everything," Nemo said.

"The whole *ship?"*

"What you call the ship."

That stopped her. She wiped one more unexamined assumption away, embarrassed to have made it without even noticing, and revised her perception of the squidmoth. J.D. had assumed Nemo was her counterpart, the individual who volunteered, or was chosen, to meet an alien being. She had assumed each of the silky craters held a being like Nemo, each in its own web.

"You're all alone here?"

"I am myself," Nemo said without inflection.

Great question, J.D., she thought. What would *you* say if somebody asked if you were all alone in your own body? "No, I'm here with a bunch of white blood cells and a liver"? But—no wonder Europa and Androgeos said squidmoths were reclusive!

She looked around with an even finer appreciation of her environment and all the other species living here, helping to repair and remake the structure, adapted or co-opted to a perfect interaction. . . .

Were they symbionts, or did they correspond to blood cells, or organs? She was still trying to put names from her own frame of reference, from her own linear language, into a system that corresponded more closely to Nemo's multidimensional communication.

"Who do you communicate with?" she asked abruptly.

"I communicate with whoever speaks to me."

"I meant . . . if you're the only one of your people in the Sirius system, how do you communicate with others? We haven't found any way of sending electronic signals through transition. Can you—?"

She stopped her excited rush of questions and waited impatiently for Nemo's reply. She imagined the anticipation of her colleagues pressing against her link to Arachne.

If Nemo knew how to communicate through transition, the deep space expedition would be able to tell Earth that it had met alien beings. That could change everything.

If we could let them know back on Earth, J.D. thought, that an interstellar civilization really exists . . .

J.D. knew it was Utopian to believe human beings would come to their senses, and end their interminable and dreadful power games, if they knew of a civilization beyond themselves. She knew it was Utopian . . . but she believed it anyway.

And if *Starfarer* could send back word that it had met other intelligences, the members of the expedition might be forgiven for taking *Starfarer* out of the solar system against EarthSpace orders.

If they could signal through transition, at the very least they could let their friends and relatives know they had survived the missile attack.

"I *am* mobile," Nemo said, "like all my people."

"Oh," J.D. said, as suddenly disappointed as she had been elated. "Then you can't signal through transition?"

"No."

"Can anyone?"

"No one I know of."

"You go visiting."

"I go visiting," Nemo agreed.

J.D. sighed. It had been a long shot. Cosmic string theory allowed only large masses to enter transition. No one—no one human—had figured how to chitchat across the transition threshold. Apparently no one non-human had made such a discovery, either.

Talking about cosmic string reminded her of something she had put off discussing for too long.

"I understand your wanting to get used to meeting people," she said to Nemo. "But if you want to meet any other human beings, you have to do it soon. *Starfarer* has to move out of the star system before the cosmic string withdraws. If it does withdraw—you'll have to move, too, or you'll get stranded."

"I will not allow myself to be stranded," Nemo said.

"Good . . . I was afraid . . ." She shrugged. She was ambivalent about bringing up the subject. "I'm surprised you'll talk to us. Aren't you afraid of being contaminated by us? You've talked to me more than Europa and Androgeos did altogether, I think."

"They were disappointed that you failed the test."

"But it was a mistake! We *weren't* armed with nuclear weapons. Or with anything else, for that matter. Nemo, we were attacked in our own system. We dragged the missile through transition because it *hit* us."

"That is a shame," Nemo said.

"And the only thing that will keep us from being attacked again, if we go home, is proof that Civilization exists."

"Your own people would kill you because you failed," Nemo said.

Another silk-spinner crept out of a fold in the wall and joined the silk worm in the new circle of fabric. The second spinner scrambled across the disk, leaving a radial trail of thread that secured the delicate, tight spiral.

"They wouldn't kill us, but they'd put us in jail." Nemo's attention to the handwork exasperated her.

Is there any way to get Civilization to *listen* to us? she thought.

"Maybe you should neither go on, nor go home, but allow yourself to be stranded," Nemo said.

"We've thought about it," J.D. said. The ecosystem could support far more people than the ship carried; it could support them indefinitely. "We could turn *Starfarer* into a generation ship, and form our own little isolated world. . . ." The whole idea depressed her. It meant abandoning Earth. She could not imagine anything more selfish. "I'd rather go back and get put in jail!" she cried aloud, and her voice broke. She struggled to calm herself.

"I did not understand that," Nemo said.

J.D. repeated herself. Her electronic voice sounded so calm, so rational.

"Imprisonment is preferable to freedom." Nemo's eyelid opened all the way around, and the tentacles extended to J.D. and touched her forehead, her shoulder. The silk-spinners, deprived of guidance, wandered across the fabric and trailed threads that left flaws in its surface.

Nemo's tentacles drew away from J.D. and returned to the spinners.

"No! But . . . we didn't come out here to found a colony. That's against everything we agreed on, everything we dreamed of! We came out here hoping to join an interstellar community. We came out here to meet *you*! And now you tell us we have to go back, or abandon Earth, because of a mistake—!"

"Five hundred years isn't so long," Nemo said.

"Not to you! You and Europa and Androgeos will still be here when five hundred years have passed. But I'll be dead. Everyone on board *Starfarer* will be dead. And if we go back to Earth with nothing but the news that we've failed . . . I'm afraid human beings won't survive at all."

"Many civilizations have destroyed themselves."

J.D. looked away from Nemo's brilliant, colorful form, with two long tentacles shepherding the spinners, the third waving delicately in the air.

"I'd hoped . . ." She started to take a deep breath, felt the tickle of acrid gases in the back of her throat, and instead blew her breath out in frustration. "I hoped you might tell me that no civilizations are ever lost. That somehow we always manage to pull ourselves out of destruction."

"Civilizations are lost all the time, J.D."

"I meant . . . a whole world's civilization." The culture she lived in had reached out for the stars, and had attained them, however temporarily. Why should that be proof against extinction?

Nemo's tentacle brushed her toe, her shoulder.

"So did I," the squidmoth said.

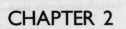

CHAPTER 2

J.D. SAT CROSSLEGGED BESIDE NEMO, THE SILK
beneath her warm and soft. She could
happily stay here for a week, just talking.
She shifted her position, resting her elbow on her knee and her chin on her
hand, looking at Nemo, amazed and en-
thralled by the being. She watched, in
silence, as Nemo guided the silk-spinners. The disk had become an iridescent
pouch, like several others lying at the
edge of the chamber.

"Tell me about Civilization," J.D.
said.

"Beings exchange their knowledge,"
Nemo replied.

The two spinners, one wormlike, one

resembling a starfish crossed with a lace handkerchief, met nose to nose.

"But there's more than that!" J.D. said. "How many worlds are there? How many people? How many *kinds* of people? What are they like? What kind of governments do they have? I want to know everything, Nemo, about Civilization and how it works, about the movements of the cosmic string—!"

The worm reared up, the starfish twisted. They touched. Each extruded a spurt of silk.

"The people of Civilization will want to describe themselves to you."

"What do they do when they meet? How do they reconcile their differences?"

The bursts of thread caught together and tangled. As the creatures danced, Nemo urged them easily around the pouch. Their motions formed the silk into a fluted rim.

"They make peace, or the cosmic string withdraws."

"That's simple," J.D. said dryly. "A little Draconian, but simple."

When the silk worm and the starfish returned to their starting point, Nemo flicked them both off the edge and into the pouch.

"Tell me what you're looking for," Nemo said.

"We're looking for answers," J.D. said. "Answers . . . and more questions."

"Tell me what answers you're looking for."

"We already found one—a big one. You. We built *Starfarer* to find out whether other civilizations exist. Or whether we were alone. Now we know that answer."

"The answer to your question is self-evident," Nemo said.

"Not to everyone. At least not to a lot of human beings. Their philosophy depends on their being alone in the universe."

"Earth has passed through a decline," Nemo said.

"I—what do you mean?"

"Europa and Androgeos knew of other beings."

"After they were rescued, after they left Earth and joined Civilization—"

"When they lived on Earth, they spoke to others."

"They had myths. They believed in gods and demigods and fantasy creatures. That doesn't count as knowing about spacefaring beings."

"Yet their myths were more accurate than Earth's current myths of solitude."

"There are lots of different myths on Earth right now. But . . . you're right. Europa and Androgeos came from a sophisticated culture. That's probably why they fit in so well with Civilization."

Nemo's feet drummed softly on the floor, a complicated rhythm. Seven against five? J.D. could not quite tell.

"If we do go back to Earth—I'm not saying we'll accept the exile, but if we do—there are lots of people who won't believe we've met alien beings."

"You'll tell them you met alien beings," Nemo said.

Several attendants scuttled and swooped nearer. Nemo rounded them up and herded them into the pouch.

"I'll tell them, but they won't believe me. They'll say we faked the records. They'll say it's all a monstrous hoax."

"You wouldn't fake information."

J.D. thought she heard shock in Nemo's voice.

"But they'd say we did. So we could claim we succeeded. So we could claim they shouldn't put us in jail because we were right all along. They'll want proof that we're right."

She waited, but instead of replying, Nemo lifted the delicate pouch and placed its fluted edge against a silk-draped wall, where it stuck.

"You could prove we were right, Nemo," J.D. said.

"If they saw me, they'd believe you'd met alien people."

"They sure would."

"If they saw me, they wouldn't put us in jail."

J.D. laughed. "They wouldn't put you in jail, that's

for sure." She stretched out her hands to Nemo. "It's a lot to ask, I know, but five hundred years isn't long to people like you and Europa. Wouldn't you at least think of visiting the solar system? You could learn everything there is to know about human beings."

"Your invitation's tempting," Nemo said.

"You'll do it?" J.D. exclaimed, astonished.

"I'm sorry, I have another commitment."

"I understand." The thrill J.D. had felt dropped abruptly into disappointment, with sad amusement that people gave the same excuses everywhere. "Five hundred years is too long."

"This time it is, I am sorry."

J.D. rose and stretched.

"I've been here for hours," she said. "I have to go back to the *Chi* for a while."

"You are leaving."

"I have to rest, and eat—" She shrugged. "Things that are easier back on the *Chi.*"

"I can offer you food," Nemo said.

Nemo snaked out one long tentacle to the far side of the chamber. The curtain there was a mass of iridescent bubbles of silk. Nemo's tentacle quivered across the surface.

It moved. The bubbles fluttered and bobbed and separated, the whole mass expanding, opening like a flower.

Each sphere was a living creature, depending from the curtain by three long slender limbs. The creatures had no heads, no other appendages, only a circular ring of spots.

Eyespots, J.D. thought, knowing she was making another assumption without much evidence.

Nemo chose one at the edge of the mass and stroked it. It released its hold on the silk and wrapped its legs around Nemo's tentacle.

Nemo extended the creature toward her.

"A decorative food," Nemo said.

J.D.'s helmet radio emitted a noise, not Nemo's voice, but Victoria's, a quick sound of protest more

quickly cut off. J.D.'s friends worried when they thought
she was in danger, but they were beginning to understand that facing the danger was her responsibility. They
were beginning to understand that they had to let her
do her job. Stephen Thomas had once offered to take
her place, but he had only offered once: her reaction
assured that. The other members of alien contact
thought of her as mild-tempered, even meek, and she
was. But when Stephen Thomas suggested that he go
out instead of her, she lost her temper.

"The food will not hurt you."

J.D. accepted Nemo's offer.

It touched her lips. The jointed legs fluttered against
her tongue; the abdomen disappeared like sea foam or
cotton candy, bursting with a flood of strange flavor:
sweet and gingery, spicy-hot enough to make her draw a
startled breath. The air passing over her tongue dissolved the spicy taste into a cool musky flavor like perfume. She crunched the delicate legs, but when she
swallowed even the legs had evanesced.

The evanescence dissolved straight into J.D.'s blood,
straight to her brain.

J.D. broke out into a sweat, she flushed from collarbone to forehead, and her heart began to pound. As
J.D. gasped for breath—and coughed violently in reaction to the air—Victoria's voice rumbled from J.D.'s suit
helmet, rising in pitch. A spot of heat appeared in the
back of J.D.'s mind, a signal from Victoria. J.D. let it in.

"J.D., I'm coming after you!" Victoria said directly
into her mind.

"Nemo, what's happening?" J.D. said.

Trying not to sound panicked, she sent a message
back to Victoria and the *Chi:* "No, don't, not yet. I'm all
right. . . . I think I'm all right."

"It's the effect of decorative food," Nemo said.

Nemo's long tentacle manipulated another creature
from the wall and carried it beneath Nemo's mustache
of shorter tentacles. The creature disappeared, with a
faint *crunch*.

Veins in the gauzy fins over Nemo's legs darkened,

and the fins rippled rapidly. The long tentacles twined around each other, leaving the silk-spinners to their own direction. The tips of Nemo's legs pattered erratically against the floor. Nemo's eyelid opened completely, then closed, then opened again in J.D.'s direction.

J.D.'s flush passed, and her heartbeat steadied. Only a quiver of sexual excitement remained, pleasurable and comforting and startling.

"Some effect," J.D. said.

"That's the decoration." Nemo's fins returned to their normal color, and settled back into their usual gentle wave. Instead of replacing the spinners on the rim of the silken pouch, Nemo let them wander in patterns across the surface.

"Did you know how I'd react to it?" J.D. asked.

"Tell me how it felt."

"Like ninety-proof champagne. Like excitement."

"Yes," Nemo said.

"How did you know?"

"Human biochemistry."

"Is that how it feels to you?"

"If excitement feels the same to me as it does to you."

"Is this what you live on all the time?"

"No one can live on decorative food," Nemo said.

"What do you live on?"

"Starlight," Nemo said. "Radiation."

"Photosynthesis—?"

The theory had always been that the metabolism of animals was too high to be sustained by sunlight alone, that fictional creations like giant, walking, talking plants could not exist—or at least that they could not walk very far, very fast, or think very much.

"The light of Sirius helps sustain me."

That would explain the other crater-nests, the ones filled with smooth silver silk in parabolic shapes: solar collectors, focusing the starlight, converting it, and funneling it to its users.

Nemo touched the silk-spinners and guided them to

the rim of the pouch. They had created a pattern of scarlet and indigo.

J.D. wiped her forehead. Her hair was damp with sweat. The first effects of the decorative food had passed, but her hands were shaking. She wondered if the food acted with a wave effect, or if it was about to give her a flashback.

I'm hungry, she thought. I'm hungry and I'm exhausted and I have a bad case of sensory overload. And like Nemo said . . . nobody can live on decorative food.

"Nemo, I must go back to the *Chi* for a while. I have a lot to think about, and I'm tired—aren't you?"

"No, I don't tire."

"You're fortunate. Would you like to visit with someone else while I'm gone?"

"I will think, until you return."

She took that as a polite refusal.

As she put on her spacesuit, she wondered how to persuade the alien being to let her colleagues come into its nest. They would be horribly disappointed if they could not.

Several of Nemo's attendants whispered past her on tiny invisible feet, and clustered around the gossamer thread that had led her in. When they passed over it, it parted. They hunkered down over the pieces, drawing in the threads.

"May I have a piece of your silk?" J.D. asked Nemo, gesturing to one of the threads.

"Tell me what you'd do with it."

"I'd give it to one of my colleagues to analyze. He studies genetics."

"You may have it."

J.D. pulled the sampling kit from the thigh pocket of her spacesuit and used the sterile tongs to pick up a thread. One of the attendants lunged, arching upward to snap with shiny jaws. Startled, J.D. snatched the sample away.

"It doesn't want me to take it," she said to Nemo.

"It doesn't have much tolerance for change."

The attendant flopped back to the floor, forgot about J.D., and headed for another loose bit of silk.

J.D. put her prize in a sample bag and sealed it.

"Thank you, Nemo," she said. "I'll come back as soon as I can."

"I will wait."

"Shall I leave my lifeline here? Then I could follow it in when I come back."

"One of my attendants will spin you to me," Nemo said.

"But that's so much trouble for you, when I could just follow the line."

"The line is essential to you," Nemo said.

"No, not really. It's for safety, for backup."

"J.D.," Nemo said, and J.D. thought she heard a hesitation in the squidmoth's voice, "the line is uncomfortable."

"It—what?"

She thought about the line, snaking back and forth through Nemo's body, pressing against, even cutting into, Nemo's tissues and organs.

"I'm so sorry!" she exclaimed. "Nemo, why didn't you say something before?" She blushed, mortified at having thoughtlessly caused Nemo pain.

"I want you to feel welcome," Nemo said.

J.D. grasped the end of Nemo's tentacle gently. "I'm so sorry," she said again. "I won't bring the line when I come back."

"Thank you," Nemo said.

As she left the bright sphere of light in the center of Nemo's nest, the long tentacles slithered after her, touching her heels. She paused at the opening between two inner curtains, glanced back, and waved. Nemo's mustache vibrated.

"Good-bye for now," she said.

"J.D."

She glanced back. "Yes, Nemo?"

"Tell me the questions you seek."

J.D. smiled. "We won't know what those are," she said, "till we find them."

.   .   .

Reeling in her lifeline, J.D. left Nemo's chamber and
entered the labyrinth. At the first switchback turn, the
line had pressed against the edge of the curtain. When
she released it, a dark welt formed. She touched it
gently, sorry for the pain she had caused.

Motion fluttered against her fingers. She started and
drew back her hand. Several palm-sized flat creatures,
the same color as the curtain and camouflaged against
it, had snugged up against the place where the cable had
lain. Now, as J.D. watched, they flowed over the welt,
covered it, and settled against the fabric. The welt vanished beneath a rough line of scar tissue.

J.D. left the labyrinth and hurried through the cathedral corridors, climbing toward the edge of the
crater. Now she noticed more of the creatures who
maintained the intricate environment that was Nemo.
They crept up every wall, spinning, weaving, unweaving;
they peered at her with eyespots or antennae from luxurious folds of drapery; they scuttled away before her so
all she knew of them was the sound they made when
they fled. And always she was aware of the larger creatures beyond the sides of the tunnels, shapes and shadows, the touch of a powerful limb tenting the wall or the
ceiling.

Maybe I should think of Nemo as an ecosystem, she
thought. Or maybe I need a whole new term.

She passed through the double sphincter that
formed Nemo's airlock, no longer frightened by the
monster-organisms that closed in to change the shape of
the tunnel.

She started up the long steep hammocks that led to
the surface.

The closer she got to the outside, the more deeply
the lifeline had cut into Nemo's fabric. In places, she
had to pull it—as gently as she could—from beneath the
healing creatures.

At the last place where the lifeline had sunk in, just
before J.D. emerged from the crater, a healing creature

had fastened itself firmly to both sides of the welt. J.D. pulled on the lifeline, but not gently enough. The creature's body ripped open. Pale fluid dripped out. The creature's edges had melded into the wall.

The lifeline fell free.

J.D. stared at the dripping tissue. The dripping slowed, and the fluid solidified. Soon the edges had healed, the walls began to absorb the two halves of the creature, and more healers came to finish covering the welt. J.D. let the lifeline reel in, glad she had reached the last steep slope.

Victoria was waiting for her at the edge of the crater, her slender, compact body radiating energy and excitement. She gave J.D. a hand up the last long step, squeezing her fingers. Behind the gilt surface of her faceplate, she looked amazed, exhilarated, relieved.

A deluge of questions and comments and exclamations poured through J.D.'s earphones. It was as if everyone had waited as long as they possibly could, till she stepped out of the alien being's home, and then could hold their curiosity no more. J.D. felt a surge of panic. Victoria must have seen it, because she squeezed J.D.'s hand again and opened a voice channel back to *Starfarer.*

"Come on, folks. J.D.'s had a long afternoon. You saw everything she did."

The cacophony eased. Someone muttered, "Sorry," and someone else said, "But it isn't the *same.*" That sounded like Chandra, the sensory artist.

"Nevertheless," Victoria said. "I'm closing down the PA for a while. We can all talk to J.D. when she's had a chance to collect her thoughts."

The monitor signals vanished, leaving J.D. in peace and silence.

"Thanks," J.D. said. "You could have said, 'Till J.D.'s had a chance to pee,' but I'm glad you didn't."

Victoria chuckled.

"You were fantastic, J.D." she said. "I wouldn't have had the nerve to do all that you just did."

J.D. smiled, exhausted but elated. No matter what

happened now, she had begun to make friends with Nemo, with an alien being.

Too many things on the deep space expedition had gone badly up till now. She needed a success. They all did.

"Let's go in," Victoria said.

"Okay."

They retraced their footprints through the dust of the planetoid's rough surface, returning to the ungainly explorer craft, the *Chi*.

J.D. unplugged the end of her lifeline from the flank of the *Chi* and let it snap back into the reel. She unhooked the reel from her suit, and handed it to Victoria.

"From now on," she said, "I'm working without a net."

Outside the spacesuit locker, Zev and Satoshi waited for Victoria and J.D.

"You have a hell of a lot of guts," Satoshi said.

J.D. knew he meant to offer her a compliment, but she also heard the note of caution in his voice.

"More guts than brains?" she said.

"Maybe," he said. "But maybe . . . that's what the alien contact specialist needs." He grinned at her, and she smiled back.

"Thanks."

Satoshi was the most restrained of the three members of the family partnership. Unlike Stephen Thomas, who said whatever he thought, Satoshi more often than not kept his opinions to himself. J.D. valued his rare comments, and rarer compliments.

Satoshi went to Victoria and brushed his fingertips against his partner's very curly short black hair, smoothing it where her helmet had pressed against it.

J.D. rotated her shoulders and stretched. Zev came to her and hugged her tight. She stroked his fine pale hair, and laid her hand against his cheek.

The diver's smooth mahogany skin radiated heat. Zev wore only light shorts and a sleeveless shirt, both too big for him, both borrowed from Stephen Thomas, who was nearly thirty centimeters taller than Zev. Zev owned almost no clothing, only a heavy wool suit, part of his disguise for boarding *Starfarer*. He would have abandoned clothing as quickly as he had abandoned his fraudulent identity, if J.D. had not told him it would be socially unacceptable. He never wore clothes back in Puget Sound.

Zev took her hand between his, spreading his long fingers to enclose her hand between the translucent swimming webs. He looked up at her, his dark eyes bright with excitement.

"When you go back, I want to go with you," he said. "I want to meet Nemo."

"We all want that," Victoria said, her voice intense. "I hope it happens."

"I do, too," J.D. said.

Her colleagues had all been disappointed when Europa refused them permission to explore her starship. J.D. hoped the same thing would not happen with Nemo.

"Where's Stephen Thomas?" J.D. asked.

"In his lab." Satoshi sounded troubled. He ran his hand through his short black hair. "I've hardly seen him all day."

"I need to talk to him before I go back out." J.D. was disappointed that he had not joined the others to greet her. She held out the sample bag with the fragment of Nemo's thread. "And I have a sample for him. Didn't he see me pick it up?"

"Maybe he thought it was for me, eh?" Victoria said. She grinned. "I would like a piece of it. It looked like it had some interesting optical properties."

J.D. held out the sample bag to Victoria, embarrassed to admit how much she had wanted to give it to Stephen Thomas herself.

"Tell him not to chop it *all* up looking for microbes," Victoria said. "Why don't you give it to him, and freshen up, and we'll get ready for the conference and meet you in the observers' circle?"

"Okay," J.D. said.

A few minutes later she hurried from her tiny cabin and headed for the *Chi*'s labs. The labs were larger than the cabins, but still minuscule. J.D. stopped in the doorway of the genetics lab. Stephen Thomas sat at the work bench, staring into the microscope's holographic image. The image rotated, then flipped over.

Another holographic projection, the image of Nemo's crater, hovered in the air where he could glance up and see it.

"Stephen Thomas," J.D. said.

"Hi, J.D." Stephen Thomas straightened and turned, hooking his elbow over the chair back. "That was some expedition."

He smiled at her.

"Thanks," she said softly, keeping back everything else she might have wanted to say to him.

He looked drawn and distracted. He had been uncharacteristically silent since they left *Starfarer*. Of everyone, he was taking Feral's death the hardest. It broke J.D.'s heart to see him so withdrawn, so deep in shock. Grief concentrated his beauty, rather than fading it, heightening the blue of his eyes and refining the planes of his classic features. He had pulled his long blond hair back and tied it very tight. His skin, so fair a few days ago, continued to darken. Except for the pale new scar on his forehead, his skin now was a smooth café au lait. Eventually he would be the same color as Zev: dark mahogany, deep brown with a reddish sheen.

"I brought you a sample." J.D. held out the sample bag. "There's not much of it, but it's less abused than the other one."

She had inadvertently pulled up a weed from Europa's ship. If she had not been running away from an aurochs at the time, she probably would have stuck it back in the ground instead of shoving it into her pocket. On the other hand, if she had not been running away from an aurochs, she would not have pulled it up in the first place.

Stephen Thomas accepted the bag. J.D. expected

him to react—with excitement, with disbelief that she had picked up no more than a discarded bit, with a profane expression of joy, with some unexpected impulse unique to Stephen Thomas Gregory. When she had given him the battered weed from Europa's ship, he had kissed her forehead.

This time, he simply held the bag up to the light. The silk caught the illumination and carried it from one end to the other. The tips of the thread glowed blue-white; the length of it shone luminous indigo. Between Stephen Thomas's fingers, the newly-formed swimming webs glowed pale amber.

"I wonder if Nemo's microflora is as diverse as the web fauna," Stephen Thomas said. "This'll be contaminated. . . . Too bad you couldn't collect it before you got out of your suit. People just emit bacteria like crazy. But it shouldn't be too hard to separate the alien bugs . . ."

"I'm sorry." J.D. blushed, both annoyed and embarrassed by the implied criticism. "I couldn't just go in and start ripping up bits—"

He shrugged. "Can't be helped." He turned toward her again. "Hey, don't get me wrong. I'm glad to have it."

"If you say so," J.D. said, and rushed to change the subject. "I want to enhance my internal link. Can I?"

"Sure, but why the fuck would you want to?"

"Weren't you watching? Weren't you even *listening*?"

"Of course I was watching. Why are you pissed off at me? Is *everybody* pissed off at me?"

"No, of course not, I'm sorry." J.D. gestured at the floating image. "I want to communicate with Nemo on Nemo's own terms. So I have to enhance my link. Can I start working on it now?"

"No, I don't have any prep here." He frowned. "You'll have to ask Professor Thanthavong if she can mix some up for you in the biochem lab. The ready-made stuff was in the genetics building, so it's under forty tons of rubble."

"Oh," J.D. said, disappointed. "Okay. I'll talk to her." As soon as I get some sleep, she said to herself. As soon as I can sound coherent. Though Professor Thanthavong was usually pleasant and invariably at least civil, J.D. always felt intimidated by the idea of walking up to a Nobel laureate and talking to her as if she were an ordinary person. Miensaem Thanthavong was not ordinary.

"Just how much are you planning to enhance the link?" Stephen Thomas said.

"As much as I can."

He knit his eyebrows. "You won't like it. You'll be a zombie whenever you use it. The synapses have to feed in *somewhere,* they'll take over all your other senses."

"I don't care," J.D. said. "It's important." Her link warmed in the back of her mind, notifying her of a message. "Excuse me a second." Her eyelids fluttered. As she went into a communications fugue, she thought, Most of us close off the rest of the world when we use our link, so what does it matter?

She accepted the message. Nemo's characteristic signal touched her mind.

"Nemo! Is everything all right?"

"The attendants are prepared," Nemo said.

"Does that mean— Are you willing to meet my colleagues? Can we visit you?"

"Yes, you may visit."

J.D. opened her eyes. "That was Nemo! Come on!"

Without waiting to explain, J.D. ran out of the lab.

CHAPTER 3

J.D. TWEAKED HER METABOLIC ENHANCER again. It flooded her body with extra adrenaline, hiding her exhaustion. She led the way to the edge of Nemo's crater.

"It looks different," Victoria said.

"It is," J.D. said.

The surface had changed, and the entrance. The tunnels were rewoven, re-formed. If J.D. had left her line in the nest, it would not simply have cut into the edges of Nemo's curtains. It would have grown into the fabric of the nest itself, like gravel in a wound.

Satoshi knelt at the edge of the crater and peered down the new slope.

"There's our guide," he said. "One of the lifeliners."

They followed the creature's thread downward. The lifeliner ambled before them, no longer trying to hide.

"The route's easier," J.D. said, with wonder. "Nemo remade all the tunnels." They were higher, the slopes shallower. She never had to stoop. She let her eyelids flicker, touched her internal link, and sent a quick message of thanks to Nemo.

"I rebuild all the time," Nemo said.

J.D. hurried between the pearly gray curtains. Without the lifeliner, without its thread through the labyrinth, she would be lost.

"It's beautiful," Zev said. "It's like anemones."

"Anemones?" J.D. said. "How do you mean?"

"On the curtains."

"Look at it in the ultraviolet," Stephen Thomas said. "It's like flowers. Jungle."

J.D.'s suit obediently displayed Nemo's web in the UV.

The web exploded.

Intricate patterns whirled into alien plants and surged with violent blossoms. Auroras chased themselves in spirals that expanded to cover every surface, then diminished to a single point, and vanished.

Dazzled, J.D. took a step forward and ran into a silken wall. Victoria grabbed her arm and steadied her.

"Whoa, careful."

She stopped and closed her eyes and canceled the suit display. When she looked again, the storm of color had vanished and the path lay clear before her again, winding between the curtains and their invisible decorations, their camouflage.

"Wow," she said softly. "That's something."

"It sure is," Victoria said.

"Can you see it?" Satoshi asked Stephen Thomas. "I mean, like Zev? Without the suit display?"

"Yeah," Stephen Thomas said. "I can see it."

The path spiraled deeper into the crater. They reached the airlock. As the shadows outside bore down on the walls, Satoshi cupped his hands against the translucent tunnel.

"Damn, I wish *I* could see *them*!"

The pocket filled with air; sound returned.

The interior end of the airlock relaxed and opened. They continued to the central chamber. The maze of curtains around Nemo remained, but the chamber extended farther upward, and the curtains reached to its ceiling. In single file, the members of the alien contact department followed the lifeline through Nemo's maze.

The gossamer thread ended. J.D. entered Nemo's chamber. Victoria and Satoshi and Stephen Thomas and Zev came in behind her.

"Hello, Nemo." J.D. unfastened her helmet. The thick, smelly air displaced the tasteless air of her support system.

Nemo's eyelid rose; the faceted eyes glittered. Nemo's central tentacle snaked out and grasped J.D.'s wrist. She gripped it, her fingers closing around silky fur. The tentacle felt hot, like the tail of a cat basking in the sun.

"These are my friends, my colleagues," J.D. said to Nemo.

"Welcome," Nemo said.

"Thank you," J.D. said.

The others took off their helmets. J.D. had warned them of the exhaust-fume smell, and they had seen the LTM analyses. Stephen Thomas wrinkled his nose in distaste, and Zev sneezed.

"Tell me if you thought new things." Nemo said.

"I sure did," J.D. said. "We all did." She and her companions removed their spacesuits and left them at the edge of the inner chamber. J.D. approached the squidmoth. "How are you? Did you think new things, too?"

"I thought of some old things," Nemo said.

"I want to introduce my friends," J.D. said. "Victoria Fraser MacKenzie, who's the head of the alien contact department, and a physicist. She discovered how to use the cosmic string to enter transition."

"I am glad to meet you, Victoria," Nemo said.

The long central tentacle snaked out and hovered. Victoria extended her hand, and Nemo laid the soft tip of the tentacle in her palm. She shivered.

"I'm glad to meet you, too, Nemo," Victoria said through her internal link.

"Here's Satoshi Lono. He's a geographer. He studies how communities interact with their environments. And Stephen Thomas Gregory, who studies genetics. And this is my friend Zev. Zev is a diver."

Nemo went through the new greeting ritual with each of J.D.'s colleagues in turn.

"You're the ichthyocentaur," Nemo said to Zev.

"That's what Europa called me," Zev said. "But the word means I'm part fish. I'm not."

"You are different from J.D.," Nemo said.

"Of course. I'm a diver, and J.D.'s still a regular human being."

J.D. was touched that he used the word "still." She would probably always regret turning down the chance to become a diver that Zev's mother had offered her.

"And Stephen Thomas is different from you all," Nemo said.

"I'm changing into a diver," Stephen Thomas said. "I'm about half and half at this point."

"Maybe someday J.D. will decide to change, too," Zev said.

A spinner crept from a fold. Nemo's tentacle snapped out and grabbed it and teased it into spinning and urged it in a tight circle and started to weave another pouch.

"Can we look around?" Stephen Thomas said.

"You would like to see other parts of me."

"Yes."

"The attendants will take you to what you wish to see."

Three lifeliners crept into the chamber.

• • •

The lifeliners led Victoria, Satoshi, and Stephen Thomas out of Nemo's chamber through the same path. At the first split in the path, two went one way and one went another.

"See you guys later," Stephen Thomas said. He strolled after the spinning creature and disappeared between two curtains.

Victoria started to call after him.

"He'll be all right," Satoshi said.

Victoria stepped back, took a shallow breath of the fetid air, and blew it out abruptly.

"I know," she said. "But I'd feel easier if our guides didn't look so much like scorpions."

Intellectually she understood all the reasons for believing they were safe with Nemo. Emotionally, she had a harder time. She was very glad Nemo had not offered them all decorative food.

I wonder how you turn it down if you don't want it? she said to herself. Maybe you say, Thank you very much, but I don't care to be decorated.

Satoshi grinned. "They do look like scorpions, don't they? Not as mean, though, or they'd be beating the hell out of each other right now."

The other two lifeliners scuttled down the path. At the next fork in the corridor, they diverged.

Satoshi grabbed Victoria in a quick, fierce hug, then hurried after his lifeliner.

Victoria descended through twisting tunnels, curving tubes of watered silk that spiraled steeply downward. The color-shot patterns quivered beneath her footsteps, and the lifeliner scuttled drunkenly along the shifting floor.

Victoria jumped, experimentally, cautious because of the low gravity. She hit the ceiling, pressing into the warm, slightly sticky fabric. She broke away from it with a faint ripping sound, bounced to the floor, and rebounded. By the time she came to a sprawling halt she was laughing at the position she was in, and even at her fear.

Above her, the ceiling darkened where she had hit it. A shape passed over the bruise. The silk dimpled from the other side as one of Nemo's attendants stepped lightly across the upper curve of the tunnel. It was like being underwater during rain. The brief shadow of the cloud, the quick touch of raindrops sweeping delicately across the surface. The shadow faded; the bruise disappeared.

Victoria continued down the tunnel.

The air grew sharp and clear. Ozone tinged it. When she touched her hair, static electricity crackled.

And the gravity grew stronger.

At first she thought she was imagining the gradual effect, but it was real.

It makes sense, she thought. Grade-school physics. I *knew* there had to be something inside Nemo's ship at least as dense as neutronium. And I'm getting closer to it.

The LTM sensors registered a slight increase in the radiation level. Nothing dangerous yet. Victoria knew she should not stay long, but curiosity drew her on.

The lifeliner scrambled onward and downward, leading her toward a lambent glow.

Victoria followed the creature around a bend in the tunnel.

The creature stopped. The tunnel ended its spiral and curved abruptly straight down.

Victoria glanced back. Her escape route was open and clear. She crossed the last few meters to the sharp curve of the tunnel, passing the lifeliner.

A thick panel of transparent webbing covered the end. She knelt on the floor and gazed down through the clear surface. It was like looking into a well, a well lit from below, or through a pane of old, wavery glass.

A shining sphere lay in the center of Nemo's planetoid. A curving pattern of pale cables suspended it and held it in place—held the planetoid in the proper relationship to it. Here and there, more of Nemo's crea-

tures crept about. They looked like the lifeliners, but
they had much heavier carapaces, shorter spinners, legs
nearly invisible. They picked their way across the suspension cables. In front of them, the white cables flexed
in response to the spinners' motion and the faint occa-
sional vibration of Nemo's sphere. Behind them, they
left dark metallic rope of twisted wire.

Victoria ignored the faint scratching noise behind
her. She wished she could see into the sphere, but she
knew it was protecting her from radiation and energy
flux that would kill her, and all her colleagues, and
probably Nemo as well. The sphere hid the engine that
powered Nemo's voyaging.

The lifeliner scratched persistently at the floor. Victoria finally noticed the sound and glanced over her
shoulder.

The creature huddled over a tangled tracery of silk.
It scratched again, ran a little way up the tunnel,
stopped, and ran back toward her. It did not turn; it ran
both directions with equal ease. Wherever it moved, it
trailed a line of silk. Its scorpion tails twitched, fore and
aft.

"Okay," Victoria said. "You're right. It's time to get
out of here."

She rose, glanced one last longing time into the center of Nemo's starship, and followed the lifeliner back
toward the surface.

"Thank you for showing me," she said aloud to the
creature and silently to Nemo, using her internal link.

"You are welcome," Nemo said.

Satoshi followed the small scuttly creature spinning
black silk before him. He wanted to get close to the
lifeliner, to pick it up and inspect it, to subject it to the
electronic gaze of the LTM clinging to his shirt. J.D. had
asked him to be careful, and he approved of her caution. But he wanted to see and understand every facet of
the environment surrounding him.

The wide, low corridor narrowed, the deep-fissured

walls smoothed, and the firm, springy floor dropped into a slope. Satoshi climbed downward. The light began to fade. The slope ended in a tall, cylindrical chamber hung with heavy, fibrous curtains and pierced with two more tunnels slanting up and out, like the one through which he had descended.

The lifeliner stopped and huddled against the wall.

Satoshi sat on his heels beside the creature. The lifeliner rubbed against the wall, severing the silk.

"Is this the end of the road?" Satoshi said softly.

He walked around the edge of the chamber, touching the long bright swaths of drapery.

They *open*, he thought.

He looked up.

Long-lidded glittery eyes looked back.

Satoshi started and spun around.

At the top of each set of curtains, a creature clung to the vaulted ceiling. If Satoshi had not met Nemo, he might not have recognized them as creatures, or the circular fissure as their eye-slits. The creatures hugged the wall, arching long legs overhead till they touched at the center of the ceiling. The legs pressed upward and outward like an arch, holding the creatures in place.

The mouth parts of the creatures, tremendously enlarged, formed the curtains.

One of the sets of curtains suddenly billowed wetly outward. A blast of oily, pungent air swept over Satoshi, knocking him down and slapping him to the floor. The pressure pushed the hot fumes up his nose. He sneezed convulsively, three times, four.

The curtains fell back and the tempest vanished.

Satoshi lay flat, catching his breath, breathing shallowly. His eyes and throat stung. A second set of curtains quivered. He ducked and buried his head beneath his arms as the curtains billowed and a second blast crashed over him.

He looked up and around just in time to see the third set of curtains quiver. He watched long enough to see them open, pulling apart in the center, remaining closed at top and bottom. Beyond the curtains, acid dripped down color-striped stone, dissolving it, releasing roiling clouds of gas.

He ducked again as the hot, polluted air filled the chamber and billowed out through the tunnels. The curtains fell closed with a wet *slap*.

He pushed himself cautiously to his feet. He felt damp and greasy. The curtains hung motionless.

"Nemo!" he said through his link. "What's going on down here?"

"Fresh air," Nemo said.

Satoshi started to laugh. "That's more fresh air than I can handle all at once," he said. "This place is amazing —but do you mind if I leave before the next storm?"

"I'll wait till you're safely away."

"How long do I have? Can I look around?"

"I must hold my breath."

"Oh. Okay, I'll hurry."

As he headed for the exit tunnel and the silken guideline, he took one last look around, at Nemo's lungs, at the symbiotic creatures who not only pumped air through Nemo's body but created the air as well.

Stephen Thomas strolled after his lifeliner. When he was well out of sight of his partners, he stopped at the intersection of several tunnels. The creature beetled on and disappeared around a curve.

Stephen Thomas deliberately turned down a different tunnel.

He made it about a hundred meters. The lifeliner's carapace scraped the floor behind him as the creature scuttled after him, spewing thread.

"Think you're going to stop me, huh?" Stephen Thomas said. "Just how the fuck are you going to do that?"

It closed the gap, spinning out a lifeline of increasing slenderness and delicacy.

"Stephen Thomas," Nemo said directly to the internal link.

Stephen Thomas stopped. J.D. had adapted easily to

direct communication. But Stephen Thomas wished he had brought a portable radio headset.

"I hear you," he replied.

"It's hard to follow you when you go so fast."

"That's all right," Stephen Thomas said. "I won't get lost, I don't need a babysitter."

"You do not wish to study genetics."

"I—What?"

"My attendant will take you to where you can study genetics."

"Can I take samples?"

"You have a sample."

Great, Stephen Thomas thought. A few alien bacteria off a shred of string. They probably have as much relation to Nemo as E. coli does to human beings.

"Thanks a lot."

"You are welcome."

"Oh, fuck it," Stephen Thomas muttered aloud.

When the lifeliner went into reverse and trailed a thread parallel to the one it had left coming in, Stephen Thomas shrugged and followed the creature wherever it wanted to take him.

"Suppose I'd kept going," Stephen Thomas said to Nemo through the link.

"I suppose you'd kept going," Nemo said.

Stephen Thomas waited. Finally it occurred to him that Nemo had done exactly what he had suggested.

"*If* I'd kept going," Stephen Thomas said, "what would you have done?"

"Nothing."

"Would you let me go anywhere I wanted?"

"I'd warn you of dangerous spots."

The lifeliner stopped in a gap among several curtains. Light shined out into the corridor, brighter than the light from the optical strands woven into the walls. The new light shimmered, like reflections from water.

The lifeliner leaped, trailing silk, and disappeared.

Stephen Thomas moved forward curiously. Warm, pungent air flowed toward him. Sulfur and hydrogen sulfide and other, more complicated chemicals made him breathe shallowly through his mouth. If the air got much worse, he would have to turn back. He tapped into the analysis of the LTM clinging to his pocket, and scanned the chemicals. None of them would kill him in their current concentrations. Not immediately.

The curtains created a spherical chamber around and above a water-filled depression, and trapped the heat and the stench. Stephen Thomas stood on the bank, inspecting the place curiously. Sweat beaded on his forehead, on the back of his neck.

The lifeliner's thread vanished into the oily, organic sheen floating on the pool. The light was so bright, the surface so obscured with rainbow brilliance, that Stephen Thomas could not see to the bottom.

Nemo likes water as scungy as the air, Stephen Thomas thought. If I'm supposed to dive in after the lifeliner, forget it.

He lifted the thread. Its end emerged, broken, from the water.

Broken or dissolved, Stephen Thomas thought.

"Hey, critter," he said aloud.

The water shivered at his feet. He stooped down, expecting the lifeliner to answer his summons.

The surface splashed upward, spraying him with the scummy soup. He shouted in shock and flung himself back. His feet slipped into the water.

"Shit!" He jerked his feet back and scrambled for the entrance. He reached safety. He pulled off his shirt. The front and the arms were stained—he was glad that for once he had worn a long-sleeved shirt and long pants—but the back was clean. He used it to wipe the liquid from his face and hands.

The pale blue silk of his shirt discolored to brown.

"Jesus, Nemo, what's—oh, fuck!"

His sandals were smoking. He snatched them off and threw them into the corridor and rubbed his feet on the remnants of his shirt.

"What's going on down here?"

"Genetics."

"Survival of the fittest?" I knew there was a good

reason to study molecular genetics, he thought. "You told me you'd warn me of dangerous places."

"But you asked to observe, not interact," Nemo said.

"I didn't mean to fall in your damned pond."

Stephen Thomas got the distinct impression that the squidmoth was laughing at him. Scowling, he sat cross-legged well above the waterline, rested his elbows on his knees, and leaned his chin on his fists.

The caustic liquid had not discolored the skin of his feet, or of his hands, even the delicate new swimming webs, so he supposed his face was not disfigured either.

The splashing creature had submerged, unseen. But the surface roiled slowly, as if gentle whirlpools drifted across it, now and then colliding, mixing, separating.

From the safety of the entrance, Stephen Thomas could not see what was going on. He rose and went cautiously nearer the edge. He bent just far enough to peer into the pool.

The lifeliner burrowed into the bottom until nothing showed but its two scorpion tails. Dark blue filaments, slender at the root, wide and flat in the center, and tapered at the ends, grew from the bottom like kelp. They stretched toward the center of the pond. Just above the root, each bore a cluster of scarlet flowers.

A tantalizing array of entities crawled and swam and burrowed among and below the kelp. Stephen Thomas wished he had a protective suit. He was not going swimming unprotected in Nemo's pool. He doubted even his spacesuit would help. It might keep out the noxious liquid and gases the pool was emitting . . . then fail catastrophically as soon as he entered vacuum.

Another unfamiliar creature ploughed toward the lifeliner. It was shaped like a sowbug, but the size of Stephen Thomas's cupped hands. Several rows of spines ran down its back. They wavered, pressed backward as the creature crossed the muddy bottom.

The spined sowbug lunged forward, straight between the lifeliner's extended scorpion tails. Silk burst from the tails, erupting onto the spines, and the tails flailed at the attacker. But the sowbug fastened on. Silt spewed up, obscuring the fight. Trails of yellow blood filmed the water. The lifeliner humped up out of its burrow, flexing its body spasmodically. One tail crushed a patch of spines. The sowbug shuddered, then clenched.

The lifeliner relaxed and grew still. As Stephen Thomas watched, the sowbug bore down on it. It fell apart in battered pieces, leaking guts and golden blood.

Stephen Thomas backed away from the pond. He felt sick. His vision blurred. He stumbled out into the corridor, fighting for breath.

Don't throw up, he told himself. Not here, not now. Whatever you've seen, whatever it signifies, don't let it affect you.

He grabbed his shirt and his sandals and fled from the soft vicious sounds of struggle.

J.D. and Zev remained with Nemo.

One of the armor-scaled creatures flowed up to Zev's bare foot and extended its frilly mantle, rippling out to touch him. Zev watched it curiously. Then, fearless, he picked it up and turned it over to look at it. Its feathery appendages waved frantically, and a stream of fluid spurted from its underside. Zev laughed. An old hand at catching creatures who used water jets and ink and even tiny poison darts for defense and escape, he had been holding it at an angle. The liquid jet missed him and spattered, pungent and oily, on the floor. Zev put the creature down, and it zipped off under one of the silk-sheet walls.

Zev crossed the distance to Nemo. He knelt down and touched Nemo's sleek side, stroking the iridescent skin. Nemo blinked slowly. The long eyelid closed. Nemo reminded J.D. for all the world like a huge mutant cat being petted. The long tentacles moved languorously, tapping against the silk floor, the spinners, Zev's leg.

Nemo plucked one of the honey ants and gave it to Zev, plucked another and handed it to J.D. J.D. ate hers slowly, preparing for the rush and dizziness. Zev popped his into his mouth and crunched it.

"Oh, I like that," he said out loud, his voice breathy. He returned to using his link. "Thanks, Nemo! I wonder if you'd like beer."

Nemo's long eyelid opened; the glittery eyes peered out. The long tentacles surrounded Zev, touching and stroking him.

"I eat only insubstantial food," Nemo said.

Zev sat quiet and interested as Nemo's tentacles explored him.

The tentacles touched and probed his body through the thin fabric of his shorts and shirt. Zev, not in the least uncomfortable, stroked Nemo's back and played his fingers along the shorter proboscises that formed Nemo's mustache.

Nemo touched Zev's face with the tip of one long tentacle.

"You have had your children."

"Me?" Zev said, startled, yet flattered. "No, I've never been asked to father a child. Not yet."

Nemo's short tentacles wuffled in a complex wave.

"You're a juvenile."

"I'm grown!"

Nemo pulled the tentacle sharply back. Zev leaned toward the squidmoth and touched the purple fur.

"I didn't mean to frighten you," Zev said.

"Zev's an adult," J.D. said. "But divers wait till they're older, usually, before they reproduce."

"Humans change to divers," Nemo said.

J.D. was having trouble following Nemo's reasoning, though the insubstantial food made her feel intense as well as dizzy, able to make great leaps of intuition. Unfortunately, figuring out what Nemo meant, or what Nemo wanted to know, was too great a leap even for J.D.

"Divers started out as human beings. But we changed ourselves. My grandparents did."

"Divers are not the adult form of human beings."

"No," J.D. said. "I mean, that's right. Humans can

change to divers and divers can change to humans, but we usually don't."

"I was never an ordinary human being," Zev said. "And we breed true. Diver genes are dominant. If J.D. and I had children, they'd be divers."

"There's another difference between Zev and me," J.D. said. "Zev is male and I'm female."

She was glad to have a relatively neutral way of bringing up the subject of sex and gender. Though Nemo had not balked at any of J.D.'s questions so far, she had felt shy of asking about the reproductive strategies of squidmoths. And though J.D. assured herself that a squidmoth would be shy of completely different subjects than the ones human beings found difficult and delicate, she did not find broaching the question of sex any easier.

"Europa is a female and Androgeos is a male," Nemo said.

"Yes. Exactly."

"This is significant for your reproduction."

"Yes. For us, and for most of the higher animals and plants on Earth. To reproduce, we need a male and a female. How does it work for you?"

"We exchange genetic material, then save it for our reproductive phase."

Male first, and then female, J.D. thought. Or hermaphroditic—

Then: You're doing it again, she thought. Trying to fit Nemo into familiar terms. Just because you think you've pinned something down, just because you've named it, doesn't mean it fits in the box you've made of the name.

"How often do you reproduce?" J.D. asked.

"One time."

"Do you have children, then? Young ones, offspring?" Nemo was a being of great age; J.D.'s impression was that Nemo was an elder of the squidmoths.

"I have no offspring yet."

"How do you decide when to have them?"

"I decide when the juvenile phase of my life is finished."

J.D. started to say something, then stopped, for she had been about to interpret Nemo's comment without double-checking her assumptions.

"Do you mean that you decide when to become an adult—when to become sexually mature?"

"I decide when to enter my reproductive phase."

"Is that when you become an adult?"

"Yes."

"Are you still a juvenile?"

"I'm still a juvenile."

"I thought you were old," Zev said. "Older than Europa, even."

"I am older than Europa," Nemo said.

"And still a juvenile!" J.D. said, amazed.

Maybe that's why Nemo's willing to talk to us, J.D. thought. Just a crazy kid.

"Nemo, how long is your lifespan?"

Nemo hesitated.

I wonder, J.D. thought, if Nemo is afraid I'll say, "Take me to your mother"?

"I'm nearly a million subjective years old," Nemo said.

Some juvenile! J.D. thought. If Nemo's a juvenile, how old and wise the adults must be!

"Did Civilization increase your lifespan, too, like Europa's?" J.D. asked. "Or do you naturally live a long time?"

Again, Nemo paused before replying. Would the squidmoth start behaving like Europa and Androgeos, withholding information because it was valuable, and human beings had so little to trade for it? She could not bear to think that after all, Nemo would send the humans away.

If everyone in Civilization is four thousand years old, a million years old, J.D. thought, no wonder they think of us as immature. But . . . do they have kids of their own? Europa gave me the idea there were a lot of different people out here. Where do they put their population? She wondered, feeling depressed, if the people of Civilization crammed themselves together, like human beings in some of Earth's cities, and comforted themselves by calculating how many people could be packed into a given area, and still have a spot of ground to stand on.

"Civilization helped my people naturally live this long," Nemo said.

"Do you build in a long life-span? Instead of prolonging it with outside treatments?"

"More or less," Nemo said.

"Who decides who gets to make those changes?"

"With enough knowledge, you can change yourselves."

J.D. sighed. "We'll have to discover the knowledge on our own, I'm afraid," she said.

"When you come back, Civilization will give you another opportunity to ask for it," Nemo said.

"We don't want gifts!" J.D. said. "Not now, not in five hundred years! We want partnership. We want friendship and communication." She stood up, too agitated to remain lounging on the soft silk floor. "I know it isn't very long-sighted to care that I'll be dead when we get another chance. But I *do* care! I want to see the interstellar Civilization for myself. Can't anybody out here understand that?"

"I understand."

Europa had referred to the squidmoths with contempt. J.D. thought Europa's assessment of Nemo's people was wrong. J.D. thought Nemo might know more about the inner workings of Civilization than Europa did, more about the power structure, more about the cosmic string.

On the other hand, J.D. could not imagine Europa living anywhere for four thousand years—for one year—and not scoping out the power structure.

"And . . . I'm selfish," J.D. said. "Now that I've met you, how can I go home and know I'll never get to talk to you again?"

"I'll be sorry when our talks end, too," Nemo said.

"They shouldn't *have* to, though, that's the point," J.D. said. "The nuclear missile was a mistake. Bad luck, and misunderstanding, and error. It wouldn't happen again in a hundred years. In five hundred! Especially if people back on Earth knew about Civilization."

"The nuclear missile was bad luck," Nemo said.

J.D. chose to interpret the expressionless comment as agreement, rather than as a question, or as skepticism.

"I have to find the other people, Nemo. The ones who came before. I have to explain what happened, so they'll stop withdrawing the cosmic string."

"There are no other ones anymore, J.D."

J.D. sank down. Androgeos had said the same thing, but J.D. had stopped believing Androgeos when he tried to steal Victoria's transition algorithm. Hearing Nemo say the same thing shocked her. She trusted and believed Nemo.

"How do you *know*? How *can* you know the other ones are gone?"

"There haven't been any in a million years."

"Maybe you just never met any," J.D. said. "The galaxy's a big place."

"Have you been everywhere?" Zev asked. Several of Nemo's attendants had gathered at Zev's feet, snuffling at his toes, at his semiretractile claws. He petted them like kittens, like the baby octopuses the divers liked to keep around.

"I haven't been everywhere," Nemo said.

"So there might be some you don't know about." J.D. smiled sadly, but she felt hopeful again.

"I don't think so."

"We've got to keep looking. Maybe I'm too arrogant, but I think our people would be an asset to Civilization. And maybe I'm not arrogant enough, but I don't think our nuclear missiles are a threat to any of you. Even our military thinks interstellar war would be stupid and unwageable."

"Stupid isn't equivalent to lacking destructive power," Nemo said.

J.D. slumped, her hands lying limp on her knees. It was essential to her, even if selfish and simple-minded, to return to Earth with a successful expedition. She was terrified at what would happen—not only to her and her renegade colleagues, but to their whole planet—if they returned a failure.

The rush of Nemo's insubstantial food had vanished, leaving her drained and shaky. She was too tired to think, too tired to talk. She could not remember the last time she had rested. She goosed her metabolic enhancer, but it too had exhausted itself.

"Where do you come from?" Zev asked.

Nemo did not reply.

"Bad question?" Zev asked.

Nemo's long tentacles writhed and coiled slowly around the half-formed bag; their sound was of waves caressing dry sand.

"No question is bad," Nemo replied.

"But you didn't answer."

"I come from here," Nemo said.

"From Sirius, you mean?"

"Yes."

"It's lonely here," Zev said. "No other people. No life on the planets."

"My people didn't evolve here," Nemo said.

"Then where?"

Nemo's tentacles twined, quivered, relaxed.

"I can't tell you."

"Why not?"

"I don't know how."

J.D. saw in her mind the glimmer of a star map. Zev brought it from the *Chi*'s onboard computer and sent it through his link. The sun was a point of light in the center; its near neighbors spread out around it. J.D. closed her eyes and looked at the map in her mind.

"Can you see this all right?" Zev asked.

"Make it bigger."

The scale changed. The dark space containing a few sparks changed into a crowded field of stars.

"How's that?"

"Make it bigger."

Zev scaled it all the way up to the Milky Way and its neighboring galaxies, bright multicolored spirals and ellipses, dark dusty clouds.

"Big enough?"

"Not that big," Nemo said.

"Can you travel between galaxies?" J.D. asked.

"We are not so advanced."

Zev showed Nemo a representation of the Milky Way.

"On the other side," Nemo said.

The galaxy rotated. But its other side was dark and empty, for no human being knew what lay beyond the crowded stars and dust clouds of the galaxy's center.

"We don't have that information," J.D. said.

"I could show you. . . ," Nemo said, then, "No, I cannot, because of your link."

Zev let the map fade. J.D. sighed, and opened her eyes, more determined to enhance her link as soon as she could.

"You've come a long way," Zev said.

"My people have."

A lifeliner scuttled into the chamber, trailing silk. Right behind it, Victoria swung around the edge of the curtain. Ecstatic, she strode toward Nemo.

"Nemo, your center—I want to know all about it! Is it neutronium? How did you build it? How does it make you move?" She switched from using her link to speaking aloud. "J.D., are you okay?" She dropped to her knees next to J.D. and put her arm around J.D.'s shoulders. J.D. leaned against her gratefully.

"Just tired," she said.

"My center's difficult to explain," Nemo said.

"Try me."

J.D. could hear the dryness in Victoria's tone; she wondered if Nemo could.

"I mean difficult physically."

"How so?"

"Your link is like J.D.'s," Nemo said.

"It's too narrow," J.D. said. "None of us can take in everything Nemo could show us."

"Arachne and I could exchange information," Nemo said, "about my center, about the galaxy."

J.D. glanced at Nemo, then quickly at Victoria.

"No," Victoria said. "No, I'm sorry, I don't think that's possible."

"Talking is enjoyable, but slow, and imprecise, and insufficient," Nemo said.

"Maybe . . . limited access to Arachne?" J.D. said softly.

Victoria twitched her head sideways, a quick, definite negative. Full access to Arachne meant access to Victoria's algorithm. Limited access . . . who could tell how deeply Nemo might delve? The algorithm was the only thing *Starfarer* had, the only thing Earth had, that Civilization had shown the least interest in. Once Civilization possessed it, human beings had nothing left to bargain with.

"I'm sorry, Nemo," Victoria said. "That isn't a decision I can make myself. I'll have to discuss it with my colleagues. Do you understand?"

"No," Nemo said.

How *could* Nemo understand? J.D. thought. All alone here, with the power to go anywhere, and do anything . . .

"Human beings and divers talk about what they do," Zev said. "And about what they did and about what they plan. Sometimes it's boring, but it's very serious."

Nemo touched Zev's forehead, then J.D.'s cheek, with one soft tentacle. The other two tentacles continued to guide the spinners around and around and around the edge of another pouch.

"I must think, and you must all talk together."

"Yes," J.D. said. "As soon as Satoshi and Stephen Thomas get back—"

"They'll meet you at the airlock."

It was the first time Nemo had interrupted her. J.D.'s gaze met Victoria's. Victoria looked thoughtful. J.D. felt stricken. She had been dismissed.

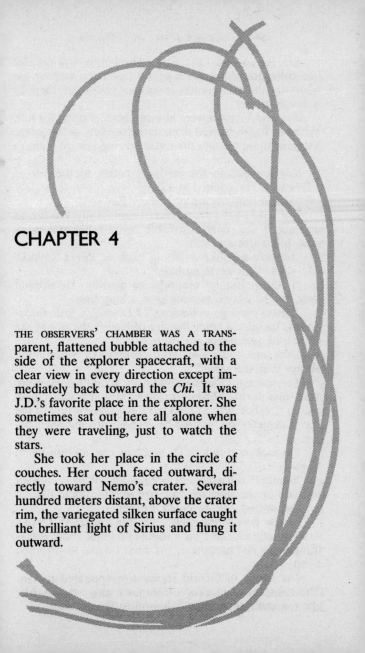

CHAPTER 4

THE OBSERVERS' CHAMBER WAS A TRANS-
parent, flattened bubble attached to the
side of the explorer spacecraft, with a
clear view in every direction except immediately back toward the *Chi*. It was
J.D.'s favorite place in the explorer. She
sometimes sat out here all alone when
they were traveling, just to watch the
stars.

   She took her place in the circle of
couches. Her couch faced outward, directly toward Nemo's crater. Several
hundred meters distant, above the crater
rim, the variegated silken surface caught
the brilliant light of Sirius and flung it
outward.

J.D. felt too tired to talk, too tired even to think. But her colleagues back on *Starfarer* had been waiting for hours for this conference. It was not fair to ask them to wait any longer.

Zev and Victoria were already there, waiting for her. With her hands shoved deep in the pockets of her jeans, Victoria stood outside the circle, gazing toward Nemo's crater.

Zev lounged in the auxiliary couch to the left of J.D.'s seat. He grinned at J.D.

"Nemo reminds me of home," Zev said.

J.D. stroked the young diver's arm fondly. His fur, so delicate it was nearly invisible against his mahogany skin, felt warm and soft.

"Nemo's not like anything back in Puget Sound," J.D. said. "Not anything like."

"I know. But he reminds me anyway. He doesn't look like he's been swimming in a long time."

"Nemo can't go swimming," J.D. said, a little impatiently. Imagine a being the size of Nemo, the size of the planetoid, swimming anywhere.

"Not *now*," Zev said. "But critters like Nemo don't always look the same."

Zev was right. Nemo could have gone through more than one form. Maybe that was why Europa called Nemo a squidmoth. J.D. added Zev's observation to the list of subjects she wanted to discuss with the alien being.

Through her link, J.D. reached out tentatively to Nemo.

"Nemo?" she asked. "I'm going to talk to everybody back on board *Starfarer*. You can join in, if you like."

She waited. She received no reply.

I know how Nemo feels, J.D. said to herself. I'd like to sit quietly all alone for a while and think about everything that's just happened. No. First I'd like to get some sleep.

The image of Gerald Hemminge appeared nearby. The assistant chancellor of *Starfarer* also acted as the alien contact department's liaison to the starship.

"Are you ready?" he asked. "Everyone's anxious to start."

"In a minute, Gerald, thank you," J.D. said. "We're still getting ourselves together."

"Very well." As he turned, he faded out.

Stephen Thomas entered and crossed the transparent floor of the circle. He had changed to a *Starfarer* T-shirt and a clean pair of long pants with the *Starfarer* logo on the thigh, unusually subdued clothes for Stephen Thomas. But he no longer looked as bedraggled as when he came out of Nemo's crater.

He stopped beside Victoria, but he did not speak and he did not touch her. He stared out the transparent side of the observers' circle, his gaze on Nemo's spiky curtains of silk. The severity of his hair, pulled tight and tied at the back of his neck, made him cold, and aloof.

J.D. wondered what he was thinking about. The alien museum, on a harsh little airless world not too different from this one, fusing and destroying itself as he watched? The collapse of the genetics department around him? The changing virus turning him into a diver? No . . . none of those, of course. He was thinking about Feral, wondering how the enthusiastic young journalist would have reacted to Nemo. He was mourning the delight Feral would never feel. Mourning Feral.

Then Victoria briefly touched her younger partner's hand, and they turned to join the circle. Stephen Thomas looked straight at J.D., completely expressionless, and she had no idea what he was thinking.

She glanced away, embarrassed to be staring at him, and blinked fast to clear her eyes of tears.

Victoria took her place in the seat across from J.D. Stephen Thomas sat at J.D.'s right.

Satoshi came in a moment later. He always moved so smoothly, so athletically: he nonchalantly carried two brimful mugs of tea. He handed one to J.D.

"Careful. It's hot."

"Thanks," she said. Trying not to move the cup, she leaned forward and took a sip so she would not spill it.

It *was* hot. She had to slurp it so she would not burn her tongue.

"You looked like you could use it," he said. He sat in his couch one place to Zev's left.

Now the members of the alien contact department were all in their places, quartering the observers' circle like the cardinal points of a compass. Zev broke the pattern, but J.D. was glad beyond words that he had joined the expedition, and grateful that Victoria had not objected when he accompanied her on board the *Chi*.

Zev enfolded her hand with his long webbed fingers. In the sea, he would have touched her more closely. He was learning land manners. J.D. was learning that on land, land manners were not always preferable. Even when they were more appropriate.

He cared more about her than about her success with Nemo, she thought. His curiosity had brought him to the expedition—that, and missing her. Maybe missing her had been the most important factor. He participated with delight in the expedition, but the most significant part of life, for divers, was the connection among friends, family, and lovers. J.D. and Zev were all three to each other.

She squeezed his hand gratefully, sipped her tea, and collected herself for the conference. She felt like she had crashed from the high of an intense long-distance swim. Besides the physical effort, the emotional exertion had taken its toll.

In principle, she supported the idea that her colleagues should be able to accompany her vicariously. She welcomed the ability to call on their knowledge and ideas and questions. In practice, she hated every minute she spent in front of cameras and recorders.

"Did you have a chance to look at my LTM recording?" Stephen Thomas asked.

"No," J.D. said. "I'm sorry." They had only been back on board the *Chi* for a few minutes. She had not had a chance to look at what any of her colleagues had seen on their excursions into Nemo.

"I think you should. It was weirder than shit. Hard

to figure out what it meant, or what Nemo intended to tell me."

"I'll look at it as soon as I can. And we can ask about it, as soon as Nemo starts communicating again."

"Okay."

J.D. folded her hands around the tea mug. A comforting warmth seeped through its insulation.

"I guess I'm ready. Shall we start?"

"Okay." Victoria's eyelids flickered and she went into a brief communications fugue to notify Gerald. "We're on."

All their colleagues from *Starfarer* could now see and hear and speak to everyone on the *Chi*.

"J.D.," Victoria said suddenly, "Nemo will probably listen to everything we say."

"Of course," J.D. said. "Yes. I hope so. Listen, and maybe join the conversation."

"We shall all bear that in mind," Gerald Hemminge said. "We'll start the questions with Senator Orazio. Senator?"

Victoria sat forward—about to object, J.D. thought, because the two United States senators were not members of the deep space expedition. They were unwilling guests. They had been on a fact-finding tour of *Starfarer* when it plunged out of the solar system, fulfilling its charter, but disobeying the orders of EarthSpace and the U.S. military.

Instead of speaking, Victoria sat stiffly back. J.D. glanced at her with a sympathetic expression.

The holographic image of Ruth Orazio, junior senator from Washington State, appeared before J.D.

"J.D., you *must* try again to persuade Nemo to return to Earth with us."

"Senator . . . my question to Nemo was hypothetical. We aren't on our way back to Earth."

Orazio had always supported the deep space expedition, and against all probability, she still did. How long her support would last was another question entirely. J.D. would not blame her when it waned; she had never agreed to leaving her family, her profession, her home world.

"We have to go home," Orazio said. "You came away unprepared, undersupplied, and understaffed, with an undependable computer web. It's dangerous to go on this way."

"And more dangerous to go back," Stephen Thomas said.

"The expedition members have already decided that question." Victoria did not soften her cold tone with the Canadian speech habit of raising the inflection of a sentence at the end, turning it into a question, inviting the listener to agree. "It isn't appropriate to argue it again now."

"Dr. MacKenzie, we all know you'll never agree to any plan that furthers the interests of the United States." William Derjaguin, the senior senator from New Mexico, spoke out of turn. "At least let us discuss the subject!"

Derjaguin had always opposed the expedition bitterly. Being kidnapped on a hijacked starship did nothing for his temper.

"We discussed it at length," Victoria said.

J.D. broke in. "It wasn't fair of me to ask Nemo to go to Earth in the first place," she said. "The cosmic string has receded from the solar system. We can still go home. But we can't leave again until the cosmic string returns."

"Unless it returns," Victoria said.

"Europa *said* squid—Nemo's people just orbited stars and listened and watched," Orazio said. "And Europa said nobody even did that once we could detect them."

The interstellar community had paid Earth very little attention at all, Europa claimed. Civilization never involved itself in the affairs of non-spacefaring worlds. Europa had found the idea of UFO reports quite amusing, which was an interesting reaction considering that she herself had been abducted by a UFO. But Civilization limited itself to the secret rescue of a few doomed

individuals, including Europa and Androgeos. It saved
them from natural disasters in order to train them to
greet the first expedition of starfarers from their own
home world.

Other than that courtesy—a courtesy J.D. thought
not only questionable but condescending—the interstellar community ignored new intelligences until they
proved they were interesting enough, advanced enough,
to bother talking to. So far, human beings did not qual-
ify.

"They've had to avoid us for two generations," Ruth
said. "What better star to orbit now than ours?"

"What better star to avoid," Stephen Thomas said,
"than the home of warlike barbarians?"

J.D. chuckled ruefully. "Good point."

Ruth smiled. "But who could resist trying to convert
a bunch of barbarians? Victoria, I'm not letting you off
the hook about going home. If we can persuade Nemo
to go with us, then the deep space expedition will have
accomplished the aim of its charter. You'll be able to
prove an interstellar community exists."

"The senator makes an incontrovertible point," Gerald said. "Under those circumstances, we'd have no
other ethical choice than to go home. Whether we could
leave again would be completely immaterial."

Gerald Hemminge was one of the few expedition
members who thought the starship should go home. He
was one of the few who had argued for following Earth-
Space orders, for converting the campus to an orbiting
spy platform.

But what he said was true.

"Nemo's already said no," J.D. said.

"But people sometimes change their minds," Ruth
said. "I intend to try to persuade Nemo to go home with
us, if I get the chance."

J.D. smiled back. She had admired Senator Orazio
before she ever met her; having met her, she liked her.

"When we do go home," J.D. said, "whenever it is,
nothing would make me happier than to have Nemo
come along with us."

"I have a question," Gerald said, in the round, high-class British tones that always managed to sound more or less disapproving, "if I may step out of my liaison position for a moment."

"Go ahead," J.D. said.

"I was rather surprised . . . that you *ate* a live animal."

J.D. grinned mischievously. "It was good, Gerald. Essence of fresh shrimp, with honey-orange sauce. Quite a rush, too. It wasn't any stranger than eating an oyster."

"If you say so," Gerald said. "There is a question from the astronomy department. Avvaiyar?"

The tall, elegant astronomer appeared in the circle. She gestured, her hands as graceful as a dancer's, and the image of the Milky Way also appeared. It turned, revealing the unmapped area beyond its core.

"We have a matter of policy to decide," she said. "Can we afford to turn down Nemo's offer to exchange information?"

"Can we afford to accept it?" Stephen Thomas said, sounding grim. J.D. wished she had had a chance to see what he had encountered in Nemo's crater. She could not spare the attention, now, to look at it, but it had spooked him badly. Her impression was that Stephen Thomas Gregory did not spook easily.

"What do you think, J.D.?" Victoria asked.

"I . . ." She took a deep breath. "I want to say yes. I trust Nemo—"

"That fact is self-evident," Gerald said dryly.

"But we aren't just talking about me. I think . . . I think we still have time to think about it and decide."

"We have only a few days till we enter transition," Avvaiyar said.

"I know." J.D. reached out briefly through her link toward Nemo. This is your chance to persuade my colleagues, she thought.

But Nemo did not reply.

"I think it's too dangerous to give Nemo access to Arachne," Victoria said.

"You're suggesting that we give up a great deal in order to protect your new transition algorithm," Gerald said.

"That's right," Victoria said.

"In other words, you feel your work may be the only thing human beings will ever have to trade that the interstellar community will want."

"What's your point, Gerald?" Stephen Thomas carried his voice with an edge.

Gerald ignored Stephen Thomas. "Rather arrogant, perhaps, Victoria."

"Yes," Victoria said.

"There's no need for personal animosity," Professor Thanthavong said.

"I meant no animosity. I'm merely suggesting that if we gain this new knowledge, we can go home—with or without Nemo—and consider the expedition a success. If Nemo takes the transition algorithm, what of it? We'll have five hundred years to develop something equally impressive."

"I can't believe you're so anxious to give up and go home!" Victoria said.

J.D. leaned back in her seat. This was an important discussion, and she was an important part of any conclusion. She had to pay attention to it.

She closed her eyes. Just for a moment.

Satoshi woke. Victoria snuggled against him, one arm beneath her cheek, the other draped around his waist. They had dozed, waiting for Stephen Thomas. The bed felt empty without their younger partner.

When J.D. fell asleep in the observers' circle, Victoria had decided not to awaken her. No one was ready to make a decision about Nemo and Arachne, so they ended the conference. Everyone, on the *Chi* and back on *Starfarer,* was as grateful for a few hours' rest.

Everyone, apparently, except Stephen Thomas.

I wonder where he is? Satoshi thought. Sleeping alone in his cabin?

Not likely.

Stephen Thomas liked to sleep with his partners. He liked to sleep in the middle, the way Merry used to.

Not that Stephen Thomas had taken Merry's place, or even tried. No one could ever do that. But after Merry's accident, only a few months after Stephen Thomas joined the family partnership, the triad had comforted them all.

I wonder if our family would have survived after Merry died, Satoshi wondered, if not for Stephen Thomas? I don't think it would have. I fell apart pretty badly, and so did Victoria.

The old ache and the numb shock returned. He hugged Victoria fiercely, desperately. The pain had barely diminished in the time since Merry's death. It hit less frequently, but it hit just as hard.

Victoria woke. She held him, stroking his smooth short hair, murmuring comfort in his ear.

"I love you," Satoshi whispered. "I don't know what I'd do without you and Stephen Thomas."

"I love you, too," she said. "And if I have anything to say about it, you'll never need to find out what you'd do without me. But where's Stephen Thomas?"

"Maybe he thought we were sleeping in his room tonight."

Victoria looked at Satoshi, askance. They seldom all slept in Stephen Thomas's room. He had a lot of good qualities, but neatness was not one of them. His room back on *Starfarer* was bad enough. The *Chi*'s forays into free-fall turned his cubicle into a disaster area.

"I'll go see," Satoshi said.

He crossed Victoria's cabin and his own, pushing the connecting door the rest of the way open to create a single space. The door into Stephen Thomas's room stood ajar. Satoshi pushed it open. Stephen Thomas was not there. His patchwork quilt, a wedding gift from Merry's family, lay rumpled across his bed.

He can't still be in his lab, Satoshi thought. Can he? Maybe he fell asleep there.

Satoshi pulled his own ratty bathrobe out of the storage net on the wall, put it on, and crossed to the laboratory section of the *Chi*.

At the doorway of Stephen Thomas's lab, Satoshi stopped. His partner tilted his chair to its limit, his hands behind his head and his feet braced against the lab table. Stephen Thomas gazed, frowning, at the magnified image of growing cells.

"Hi, Satoshi," Stephen Thomas said without turning around. He took his feet off the table and let his chair drop forward.

Satoshi put his hands on Stephen Thomas's shoulders.

"Coming to bed?"

Stephen Thomas shrugged.

If Stephen Thomas had asked him to go away, he would have complied. Stephen Thomas could be moody, and he could say, often bluntly, what he wanted. But he had been so quiet recently that Satoshi worried. They had been through a lot. Maybe it all was catching up with Stephen Thomas. Maybe he was still in shock because of Feral's death.

Or maybe turning into a diver was not as benign a procedure as Zev thought.

It troubled Satoshi that Stephen Thomas had chosen to let the changes proceed. They had begun by accident, by mistake. Satoshi wished the accident had never happened.

You don't have any right to tell him what to do with his body, he told himself sternly.

Don't I? he replied to himself. I love him. I care what happens to him.

And I think this is crazy.

"I don't understand what's going on with these cells," Stephen Thomas said.

"Which ones are they?"

"From Europa's weed. Ordinary soil bacteria. Same as back on Earth, she said."

"But?"

"But not quite. They'll grow on dirt from *Starfarer,* if I sterilize it. Not otherwise. I must have missed something."

"It's late, you're tired. You're working too hard."

"I'm not working hard enough." Stephen Thomas slapped the lab table with a sharp, shocking strike. "Or I'd be able to figure this out. Everything I've done since we left home has been crap."

"Come to bed."

"I wouldn't be good company."

"Are you okay?"

"Twitchy. Achy. I'll probably thrash around. I'd keep you both awake."

"I don't care," Satoshi said.

Satoshi looked at Stephen Thomas for a long moment. He was as susceptible to his partner's extraordinary beauty as anyone. As everyone. He stroked Stephen Thomas's long blond hair. It had, as usual, come untied. It curled around his partner's face and tangled down over his shoulders.

"Is your hair going to change color?"

"Probably not," Stephen Thomas said. "No reason it should. Zev says I should cut it, to be a proper diver."

"You never cut it to work in zero g, why should you cut it now?"

"I'm not going to. *Starfarer* doesn't have a proper ocean, so I can't be a proper diver no matter what."

Most divers had dark eyes. So far, Stephen Thomas's eyes remained brilliant sapphire blue. Satoshi hoped they would not change. He started to ask. But if they were going to change, he did not want to know.

Satoshi slid his hand beneath the collar of his partner's shirt, a deliberately arousing touch. His fingers stroked the soft new fuzz of fine, transparent diver's fur.

Satoshi froze. He willed himself to leave his hand where it was. He could not tell if Stephen Thomas noticed his reaction.

Stephen Thomas put his hand on Satoshi's. The

swimming webs felt warm against Satoshi's skin. Satoshi shivered. Stephen Thomas tensed and closed his eyes.

"What's wrong?" Satoshi asked.

"I've just beat my body up pretty good the last few days," Stephen Thomas said.

"But Zev said—"

"I had a run-in with a silver slug, all right?" Stephen Thomas said angrily.

"What? How? When?"

"When I tried to get into the chancellor's house."

"Why?"

"Why the hell do you think? He killed Feral! I wanted . . . I don't know what I wanted. I don't know if I would've killed him. But the slugs make fucking good watchdogs. It just about squashed the crap out of me. For a while I thought it broke my pelvis."

"Are you sure—"

"It's just bruises."

"Good lord," Satoshi said. The lithoclasts guarding Blades were the size of rhinoceroses. "You could have been killed."

"I know. I won't do it again." He moved Satoshi's hand away, gently but firmly. "I want to sleep alone tonight." His voice was careful, neutral.

Satoshi hesitated. "Okay," he said. He was upset and confused and he had no idea whether he was relieved or disappointed that Stephen Thomas would not come to bed with him. "See you in the morning."

He started out of the lab.

He could still feel the fur against his fingers.

"Satoshi!"

"Yeah?" He turned back.

"Don't tell Victoria," Stephen Thomas said, his voice intense. "About the slug."

Satoshi frowned. "I hate it when you ask me to keep things from Victoria."

"I shouldn't have told either one of you, dammit! I knew it would just upset you both—"

"All right. All right! I won't tell her."

He left his younger partner alone.

He returned to Victoria. She lay on the sleeping surface of her cabin, one knee drawn up, the other leg extended, her fingers laced behind her head, her eyes half closed.

"He wants to sleep by himself tonight."

Her expression was her only question.

"He said he was achy, he said he'd thrash around. . . ." Satoshi was not lying. Not technically. "I don't know," he said.

"One of his moody spells," Victoria said. She had learned to overlook them, as Stephen Thomas preferred. "He'll be okay in the morning."

"Victoria," Satoshi said, "he's growing *fur.*"

"I know. I saw." She grinned. "I think it's kind of sexy, don't you?"

She reached out to him. He grasped her long, slender fingers, lay beside her, and pulled the blanket over them both. Victoria hooked her foot over his leg, sliding her instep up his calf. She pulled him closer and kissed him, hard and hungrily. He opened his mouth for her tongue, and rolled over on his back, drawing her on top of him, abandoning himself to her, abandoning his worries and his fears.

And yet, making love with Victoria in the starlight, in the harsh reflected shine of Sirius, Satoshi missed the touch of Stephen Thomas's body, the strength of his hands, his voice.

After Satoshi left, Stephen Thomas stared at the cell cultures for a few more minutes. He did not want to move. His whole body hurt.

Just ignore it, he said to himself. You'd feel worse after a rough soccer game.

He was used to recovering quickly. He still did recover quickly: a few days ago he had had two black eyes and a livid cut across his forehead. Those bruises had vanished and the scar was fading.

The ache of the changing virus remained. And once in a while, completely unexpectedly, real pain ambushed him. Before he realized how badly the slug had bruised him, he had feared something was going wrong with the changes.

He wished he could just take to his bed and get his partners to bring him chicken soup. They would do it, too . . . except that then he would end up having to tell Victoria what had really happened. Admitting to Satoshi what a fool he had been was bad enough. He did not think he could stand to admit it to Victoria.

He swore out loud, shut down the lab, and went across the *Chi* to his cubicle. In the far cabin, Victoria and Satoshi murmured to each other. An ache radiated from the center of his pelvis. It spread in a wave. He quietly closed the door that joined his partners' cabins to his own.

He stripped off his clothes, untangled his quilt, and lay down on the sleeping surface. He pulled the quilt around his shoulders. It used to smell like Merry, but it did not anymore, even in his imagination.

He was wide awake. He flung off the quilt, turned over, stretched, and looked at himself.

His body proportions were similar to Zev's: he was slender, narrow-hipped; he had good shoulders. But Zev, like most divers, was rather short. Stephen Thomas liked being tall. He hoped that would not change.

So far, his toenails had not begun to change to semiretractile claws. He curled his toes. His feet were about the only part of him that did not hurt.

His skin changed from day to day. Not only its color. He had traded the maddening itch between his fingers, while the webbing formed, for a milder itch all over his body as the fine, nearly invisible hair grew in.

He liked the delicate pelt. He thought he would find it sexy on another person. He rubbed his hand down his forearm, down his side. He hoped Victoria and Satoshi would get to like it, too.

I wonder whether Merry would have liked it? Stephen Thomas thought. Probably. Merry was always the one who wanted to experiment.

The partnership had never quite perfected the com-

plex, erotic chaos of four people making love to each
other in the same bed. They had needed more time.
They had all been looking forward to trying sex in free-
fall. But they never got to try it as a foursome; Merry
died before their first trip into space.

With a sharp pang of loneliness, Stephen Thomas
wished he were sleeping with his partners. But all his
reasons for sleeping alone remained. He hurt, he was
restless, he would keep them awake. Besides, he liked to
please them, and for the past couple of days his interest
in sex had been very low.

That worried him. He explained his lack of interest
to himself with the bruises, the persistent ache, the oc-
casional intense pain.

He told the lights to turn off, curled up in his quilt,
and hugged his knees to his chest. That eased him a
little.

His mind spun around the strange behavior of his
cell cultures, the disturbing encounter with Nemo's
pond creatures.

Trying to take his mind off his work, Stephen
Thomas thought about Feral.

Feral liked change, just like Merry did. That was one
of the reasons Stephen Thomas had been attracted to
him. Feral had joined the expedition's revolt without
hesitation. He had been excited when Stephen Thomas
decided to finish turning into a diver. He had even been
envious.

Stephen Thomas smiled wryly to himself.

Some of these changes you wouldn't be envious of,
my friend, he thought. But I bet you would've liked my
new fur.

On impulse, he opened a private channel back to
Starfarer. In response to his call, Gerald Hemminge appeared, his dark hair mussed. A wrinkle, the image of a
crease in his pillow, was imprinted across his cheek.

"Did I wake you up?"

Gerald glanced sideways, realized he was transmitting his image, and snapped a command to Arachne. He
faded out.

"What is it? Has there been a new development?"

"No," Stephen Thomas said. "Nemo's still quiet."

"Then why did you call me? Don't you ever sleep?"

No, Stephen Thomas thought, I don't, these days.

"I called you because I want to talk to you for a minute. Why'd you answer, if you were asleep?"

"Because I'm your bloody liaison!"

"But I marked the message private—"

Stephen Thomas stopped. No point in deliberately getting into an argument with Gerald. They argued enough anyway.

"It's about Feral."

"What about him?"

Gerald's image reappeared. He had combed his hair and put on a shirt. Except for the crease across his cheek, he looked wide awake and professional.

"His funeral. We should do something—"

Gerald stared at him. "You never cease to amaze me. You're in the midst of humanity's first alien contact—"

"It's only the first if you don't count Europa," Stephen Thomas said.

"Europa isn't an alien."

"Europa's the first human to meet aliens—Look, Gerald, forget Europa, I want to talk about Feral."

"There's nothing we can do here and now."

"I know, but when I come back—"

"When we return to Earth, we'll turn his body over to his family."

"*What?* That might be years!"

"I sincerely hope not."

"Besides, he hasn't got any family."

"The proper authorities, in that case."

"But—"

"I'm sorry. There's nothing to be done. I haven't any authority to make any arrangements. It will have to wait till we go home."

Stephen Thomas started to object again, but Gerald interrupted.

"And now, if you don't mind, some of us would like to be fresh for the next conversation with Nemo."

He broke the connection.

"Shit," Stephen Thomas muttered to the air where Gerald's image had faded.

J.D. woke, disoriented. Stars and darkness surrounded her.

It was nearly morning. She was still in her couch in the observers' circle, but the couch had been extended flat. A blanket covered her.

Oh, no, she thought. I fell asleep during the conference. I was just going to close my eyes. . . .

Zev curled nearby, on his own couch. He woke and drew in a deep gasp of air. Divers slept like orcas, napping till they needed another breath, waking, breathing, drifting back to sleep. Zev turned toward her, his dark eyes reflecting light like a cat's, his fine fur catching the starlight. He looked like a gilded statue, with eerie emerald eyes.

"Hi, Zev."

In silence, he left his couch and joined her in hers, snuggling close. His webbed hand slid beneath her shirt and over her full breast. In a moment of embarrassment she started to draw away. But the sensors and the cameras and the microphones were all turned off. No one could watch them through the transparent walls of the circle. The *Chi* was quiet, Victoria and Satoshi and Stephen Thomas asleep together in their cabin.

J.D. hugged Zev closer, and kissed him. Her tongue touched his sharp, dangerous canine teeth. He nibbled at her lips, at her throat, at her collarbone, unbuttoning her shirt with his free hand. She pressed her hands down his muscular back, beneath his loose silk shorts. His body was hot against her, urgent with his insistent, ingenuous sexuality.

He wriggled out of his shorts. He straddled J.D.'s thighs while he unfastened her pants and pushed them down over her hips, then when she had kicked them to the floor he moved between her legs. Among divers, men as well as women produced a sexual lubricant. As J.D. and Zev played and caressed and teased each other, Zev grew slick just like J.D.

J.D. kissed Zev's shoulder. His fur felt soft and bright against her lips. She gasped as he stroked her inner thigh with his warm webbed fingers.

They moved with each other in the slow, luxurious rhythms of the sea, leading each other on. The rhythm quickened, grew desperate and joyful, and they loved each other beneath the alien stars.

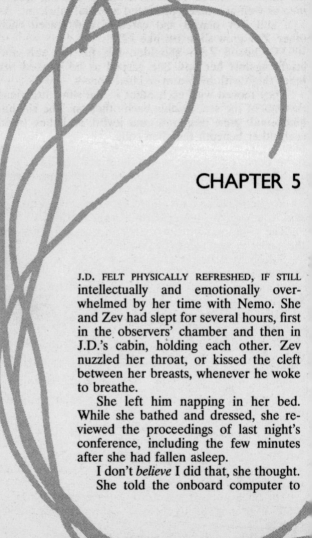

CHAPTER 5

J.D. FELT PHYSICALLY REFRESHED, IF STILL intellectually and emotionally overwhelmed by her time with Nemo. She and Zev had slept for several hours, first in the observers' chamber and then in J.D.'s cabin, holding each other. Zev nuzzled her throat, or kissed the cleft between her breasts, whenever he woke to breathe.

She left him napping in her bed. While she bathed and dressed, she reviewed the proceedings of last night's conference, including the few minutes after she had fallen asleep.

I don't *believe* I did that, she thought. She told the onboard computer to take away that display and show her the recordings of her colleagues' experiences with Nemo.

Nemo had tempted Victoria with the inner workings of a starship, and tantalized Satoshi with more hints of the complexity of the web community.

What Nemo had offered Stephen Thomas, J.D. did not understand any better than Stephen Thomas did. The violence of the inner pool shocked her.

We were visiting an alien, she thought. We have to expect encounters that are . . . alien.

And . . . if I were inside my own body, watching blood cells attack pathogens, watching osteoclasts break down bone, I'd be just as surprised, and repelled.

She kept waiting for a message from Nemo. It worried her to have heard nothing.

You're thinking hard and long, Nemo my friend, she said to herself. I wonder what that means for us?

The computer put away the displays. J.D. went to the galley to find some breakfast.

Satoshi hunched over a cup of coffee, staring into the steam.

"Good morning," J.D. said, surprised to see him. Satoshi was not known as an early riser.

"Hi," he said shortly.

"I'm sorry about yesterday," she said.

He raised his head; his expression remained blank, distracted.

"Huh?"

"For falling asleep."

"Oh. God, don't apologize. You've been going flat out for days."

J.D. reconstituted some milk—*Starfarer* did not have any cows, and she had not worked herself up to making hot chocolate with goat's milk—and heated it.

"Satoshi . . . do *you* think we ought to let Nemo into Arachne?"

He sipped coffee, his strong square hands wrapped around the mug, lifting it slowly, putting it down deliberately.

"Yes," he said. "As a matter of fact, I do."

"You do!"

"I think the potential's worth the risk."

"That's my reaction, emotionally," J.D. said. "But intellectually I keep telling myself it's a terrible idea."

"I understand Victoria's point of view," Satoshi said. "But the trade . . . a million years of observation, even if it's limited observation—"

"Who knows about that," J.D. said.

"Right."

"What does Stephen Thomas think?"

"I don't know *what* Stephen Thomas thinks or feels or wants!"

Satoshi's outburst startled J.D.

Satoshi lifted his mug, but set it down hard instead of drinking.

"He spends all his time alone, in his lab, or—" His hands clenched around it. "He's changed so much."

J.D. sat down across the table.

"Because of Feral? Because of turning into a diver?"

"I don't know," Satoshi said sadly, more calmly. "Feral, being a Changeling, misjudging Blades . . . that's all part of it. But not all." He stopped and sat back, embarrassed. "You don't need to hear this."

"It's all right," J.D. said.

Victoria's voice flowed through the intercom.

"Hey, you guys, anybody up? Come look at this!"

J.D. and Satoshi hurried to the observers' chamber, where Victoria sat with her couch turned to face the curved glass wall.

J.D. saw what Victoria was watching. She whistled softly through her teeth as she slid into the auxiliary couch next to Victoria's and turned it toward the outside.

A protrusion of silk led from the crater, across the rocky surface of the planetoid, nearly to the *Chi*. It looked like a thick, rumpled carpet. As J.D. watched, it extended itself another handsbreadth. The leading edge roiled and quivered as silk-spinners created it from the inside out.

"It worried me at first," Victoria said, "but Nemo's

making no attempt to camouflage it. I tested the silk—
it's strong, but it wouldn't withstand the *Chi*'s engines if
we lifted off. I don't think it's any danger."

"I wish Nemo would answer my transmissions," J.D.
said. "I could ask about it. And about what Stephen
Thomas saw. I'm worried. . . . I don't know what to
think about the silence. Or the way Nemo dismissed us
yesterday."

"Nemo hasn't given up on us entirely," Victoria said.
"The planetoid is following *Starfarer* toward Europa's
transition point."

"Nemo's coming after us?" J.D. exclaimed, surprised and delighted.

"Mm-hmm. Following, but not closing any distance.
That's probably a good thing. *Starfarer* doesn't need any
more gravitation perturbations."

"I'd love another expedition into the web," Satoshi
said. "I have a good start on an analysis. But only a
start."

"We might have more time, if Nemo follows us all
the way through transition—"

"Nemo can leave from the same point and come out
at the same place on the other side," Victoria said. "But
without my algorithm, the route will be different."

"Tracking Europa?"

"Probably. I suppose it's possible Nemo has another
algorithm."

"Europa gave me the impression everybody in Civilization uses the same one. The best one they've found
yet."

"Yes. Me, too. If that's true, however long it takes
her to get wherever we're going, that's how long it'll
take Nemo. It will take us less time. But I don't know
how much less time. Whether we'll catch up to the alien
humans or not . . ."

"Wait, back up a minute," J.D. said. "You don't
know where we're going?"

"Not yet, eh? It's complicated. Arachne hasn't
solved it yet."

J.D. looked at her, astonished.

Victoria smiled, contentedly.

"It's okay, eh? The algorithm shows that wherever we're heading, it's full of cosmic string. So even if we lose Europa, we can keep going."

J.D. stared through the transparent wall. The tube of silk reached the foot of the *Chi*. There, it paused.

"What will we do, if we lose Europa's trail?"

"I don't know," Victoria said. "I just don't know."

They sat side by side and stared at the projection from Nemo's crater.

The projection began to inflate, like a balloon blowing up.

What *is* that thing? J.D. thought.

"Do you want me to open Arachne for Nemo?" Victoria asked abruptly.

"Yes," Satoshi said.

Victoria gave him a surprised look.

"Could you take your algorithm out first?" J.D. asked.

"No. Not anymore. Arachne's still finding the solutions we'll need. And by now the algorithm's hardwired in. It's part of the computer's thought patterns."

"Then . . . I guess you'd better keep Nemo out for the time being."

"Yeah. That's what I think, too."

Suddenly Nemo's tube reared up like a snake. Satoshi leaned closer, fascinated.

Victoria jumped to her feet. Her eyelids fluttered as she touched the *Chi*'s onboard computer, preparing for emergency liftoff.

"Wait, Victoria!"

Victoria opened her eyes, frowning.

"It's an airlock," J.D. said.

As they watched, the swaying tube draped itself against the *Chi*'s outer hatch. Its puckered end opened, crept outward, and its edge fastened itself around the seal of the hatch, trembling with the workings of small creatures within its walls.

A spot of heat appeared in the back of J.D.'s mind. She opened herself to the transmission.

"Nemo? Is it you?"
"J.D., please come to me."

Alone, J.D. hurried through the airlock and into the new tunnel. She did not even stop to put on her spacesuit; she simply grabbed a pocketful of LTMs and headed for Nemo's crater.

At the edge, she paused. A frayed bit of silk led downward. It was the same lifeline that she had followed yesterday. No lifeliner waited to spin her a new thread.

She descended, expecting the thread to vanish into a reshaped curtain. Each time she rounded a curve, she expected to see a lifeliner hunkered down waiting for her. But the configuration of the nest had not changed. The corridors were very quiet. J.D. saw none of the spinners and weavers and scavengers that had been so common yesterday. The curtains looked drab and dusty. She tapped into an LTM perception of the ultraviolet. Instead of bursting around her in patterns and colors, it faded into a gray moiré. The shimmering blossoms had faded to blurs.

The larger attendants no longer haunted the spaces between the corridors, throwing their shadows against the tunnel walls. The nest felt deserted. Even the lightlines had faded, as if their optical properties had deteriorated.

J.D. climbed and slid down a long slope. At the bottom, an attendant with several broken spines tried valiantly to drag away a fallen curtain. The curtain's edges shredded as it moved.

The attendant gave up trying to move the disintegrating fabric. Scrambling over wrinkles and folds, it crawled to the center, and picked and chewed at the material.

J.D. sat on her heels and watched it; in a moment it had eaten a fist-sized hole. She rose quickly and continued deeper into the web.

She reached Nemo's chamber. The squidmoth lay

motionless, eyelid closed, beside the line of silken
pouches. Still another pouch lay nearly completed beneath Nemo's limp tentacles. The spinners wandered
around the top, stumbling into each other, creating the
lacy edge.

"Nemo?"

The squidmoth's eyelid opened slowly. The long tentacles moved lethargically in a tangle; the short tentacles
hung limp. A fine mist of silken strands covered Nemo's
lower body, restraining the last couple of pairs of vibration-sending legs.

"Are you all right? Were you asleep?—But you
don't sleep."

"In this form, I don't sleep." Nemo extended the
long tentacles toward her. She grasped one; the others
curved around her body. Their warmth soaked into her.

"I'm glad you're still talking to me," J.D. said. "I was
afraid you weren't."

"You've decided not to trade information with me."

Here in Nemo's crater, J.D.'s impulse to give Nemo
access to Arachne felt much stronger than her thoughtful decision to protect *Starfarer*'s computer web.

"I'm sorry," she said. "Europa and Androgeos—Androgeos mostly—scared us. Give us all a little more time
with you."

"You're different," Nemo said.

"In what way?" J.D. was afraid Nemo would say, I
misjudged you, I don't want to talk to you anymore, go
away.

Nemo's proboscises regained their normal activity;
the mustache began to ripple.

"It's your scent that's different."

J.D. was not wearing perfume—she seldom did—
and she had used the same soap as always.

She supposed she smelled strange to Nemo, as
Nemo smelled strange to her. But . . . Nemo had not
said strange, or unpleasant. Nemo had said "different."

She started to blush. She did smell different today,
even to herself, with a trace of the deep sexy musk that
remained after she and Zev made love.

"I suppose I do," she said. "Human beings smell different depending on what they're doing, or what they've eaten, or the state of their health." She hoped that would do for now. She supposed she should tell Nemo in detail why and how she smelled different from yesterday. She might have been able to do so if they had been alone. But they were not alone. They were under the eyes of the LTMs and everyone on *Starfarer*.

Why, she thought, is it harder to tell other human beings about intimate actions—actions we share, after all—than it would be to tell someone completely alien? Because an alien would be objective about it? Because if an alien said, "How extremely strange," it would hurt less than if a human said the same thing?

"Does it bother you that I smell different today?" J.D. asked.

"Your new scent makes you a different shape in my mind."

J.D. smiled. She hoped her new shape in Nemo's mind was not quite as undignified as it had been when she was with Zev. At least they had been making love within a gravity field. In zero gravity, sex could be hilarious.

"Today you're different, too," J.D. said. "Are you . . . wearing clothes?"

"No," Nemo said.

Nemo reached up to the bank of honey ants and plucked one. Only a few remained. A burst of saliva flooded J.D.'s mouth. She could taste the sweetness and feel the rush. But instead of offering the honey ant to J.D., Nemo stroked the creature till it folded its legs. Nemo slid it into the silken pouch. Disappointed, J.D. watched it vanish.

A spinner emerged from beneath Nemo's vibration-sending legs. It crawled up the side fin and over Nemo's back, trailing a strand of silk. J.D. tapped into an LTM perception in the ultraviolet. The blanket of silk around Nemo's tail section rippled like water, like sunlight pouring through leafy trees and dappling the ground.

Several more spinners climbed up Nemo's side, helping create the layered fabric.

"You are so beautiful," J.D. said.

"I'm changing," Nemo said.

"But how? Why?"

"I'm changing myself into an adult, because I'm very old."

"But you said you're just a child."

"No, I told you I'm a juvenile."

"But when you said you'd lived for a million years— I thought you were just at the beginning of your life!"

"You asked my life span."

J.D. grasped Nemo's tentacle suddenly. She sank down beside the squidmoth and stroked the soft, brilliant skin. She *had* asked Nemo's life span. Nemo had lived a million years.

"How long do you live, after you become an adult?"

"Until I reproduce."

"In a hundred years?" She was afraid to hear the answer. She made up one she hoped to hear. "Five hundred?"

"In a few hours."

"Oh, no—!"

I keep making assumptions! she shouted, angrily, to herself. Assumptions!

"You're protesting my decision," Nemo said.

"Not your decision, just the timing. I just met you! I like you, I don't want to lose you!"

"If I'd known you were coming, I'd have waited to change."

"Can't you wait *now*?"

"No, I've been preparing for too long."

"You can't go back?"

One of the attendants that cleaned Nemo's skin scuttled across the floor.

Nemo's tentacle snapped out of J.D.'s hand and caught the creature. It struggled as Nemo placed it in the gray silk pouch. Holding the pouch with all three tentacles, trembling, Nemo sealed its edge to the curtain.

"All my attendants are parceled out." Nemo touched the bulging pouches.

"Parceled out? Why? What *are* those things?"

"They are egg sacs for my children."

"Can't you change your mind?"

"Do you wish me to change my mind?"

J.D. wanted to say, Yes! Don't change, don't die.

"What would happen if you stayed a juvenile?" she asked.

"My attendants would die."

"And your children?"

"They'd never be born."

"What about you?"

"I would leave nothing behind me."

"Tell me your life cycle," J.D. said.

"I awoke, I remembered my parents, to thank them, and I listened and I learned and I grew into my body."

J.D. clutched at a hope. "You listened to your parents? You learned from them? They were there to teach you?"

"They weren't there, but I remembered what they left for me, and I added to what they had learned."

"Were they dead?"

"My juvenile parent might still be alive, but my adult parent died, of course."

"When you exchange genetic material with others of your people—that's being a juvenile parent?"

"Yes, we're the juvenile parents of each other's children."

"But you don't bear the children until after you metamorphose into an adult," J.D. said, beginning to understand.

"That's right."

"And then you'll die."

"I'll die."

"And you can't delay the change."

Nemo touched the sacs again, handling them delicately so as not to damage the hibernating attendants and groomers, spinners and honey ants and silk-eaters. Nemo's legacy, parceled out into each offspring's cradle.

"I could stop the change."

"Then what would happen?"

"I'd never change at all."

"Never? You'd be immortal?"

"Until I got bored."

"That could be a long time, Nemo."

"But I'd have no offspring, and then no one would remember me."

Nemo's tentacles withdrew from the silken sacs. The long tentacles twined together, apart, and circled J.D.'s body, quivering, brushing her body with quick, delicate touches.

"I'd remember you," J.D. said sadly.

"You aren't immortal."

"No," J.D. said.

"It's important for my children to remember me."

"Will your children be identical to you, with identical memories—" She stopped. "No, of course not, they have another parent. A juvenile parent."

"They'll know all I know, but they won't be identical to me."

"I understand." She let Nemo's tentacle curl and cuddle in her hands, like a warm, furry snake. "I wish we'd met sooner. I would have liked more time to know you." She tried to smile. "About a hundred years."

"Maybe you'll know my children."

"I hope so."

The silk-spinners continued to crawl around and over Nemo, guided and encouraged, now and again, by one of the long tentacles.

"What will happen now?" J.D. asked.

"Soon I'll sleep, and you'll return home, and when I awaken I'll be changed."

"What will you change to?"

"You can see, if you want."

"I'd like that. Thank you. How will I know? When will it be?"

"It's different for everyone."

"I'll wait."

"No, go home, I'll call you to return."

"All right," J.D. said reluctantly.

J.D. watched the silk-weavers flow back and forth and around Nemo's body.

We could have kept Feral's body alive, she thought. We could have regenerated his burst arteries and damaged brain, but he wouldn't've been Feral anymore. He would've been a child in an adult's body, with part of his life already spent.

Trying to persuade Nemo to stop changing would have been the same as reviving Feral's body after Feral himself was gone. J.D. thought about the rhythms of life. Nemo's rhythms differed from the rhythms of a human lifespan, but they were no less demanding. For all her disappointment, J.D. respected the decision Nemo had made.

Nemo's eyelid closed completely, nearly vanishing against the shimmering peacock pattern.

"Nemo!" J.D. said, startled, afraid the squidmoth had gone to sleep without saying goodbye. "Nemo?" She sent the message softly through her link, an electronic whisper.

The eyelid quirked open.

"I'm sorry—I was afraid you'd gone already."

"I'm curious about sleep." After that, Nemo said no more.

J.D. sat beside Nemo for a long time, until the spinners finished the dappled chrysalis. The LTMs watched the scene. They would record everything, even changes that happened too quickly, too slowly, too subtly for a person to notice. J.D. put them on the floor and turned them all away from herself so she had a semblance of privacy.

The silk covered Nemo, except for the bright furred tip of one tentacle.

"J.D.?"

"I'm here, Victoria."

"Shall we go home?"

J.D. shivered. The web cooled as the light dimmed,

as if the fibers of Nemo's construction were metamorphosing along with their creator.

J.D. replied reluctantly. "Sure. I'm coming."

The *Chi*'s outer hatch closed. Nemo's tunnel loosened its seal, dropped away, and withdrew. J.D. watched it, wondering if it meant Nemo was still aware of events and surroundings.

She tried to send Nemo one last message. She received no reply.

The *Chi* returned to *Starfarer*. At first the starship was a tiny dark blot against the huge silver expanse of its distant stellar sail. It resolved, gradually, into the two enormous rotating cylinders that formed the starship's body. The *Chi* oriented itself to the hub of the campus cylinder, then approached the dock.

Slowly, perfectly, it connected.

J.D. took a deep breath and let it out, returned the reassuring pressure when Zev squeezed her hand, and kicked off gently from the *Chi*'s access hatch into *Starfarer*'s waiting room. Her overnight bag bumped against her leg; she wished she had a backpack like Satoshi's. They had called for an artificial to take their gear back into *Starfarer,* but none answered. Victoria had a small neat shoulder bag. Stephen Thomas carried a sample case on a strap, and his quilt, folded up and tucked under his arm. He no longer looked at all awkward in zero g, as he had when she first met him.

J.D. floated in amidst a crowd of people: *Starfarer*'s faculty and staff. Professor Thanthavong. Senator Orazio, whom J.D. had expected to see, and Senator Derjaguin, whom she had not. Gerald Hemminge, trying to shush the racket so he could moderate the discussion. The sailmaster, Iphigenie Dupre, who had for once come down out of the sailhouse. Avvaiyar Prakesh, whose work dovetailed with Victoria's at the point where astronomy and physics intersected. Crimson Ng, the sculptor, and Chandra, the sensory recorder, both from the art department. Nikolai Petrovich Cherenkov, the cosmonaut, hero of his homeland, refugee from his homeland. Griffith, who claimed to be an accountant from the General Accounting Office, even though no one believed him, as usual tagging along after Kolya. Infinity Mendez, whose actions after Feral's death had probably kept more people from dying. Esther Klein, the transport pilot. Floris Brown, the first member of Grandparents in Space. A gaggle of graduate students: J.D. recognized Lehua and Mitch and Fox. J.D. had no grad students of her own. Job prospects for alien contact specialists were rather low.

They all floated in the barely perceptible microgravity of the waiting room at the hub of the cylinder, surrounding the members of the alien contact department. The noise rose to a painful level as everyone burst out talking at once, asking more questions, making more comments.

"I'm sorry," J.D. said. "I can't hear you all."

Chandra, the sensory artist, pushed herself in front of everyone else and ignored Gerald's efforts to organize. She turned her strange opaque gray eyes on J.D. She looked blind, but her vision was more acute than any ordinary person's, and she could store and recall any image she perceived.

"Weren't you scared?" Chandra asked,

"Now and then," J.D. said. "But Nemo seems very gentle to me."

"Gentle! Did you see what happened to Stephen Thomas?"

"Nothing happened to Stephen Thomas," Stephen Thomas said, drifting between Florrie Brown and Fox. "I don't know what was happening to those critters, but nothing happened to me."

"It could have. We don't know what Nemo wants. Maybe when it reproduces it needs a nice warm body to lay its eggs in."

"I don't think so," J.D. said.

"Why not?"

"Because Nemo's a civilized being."

Chandra shrugged. "And we're half-evolved exiles. Why should Nemo care what happens to us? Europa didn't care if she stranded us in orbit around Sirius and we never got home."

"Nemo only eats insubstantial food," J.D. said.

"Who said anything about eating? Besides, Nemo's metamorphosing. Lots of critters eat one thing during one stage of their lives—I don't know, leaves or grass or flower nectar—that eat other stuff, other times."

"This is a subject worth discussing," Victoria said, "but let's not be morbid about it."

"I'm not morbid."

Stephen Thomas looked at her askance. "Have you taken a look at your own work lately?"

"Screw you, Stephen Thomas Gregory. And how are *you* going to feel if J.D. comes back full of maggots?"

"That's her job," Stephen Thomas said easily.

"Stephen Thomas!" Professor Thanthavong exclaimed.

J.D. laughed. "I asked for that one, Professor—Stephen Thomas is quoting me. But, Chandra . . . there's a principle of astronomy that says you aren't likely to be in the right place at the right time to observe an event of cosmological significance. Considering Nemo's age, the principle applies. It'd be a tremendous coincidence if I arrived just in time to feed Nemo's offspring."

"Unless it isn't a coincidence at all."

"What—? Oh. I see what you mean."

"Nemo *chooses* when to become an adult. So maybe squidmoths hang around waiting till there's somebody just right, and then . . ."

"I think," J.D. said, "that you've been watching too many old monster movies."

"Maybe you've written too many sentimental sci-fi novels!"

"Sentimental!" J.D. exclaimed, affronted.

"Yeah, in the end *everything* comes out right for *everybody.*" Chandra made a noise of disgust.

J.D. almost laughed and almost cried.

I think I'm too tired to be having this conversation, she said to herself.

"Er," Gerald said, at a loss and trying to make the best of it, "perhaps it would be better to postpone literary discussion until a later time? Now, we shall break into smaller groups and meet separately. That way our colleagues won't be quite so overwhelmed."

Hearing the murmurs of agreement, J.D. gave Gerald a grateful glance.

With that, the tight sphere of people broke up into smaller clusters, sorted broadly by occupation: physical sciences around Victoria, social sciences with Satoshi, biological sciences with Stephen Thomas. The group around Stephen Thomas included Florrie Brown. When she joined him, he took her frail hand and kissed it gallantly. She smiled, and J.D. realized that beneath her remarkably quaint heavy black eye make-up, beneath the pink and green and white braids drifting around her mostly shaved head, Florrie Brown was beautiful.

Professor Thanthavong joined J.D. briefly.

"Are you certain about changing your link?" she asked.

"Yes," J.D. said. "I want to enhance it. There still may be time to use it."

"Very well," Thanthavong said. "I've made the preparation. See me when you're ready."

"Thank you," J.D. said, as Thanthavong touched the wall, pushed off, and floated toward Stephen Thomas's discussion section.

Stephen Thomas led his group out of the waiting room, heading down into *Starfarer*'s main cylinder and out of zero g.

The group was much smaller than it should have been. Many of the scientists of the multinational faculty had been recalled by their governments, protesting the threat of change in *Starfarer*'s purpose. So they had all been left behind when *Starfarer* fled.

Stephen Thomas was glad Florrie Brown had joined his group. He liked her; he only wished she and Victoria had not started out on the wrong foot.

Besides Stephen Thomas, the scientists included Professor Thanthavong, a couple of biochemists and a botanist, and a dozen graduate students: Lehua, Bay, Mitch, Fox—

"Fox, what are you doing here?"

Fox was one of Satoshi's graduate students.

"Satoshi isn't talking to me."

"What?" he asked, incredulous.

Both Satoshi and Stephen Thomas had good reason to be annoyed with Fox. She was only twenty, too young to apply for a place on the deep space expedition. She had refused to return to Earth. Stephen Thomas and Satoshi had been in the genetics building, trying to persuade her to get on the transport and go home, when the missile hit *Starfarer* and brought the hillside down around them. But the missile might have hit anywhere. Stephen Thomas found it impossible to blame Fox for staying behind, and he assumed Satoshi felt the same. So what, if they got charged with kidnapping when they got back home? Their prosecution for hijacking the starship would probably take precedence anyway.

Unless kidnapping the niece of the president of the United States took priority over everything.

"Satoshi thinks it's my fault you're turning into a diver!" Fox said.

"Oh, bullshit."

"Don't make me leave," she said.

He shrugged. "Doesn't make any difference to me."

Stephen Thomas was tired and distracted. Most of his body had stopped aching for the moment, but his toes hurt fiercely. He wanted a hot bath. He thought it might help.

Thanthavong watched him with concern. "Come

along, Stephen Thomas. Questions can wait till we're back on solid ground."

"It doesn't matter," he said. Everyone was used to his bitching about zero g, but he had spent so much time in weightlessness recently that he had overcome his aversion to it. Or . . . his body was preparing him for living in water.

He followed Thanthavong obediently. He was in the habit of complying with her requests. Like everyone else, he admired her to the point of awe. When the changing virus infected him, and she prepared to treat him against it, saying no to her was one of the hardest things he had ever done.

They made their way to the long hill that formed one end of *Starfarer*'s campus cylinder. The hill, with its winding switchback paths, led down from the axis to the cylinder floor, the living surface. The air was sharp and cool with rain. Overhead, puffy clouds softened the sharp bright line of the sun tube and, beyond the tube, the cold glitter of lakes and streams on the far side of the cylinder. *Starfarer*'s small shallow ocean, gray and foggy, circled the opposite end of the cylinder. Stephen Thomas kept waiting to feel some primeval call to the sea, but it did not happen.

You aren't turning into a fish, he said to himself, repeating Zev's distressed protest to a joke about what was happening to Stephen Thomas. You aren't turning into a fish. You aren't going to get pulled to the sea to spawn.

At a hairpin turn of the trail, halfway to the floor of the cylinder, benches clustered in a small circle. The false gravity was about half of *Starfarer*'s regular seven-tenths g. One could sit without bouncing into the air.

Thanthavong took a seat and motioned the others to join her. Stephen Thomas limped to a nearby bench, lowered himself gratefully, and stretched his long legs. He curled his toes, pressing them against the soles of his sandals, straightening them quickly when the ache turned to a raw jolt of pain.

Everybody else joined the circle and watched with anticipation as Stephen Thomas slipped his carrying-case strap off over his head and held the case in his lap. The grad students had been waiting for something new to work on. J.D. had brought Stephen Thomas a crumpled plant from Europa's ship, but the plant was, as Europa said, of Earth origin. Though the bacteria associated with it were still acting strange, they matched ordinary Earth species. He was glad he finally had something for his students.

"Stephen Thomas?"

He opened the sample case. He had not transmitted any of this information, or discussed it on the public access. Europa and Androgeos had made him more cautious—more sneaky—than he had ever been before.

"The optical fiber J.D. picked up is just a polymer. Organic. Similar to silk, a little stronger." He shrugged. "Most of its interesting qualities are optical. But it was shed into a living ecosystem. Good and nonsterile. Particles in the range from viral to amoebic. I made some slides, and . . ."

He pulled the cushioned isolation chamber out of the case and held it up, letting light flow through the windows of the sample vials.

Tiny cell colonies traced one inoculation stab.

He had not expected—not dared to hope for—the growth to appear so quickly. He had been afraid to hope for any growth at all.

Most of the tubes of growth medium remained clear. No surprise: he had no way—yet—of knowing what to feed an alien cell.

But something, some alien equivalent of a bacterium, was an autotroph: an organism that could grow and replicate using only simple sugars, oxygen, water. . . .

He offered the isolation chamber to Thanthavong.

"No," she said. "No. You carry it. I'm afraid my hand . . . might not be steady enough."

They had met the alien humans. They had encoun-

tered an alien species of intelligence. But this micro-
scopic quantity of life was the first alien cell they could
look at, grow, and study.

"Maybe some of the other microbes feed on the
autotroph," Lehua said.

"Right." With a little luck, he could end up with a
self-sustaining mixed colony of alien microbes.

"Did you have enough to do any tests?" Thanthavong asked.

"Just one." He paused. "Whatever Nemo's ecosystem uses to make whatever it uses for genes . . . it isn't
DNA."

J.D. and Zev found themselves among a diverse group
of faculty and staff, including most of the artists, Jenny
Dupre, and Senator Orazio.

J.D. wished she did not have to meet with them all
so soon after getting back. She was tired, and sad. Still,
she understood why her colleagues were here waiting
for her. She would have been with them, if she had not
been a member of the alien contact department.

"There's no question of letting the alien into
Arachne," Jenny Dupre said.

"I don't think so," J.D. said sadly. "And I'm beginning to think that's a mistake."

"The web's still too fragile to risk it!"

J.D. did not blame Jenny for her concern. She had
nearly died in Arachne's crash, the crash that killed Feral. If Feral's death was murder rather than accident, as
Jenny believed, then Jenny had probably been the target.

Nevertheless, the more J.D. thought about it, the
more she disagreed with keeping Nemo out.

She wanted to be back with Nemo.

She was still moving through microgravity, so she
tried to keep her eyes from closing as she went into a
communications fugue. She did not want to crash into a
wall while she was not looking.

She touched Arachne, sending a gentle message to the squidmoth. Nemo made no reply.

J.D. forced her attention back to the group she was with, to their questions and curiosity.

All she could do now was wait.

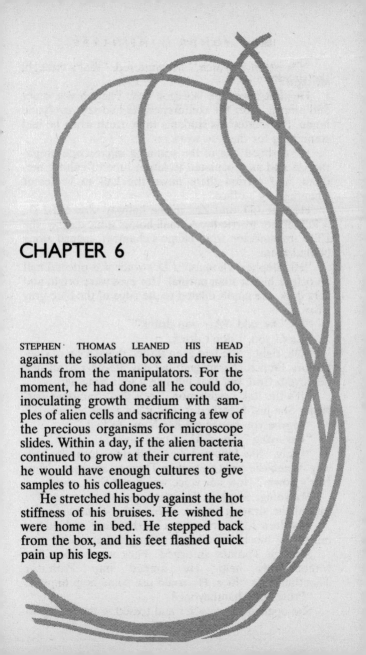

CHAPTER 6

STEPHEN THOMAS LEANED HIS HEAD against the isolation box and drew his hands from the manipulators. For the moment, he had done all he could do, inoculating growth medium with samples of alien cells and sacrificing a few of the precious organisms for microscope slides. Within a day, if the alien bacteria continued to grow at their current rate, he would have enough cultures to give samples to his colleagues.

He stretched his body against the hot stiffness of his bruises. He wished he were home in bed. He stepped back from the box, and his feet flashed quick pain up his legs.

"Christ on a crutch," he muttered, "that's enough, all right?"

He shut down the isolation box. The lab was quiet and empty. After the conference, he had sent everyone home. He wanted his students to be fresh when he had something for them to work on.

He grabbed one of the scanning microscope preparations and an inoculated isolation tube of culture medium, and carried them down the hall to Professor Thanthavong's office.

He met J.D. and Zev in the hallway. Zev led J.D., watching her worriedly. A small holographic display, the LTM transmission from Nemo's chamber, tagged along behind them.

"Hi, Stephen Thomas." J.D.'s voice was pitched half an octave higher than normal. Her eyes were bright and very dark, the pupils dilated to the edge of the blue-gray irises.

"Hi," he said. "Are you drunk?"

"I *told* you, I don't drink."

"Oh, right." She had even turned down a sip of celebratory French champagne, the day *Starfarer*'s sail first deployed. God, but that felt like a long time ago.

"It's the link preparation," Zev said, sounding worried. "She just breathed it, and it's making her weird."

"Maybe you better get her home to bed."

"I'm *trying,*" Zev said. "Come on, J.D., okay?"

"Okay." She followed Zev obediently down the hallway. When she passed Stephen Thomas, she said, "Your hair's down." Now her voice was lower than usual.

Frowning, Stephen Thomas watched them go. He tucked the straying strands of his hair behind his ears.

Zev drew J.D.'s arm across his shoulders and led her out of the biochem building, talking to her softly.

Stephen Thomas shrugged. They were doing fine without his help. He limped into Professor Thanthavong's office. He could use some help himself.

"Professor Thanthavong?"

She opened the recycler and tossed in the prep bottle and the inhaler by which she had administered the link enhancer to J.D.

"Hello, Stephen Thomas." Nearby, a couple of holographic images hovered, frozen. When her attention returned to one, it would continue its report.

Stephen Thomas put the slide and the chamber on her desk. "I should have enough samples for everybody soon. But here's one, to start."

"Thank you," she said. She gestured to a chair. "Sit down. You look footsore."

Footsore was hardly the word for it, but he held back from complaining to Thanthavong. She probably would not say, "I told you so," but she was not likely to offer much sympathy, either. She had not wanted him to turn into a diver in the first place.

He sat down, wondering if he would be able to get up again. Professor Thanthavong was small, and all her furniture was too low for him. Sitting down eased the pain in his feet, but renewed the ache in his body. He did not mention that to Thanthavong, either. She had rescued him from the slug. She had probably saved his life. Then she had read him the riot act about his behavior.

She gestured to one of the displays, the report Stephen Thomas had made on the alien microbes.

"This is good work," she said.

"More questions than answers," Stephen Thomas said.

"That's why it's good work. You got a lot accomplished while you were gone." She paused. "You weren't able to collect more samples," she said, a question rather than a comment.

"I was tempted," Stephen Thomas said. "But I didn't want to screw J.D. up with Nemo."

"Ah."

"But maybe . . ."

"Out with it, Stephen Thomas."

"I tried taking a culture off my shirt. The stuff I wiped up from the pool. Nothing's growing. Yet. Maybe it will."

"We can hope."

"Yeah."

"These other experiments you're doing," she said. "With the soil bacteria from Europa's ship."

"I haven't figured those out yet. Any ideas?"

"Their DNA fingerprints are very close to normal. About what you'd expect if they diverged four thousand years ago."

"They look the same," Stephen Thomas agreed. "But the buggers act different."

"Have you sequenced them?"

"Not yet. I was resequencing bacteria from J.D. From all of us in alien contact."

"You suspect contamination?" she said sharply.

"No. I was double-checking. It's strange, though. You'd expect *some* exchange between us and the alien humans. Nothing pathological. The normal skin microbes and so forth."

"But you found none."

"No. Europa told the truth about something, anyway."

"Or we're blessed with unusually robust microbial flora," Thanthavong said dryly. "Your students could have done the sequencing."

"I didn't have the heart to make the kids stop watching the reports."

"Graduate students expect to work," Thanthavong said. "You're perhaps a bit too indulgent of yours. The sequencing should be done soon."

"Do we have a machine to use?"

"Biochem's is at your disposal."

"Good. Thanks." He had not been looking forward to the commute up the hill to use the sequencer in the *Chi.* "I'll go—"

"Go get some sleep, Stephen Thomas! I said 'soon,' not 'instantly.' Leave instructions for your students to do it. You look worn out."

"Yeah. Okay. I'll see you tomorrow. Today. Later." His time sense was completely skewed.

Stephen Thomas went outside. He paused in the

dawn air, enjoying the coolness. The daytime temperatures on *Starfarer* had been warm for spring. He touched Arachne and left a message for his students, obeying Professor Thanthavong as far as that went.

But he did not go home to bed. He had something to do. If he did it now, while everyone was still caught up in the reports from the Nemo expedition, no one would stop him. If he waited, he might not be able to carry out the task at all.

Infinity Mendez dozed on his futon, drifting in and out of sleep, telling himself he should get up and go to work. Beside him, Esther Klein slept soundly, her snore a soft buzz.

By this time of the morning, Infinity had usually been up for a couple of hours. He liked to be outside in the gray foggy dawn while the light tubes slowly brightened. But he and Esther had sat up late talking to J.D. Sauvage.

Every so often, Infinity stopped and said to himself, We've met an alien being. No matter what happens now, we did what we said we were going to.

Like just about everyone else on board, Infinity would have liked to tag along with J.D. He wished he could lie here all day, cuddle with his lover, replay the transmissions from the *Chi*, and wait to see what happened next.

But anticipating what happened next meant anticipating the death of Nemo.

Come on, he said to himself, suddenly restless. Get up, you have things to do.

Esther curled on her side, facing him, her knees drawn up beneath his legs, her small square hand draped down between his thighs.

Light washed the room. *Starfarer*'s light always came from high noon, straight overhead, from the light tubes along the axis of the campus's cylindrical body.

Infinity had gotten used to the unchanging direction of the light before the campus was even finished. He had belonged to the construction crew that built the starship. Infinity knew *Starfarer* from the outside in. Having helped build its shell, he now helped maintain its ecosystem.

Infinity covered Esther's hand with his own. She snuggled closer, still asleep. Moving away from her warm touch, Infinity slid out from under the covers, drew the blanket up around Esther's shoulders, and looked for his clothes.

It's sure harder to keep track of things without the artificial stupids, Infinity thought. They *should* have been released by now. . . .

Chancellor Blades had impounded them, but he could not control them anymore.

Maybe Gerald's been too busy to let them loose, Infinity thought. He smiled to himself. Big job, being acting chancellor of a bunch of revolutionaries.

Probably Gerald had just not got around to the task. When Chancellor Blades impounded the machines, he got everyone's attention. The ASes did the kind of work nobody noticed till it did not get done. It was annoying to order dinner and get nothing; to find dirty clothes still lying around instead of washed and pressed and returned to the shelf.

What a lot of people did not realize was how important the ASes were to the health of *Starfarer*. The faculty thought of the ASes and mobile AIs as conveniences. But the machines also watched and maintained and repaired the complex structure of the starship.

Infinity threw on his jeans and sandals and his leather vest, combed the tangles out of his long black hair, and left the coolness of his house.

Outside, in his garden, bees buzzed loudly and birds called and chirped and rustled the bushes. The morning was warm for spring. The afternoon would be uncomfortably hot.

The quality of the light made him uneasy. Arachne filtered it so the radiation of Sirius resembled the light of the sun; still, its white harshness remained. It worried him. He belonged to the staff, not the faculty, so under normal circumstances his responsibility was low and his authority negligible. Alzena Dadkha, the director of the ecology department, should have been in charge.

But Alzena was gone. Unable to reconcile her conflicting loyalties to her family on Earth with her responsibility to the deep space expedition, she had fled with Europa and Androgeos. Europa had taken pity on Alzena's despair.

Infinity touched Arachne through his link, asking for access to the interior spectrum. The computer gave it without hesitation.

A bee whizzed past him, flying fast with an angry buzz.

Whether Arachne would or would not permit him to alter the light filters made no difference at all. The filters pegged out at their limits. He could have less light, or more. But he could not get a spectrum any closer to real sunlight than he already had.

The bee circled wildly. The frantic buzz stopped short. Infinity frowned. The fat honeybees were usually as placid as cows. He worked around them all the time, moved the hives, collected the honey. He had never even been stung.

He moved cautiously toward the last place he had heard the bee, expecting to find it nuzzling the center of a flower for pollen and nectar. But the flowers were still in the breathless morning.

A faint sound, not even a buzz, caught Infinity's attention. He found the bee lying on the ground, upside down, its wings battering uselessly against the earth. Its short life span ended in a burst of angry energy; its motion stopped and its legs curled up against its body.

I'd probably run around yelling, too, Infinity thought, if I realized I was about to die. But bees don't usually act like that. . . .

In the driest corner of his garden, he stooped to look at a barrel cactus. For a while it had flourished in this microenvironment. Something about it troubled him: the spongy feel of its skin when he carefully slipped his finger between its hairy spines.

Infinity's mother came from the American south-west, but she had fled to Brazil, a refugee, before Infinity was born. Infinity had never grown a cactus before, never lived where cactuses grew wild. His memories from childhood, before he came into space, were spotty and disjointed, of eroded land struggling to re-establish itself as forest, of displaced people grieving for land they had loved and disconnected from the new land where they now scraped out a living.

Information on cactuses was only one of the many things Arachne had lost when the system crashed. He wondered if anybody had hard references, if Alzena had left anything in her office when she fled. With plants, hands-on experience was best. But references were better than nothing.

He remembered what Esther had told him about her potted cactus. She only realized it had died when her cat knocked it over and it had no roots. He pushed gently at the barrel cactus. Was it releasing its grasp on the soil? Or was the soil just loose? He could not tell.

Better to leave it alone and keep watch on it. If he worried at it, he might damage it.

He headed for the administration building, trying again, as he walked, to ask Arachne for information about the artificials.

Arachne replied, but the reply contained no information.

It's like they don't even exist, he thought. What if Blades destroyed them, or threw them out into space? That would be crazy . . . but a lot of crazy stuff has been happening recently.

A holographic triptych, a replay of J.D.'s alien encounters, occupied the center of Chandra's large living room, hovering above the thick Berber carpet.

While most people on board *Starfarer* lived austerely, Chandra lived in a house full of stuff. When she decided to join the deep space expedition's art department, she had ordered a lot of expensive furniture and sent it on ahead. Other people built their own furniture of bamboo and rock foam and canvas. They covered the floor with woven mats. Chandra saw no reason to limit herself to local materials and amateur labor. She made plenty of money; she could afford to indulge herself. Back on Earth, her name on a new production guaranteed attention, reviews, and more royalties than she could spend.

Crimson Ng sat companionably beside Chandra. She watched the replays of Nemo's nest, toying idly with a model bone, part of her newest sculpture. Crimson held the bone up between her and the holographic replays. When she moved the bone, Chandra could see the muscles, the skin, the soft sleek pelt of the animal in Crimson's imagination.

The remains of dinner littered the mosaic table. Chandra had also imported a supply of exotic food; she had been afraid that the meals on board *Starfarer* would be pedestrian. She had been right. And now, the campus was in such disarray that the central cafeteria could not produce even pedestrian meals.

"Did you get enough dinner?" she asked Crimson.

"I sure did. It was great."

One of the displays repeated J.D.'s first meeting with the squidmoth.

Chandra sprawled naked on her leather couch. She could take in her surroundings with her whole body, if she chose, but there was absolutely no point in recording J.D.'s experience secondhand.

Chandra felt jealous of J.D.: not simply envious, wishing to have the experience herself, but flat out jealous.

I should have been there instead of *her,* Chandra thought. Holographic recordings. Big deal.

Visual and audio recordings could never convey exactly what J.D. had experienced, the way a sensory artist could.

I *should* have been there, Chandra said to herself. I can see and feel and taste and hear and smell everything, and everybody could experience it again, through me.

No one else on board resented the alien contact specialist's position. They were all perfectly happy to back her up, to support her, to be good obedient members of the team.

Fine for them. Chandra always worked alone.

She had barely recorded a thing since coming on board *Starfarer,* since giving her life up to this pastoral, small-town campus. *Starfarer* was as boring as a village back home, despite being a stone cylinder four light-years from Earth. As soon as it was too late to change her mind, Chandra had realized her mistake.

The other experience she would have wanted to capture had also passed her by: transition. When *Starfarer* fled Earth, she had been connected by hard link to a backup computer, storing a full load of sensory recordings. If Arachne had been up, she could have been ready for transition, and for *Starfarer*'s arrival at Tau Ceti. But she had missed that chance. The Tau Ceti to Sirius transition had been just as bad. Arachne crashed again, Feral died, and Stephen Thomas and J.D. caught Blades at sabotage.

I should have been part of the hunt, too, Chandra thought. But J.D. didn't even consider trusting me.

Chandra's body still had not recorded transition. She needed a calm, controlled approach to the transition point, not the chaotic flights they had made so far, with the computer web crashing around them.

When J.D.'s recorded image took off her spacesuit and let Nemo touch her, Chandra groaned in exasperation. The swollen nerve clusters all over Chandra's body throbbed and engorged with anticipation.

"Why didn't you take off your clothes, you stupid bitch?" Chandra shouted. She flung herself against the back of the couch.

"Chandra!" Crimson exclaimed. But at least she spared a little of her attention from the replay, and from her sculpted bone.

"She should've," Chandra said irritably. "She's seen

too many old sci fi movies. She thinks aliens want to
have sex with human beings, and she's scared."

"That's silly. Would *you've* taken your clothes off?"

"You bet I would."

"Wouldn't you be embarrassed?"

"No. Why should I? I let people experience my body
from the inside out. Damn! They should've let me go
along! Or at least made *her* make a sensory recording."

"Now I understand," Crimson said.

"What?"

"Why you kept trying to scare J.D. into not going
back."

Chandra shrugged. "It was worth a try."

"No, it wasn't. If you wanted to be in the alien contact department, why didn't you apply there instead of
the art department?"

"I joined *Starfarer* at the last minute, it was too late,"
she said belligerently.

Crimson gave her a skeptical glance.

"I didn't think they'd take me—all right? But I knew
I could get in the art department. Will you stop *playing*
with that?"

"I'm not playing." Crimson did not press the point
of Chandra's *Starfarer* affiliation, or her ambitions. "I'm
figuring out what it ought to look like. I have to hold it
and carry it around and change it till I get the model
right. I can't fossilize it till I get it right."

But she put the strange model bone aside and knelt
on the couch beside Chandra, gazing at her with concern.

"It would have made more sense for them to let me
go than for them to let Zev tag along," Chandra said.
"It isn't fair! He'd never've gotten up here if I hadn't
smuggled him on board."

"I'd like to go on the *Chi,* too, you know," Crimson
said. "Everybody would. But J.D.'s the alien contact
specialist."

"So she's first."

"You've done a lot of other things first. And recorded them for us."

"I've recorded a lot of things *best,*" Chandra said. "But not first. I don't think there's anything left on Earth to do and be, first. That's why I came out here!"

"I don't care if you're first or not."

"I'm glad you like my stuff," Chandra said. "Nobody else on this heap pays it any attention. Maybe three whole people have accessed it in the past two weeks."

"You *are* in a bad mood," Crimson said, out of patience. Then she laughed.

"What's so funny?"

"Chandra, who's had a chance in the last two weeks to spend any time—"

Chandra thought Crimson was about to say "to spend any time playing." Bristling, she readied a retort.

"—on anything but the real world?"

Chandra cut off the sharp words she had planned when she heard what Crimson really said. Finding another reply took her a moment.

"Yeah," Chandra said, reluctant to be placated. "I guess you're right."

On the crater replay, J.D. scrabbled her way up a steep silky slope. The LTMs had caught a glimpse of several of Nemo's attendants, but the recording pitched and yawed till Chandra closed her strange all-over-gray eyes.

"It's making me seasick! They'll have to edit that to death!"

"Shh, look, there's another one of those spider things. I want to watch it."

The creature left off creating a shimmery sheet of new white silk, rappelled to the floor, and snaked off on half a dozen ropy limbs. It looked like a cross between a brittle star, with long whiplash tentacle-legs, and a crustacean, with a shrimplike head and a ring of eyes.

Crimson stroked her model bone again. She examined it intently, turned it over, put it down, glanced at the image of Nemo's attendant.

"It's too conventional," Crimson said.

"Huh? *My* stuff?"

"No, mine. The fossils. They're all on an ordinary vertebrate body plan."

"Oh, right. Six-legged, winged, fanged, twelve-eyed vertebrates."

"Even if I did that all at once, they'd be too much like us."

Chandra sat crosslegged on the sofa, enjoying the soft warmth of the leather, and the way the leather stuck to her skin.

"You sure pissed Gerald off when you told Europa you're a paleontologist," she said. "I think you really got her to believe we'd found alien bones on the moon."

"Gerald just doesn't get it," Crimson said. "I *am* a paleontologist."

Chandra laughed. "I like the way you never go out of character."

"Seriously. My degree's in paleontology. But it got so I couldn't do field work. When the Mideast Sweep started expanding again."

Chandra sobered and looked at Crimson, tilting her head thoughtfully to one side. She was not sure if Crimson was pulling her leg or not.

"Androgeos took one of my fossils," Crimson said.

"What? Why'd you let him get away with it?"

"Because that's what they're for." Crimson laughed with delight. "I hope I get to find out what he thinks of it."

"He probably got the twelve-eyed fanged one. He'll just think it was one of our ordinary ancestors."

Crimson laughed again, then fell silent.

Gazing into Chandra's eyes—most people did not gaze into Chandra's featureless silver-gray eyes—Crimson touched Chandra's wrist, stroking the bright blue rope of vein that throbbed just beneath her translucent tan skin. Crimson's hands were rough from sculpting, from digging in *Starfarer*'s coarse new ground to bury her fossils in an artificial but convincing stratigraphy. Her fingers circled gently in the sensitive hollow of Chandra's palm.

The nerve clusters pulsed.

Chandra drew away.

Crimson let her hands fall into her lap. She frowned, confused and disappointed.

"What's the matter?"

"I don't *do* that." Chandra was tempted. But Chandra had made a career of resisting temptation.

"What do you mean? With me? With women?"

"I don't do it at all."

"Why? Why not?" Crimson asked, shocked.

"Every sensory artist in the universe does sex scenes," Chandra said.

"You don't have to record it!" Crimson exclaimed. "I didn't want you to record it!"

Chandra squinted at her, trying to see her in a different way, trying to see her even more clearly. She decided Crimson was serious about not recording.

"You'd better go," Chandra said.

Crimson sat back. She picked up the model bone, clenching her fingers around the shaft. Chandra wondered if Crimson would try to hit her with it. That might be interesting.

But instead, Crimson rose slowly, turned, strode across the rich carpet, stooped down and picked up her shoes, and walked out the door without a backward glance.

When Stephen Thomas reached the entrance of the health center, he hesitated. He did not want to go into the deserted, silent place.

He wished he could go back to Blades's home, push past the silver slugs, drag the chancellor out, and force him to come here and see what he had done. Did he even care that his sabotage had killed an innocent man?

I *liked* Blades, Stephen Thomas thought. How could I be so wrong about someone? His aura was clear and bright, transparent and guileless. I thought. I stuck up for him, to everybody, even Satoshi and Victoria.

Stephen Thomas remembered the chancellor's welcoming party—

It had been several weeks ago. Victoria had been back on Earth, giving a speech at the Houses of Parliament in British Columbia and meeting with the Canadian premier. Everybody thought she was lucky not to have to go to the party, because most of the faculty believed Blades had been forced on the deep space expedition in order to dismantle it. No one had more evidence than campus gossip, but most people believed it anyway. Stephen Thomas believed it. Gerald Hemminge swore it was not true, which was almost enough in itself to make Stephen Thomas believe it. Satoshi did not take much stock in campus gossip.

Stephen Thomas and Satoshi had to go to the party. It would have been an inexcusable breach of academic etiquette not to. It would have been a direct insult.

Gerald, of course, had indulged his prerogatives as assistant chancellor and hosted the welcome party. He had even gone to the expense of importing decent wine from one of the O'Neill colonies. In a few years, *Starfarer*'s vines might produce a drinkable vintage, but for now the homemade brew was beer.

Stephen Thomas went to the party expecting to despise Chancellor Blades. Satoshi went with an open mind. To his surprise, Stephen Thomas found the new chancellor pleasant and interesting and rather shy. But Satoshi took an instant and uncharacteristic dislike to him. Satoshi got along with everybody. Satoshi even got along with Gerald.

When they went home, late, Stephen Thomas was cheerfully drunk. Even drunk, he noticed Satoshi's irritation. He could hardly miss the angry blue sparks.

They lay together in bed. The moonlight reflected through the open French doors of Satoshi's room. Carnations scented the cool breeze.

"You didn't like the chancellor much," Stephen Thomas said. "And you were about the only one who didn't arrive intending to hate him."

"He's a snob," Satoshi said. "He stood off in the corner and watched us like we were experimental animals."

"Not when he was talking to me, he didn't."

"He didn't talk to you all evening." Satoshi stroked Stephen Thomas's hip. "Just most of it."

"Is that what bothered you?" Stephen Thomas asked, surprised. "That you thought he was coming on to me?"

Satoshi smiled. "He was."

"Yeah, true, but he wasn't obnoxious about it. He can take no for an answer."

"If it bothered me every time you got involved with somebody," Satoshi said, "I'd be bothered all the time. And if it bothered me every time somebody made a pass at you—I'd be nuts. Why would I pick Blades to get jealous of?"

"How should I know? You won't tell me why you don't like him. So I'm making wild guesses."

"I wasn't jealous," Satoshi said. "But Gerald was."

"Of the pass?" Stephen Thomas asked, skeptical.

"Of the time he spent with you."

That made more sense. One of Gerald's duties, a duty he relished, was to squire dignitaries around. He would expect to introduce *Starfarer* to the new chancellor.

"Great," Stephen Thomas said. "One more reason for Gerald to dislike me."

"Let's forget about Gerald."

Satoshi kissed Stephen Thomas's lips, his cheek, his throat, nibbling at the thin gold chain around his neck. The crystal slid along the chain and landed against his collarbone, cool as water. Stephen Thomas pulled Satoshi closer, and rubbed the small of his back with one hand. He loved the way Satoshi's muscles moved beneath his fingers.

"You still didn't tell me why you don't like Blades."

"I don't *know* why I don't like him. I just don't. Maybe I don't like his aura."

"Very funny," Stephen Thomas said. Satoshi did not believe in auras. "His aura was just fine."

"Hmm." Satoshi kept his voice neutral. He knew

when he had teased Stephen Thomas enough. Neither Satoshi nor Victoria would even try to look for auras.

The blue sparks of anger faded from Satoshi's aura. A gold glow of excitement flashed around him, and scarlet contentment shimmered beyond the gold.

Satoshi pushed Stephen Thomas's hair away from his forehead, caressed his face with both hands, and kissed him again, quickly, then harder. He slid his knee up Stephen Thomas's thigh. Stephen Thomas dragged his fingers down Satoshi's belly and ruffled his dark pubic hair with his fingernails. Satoshi's body was like a furnace, blasting out heat, when he was sexually aroused.

"Blades—"

"I don't want to talk about Chancellor Blades anymore," Satoshi said. He clenched his teeth and his back arched. He drew in a long, shuddering breath. He laid his hand over Stephen Thomas's, guiding him. Stephen Thomas forgot about everything except his partner's pleasure.

—Now, in the health center, Stephen Thomas closed his eyes and brought himself back to the present. Leaning against the doorjamb, he imagined making love to Feral.

Though they had never had a chance to go to bed together, they had made an immediate connection. It would have happened. And they had been well on the way to a close, solid friendship. Stephen Thomas had imagined their making love, and he had imagined inviting Feral to join the partnership. Satoshi and Victoria liked him. The family needed another member, and Feral fit in well. Someday they all had to stop grieving over Merry.

But what Stephen Thomas had done, by making friends with Feral, was put him in danger.

The health center was warm and pleasant and deserted. All the people injured in Arachne's first crash had recovered and gone home. Only one person was hurt in Arachne's second crash, and the one person was Feral.

Stephen Thomas passed through the deserted rooms. No one was around to ask him what he wanted, or whether he needed help. The mobile health AIs had been disabled just like the ASes.

He expected the morgue to be cold, but it was the same temperature as the rest of the health center. When he opened the drawer where Feral lay, chill air washed over him.

He drew back the shroud. Feral stared up at him with dull, open eyes. Dry blood smeared his face and streaked in caked rivulets from his nose. Blood from his ears matted his curly chestnut hair.

Stephen Thomas stepped back, in grief and despair.

Everybody had too much to worry about when Feral died, Stephen Thomas thought. Too much to do, to think about one dead man, to worry about what death would do to his gentle brown eyes.

And what did I do? I shut down, got on the *Chi,* and flew away.

Stephen Thomas took a ragged breath and returned to Feral's side. He touched his friend's cold cheek, his forehead; he drew his webbed hand down over Feral's eyes. The stiffness of death had passed from Feral's body, and his eyelids closed easily.

Stephen Thomas got a washcloth and cleaned the dry blood from Feral's skin and hair. Feral's expression was somber, but Stephen Thomas could imagine his full, mobile lips ready to smile. His chestnut hair curled around his face.

Stephen Thomas had been telling himself all along that he only planned to come to the health center and say goodbye to Feral. But he had been lying to himself.

"Gerald can go fuck himself," Stephen Thomas said. "I'll be damned if I'll leave you here."

Feral's clothes had been ripped and cut away during the attempts to revive him. Livid bruises mottled his chest. Stephen Thomas found a clean sheet and wrapped it around Feral's body. The health center lay well up the side of *Starfarer's* end hill, where the gravity was very low. When Stephen Thomas picked Feral up, his body felt absurdly light, as if death had taken away his substance.

Stephen Thomas easily carried Feral's body to the hub of *Starfarer*. The gravity continued to diminish, till it was barely perceptible. He floated himself and his burden to the ferry station, boarded the capsule, and strapped Feral's body on the back platform.

He had not been to the wild side since the wild side's previous spring. Spring on the wild side was fall in the campus cylinder. Summer had passed in the wilderness, winter had passed on campus. A short trip would take him from campus spring into wild side autumn.

Infinity crossed the lawn in front of the chancellor's house. Three exterior ASes, silver slugs, sprawled like shiny boneless rhinoceroses in front of the building and guarded its front door. All the house's other doors, its windows, its balconies, had been covered with ugly, irregular slabs of overlapping rock foam. The secret tunnels leading from it had been plugged with rock foam.

The exterior ASes were the only mobile artificials left working. The chancellor had disrupted the campus by recalling the service machines. He must have thought that would be a minor irritation compared to Arachne's crash; maybe he thought it would be the last straw for the expedition members.

But his petty irritation had backfired on him. He had not realized the silver slugs could work inside as well as outside—they could work almost anywhere—and had released them to finish repairing *Starfarer*'s damaged hull.

The oversight had been his downfall, for once Stephen Thomas and J.D. traced the sabotage of Arachne to Blades, the silver slugs had driven the chancellor from the administration building, through the underground tunnels, and trapped him in his house. He was cut off from Arachne now. The computer had activated its immune system and destroyed Blades's neural node, and the silver slugs had cut the house's hard links.

Infinity wished Blades had been stopped before any-one died.

Blades could communicate by note. He could ask for anything he liked, and a silver slug would carry it to him. Anything but electronic communication, or company. The slugs guarded his door for the protection of the expedition, and for his own protection as well. They let no one pass in either direction.

Infinity approached the chancellor's house, crossing behind a rough sculpture of tumbled chunks of raw moon rock.

Like the manicured yard in front of the administra-tion building, the green turf around the chancellor's house showed the scars of an angry, milling crowd. The tracks of the silver slugs gouged wide, shallow trenches in the earth.

Infinity paused at the edge of the swath of grass. All three silver slugs lay facing the same direction, an odd alignment.

Curious, cautious, he moved forward. One of the silver slugs, a lithoclast, reared up to sense him. The slugs knew him. He had called them in from repairing *Starfarer*'s outer surface; he had set them to guarding Blades. But they would not let him into Blades's house, even if that was where he wanted to go.

The lithoclast subsided. Its bulk eased onto the ground and spread out, shimmering. It rested, waiting, its senses trained on the group of rocks. The smell of crushed grass, green and light, filled the air.

In a recess in the tumbled stone, Iphigenie Dupre sat staring past the silver slugs at the open door of the chancellor's home. Infinity watched her uneasily, reluc-tant to disturb her solitude, but more reluctant to leave her here alone.

It was unusual to see her on *Starfarer*'s inner surface. She preferred zero gravity, and stayed in the sailhouse or near the axis as much as she could. Arachne ordered her out of free-fall every so often. She complied, reluc-tantly.

Infinity had not been surprised to see Jenny Dupre

in the waiting room, when the *Chi* returned from Nemo's web. But he had been surprised when she joined the discussion group. He was more surprised to see her still here.

She leaned against the rock, her long, delicate hands lying with fingers outspread beside her. She wore her hair in narrow black braids caught up at the back of her head. They fell to her shoulders, the bright glass beads an uneven fringe. In weightlessness, the braids fanned out and the beads clicked together softly, constantly.

Infinity joined her and sat beside her, watching Blades's house. The chancellor remained out of sight. The slugs would let him come to the door, but no farther. He could not cross the threshold.

He had been nearly as reclusive before they penned him in.

"Something has to be done," Iphigenie said abruptly.

The sailmaster hated the chancellor with cold outrage. She believed, with good reason, that he had tried to kill her. His attack on Arachne had caused the first system crash, which injured Iphigenie. His second attack had killed Feral.

Infinity considered her statement, careful not to answer too fast, too certainly.

"Isn't that enough?" He gestured to the foam-covered house with his chin.

"No," she said. "No. It isn't. He murdered Feral. He meant to kill me. He's dangerous."

"Not anymore."

"What if he gets back inside the web?"

"Arachne's immunized against him."

"And the web was uncrashable!" Iphigenie snorted in disgust. "He's been talking to Gerald. And to the American senators. I saw them from the hill." She gestured back toward the end of *Starfarer*'s cylinder. "But when I came down here, they went away."

The two senators had been passengers on Esther's transport, heading home after a fact-finding tour of

Starfarer. They were along for the ride, now, and none too happy about it.

"What do you think we should do?" Infinity asked. Isolating Blades in his house had felt like a good compromise to him, when he had thought of it. At least it had stopped the riot Iphigenie had tried to start, and no one else had been hurt.

"I think," Iphigenie said, "that you don't want to know what I want to see. The best I can hope for, I suppose, is a trial."

"We aren't exactly prepared to try anybody. Is anybody even a lawyer?"

Iphigenie shrugged.

Starfarer had left Earth orbit precipitously, six months early, without the long burn-in period the faculty and staff had planned. Maybe during the burn-in, they would have had to handle antisocial, even criminal, behavior. Maybe then they would have been better prepared for it. But the glow of optimism and cooperative spirit led them to the tacit, naive assumption that every problem could be solved by talking about it, by the meetings they held to discuss other sorts of problems.

The faculty and staff had agreed to continue the deep space expedition, in defiance of orders from EarthSpace, at a meeting. They had held a meeting to decide whether to go after Europa and Androgeos.

"I'm worried about you," Infinity said.

Jenny looked directly at him, gazing at him intently. Always before, until he broke up the mob she created, she had glanced at him briefly, dismissing him. People liked to pretend *Starfarer* had no hierarchy, but it did. And the hierarchy separated a millionaire solar sail designer from a gardener by quite a distance.

"You are remarkable," she said.

He looked away, embarrassed. He did not like to stand out. He was not sure he wanted to know exactly what she meant. She probably did not mean what she said as a compliment.

"Feral shouldn't have died," she said.

"Nobody should have died."

"I mean—if anyone died, it should have been me. A sacrifice to Artemis, to the wind. Maybe that's why Blades directed his sabotage toward me."

"A *sacrifice*?" Infinity said.

"Yes. My namesake escaped, but the gods always take their due, in the end—don't you know your mythology?"

"That isn't *my* mythology," Infinity said.

"Oh," Jenny said. "No, I suppose not. I'm sorry."

"If you want to know about Amaterasu, or Coyote . . ." Infinity shrugged. "But not Iphigenia."

"Her father was supposed to sacrifice her to Artemis, for a favorable wind. She escaped. Artemis waited. I escaped. Artemis tired of waiting. She took my young wild friend instead."

"Everybody feels lousy about what happened to Feral," Infinity said. "But if any one of a dozen things had happened differently, he'd be okay."

"Blades is responsible." Her eyelids flickered as she cut off her conversation with Infinity to communicate with Arachne.

The faint perception of a small spot of heat told Infinity he, too, had a new message. It was Jenny's meeting proposal, broadcast through Arachne to everyone on board.

Infinity did not add his second. He thought things would be just fine the way they were. For as long as it took *Starfarer* to be able to return home. Then the legal system could deal with Chancellor Blades.

On the other hand, it was just as likely that the United States would give the chancellor a medal and arrest everyone else as hijackers and terrorists. Maybe Jenny wanted to be certain of some justice, or revenge.

Infinity still did not want Blades prosecuted here. The memory of the mob stayed with him. His friends and acquaintances had put on unrecognizable masks of anger. He did not want to see that again.

He stood up.

"Are you okay? Do you need any help?"

"No," Jenny said.

"Then goodbye, I guess."

He left her sitting among the rocks, and continued on to the administration building.

As soon as J.D. ended the discussion group, Nikolai Petrovich Cherenkov slipped away from the clump of people and fled to the nearest access hatch. He had not been able to resist listening to J.D. as long as she would talk about Nemo. But the press of people made him uncomfortable and nervous.

Kolya climbed down the ladder, past ground level, into *Starfarer*'s skin. He strode along the dim, cool-smelling corridor, toward the nearest elevator.

Until he reached the safety of the elevator cage, he expected at every second to see Griffith behind him, hurrying to catch up. He was sick to death of Griffith's following him around, trying to worship him.

He was rather surprised to have escaped Griffith. He would probably be pleased with himself, if he did not feel so dreadful.

He had not had a cigarette in two days, and he was at the height of nicotine withdrawal.

The elevator slowed and stopped and the floor settled beneath his feet: Kolya perceived gravity as pulling backwards against him, then sliding down to settle in the proper place.

Does anyone ever get used to the sensation of riding an elevator inside a rotating space station? Kolya wondered. I've lived in space longer than anyone, and I never have.

He put on his spacesuit, entered the airlock, and climbed down through the outer shell of *Starfarer*'s campus cylinder. The airlock opened. He climbed down onto the inspection net.

Starfarer loomed over him; the stars spun beneath his feet. The motion of the cylinder took him through darkness, into the hot white light of Sirius, and back into shadow as he plunged into the cleft between the campus cylinder and its twin, the wild side. On the far edge of

the valley, he burst into the light reflected by the solar
sail. If he looked in just the right place he could see the
bright crescent of Nemo's starship, tagging along with
Starfarer toward transition.

Kolya eased himself down onto the cables of the
inspection web, grateful to be back out in space. He had
spent too much time with other people lately, too much
energy trying to understand them. They admired him
for reasons that had very little to do with him and much
more to do with situations in which he had found himself by chance and luck.

Usually bad luck, he said to himself.

It felt good to be alone. He looked forward to re-
claiming his hermit status, now that the controversy was
over and *Starfarer* was safe in the hands of people who
would use it for its true calling.

Infinity ducked through the hole in the front door of the
administration building. The door had not yet been repaired. When Chancellor Blades locked himself inside,
the silver slugs, the lithoclasts that dissolved rock, had
munched their way through the wood-finished rock
foam.

The trail of the slugs led through the wide foyer and
up the curving stairs to Blades's office. They had eaten
through his door, and herded him through the underground tunnels to his house.

But the ASes and the mobile AIs would not be on
the upper floors. The only place big enough for them all
was the basement.

Infinity went through the building to the back stairs.
The halls were cold and deserted.

"Lights on," he said, and the stairwell brimmed with
light.

In the basement, hundreds of small robots hunkered
together in a random pattern, motionless and silent, like
paralyzed hands and blinded eyes.

Infinity blew out his breath in relief. The chancellor
could have destroyed all the mobiles while he was

locked in with them. They were sturdy, but they were
not designed to stand up to deliberate abuse.

But as Infinity moved between several squatty
housekeepers, a carrier, and a plumber, he felt like he
was walking among dead things. The usual faint electronic sound and electromechanical smell had vanished.

Infinity sat on his heels beside a housekeeper. Out of
habit, he tried to touch it through his link to Arachne.
He got no response. After a moment of fumbling, he
found the power switch. It was off. He turned it on. No
one *ever* turned household robots off. No one noticed
household robots enough to think of turning them on
and off. The ASes went about their business and
plugged themselves in to recharge when they had nothing else to do. They were practically invisible.

This housekeeper had nearly a full charge, yet Infinity could not get it to respond.

When he tried the housekeeper's self-test, nothing
happened. Nothing at all. No motion, no signal to
Arachne. Not even any error messages.

Infinity stood up.

This was bad.

Griffith paused outside General Cherenkov's front
door. He had never been to the cosmonaut's house; he
had never been invited. He knocked, and waited.

No answer.

Griffith had been sitting with the general during J.D.
Sauvage's discussion. He could not figure out where
Nikolai Petrovich could have disappeared to. Griffith
was trained to keep an eye on people.

He knocked again. His impatience got the better of
his shallow courtesy. He moved across the balcony that
fronted Kolya's house, in the third story of the hillside.
He looked through the floor to ceiling windows, cupping
his hands around his face to shield his eyes from the
reflected glare of the sun tubes.

The front of the house was deserted. The floor plan
of Kolya's house was probably the same as Floris

Brown's. Three front rooms with a wall of windows, a
back hallway, a bathroom, and storage space. The two
houses probably were alike, since Brown's was on the
first level of this stepped back triplex arrangement. Like
most houses on *Starfarer,* it was built within a hill. Griffith had been inside Brown's house, during her welcoming party, and he had taken the opportunity to snoop.
He had been through a couple of deserted houses, too.

Griffith waited; still, Kolya did not appear.

Griffith returned to the front door, hesitated, and
reconsidered. He had been good at his job. Good
enough to be wary of a man who had been a guerrilla
fighter. Or a terrorist, according to the government that
had put a price on his head.

Griffith did not expect Kolya's house to be booby-
trapped. Kolya lived in space because he wanted peace.
He had told Griffith that he was the only human being
who was safer on the deep space expedition than on
Earth. The Mideast Sweep was still very much in power
in Kolya's homeland, and it had a long memory.

Griffith did not expect to encounter traps. But he
did expect Kolya to leave ways of detecting intruders.
He did not want to risk his fragile new friendship with
the man who had been his hero all his life.

If we *are* friends, Griffith thought bitterly. Some
kind of weird friend. He talks to me. He advises me. He
asks for my opinion. Then threatens to kill me because
of it. Then he apologizes. And then he disappears.

At least he admitted I was right.

Fuck it, Griffith thought. Why do you keep trying to
make friends with these people? Most of them still believe you crashed the web. Even though they know
Blades was responsible. None of them care that you sac-
rificed your career and your marriage for their expedition. They don't care that you'll be the first one in jail
when—if—we ever get back to Earth.

He turned away from Kolya's deserted and probably
unlocked home—no one, except Griffith, locked doors
on campus—and headed down the long curving flight of
stairs.

As he passed Floris Brown's apartment, a dapple-gray miniature horse squealed and kicked up its heels and galloped away from Brown's front porch. The yearling filly raced across the open field and past the herd, alerting and exciting them. The whole bunch of them burst into a run, tangled manes and tails flying and bobbing like dreadlocks.

Floris Brown sat in the shadows of her deep porch, bits of carrot bright against the black of her knee-length tunic. She blinked at him like an aged, prehistoric lizard, her eyes beady within their rim of dark eye makeup. Fox, one of the graduate students, sat at Brown's feet and leaned companionably against her leg.

"You always frighten things," Floris Brown said to Griffith, her voice accusatory. "You frighten people and you frighten creatures. Why didn't you go home?"

He almost said, Because I was trying to figure out a way to keep you disorganized anarchists from getting blown out of the sky.

Instead, he said nothing, but turned away and strode stiffly back toward the guest house.

If he had told her what he had tried to do, she would not believe him anyway.

These people, Griffith thought, are driving me crazy.

Infinity left the administration building and hurried along a path that spiraled around the interior of *Starfarer.* The anomalies he kept seeing in the growth patterns of the plants added to his distress. A lot of the flowers had been bred for long-lasting blooms: the snow irises and the crocuses lasted well into spring; the daffodils came up so early that back on Earth, the threat of snow would not have passed. On *Starfarer,* it seldom snowed more than an artistic sprinkle.

He had gotten used to the long bloomings, when *Starfarer* was half finished, during its muddy first spring.

But other plants had other rhythms, and many of these were disarranged. Crossing a warm microclimate, he entered a grove of orange trees. They were heavy with fruit. Though the cafeteria was empty of fresh food, in the absence of the ASes, no one had thought to pick any oranges. Infinity smelled not just the sharpness of the oranges, but the heavy sweetness of a profusion of orange buds and blossoms.

The orange trees looked healthy, but their burst of blossoms worried Infinity. Plants under stress reacted like this, with an extravagance of reproduction.

Honeybees harvested the pollen, and more dead bees lay on the ground.

Farther along the path, in a cooler microclimate, Infinity passed through a field of spinach that had already begun to bolt.

He was worried for a lot of reasons when he reached the edge of the tumbled patch of ground where the genetics department had been.

Lithoclasts crawled through the broken building, dissolving the shattered walls, eating them away. The place had been disinfected. Everything that could be salvaged had been brought out. A great deal of work had been lost, not only experiments in progress but some of the back-up embryonic tissue meant to support *Starfarer*'s biological diversity.

Miensaem Thanthavong, the head of the genetics department, stood at the edge of the broken building, staring at it, her shoulders slumped.

Infinity glanced at the lithoclasts again, gauging their progress. It would be a while before they finished cleaning up. After that, the geneticists would call in the lithoblasts, the rock-makers, to rebuild the shell of their building.

Every silver slug that came inside, whether to work or to carry out someone's whim, meant one less attending to the constant job of maintaining the strength and stability of *Starfarer*'s main cylinders. He wondered if the scientists had thought of that.

Professor Thanthavong saw him and greeted him. She looked tired.

He was used to seeing her on a screen, or in a holographic projection. He always forgot how slight and delicate she was. Informal as *Starfarer* could be, he never knew what to call her. Few people called the Nobel laureate by her given name.

"I found the artificials," he said.

"Oh, good. We can use some here. Are they—" Her eyelids flickered as she linked to Arachne's web.

"I'm still not getting . . ." She stopped. "What is it?"

"I think their brains are fried."

Stephen Thomas smoothed the earth over Feral's grave. He leaned against the shovel and rested his forehead against his hands. Sweat dripped down his face and over the sensitive webs between his fingers.

He had chosen a spot on a hilltop within a grove of young oak trees. He chose the spot because he liked it, not because he felt certain Feral would have liked it. He had not known Feral long enough, well enough, to be sure what he would have wanted. Feral had left no instructions. Arachne preserved a record of his Earth-Space waiver, accepted and agreed to, probably without a second thought. Where the record asked for next of kin, Feral had written, "None."

Stephen Thomas sat down and rested against one of the oak saplings. The thin trunk would grow into a mature tree in twenty years, fifty. If *Starfarer* survived, the oak trees would still be here at the end of the exile.

Sunlight poured down between the brilliant red and yellow leaves. Just as spring was hot back on campus, autumn was hot on the wild side.

"Feral, I wish I had a marker for you," Stephen Thomas said aloud. "I'll get somebody to make you one, as soon as I can. I just couldn't stand to think of you lying there in the morgue. . . ."

He hooked his finger through the thin chain around his neck. The delicate links made a cold line of pressure across the nape of his neck. The crystal pendant swung against his thumb. In some light it was red, in some it was blue, and once in a while it turned black. He stared into it, twisting it back and forth, watching the colors change.

Stephen Thomas thought about Feral; he thought about looking for his aura. Feral had been unique, surrounded by changing rainbows.

"Victoria's probably right," Stephen Thomas said. "There's no such thing as auras. I make them up to go along with my feelings. To explain them, maybe."

Stephen Thomas wrapped his fingers around the crystal and tugged at it, gently at first, then harder.

"When I met you, I felt the same way I felt when I first met Merry," Stephen Thomas said. "I love Victoria and Satoshi. But that's different. That was slower, and steadier. We all had to work at it. Merry, though . . . sparks. Explosions. All those clichés.

"But Merry's dead. And you're dead. God *damn* it, Feral, I'm so sorry. . . ."

The chain snapped in his hand. He stared at the broken necklace. A film of blood reddened the gold along a finger's length near the clasp. Stephen Thomas touched the back of his neck and found the long scratch where the clasp had cut his skin. Salty sweat stung the shallow abrasion.

The bloody red-gold chain lay in his hand, tangled around the crystal.

Stephen Thomas spilled the necklace onto the bare earth of Feral's grave.

Nearby, a silver slug rustled the scatter of dry gold leaves on the ground. Stephen Thomas had called it inside to help him carry Feral's body. Stephen Thomas had been able to manage in the microgravity of the hub. Even coming down the hill, where the perception of weight increased with every step, Feral's weight had been manageable. But he had needed some help in regular gravity.

The lithoclast rippled uncomfortably, impatiently, waiting for him to tell it what to do.

Stephen Thomas did not need it any longer. He dismissed it and watched it crawl away. He only wished he could as easily command the slugs guarding Blades's house.

How could I have been so wrong about that guy? he wondered.

The heat enervated him. He asked Arachne the reason for producing such an intense Indian summer here in the wild cylinder. Both cylinders ordinarily had mild weather. The temperature range of winter overlapped the temperature range of summer. It seldom froze, and seldom came within complaining distance of body heat. People did sometimes complain that the weather bored them.

Arachne replied that steps were being taken to moderate the temperature.

Satoshi would like it over here today, Stephen Thomas thought. Being from Hawaii, Satoshi often complained that *Starfarer*'s weather was too cold. Victoria, on the other hand, had spent much of her childhood in Nova Scotia. She thought that *Starfarer* had no weather worth mentioning, merely climate.

At the bottom of the hill, an access tunnel opened. The silver slug oozed through it and disappeared, on its way back to its regular maintenance job on the cylinder's outside skin. The tunnel closed. Its hatch, disguised by rocks and dirt and a wilting flower, disappeared against the hillside. The sharp cry of a bird made Stephen Thomas glance up. When he looked down the slope again, he could barely see where the hatch had opened.

He should go home. He should go back to the lab, where the alien cells grew and divided on nutrient plates. By now they had probably produced enough for some analyses to begin. Stephen Thomas tried to find the excitement he should be feeling, but it was too remote. In order to experience elation he would have to open himself to grief as well, grief for Feral and grief for Merry.

He had not been able to fall apart when Merry died and he could not fall apart now. The partnership could not afford it.

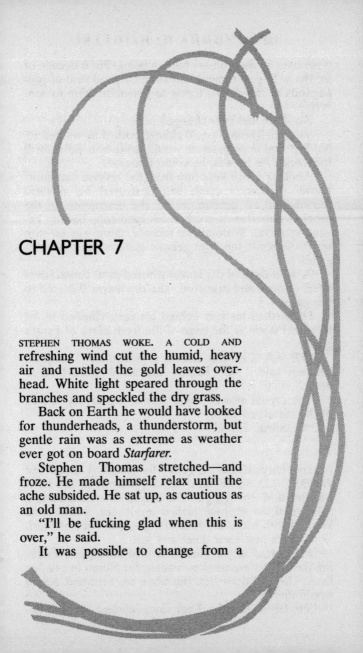

CHAPTER 7

STEPHEN THOMAS WOKE. A COLD AND refreshing wind cut the humid, heavy air and rustled the gold leaves overhead. White light speared through the branches and speckled the dry grass.

Back on Earth he would have looked for thunderheads, a thunderstorm, but gentle rain was as extreme as weather ever got on board *Starfarer*.

Stephen Thomas stretched—and froze. He made himself relax until the ache subsided. He sat up, as cautious as an old man.

"I'll be fucking glad when this is over," he said.

It was possible to change from a

diver back to an ordinary human being. For a decade or
so, the U.S. government had aimed a good deal of pro-
paganda at the divers, trying to persuade them to convert.

No diver had ever changed back.

Stephen Thomas could change back if he wanted to,
but the viral depolymerase would make him violently ill
for weeks. As he was, he could function.

Another factor kept him from the reverse metamorphosis. Arachne's crash had destroyed his medical
records and his genetic profile; the destruction of the
genetics department crushed his hard-copy backup beyond retrieval. Without the records, there was no sure
way to separate the diver genetic material from his own
genes.

A wind devil of dry leaves whirled past, paused over
Feral's grave, and dissolved. The dry leaves fluttered to
the ground.

He pushed his hair behind his ears, climbed to his
feet, and stood at the edge of the fresh earth of Feral's
grave.

"I'll ask Crimson about a headstone," Stephen
Thomas said. "And Infinity will know something to
plant."

The crystal glowed black against the drying surface
of the disturbed earth.

"Goodbye, Feral."

Nemo's chrysalis pulsed gently for hours. It shuddered
violently. J.D. sat forward, staring intently at the LTM
transmission, enlarging it. The chrysalis hardened into a
solid shell, an abalone turned inside out, swirled and
knotted with iridescent blue and green mother of pearl.

Nemo's nest grew quiet and still.

J.D. rested in the window seat of her house, watching the LTM transmission, waiting for Nemo to call her
back. The nest drew her. But when she returned, Nemo
would die.

She felt so strange. Ever since inhaling the link enhancer, she had disconnected from her body as if she were drunk. Arachne informed her that the reaction was within the tolerable range of effects.

"Tolerable for you," J.D. said aloud. Arachne, of course, did not reply. *Starfarer*'s computer did not engage in rhetorical conversations.

Getting the metabolic enhancer was so easy, she thought. After a couple of days, a couple of biocontrol sessions, I could already call on more energy. I thought enhancing the link would be the same.

She shifted her position in the window seat.

Her head spun. The light felt too bright. The light *was* too bright, but it had not bothered her so much before.

A faint breeze drifted through the open windows. It felt good. The weather was too hot.

Zev crossed the yard, coming from the river, a fish in one hand and J.D.'s string bag in the other. He saw her, grinned, and waved the fish. J.D. waved in return.

He took the steps to the porch in one stride.

"Are you hungry?"

"I am," she said. That was a difference from being drunk. If she were drunk, she would not be interested in food.

He came into the living room and sat down at the other side of the window seat. He offered her the fish.

"Zev . . . I'd like to cook it, if you don't mind."

She tried to get up. She nearly ran into the LTM display.

Whoops, she thought, bad manners!

She giggled, blinked the display out of her way and reappeared it at arm's length.

Her knees shook. A wave of heat passed up her face. She began to sweat. She sat back down.

Zev watched her with alarm.

"Maybe I won't cook it," she said.

"I'll cook it," Zev said.

"You'll cook it?"

"Sure. We do, sometimes."

"You never did when I was with the divers."

"It was summer."

"Oh." I guess that explains it, J.D. thought, wishing her head would clear.

Zev handed her an orange from the bag.

"Eat that while I cook. There's not very much growing that's ripe yet, it's too early. But there's lots of oranges."

"You didn't have to forage," J.D. said. "I'm sure the central cafeteria has plenty of supplies."

"I guess," Zev said doubtfully. "But I went by, and nobody's there to ask. It was easiest to go fishing."

He took the fish into the kitchen nook. J.D. lay back in the window seat, enjoying the unusual occasion of having someone make lunch for her.

"That smells terrific, Zev."

She peeled the orange and ate a section. She pressed the spicules against the roof of her mouth; they burst, and the sweet, tart juice flowed over her tongue.

To her relief, her head stopped spinning. She did not much like the sensation of being drunk, of having the world whirl around while she stayed still.

She suddenly groaned.

"Did I really say that to Stephen Thomas?" she said in distress.

"Say what to Stephen Thomas?"

"That his hair was down."

"You did say that." Zev joined her, carrying two plates of broiled trout.

"Oh, no."

"His hair *was* down, what's wrong with telling him? You ought to tell him to cut it."

J.D. touched Zev's pale hair fondly. It was short enough to stay out of his eyes when he swam, long enough to fan out around his head when he was in the water.

"I think he likes it long," she said.

Zev rested his head against her hand, then quickly kissed her palm.

"I think you like him," Zev said. He handed her one of the plates. J.D. gave him part of the orange.

"Of course I like him. I like Victoria and Satoshi, too."

She thought she had mastered her reaction to Stephen Thomas. She did not want to talk about it. In her present state, she would say more than she meant to.

She could say it all to Zev. He would find it perfectly comprehensible and natural. Except for her reluctance to admit how she felt. He would find it so natural that he would probably tell Stephen Thomas. J.D. could see nothing coming from that but embarrassment all around.

She took a bite of the fish. It was perfectly cooked; the flakes evaporated in her mouth.

"This is wonderful," she said to Zev. "What did I ever do without you?"

He grinned. "You were an ordinary human being before you met me," he said. "And I was an ordinary diver."

Infinity showed Professor Thanthavong what he had found in the administration building. She called the assistant chancellor.

Gerald Hemminge arrived a few minutes later. He hesitated halfway down the stairs, then strode purposefully the rest of the way to the basement.

Infinity explained what had happened. As Gerald listened, he shifted his weight from one foot to the other.

"How can we remedy this?" Thanthavong asked, her voice sharp. "How could the chancellor do something so stupid, so petty—"

"Please don't yell at me, professor," Gerald Hemminge said. He looked as unhappy as she did. He glanced across the dark basement, over the heads of the artificials, toward the shadowed corners. "I didn't know Chancellor Blades had done this. I would have stopped him if I could."

"We may have to get along without them," Thanthavong said. "Regrowing the brains . . . that may take resources we can't spare. We'll have to do their work ourselves."

Gerald made a sound of satisfaction, and a wry grin cut through his distress.

"It *will* amuse me to see Stephen Thomas Gregory beating his shirts against a rock in a stream."

"You and Stephen Thomas should put aside your differences," Thanthavong said. "The expedition can't afford them."

"I would if he would. It won't hurt him to do his own laundry. He has too high an opinion of himself, and his provocative manner—"

"He has a right to his high opinion," Thanthavong said. "He's a talented young man. My observation is that you provoke each other."

"It isn't just the *laundry,*" Infinity said, feeling provoked himself.

Thanthavong and Gerald stopped their back and forth needling. They both looked at Infinity. Gerald had a habit of cocking his head and listening with an expectant, faintly skeptical expression, as if he already knew everything anyone could say to him, as if he were merely waiting to dismiss it.

"The ASes clean up, sure," Infinity said. "But that's just part of keeping everything working. They *repair* things. They plant the gardens and weed the vegetables and harvest them and cook them—when's the last time you had a hot meal?"

"I've been eating crackers and cheese," Gerald said. "On the run. I haven't used the central cafeteria—are you saying nothing can be cooked?"

"I'm saying we'll have to do a lot more work than you think if we can't fix the ASes."

Thanthavong rubbed her chin thoughtfully with one knuckle.

"Somebody's got to grow the food," Infinity said.

"Dig in the *dirt*?" Gerald said.

"If you want to stay out here longer than the preserved stuff lasts."

"And how long is that?"

"I don't know. Arachne doesn't even know exactly what we came away with and what we left behind—"

"For heaven's sake—"

"Don't blame Infinity," Thanthavong said sharply to Gerald. "I told you Arachne lost backup information in the crashes. Some of this data the web may never even have had. We'll have to take inventory. We'll have to . . ." Her voice trailed off as she considered, then she brought herself back abruptly. "We're lucky someone is looking past the boundaries of their responsibilities," she said to Infinity.

"I suppose so." Gerald stared at the dead artificials again, but the dark corners drew his gaze. He caught his breath, but covered the reaction with a cough. *"Can* you repair the artificials? Or must we turn *Starfarer* into a primitive hunting tribe?" He glanced at Infinity. "No offense."

"What?" Infinity kept himself from laughing. What could he say? That his mother's people had been agriculturalists for thousands of years? That the hunting tribes had been a lot of things, none of them "primitive"? That he would truly like to see Gerald in the wild cylinder, trying to play pukka sahib with the shy, rare deer?

They would all be much better off gathering than hunting. A large proportion of the plants growing within *Starfarer* were edible. He wondered if Gerald had noticed that.

Infinity settled for a shrug. "I'd prefer hunting and gathering to cultivating rice by hand," he said.

The other half of Infinity's heritage was legally Brazilian and ethnically Japanese, but Gerald obviously had no idea what Infinity was talking about. He gave Infinity a blank look.

"Can you repair the artificials?" he said again to Thanthavong. He was sweating.

He doesn't like it down here, Infinity thought. He doesn't like it down here at all.

"Theoretically, of course I know how to regrow the brains," Thanthavong said. "But the technical aspects . . . Obviously, Infinity is correct. We shall have to free resources to repair these creatures. If Arachne's memories of their training are whole, the problem may not be too difficult. If the architecture has to be redesigned from scratch . . ." She lifted her hands, palms up, in a gesture of resignation.

Once more, Gerald glanced around the dark basement. The shadowy artificials surrounded them like a ghostly band of supplicants. Gerald hunched his shoulders.

"I shall have to research the best way to go about the repair," Gerald said. "If you'll excuse me." He hurried up the stairs and disappeared.

"We'd be in a pretty mess," Thanthavong said to Infinity, "if you hadn't noticed this."

"Somebody would have."

"I wonder. We're so wrapped up in what J.D. experienced. . . . Would we all of a sudden look around and see it was too late?"

What she had said to him she had meant as a compliment. But she made him wonder if he had badly overstepped his bounds, and she made him wonder if she thought he was uninterested in Nemo and the alien ship-nest.

He wondered if aristocrats always had that kind of effect. . . .

"Your mother is Japanese?" she said.

"My father."

"How did you come to be named Mendez?"

"My whole name's Infinity Kenjiro Yanagihara y Mendoza. But Mendez is easier for people to remember, and it's the original spelling. From before my mother emigrated."

"Why do you use your mother's name?"

He shrugged. "It's less confusing. I don't look very Japanese. In Brazil it didn't matter, there are a lot of us mongrels around. Most folks knew me as Kenny Yanagihara."

"Did your father grow rice?"

"No, ma'am," Infinity said. "He's . . . he's a lot of

things, but not a farmer. *Ronin* is more like it. He doesn't grow rice. His family probably never grew rice."

"My father did," Thanthavong said. "In Cambodia. A hundred years ago. With a water buffalo."

She brushed her fingertips across the carapace of the artificial, a touch of sorrow or farewell, and walked toward the stairs.

Infinity followed her out, nonplused by her comment. A hundred years ago? With a water buffalo?

He was not sure of her age, but he knew she was old. Eighty, maybe.

Her father *could* have been a rice farmer, in Cambodia. A hundred years ago.

With a water buffalo.

Carrying the shovel, Stephen Thomas headed home. He had not meant to stay so long, and he wondered how things were going in the genetics department. He checked with Arachne, but found no messages from his students or from his boss.

Involved with Arachne, he stumbled on the rough trail. He dropped the link and put his attention to negotiating the path. He had forgotten how quickly darkness fell in late autumn on board *Starfarer*. Back in the campus cylinder, where it was spring, the twilights as well as the days were growing longer.

He could not get lost: the sun tube reflected starlight at night, and Arachne could always guide him back to the access if the sky clouded over. As it was doing now. The clouds were thicker and darker than any Stephen Thomas had ever seen here. The temperature had fallen rapidly.

He kept going, following the trail in the darkness as best he could. He touched Arachne now and then to be sure he was headed in the right direction, but he could not stay in constant contact with the computer. He had to keep most of his attention on the trail.

The rain began, a few scattered drops that patted

against the dry leaves of the young trees. A rumble of sound rolled over the land.

Thunder.

Stephen Thomas looked along the length of the wild cylinder, amazed to see lightning flicker across the clouds. A break in the sky cover exposed the sun tube, bright with stars, and the far-overhead clouds.

Lightning spiraled down the length of the wild side.

As thunder rumbled around him, Stephen Thomas cursed the lightning, the rain, and Arachne. The trail led up a small hill. He stopped, looking for a way around the base. He had no intention of becoming a human lightning rod. He asked for directions to an access hatch, so he could find shelter underground, but received no reply. The storm cut him off from the web, isolating him from any help. The wind rose, whipping fallen leaves past his ankles. The raindrops hit the ground, coated themselves with dust, bounced back and splashed his legs, and turned into mud. His sore feet slid around in his wet sandals.

The clouds opened. Rain crashed down: the huge, heavy drops fell so fast the air felt like solid water.

A bolt of lightning blasted the earth nearby. The air reeked of ozone, broken cedar, smoke. The rain sizzled and hissed against flames; the fire died with a stench of wet ashes.

Rivulets coursed down the hillside and coalesced into a stream. Stephen Thomas followed the rippling water, looking for shelter. He was soaking wet, and cold, his long hair plastered against his face and straggling down his neck. He wiped rainwater from his eyes.

A lightning flash illuminated the land around him. His eyes and his mind retained a high-contrast picture. The stream was leading him into a gully: he was about to trade being a target of the lightning for being the prey of a wall of water. Even a diver might not survive a flash flood. He dropped the shovel and climbed the rough slope to higher ground, scrabbling up the rock, cursing, scraping his hands on stones.

Out of the reach of the gathering flood, he hunkered

under a scraggle of prickly scotch broom. It gave some protection from the wind, but none at all from the rain. The crisp colorful fallen leaves had turned to a slick, sopping brown mat.

The rain stopped as it had begun: a deluge abruptly changing to a scatter of droplets, then nothing. Stephen Thomas looked up. The clouds had rained themselves away, and the stars bloomed brightly all along the sun-tube.

Rushing brown water washed through the gully below him.

When Stephen Thomas stood up, the scotch broom swept him with another shower. He swore at it, looked around to get his bearings, and picked his way along the edge of the gully toward the trail. The electrical interference with his link had disappeared, for all the difference it made now. He did send a general, irritated note to Arachne about the weather. Arachne noted that the fire danger had ended.

Stephen Thomas hiked through a stand of bushy young trees that showered him with water and dead wet leaves. The trees ended abruptly at the edge of a meadow. The meadow stretched to the steep hill that formed the end of the cylinder. The ferry back to campus waited at the top of the hill, the axis of the cylinder.

When he reached the edge of the boggy field, Stephen Thomas saw someone halfway up the hill, descending in long strides through the low gravity.

Stephen Thomas stopped in the shadows of the trees. The person coming down the hill probably could not see him.

It was Griffith.

Griffith unnerved him. Stephen Thomas reminded himself that auras were a figment of his imagination. His perception of Griffith as lacking one meant absolutely nothing. As Victoria had pointed out, Florrie Brown told them all that Griffith was a narc before Stephen Thomas ever thought to look for his aura.

Griffith made him nervous because Griffith made

everybody nervous. He had been the first suspect in
Arachne's crash. He was innocent of that charge.

Griffith said he was an accountant for the General
Accounting Office. Few believed he worked for the
GAO, and nobody believed he was an accountant. Like
everyone else, Stephen Thomas believed he had worked
against the expedition.

Stephen Thomas moved deeper into hiding among
the trees.

Griffith crossed the meadow. He carried a makeshift
bedroll. Stephen Thomas wondered why he had not
taken a tent and sleeping bag from the storeroom. It
was communal property—but Griffith probably had
even less conception of communal property than he had
of governing by consensus.

What do I care if he gets wet on his camp-out? Stephen Thomas said to himself.

He stood very quiet as Griffith approached. He was
only a few paces from the government agent, and he felt
a spark of satisfaction in watching the man, unobserved,
from so close a distance.

Griffith stopped.

"Come out of there." He faced Stephen Thomas.

Stephen Thomas hesitated, then shrugged and
stepped out from beneath the trees. What could Griffith
do to him? Arachne knew he was out here. Stephen
Thomas made sure the computer knew Griffith was out
here, too.

"You look like hell." Griffith sounded annoyed.
"What are you doing in there?"

"Avoiding you," Stephen Thomas said.

Griffith's expression froze.

"What are you doing out here?" Stephen Thomas
said.

"None of your damned business." Griffith started
away, his shoulders stiff with anger.

"Hey," Stephen Thomas said.

Griffith's pace checked, but he kept going.

"How'd you know where I was?" Stephen Thomas
called after him.

Griffith turned back. He looked Stephen Thomas up and down, critically, contemptuously.

"You *could* have been more obvious," he said. "But . . . only if you'd left your scat."

Victoria hesitated on the path to J.D.'s yard. It was later than she had thought. She had spent all day in Physics Hill, analyzing her journey into Nemo's interior. What a strange conglomeration she had come back with. Neither she nor Avvaiyar knew quite what to make of it.

Delicate light poured through the tall windows of J.D.'s main room, and flowed over the wild garden. The huckleberry bushes rustled, their small oval leaves quivering, and *something*—an owl, a bat?—flew past on whispered wings.

Victoria knocked on the front door of J.D.'s house. Like most of the houses on *Starfarer,* it had been built and then covered with a hill. Its whole front was windows, except the door. Looking in someone's open windows was bad form.

Backlit by the cool glow, Zev opened the door.

"Hi, Victoria."

"Hi, Zev. Where've you been all day?"

"Professor Thanthavong told J.D. to rest."

"Is that Victoria?" J.D. asked.

"Hi," Victoria called.

Zev stood aside and let her in. She kicked off her shoes at the door.

Larger than life, the image of Nemo's chrysalis filled the center of the room, illuminating it. Victoria had kept the same image, much smaller, hovering nearby all day while she worked.

Nothing had changed.

The image overlapped the boxes that remained stacked in random piles in the main room. J.D. had not been here long enough to unpack all her belongings.

Victoria felt comfortable with J.D., and fond of her. It surprised her to remember how brief a time the alien contact specialist had been on board the starship.

J.D. sat in the windowseat, leaning against the side so she could look out the window or at Nemo's image. She had arranged a few things around her: some of her books, a reading light limpeted to the wall, the woven mat Satoshi had given her at her welcoming party. The light was off; J.D.'s attention was on the image of Nemo.

Zev joined her, sitting right-angled to her in the center of the cushioned seat.

Victoria smiled. "You look comfy."

"I feel so strange," J.D. said. "Like I've had too much to drink. I was saying silly things to everybody I saw. I thought I'd better hide out till I felt like myself again."

"Your system's taking a bit of a shock," Victoria said. "I got so involved in analysis—I should have come by to see you earlier."

"I'm okay. Come sit down."

Victoria perched on the other side of the windowseat, drawing her knees up and wrapping her arms around them. Zev's body radiated heat.

Stephen Thomas will be like that, soon, Victoria thought.

Zev curled his feet over J.D.'s; his claws gently dimpled her skin above the instep.

"I know the prep is working," J.D. said. "But I don't feel any change in my link."

"Arachne's not set up to dump more information to a person than the regular link can handle," Victoria said. "Not . . . not under normal circumstances."

The safeguards had not worked for Feral. It should have been impossible, but somehow Arachne *had* overloaded him. His blood pressure had soared, so fast and hard that it blasted open his arteries, his capillaries. The bleeding had simultaneously crushed his brain, and starved it.

J.D. was attempting something *very* risky.

"Please tell Nemo to be careful when you try this," Victoria said. She knew better than to ask J.D. to reconsider.

"I will. Don't worry." Her gaze drifted to the image of the chrysalis. "It's so *quiet,*" she said. "I got used to the attendants always fluttering around. Did you notice, you could always hear them even if you couldn't see them?"

"No," Victoria said. "I guess I wasn't in the nest long enough."

They talked for a while about Victoria's analysis of Nemo's center. Zev sat between them. Despite his youth, his exuberance, he was content to listen and watch in silence and without trying to draw their attention to himself. He impressed Victoria more and more, the longer she knew him.

"Is it what you thought?" J.D. asked. "Neutronium?" *Something* had to give the planetoid its mass. A normal asteroid its size would have negligible gravity. A person would be able to leap off its surface and orbit it before coming down again.

"I don't think so," Victoria said. "I think the gravity source . . . the power source . . . is even more dense."

"A black hole?" J.D. exclaimed.

"Economy quantum sized."

"Pick one up in any hardware store," J.D. said dryly.

"Right. Plus a nice iron shell for it to eat, a drip charge, and an electrostatic field generator. . . . But what the *hell* do you do to it to make it carry you around the galaxy?"

"A mere trifle," J.D. said.

They fell silent. A pleasurable tension rose between them; the affection and possibility Victoria always felt around J.D. increased. She extended her hand to J.D. J.D. gazed at her, then enclosed Victoria's long dark fingers in her strong square hand.

"Is everything all right?" J.D. said. "I mean . . ." She gestured with her free hand, encompassing all of *Starfarer.*

"I wanted it all to be perfect," Victoria said softly. "We'd take off with a fanfare, and explore, and come back with . . . I didn't know what, but some treasure.

Not a material treasure, an intellectual one." She rested her forehead against her knees. "Some fanfare. Some treasure." She looked up again; if she did not hide her face maybe she could keep from crying. "And I'm worried about my family back home, my great-grandmother especially. I wish you'd gotten to meet her. I wish she'd come on the expedition."

"She'll be all right," J.D. said, her voice reassuring. "They won't blame our families for what we've done. Surely."

"Grangrana has no way of knowing if we're still alive," Victoria said. "She'll be so worried. . . . And Satoshi's parents. They're wonderful. They'll stand up for us. But they'll be scared for us, too."

"What about Stephen Thomas? Doesn't he have family back home, too?"

"Just his dad. I mean, I guess he could find his mom if he really wanted to, but he never has. And Greg is . . . kind of self-centered. He knows all the right buttons to push." She sighed. "I try to like him, I really do. But it's hard to get worked up over worrying about him."

J.D. squeezed Victoria's hand.

"And I miss my cat!" Victoria said suddenly. "No matter what I said to Alzena, I couldn't persuade her to let me bring Halley along." Sometimes she dreamed of petting the sleek black cat; she would wake remembering the soft vibration of Halley's silent purr. Victoria laughed. "Isn't that ridiculous? Everything that's happened, and I think about missing my cat!"

"It's all right," J.D. said. "It's understandable."

"You don't need to hear all this!" Victoria said. "I meant to come and see how you're feeling, not to whine all over you." She let go of J.D.'s hand and pulled herself back, hugging her knees. In a moment she would leave. She would leave J.D. and Zev alone.

"J.D. and I are going swimming in the morning," Zev said. "In the ocean."

Victoria glanced up again. At first she thought Zev's comment was a complete non sequitur. But J.D. and

Zev were looking at each other with understanding, with happiness.

"Would you like to come with us?" J.D. said.

"I'd love to," Victoria said, surprised and pleased by the invitation.

"We'll stop by for you. Five a.m."

"Five!" Victoria said.

J.D. grinned. "Second thoughts?"

"Not at all. If you're sure you want company—?"

"I'm sure," J.D. said.

Alone in the dark basement of the administration building, Esther Klein put a box of probes and regenerators on the floor and tossed her lime-green baseball jacket beside it. The hot afternoon had even penetrated to the basement. Repair supplies and the dead artificials surrounded her. Over the dank scent of the basement lay the hint of mycelial growth, and ozone, and decay.

"I'm going to kill Infinity," she muttered. "I'm going to *kill* him."

Esther could have—*should* have—been out on the surface of the cylinders, in space, checking damage and making sure the silver slugs were properly maintaining the starship. Instead, she was stuck down here nursing sick artificials. It was all Infinity's fault. He was the only person on board who knew she had worked as an artificials tech.

But somebody had to do it, and she was the only person here with any experience. How the administration could let all the techs get recalled and not replace them . . . Esther supposed that was part of Blades's plan. It was convenient for him to let the techs go unreplaced. If they had remained on *Starfarer,* he would have chosen some other subsystem to disable. Esther remained with the expedition only because she had been piloting the transport that was trapped in the dock when *Starfarer* plunged into transition.

Fixing the artificials is the least I can do, I guess, she thought. Considering how much trouble I made by following orders. *Following orders!* I'm lucky Gerald or one of the senators hasn't punched me out for dragging them along on the expedition.

On the other hand, if I *had* undocked, I wouldn't be along on this trip, and I'd probably be in jail.

She rubbed her hands down the seat of her pants, rummaged for a probe in her toolbox, and set to work on the first artificial stupid.

She cracked the seal on its brain pan. Nothing. Blowing out her breath in relief, she opened the bioelectronic brain the rest of the way. Not too bad. Desiccated, like a crust of algae on a mudflat. If all the artificials were like this, she could resuscitate them in short order. She hooked up a rehydration tube and watched for a few minutes. The rumpled surface engorged with saline and fructose and salicylic acid, responding to the rich mix of hormones and growth factors. The fissures deepened.

Esther patted the artificial.

"You're going to remember everything, aren't you?" she asked it hopefully. "Arachne isn't going to be much help, so I'd appreciate it if you'd come out of this with your memories intact. You aren't gonna be much use to me as a stupid vegetable."

She went on to the next artificial and broached its seal.

The brain case hissed and burst open. Esther jumped back. Putrid bits of bioelectronic conductor sprayed her chest. Esther gagged and stripped off her shirt. It fell with a soggy thud. Bioelectronics rotted with all the worst qualities of animal, vegetable, and fungal matter: the sweet and nauseating smell of decomposing meat and the slimy deterioration of plant cells, all held together in a yeasty matrix.

First she hosed herself down, then her shirt, and finally the artificial, sluicing the spoiled brain tissue into the waste digester. The smell hung thick around her. It was not very toxic, but it sure was nasty.

She was soaking wet. Now she was glad of the day's

warmth. If she had been working in her jacket, the unofficial uniform of transport pilots, it would be ruined.

I bet *Starfarer*'s storeroom doesn't have any fluorescent chartreuse baseball jackets, she thought.

Esther set to the laborious task of cleaning the brain case. She sterilized it, seeded and sealed it, and hooked it to a feeder tube. That one would be a week regrowing. Then someone would have to retrain it.

She had Arachne display the transmission from Nemo's chamber next to the AS brain schematics. It had not changed since the chrysalis hardened; Esther had practically memorized it. She asked for some music. Trash rock. At least the recent music archives had not been wiped out in the system crash.

She set to work on another brain.

After eight hours, she was cursing Infinity under her breath. The first artificial had been a stroke of cruel good luck. Of the five open ASes, only the first had survived with any usable brain at all. Eighty percent complete destruction rate. Hands on her hips, she gazed around at the hundreds of robots that waited for her attention.

She felt like a cross between Dr. Frankenstein and an AS housekeeper. Or, maybe, considering the spatters of gunk on her clothes, she was more like Dr. Frankenstein's assistant Igor. She wiped a smudge off her wrist, thinking, The doctor never got brains all over his nice white lab coat.

"I need some help here, guys," she said to the deaf and blind and mindless robots.

She could hardly ask Infinity for help. He had more than enough to do. But Esther knew almost no one else on board. Except Kolya Cherenkov, and she was *not* going to ask the cosmonaut to do this job.

She only got over to *Starfarer* once a month or so. Most of Esther's piloting had been between O'Neill colonies. She always accepted the *Starfarer* run with pleasure.

Esther travelled a lot, she seldom stayed long in one place, and she did not like to sleep alone. Whenever she boarded *Starfarer,* all she wanted to do was take Infinity Kenjira Yanagihara y Mendoza to bed with her. He was one of her favorite lovers.

But that had not left her much time for making other friends on board the starship.

She asked Arachne to send out a general request for help for tomorrow morning. She cleaned off her tools and put them away. She let the brain schematic fade, and took one last glance at Nemo's chamber. In all the time she had been working, the squidmoth's chrysalis had not changed.

Her shirt lay in a scummy puddle. She had hosed off most of the crud, but doubted she would ever want to wear it again.

Esther shrugged, grabbed her jacket, and left the shirt where it was. Outside the basement, the evening would still be hot. Too hot for her jacket, and she would not even need her shirt.

She ran up the basement stairs, eager to get outside. She was tired and hungry.

She emerged into air so cool it surprised her.

The chill felt wonderful on her bare shoulders and breasts. It had been too hot lately. She set off for Infinity's house with a spring in her step.

A cold breeze hit her. The skin on her arms turned all gooseflesh, and her nipples hardened. Even then she resisted putting on her jacket.

Don't be a jerk, she said to herself. It's dumb to feel so cold just because it was so hot earlier. She slipped into the lurid green satin.

Arachne must be fixing the weather, she thought. Glad to hear it.

Stephen Thomas returned home, dirty and sore. It was very late—or very early—and he guessed Victoria and Satoshi had already gone to bed.

Instead of taking a shower, he told the house to fill the bathtub. As he watched the water rise along the sides of the azure tub, he tried to remember when the

last time was that he had taken a bath. He usually showered, preferably with one or both of his partners. Sometimes they sat together and soaked afterwards, lounging
in clean hot water.

He dropped his shorts and shirt on the floor and
stepped into the big blue tub.

The mud swirled away from his dirty feet.

Oh, shit, he thought, I should have at least rinsed
off. . . .

But the hot water felt so good, rising around his
hips, sliding up his back and belly and chest as he lay
down, that he could not bring himself to start over
again. He stretched out and let himself relax.

He spread his hands out on the surface; the translucent webs between his fingers nearly disappeared. Today
his skin was the color of strong tea. He pulled his hand
through the water, feeling the new power of his swimming stroke.

Like his hands and his skin, his lungs were changing.
Soon he would be able to store more oxygen, and hold
his breath much longer than normal. If "normal" meant
anything anymore, in relation to Stephen Thomas.

When the changes were complete, he would possess
an ability unique among aquatic mammals: he would be
able to extract oxygen directly from the water. In an
emergency, breathing like a fish would support the life
of a mammal for a little while.

Stephen Thomas halfway expected to be possessed
by an overwhelming urge to return to the primordial
sea, but that had not happened.

Except, he thought, I'm taking a bath.

"The call of the sea," he muttered sarcastically.
"Maybe I ought to add some salt."

Zev talked about swimming all the time, but the talk
was habit, and homesickness. Staying dry did not harm
his health; he had no gills that had to stay wet.

Air bubbles caught beneath the fine new hairs on
Stephen Thomas's arms and legs. They tickled. As they
escaped and rose to the water's surface, they made a
faint, cheerful crinkling noise. Stephen Thomas rubbed

his hands down his legs, down his arms, down his belly, currying the bubbles away.

His skin did not itch so badly, now that his transparent gold pelt had finished growing. His joints had stopped aching, though his shoulders hurt from digging Feral's grave.

He was beginning to wonder if the pains inside his body were all from his encounter with the silver slug. They should be fading. Instead, they had intensified. His pubic bone hurt with a sharp, hot stab and even his penis felt sore. Would he grow fur there, too? That would be too weird.

He knew as much about divers, or as little, as any average ordinary human being. He had never been fascinated with them, as J.D. was, and none of his work as a geneticist had included Changelings. No one worked on Changelings anymore. First it became impossible to get grants for the research, and then the changes themselves became illegal in the United States.

Stephen Thomas told the house to warm the bath. Warm water gushed from the faucet onto his feet.

His toes shot pain up his leg. He snatched his foot away, thinking the tub had burned him. But the water was only comfortably hot. He sat up in the tub and raised his foot to look at it.

Dark bruises arced across the base of each toenail, and the nails felt loose. Stephen Thomas wiggled the nail of his big toe. He grimaced.

It hurt, but it hurt in a way he remembered from his childhood. It was the itchy pain of a loose baby tooth.

Zev's feet had sharp semiretractile claws that curved over the ends of his toes, recessed into the flesh. Stephen Thomas had not thought much about how his nails would turn to claws, and he found that he did not want to think much about it now. He stopped wiggling his toenail and let his foot sink back into the heat.

The idea of being able to breathe underwater intrigued him. He wondered how far the changes had gone. He lay back in the bath, letting the water rise around his head. His hair fanned out, tickling his neck, drifting between his shoulder blades. Warm water crept up his face, covered his lips, covered his eyes. He could hardly tell the water from the steamy, humid air.

Stephen Thomas plunged his head the rest of the way underwater and took a fast, deep breath.

The water filled his throat and gushed into his lungs, choking him. He erupted from the bath, gasping. He leaned over the side of the tub, coughing water onto the floor. He nearly threw up.

Finally he collected himself, and hunched in the cooling bath. His chest and his throat hurt. The ache travelled downward and lodged in his belly.

I guess I'm not a diver yet, he thought.

He opened the drain, stood up, and splashed out of the tub. Droplets of water sparkled all down his body, trapped by the gold pelt. He curried off the water as he had curried away the air bubbles. He needed a sweat-scraper, the kind grooms used on horses or on Bronze Age athletes.

Rubbing himself with a towel, he went down the hall to his room. But in the doorway, he hesitated. He turned away from his comfortable, familiar mess and went to the end of the hall, to the room that would have been Merry's, to the room Feral had slept in. The partnership had never used it before Feral came to visit.

The futon was made up; the shelf doors were closed. It was as if no one had ever stayed here. As if Feral had never existed.

Stephen Thomas slid open the door to the built-in shelves. Feral's few extra clothes lay in a neat stack.

Stephen Thomas closed the shelf door again. He hung his towel carefully on the rack, got into Feral's bed, curled up around the deep pain of his pelvic bone, and fell asleep.

CHAPTER 8

LIKE THE STROKES OF A BRUSH PAINTING, beach grass covered the soft dunes. Beyond the dunes lay *Starfarer*'s ocean.

J.D. walked along a path too narrow to have been made by human feet. She wondered who or what had formed the path—and saw a tiny hoofprint, a small pile of horse droppings. The tough, sharp-edged grass would be little temptation for the miniature horses, but they might like the salt, and the flat freedom of the beach.

J.D. climbed the gentle rise of the dune. At the top, she paused to look across the shore.

The ocean circled the park end of

Starfarer's campus cylinder. It was the pulse of the starship's ecosystem, and the breath of its weather. The smell of salt sparkled in the onshore breeze, and the dry grains of sand hissed as they spun past J.D.'s feet. Open ocean created long crescents of white beach, separated by headlands and smoothed by the surf. Far overhead, on the shore beyond the sun tube, opposite this point on the cylinder, barrier islands protected salt marshes. The lowlands buffered the air and the water and offered shelter and spawning grounds to many of *Starfarer*'s creatures.

The hill that formed the cap of the cylinder rose from the far edge of the ocean, at the rim. The hill supported an ice field on one slope, hot springs on another. Their cold and warm currents circulated the seawater and helped drive the weather.

Zev stopped beside her, staring out at the ocean. He glanced at J.D., his face glowing.

"You go on ahead," she said softly. "I want to talk to Victoria for a minute."

He hesitated, then whooped in excitement and took out for the sea. He skidded down the face of the dune and dropped the beach blanket. Racing across the narrow crescent beach, kicking up bright showers of dry sand, he flung off his shirt; he hopped on one foot, then the other, while he stripped off his shorts.

Zev splashed into the shallow water, pushed forward, swam a few strokes, kicked his heels in the air, and vanished.

"He's eager," Victoria said, a smile in her voice. She stopped beside J.D.

"He's homesick, I think."

"He doesn't act it."

"He doesn't mope . . . but . . . when you spend time with the divers, you get used to a lot of contact. A lot of touch. He doesn't get that here."

"He doesn't?" Victoria sounded skeptical, and amused. "Could have fooled me."

"Not like back at his home."

The dune grass ended abruptly. J.D. and Victoria

crossed the beach: soft deep dry white sand, a narrow line of drying seaweed and small shells, then damp, yielding dark sand. It was easier to walk, here where the tide had just gone out, where the siphon-holes of clams pocked the surface and squirted when J.D. stamped her foot.

Out in the low breakers, Zev surfaced, waved, beckoned, and disappeared again.

"Are you going to join him?"

"In a while," J.D. said. "Let's go over by that piece of driftwood." She scooped up the beach blanket, and then she thought: *Driftwood?*

The huge, gnarled tree trunk lay above the high-water line, down where the beach began to curve out to a low headland. Its twisted, weather-silvered roots reached into the air. The trunk itself was larger in diameter than J.D. was tall. The top of the trunk had been broken off in a jagged point, as if wind had uprooted it and the fall had shattered it.

If it had ever lived.

J.D. touched the trunk. It felt like wood, and when she knocked against it with her knuckles, it resounded with a familiar, woody *thunk*.

"It *is* wood! I thought it'd be rock foam. How—?"

Victoria grinned. "Realistic, eh? Cellulose and lignin and what-all. Crimson sculpted it. She said any self-respecting beach should have cedar driftwood on it."

"It's handsome." J.D. stroked the smooth, weathered surface. "I miss big trees."

"There are some, over on the wild side. Twenty years old, from one of the O'Neills."

"Twenty years old?" J.D. smiled. The broken end of the driftwood revealed the sculpted growth rings. "This would be hundreds of years old."

"Crimson's good, isn't she? She told me she'd grown it layer by layer, and cooked the sculptural material so even the isotopic ratios would be right."

"She's very talented." J.D. let her day pack slide off her shoulders, spread out the blanket beside the tree trunk, and sank down crosslegged.

"I don't remember the last time I went swimming," Victoria said. "I've never swum in *Starfarer*'s ocean." She took off her floppy red T-shirt and kicked off her sandals. She was wearing a shiny blue two-piece bathing suit.

Zev had paced them as they walked along the shore. He waved again, called to J.D., bodysurfed halfway to the beach, then did a flip-turn and vanished into the waves again.

"Good lord, he's going to break his neck!" Victoria said.

"No, don't worry. He knows where the bottom is."

"Shall we swim?"

"I want to talk to you for a minute, first."

Victoria knelt beside J.D.

"I'm listening."

Zev was used to older adults gathering to talk while the younger adults swam and played. He was patient, and he knew J.D. would join him soon. He looked forward to casting off the restrictive land manners for a few hours, and he wished he had someone to swim with now while he waited for J.D. and Victoria. He wondered if Victoria's presence meant he and J.D. would have to maintain land manners. How would Victoria know diver manners?

Victoria's intensity both scared and intrigued him. He knew she did not altogether approve of his being along on the expedition. Still, she had let him accompany the alien contact department, so she must like him just a little.

Among the divers, Zev had spoken for J.D. to Lykos; J.D. must have spoken for him to Victoria.

While he waited for J.D., he swam through the shallow ocean.

The starship spun one direction; he swam the other direction, minus-spin, because it felt as if he were swimming downhill. The sensation amused him.

Paralleling the shore, he followed the wide curve of

the crescent beach, rounded the headland, and skirted close to the dangerous and exciting rough water. He probed the ocean with sound. He heard and tasted the weathered gnarls of the rock, and the seaweed and barnacles, periwinkles and limpets, anemones and starfish that inhabited the intertidal zone. Offshore, a school of fish scintillated past.

On the other side of the headland, the beach sloped shallowly into the sea, then rose again to form a barrier island half a kilometer offshore. Zev swam through the channel, staying on the surface. The water was silty and brackish and the bottom sand turned to mud. The taste of algae and reeds, shrimp and crabs and the bottom-dwellers of sheltered bays, filled his mouth and nose. He stroked toward shore till he could stand, chest deep, in the water. He put his feet into the deep warm mud of the river delta, for the pleasure of feeling the life it succored vibrating against his skin. He pushed off backwards and kicked along like an otter, looking up, tracing out the shore of *Starfarer*'s ocean belt.

He passed the end of the island. Another headland stretched into the sea, separating the delta from an open beach. Zev swam around it and into cold, exhilarating water. He dove, touched bottom, pushed off, exploded all the way out of the water at the apex of his jump, and splashed back into the waves.

Ahead he heard the steady splash of another swimmer. Not J.D. or Victoria, someone swimming near the small crescent beach. Zev turned over and swam hard, glad to find a swimmer to play with. When J.D. was ready, she would call his name and he would hear her.

He reminded himself to maintain his land manners, even though he was in the water. The ordinary humans owned this place, and the customs of divers carried no weight.

Even J.D. had taken time to get used to diver manners. He remembered how shy she had been at first. For at least a week, when she came to live with his family back on Earth, she had worn a bathing suit that covered most of her body. Sometimes she even wore a wet suit.

Zev could not imagine swimming in clothes. Now J.D. swam naked, just like a diver. She was not shaped like a diver, but that was all right. He remembered the first time she had joined in playing with him and his siblings and cousins; he remembered the first time he had swum beneath her and stroked her body from her throat to her knees. He loved the way her body felt against his hands, against his skin. He loved the weight of her breasts, the taste of her tongue. He liked it when they played together in the water, and he liked land sex as well. It felt more serious to Zev, somehow, though that might be because it was just him and J.D. and they concentrated only on each other.

He felt excited. The tip of his penis protruded from his body, into the cold water.

He gave up trying to figure it all out. Making love seriously, making love playfully: he liked both.

Ahead of him, the other swimmer churned the water. Zev remembered how astonished Chandra had been by the differences between male divers and male human beings. He did not want to startle the other swimmer. He let his penis withdraw again.

He touched the second swimmer with his voice. She did not react: she did not know how to listen.

At first he did not recognize her. She looked different underwater. People always did, with their bodies made transparent by echoes. But he was close enough to see her with his eyes. It was Ruth Orazio, the United States senator. Suddenly wary, Zev wondered if she had been involved in deciding that divers should work for the military.

He hung back, ready to dive and disappear, but willing to be friends. He cried out, in the air, with a questioning whistle, a sound of greeting.

She glanced over her shoulder, saw him, and stopped swimming. She turned toward him, treading water, and lifted one hand above the surface in a tentative greeting. Zev ducked, stroked once, and came up beside her. While he was underwater he traced her with his voice more completely, so he would be sure to recognize her immediately next time he saw her swimming. Her bathing suit made it harder to see all the way through her. But not impossible.

"Hi," she said. "Getting some exercise, too?"

"Exploring the sea," he said. He reached up and pushed his wet hair off his forehead with his webbed hand.

"You're Zev, right?"

"Yes. And your name is Ruth Orazio." A strange way to be introduced, by speaking the other person's name, Zev thought. He wondered how two land people introduced themselves if they did not know each other. In the sea, when divers or orcas met, they gave their own names.

"Just Ruth. I'm beat. God, the water's cold today. I need to get where I can sit down, okay?"

Zev followed her toward shore. The waves were very gentle here. Soon Ruth could stand up and walk. She wrung the water from her hair.

Zev stood up and waded beside her. When she was thigh-deep in the gentle surf, she turned to look out over the sea, toward the rocky cliffs of *Starfarer*'s end.

"It's so beautiful down here, I'm surprised there aren't more people. And more houses."

Zev fell to his knees before her, hugged her hips, and pillowed the side of his face against her belly. She stiffened, startled, then relaxed a little and looked at him curiously.

"What are you . . . ?"

"I can't hear it, not yet." Zev smiled at Ruth Orazio, blissfully. "It's *very* little!"

She paled. "How did you . . . ?"

"I saw, of course. Can I help teach it to swim?" It would be wonderful to have some youngsters here. He missed his little sister and his cousins. He splashed back in the water, gazing up at Ruth.

"You *saw*?"

"Underwater."

She did not understand.

"Everything's *transparent*," he said.

"Oh. Sound. Of course. Everything would be."

Her expression was so different than what he expected: he was afraid he had misunderstood. He stood up.

"Aren't you . . . aren't you going to keep it? I—I thought since you chose it, you would . . ." He stumbled to a stop.

He had not discussed this with J.D. But he had told her, as it was only polite to do, that he had not chosen to be fertile. She had assured him in turn that she too was in control of her reproductive abilities. So ordinary humans were like divers in the matter of deciding to bear children. Or J.D. was even more extraordinary than Zev already knew.

Or something had gone wrong, and Ruth had to make a decision about it.

He felt confused and embarrassed, when he only wanted to feel joy for Ruth Orazio and her coming child.

"*Did* you choose?" he asked.

"Yes—of course I did. I want it . . ." She stopped and took a long, deep breath. "Zev, promise me something."

"If I can."

"My lover and I have been trying to have kids for a long time. I've had a couple of miscarriages." She hesitated. "Do you know what that means?"

"Yes. I'm sorry." Divers had an even higher rate of miscarriage than ordinary human beings. That did not make the loss any easier.

"It's hard to handle, when that happens," she said. "It's even harder when everybody knows, and then you have to tell them you've lost it."

No diver would have to be told; it would be obvious.

But it *would* be hard, Zev thought, if someone tried to congratulate you on your happiness, and you had to tell them you were sad instead.

"Yes," he said again.

"So . . . please don't tell anyone you know. Till I'm sure I won't lose it. All right?"

He could not help feeling that she was not telling him something—but he could not think what it might be.

"All right." He agreed reluctantly; he did not know what else to do. "I have to go. A friend is waiting for me."

"Go ahead," she said. "And—thanks for giving me your word."

He waded toward deeper water. When the waves rose around his chest, he glanced back.

"I didn't mean to . . . to trouble you," he said. "Do you have friends to be with?"

"Sure," she said quickly. "Sure I do. You go on, now."

He stroked forward through the waves, and dove.

J.D. wondered why it was so hard to discuss, on land, a subject that was so easy and natural in the sea. She wondered why it was so hard to discuss it with Victoria, who found her attractive, whom she had kissed.

"Divers and ordinary humans have different manners," she said to Victoria. "Zev behaves differently on land than in the water. So do I, but it's easier for me. The land manners, I mean, because they're what I'm used to. It took me a while to get used to the way divers behave with each other, back on Earth. They play a lot. And their play's very sexual." The words for sex and play were nearly indistinguishable in true speech, the language divers learned from the orcas.

"Yes?" Victoria said.

J.D. glanced out at the sea, and obliquely overhead. The ocean extended in a blue and silver circle all the way around this end of *Starfarer*. She could see nearly three-quarters of the circle; directly overhead it vanished behind the brilliance of the light tube, and she could not look in that direction.

"If it will make you uncomfortable," J.D. said to Victoria, "for either of us to touch you while you're swimming, I'll tell Zev that we're using land manners in the ocean today."

"It wouldn't make me uncomfortable to touch you," Victoria said. "Quite the opposite. And Zev . . . intrigues me. The question is, what do *you* want to do?"

"I'd like . . . I'm looking forward to playing. With both of you."

Victoria grinned. "That sounds like fun, eh?"

J.D. smiled in return. "Yes. It does. Let's go swimming."

She flipped off her sandals with her toes, stood up, and unbuttoned her shirt. She was not wearing a bathing suit, and she felt shy about undressing in front of Victoria. She faced the ocean and took off her pants. She was built like a long-distance swimmer, medium tall and stocky. She had done competitive endurance swimming when she was in school. Recently her endurance swimming had consisted of trying to keep up with the divers, a task an order of magnitude harder than swimming a sea race. Taking a deep breath, she let it out and dropped her shirt. Nearby, Victoria dropped her bathing suit on the sand.

"Let's go!" She sprinted for the water, laughing, free and excited.

Swimming underwater, Zev heard his name-sound, in J.D.'s voice with her unique true-speech accent. He replied. He could hear her from both directions: without mechanized craft making engine noises, sound could bounce around and around the cylinder. He could hear multiple sets of echoes, each one fainter than the last.

J.D.'s voice came a moment sooner from in front of him than from behind him. He had swum more than halfway around the cylinder. The shortest way to return, and the most fun, was to swim the rest of the way around in the minus-spin direction. He plunged ahead. The faster he swam, the steeper downhill slope he perceived. He would be back to his starting point in a short time.

Suddenly aware of the restrictions in his movements, the small size of *Starfarer,* Zev felt closed in. Orcas could travel a hundred kilometers in a day. He was on board a vessel a few kilometers in circumference, twice that in length. Its ocean took up only a narrow ring along one end.

Swimming hard through the cold water, anxious to meet J.D., Zev passed the source of the chill current: a small glacier, flowing and dripping down one narrow angle of the cylinder's end. Zev swam as fast as he could. Bits of ice, calved by the glacier, bobbed on the waves. They were too small to be icebergs, or even ice floes. They were ice cubes, nearly freezing the water, chilling the air. His breath steamed.

Zev was not arctic adapted. Divers had discussed adapting themselves for polar life, but Zev liked the temperate climate of the Puget Sound wilderness. During most seasons back home, the water was cold. But not *this* cold. He had never swum in such cold water before. His body reacted, his metabolism kicking into high gear, pumping out heat as fast as the cold drained it.

The webs between his fingers paled as his capillaries contracted, conserving heat within his body. He pushed himself to keep going. He could hear the end of the cold water, not very far ahead: his searching voice echoed against the rough interface where the cold current plunged beneath the warm gulf stream.

In the distance, J.D. swam toward him. But she was slower than usual. She was swimming plus-spin. She would feel as if she were going uphill.

Zev asked Arachne if the current was always this cold, and found that the computer web was attempting to solve the problem of the unseasonably warm weather. He began to shiver, deep and hard. He called out to J.D.

She answered, greeting him, teasing him. New energy propelled him.

J.D. heard Zev's call. She replied to him, caressing him with her voice. She heard a change in the water.

She paused for a moment to look ahead. The surface turned from soft blue to dark, dense blue. Zev was fifty meters past the boundary. She did not know what the difference was until she plunged into the frigid current. She gasped and nearly stopped, kicked her metabolic enhancer, and ploughed into the swirling mix of currents.

Zev swam doggedly forward, his stroke rough and noisy instead of smooth and silent.

"Whew!" J.D. said in true speech. "It's cold over here!"

She flip-turned beside him and matched his speed and direction. She laughed in delight at the change from plus-spin to minus-spin, as if she had caught a wave.

She swam very close to Zev, letting her motion pull him along. Zev let his arms relax against his sides, and rode J.D.'s strength through the rough boundary.

They broke out of the cold, into a current so warm it felt tropical. Zev whistled in pleasure and relief, spiraled out of J.D.'s wake, and let himself sink.

J.D. sank beside him, immersing herself in the heat. "Are you okay?"

"Just cold," he said.

"Your hands are freezing!" She chafed his chilly fingers, then rose with him to the surface, expelled her breath, and drew in fresh air. She wished she had the artificial lung that had aided her when she lived with the divers. She had left it back in the wilderness. Zev had lent the lung to Chandra, then released it.

J.D. put her arms around him. He held her tight, his head on her shoulder. They drifted downward again.

"You rescued me!" Zev said.

"Nonsense." She blew a stream of bubbles at him. "You were all of thirty meters from the gulf stream."

"I didn't know it would be so cold," he said. "Or maybe I wouldn't have swum all the way around."

"It *was* cold back there, wasn't it?" J.D. said.

Zev warmed up quickly.

"Do you want to rest?" J.D. asked. She felt full of energy, exhilarated with the effort of the swim.

"No," he said. He grinned. His eyes were bright. "It's good to know everything isn't safe on *Starfarer.*"

They surfaced and sidestroked against the warm current, facing each other. J.D. let her fingers caress Zev from collarbone to groin. She kissed him. He had just learned to kiss. She explored his lips and his sharp canine teeth with her warm, soft tongue, then reluctantly drew away.

"Come on, let's go meet Victoria."

"Do we have to use land manners?" Zev said.

"No," J.D. said. "Not here. Not at all."

Victoria was a strong but inexperienced swimmer. J.D. had not wanted to criticize her, but she lost a lot of the power of her stroke because she did not know exactly how to place it. She churned valiantly ahead. J.D. was impressed that she had kept swimming through the open water, rather than heading to shore and waiting in the shallows.

Zev dove. The pressure of the water caressed J.D. as he passed her. He swam close beneath Victoria.

He startled her: she stopped swimming and trod water, kicking hard. He surfaced. Victoria grinned at him, and then, to J.D.'s surprise, jackknifed and dove beneath them both. Victoria's back touched J.D.'s knees, her feet. She surfaced, sputtering water. J.D. faced her, astonished, delighted, and Victoria flicked drops of water from her fingertips into J.D.'s face. Zev circled them both, reaching out with quick touches of his long-fingered hand, his sharp-clawed toes.

J.D.'s body produced energy, heat, adrenaline. She dove, swam between Victoria's feet, and kicked toward the surface. She slid up behind Victoria, stroking her from her heel up her leg, along her buttocks and her spine. Victoria turned to catch her. Their bodies pressed together.

They sank beneath the surface. Bubbles escaped from J.D.'s mouth and nose, tickling Victoria's face.

Victoria broke away and kicked toward the surface. J.D. and Zev rose beside her.

"It's okay," J.D. said. "We're right here."

"I know," Victoria said. She was apprehensive, but not panicked. "It's too deep for me. Let's go closer to shore."

"I wish we had swimming lungs," J.D. said. But even artificial lungs were not the same as swimming free, like a diver.

Victoria set out toward a calm, sandy cove, a small sheltered beach, making good speed despite her thrashing swimming stroke. Zev glided up beside her and J.D. swam on her other side, helping draw her along.

"Swim smooth," Zev said. He showed her a good surface stroke. "You won't get tired so fast, and you won't attract sharks."

"Sharks!" She took in a mouthful of water and sputtered it at him. "There aren't any sharks! The biggest predator is tuna fish."

"Maybe you'll attract tuna fish," he said.

J.D. deliberately put some splash into her swimming stroke. "I love tuna fish," she said. "Is this all I have to do to get one?"

Exasperated, Zev dove. J.D. felt him swimming below her. Soon she noticed that Victoria was swimming more smoothly.

The bottom shoaled up beneath them. The water was blue and clear and warm, the bottom bright with coral and fish.

"It's so beautiful here," J.D. said.

Victoria turned to float face down, her eyes open, gazing into the bright water. J.D. dove beneath her and swam face to face. She reached up. Tentatively, they touched hands. J.D. let herself rise. She kissed Victoria, quick and soft. Zev joined them, brushing his hand up Victoria's back and down across her small breast, her dark nipple. He dove between them, stroking them both with his body and his hands.

J.D. spun out and surfaced to breathe. The sea bottom shoaled up again. The coral gave way to soft bright sand.

They reached a spot where Victoria could stand. The water reached to her shoulders. J.D. came up behind

her. The sea buoyed J.D.'s heavy breasts. She put her
arms around Victoria. Victoria turned and drew her
down to kiss her, deep and long.

"Is this how divers play?" Victoria whispered, holding her, pressing her body close to J.D.'s.

"Yes."

"Serious play." She smiled.

Zev surfaced behind J.D. He slid his hand over
J.D.'s shoulder and around to trace the lines of her collarbone. He nibbled the nape of her neck. Victoria
placed one hand over his, and slipped her other hand
down J.D.'s side, from her waist to her hip and between
her thighs. J.D.'s nipples hardened and her heart
pounded. The rhythm reached her center, and flowered
like a whirlpool, opening.

At her garden gate, Victoria kissed Zev and J.D. Zev's
lips were very warm, J.D.'s cool and soft. Victoria held
J.D., letting herself relax for a moment within J.D.'s
embrace.

"See you later, okay?"

"Soon."

She smiled and watched them walk together, hand in
hand, along the path to J.D.'s house. Arachne's holographic image of Nemo's chamber appeared nearby,
and paced them.

Victoria asked the computer web to show her the
alien scene. It had remained static since Nemo's chrysalis hardened.

Victoria turned through the opening in the rounded
earth wall that bracketed her yard. Carnations covered
the slopes, blooming wildly, pink and white and red,
filling the air with their spicy fragrance. Crocuses and
irises covered the lawn. This was Victoria's first experience with planting flowers. She felt a surprising sharp
shock of pleasure every time she saw them.

She stepped up on the porch, beneath the roof of
shaggy grass that drooped to make the house look like it
had eyebrows.

Victoria felt exhilarated, hungry, and scratchy with dried salt water. It was still very early. She entered her quiet house through the open French doors of her room. Satoshi snored softly in her bed. He had not moved since she left to go swimming. She glanced into Stephen Thomas's room; it was empty.

Now she was worried about him. It was not unusual for him to spend all night working in his lab, but no one from the genetics department had seen him since yesterday. Nor was it unusual for him to spend the night with someone else. But it was unusual for him to disappear without a word about where he had gone or who he was with.

Besides, Feral was the only person Victoria knew of who had attracted his attention recently. Feral's death had affected him deeply. But he had pulled himself together quickly after Merry's death. He surely would not fall to pieces now.

He managed better than I did, when Merry died, she thought. Better than Satoshi did. I don't know how he did it, but I'm grateful that he could.

As she headed for the shower, she decided that if he had not come home or left a message by midday, she would ask Arachne where he was. She seldom resorted to having the web chase someone down.

She walked into the bathroom, slipped in a puddle, and nearly fell. Even as she thought, At least I know Stephen Thomas has been home, she saw the damp towels he had left in a tangle and the muddy clothes he had left in a heap.

She kicked the dirty laundry aside, annoyed, and glared at the tracks her younger partner had left on the floor.

Dammit! she thought. I know you're upset and distracted and excited and everything else. But that's no excuse—!

A line of clayey mud ringed the tub. Now she was mad. She was particularly irritated to have anything spoil this morning.

And why do I have to scrub the bathroom down

twice, she thought, because Stephen Thomas can't bother to do it once?

She sprayed out the bottom of the tub so at least she had a clean place to stand.

She washed her hair and rinsed the salt from her skin. The tub was luxuriously large, with a rim wide enough to sit on, and a heater that would turn the enclosure into a sauna. Victoria wondered if *Starfarer* would ever have enough cedar trees to allow a few to be used as lumber. Or maybe Crimson's driftwood technique could grow some cedar boards. A sauna that did not smell like cedar was no sauna at all.

She had to use the last clean towel; damned if she would try to dry herself off with the cold clammy dirty ones Stephen Thomas had left on the floor. Grumbling, she gathered up all the dirty laundry she could find. Her house had no laundry facilities; the AS housekeeper was supposed to take care of that.

Satoshi was up now, sitting in the main room with a cup of coffee. He always took a while to get going in the morning. Victoria dumped the laundry by the front door, then turned on the kettle to make a pot of tea. Today the coffee smelled almost good enough to drink. Feral had made good coffee, and he had showed Stephen Thomas and Satoshi how to make it, too.

"Don't take a shower," she said to Satoshi.

"Huh?" Satoshi sounded sleepy—not surprising, since he had been over at the geography department till two o'clock in the morning. But he was awake enough not to be grumpy.

"No clean towels."

"Again?"

"Yeah."

"He promised."

"I know."

Satoshi sighed. "He promised to give the laundry to the housekeeper. No housekeeper—"

"I'd split hairs for him, too. Usually. But he *did* promise. And the tub was filthy."

"So much for learning quaint Japanese customs,"

Satoshi said. "He forgot the one about showering first
and soaking afterwards." Stephen Thomas was studying
the partnership's ethnic background. Satoshi's mother
was of mostly Japanese ancestry, though that branch of
his family had been in Hawaii almost as many generations as Victoria's family had lived in Canada. The other
side of Satoshi's family, being Hawaiian, had been in
Hawaii since people started living there.

Victoria could not help but chuckle. "He must have
skipped that chapter."

Satoshi sipped his coffee and Victoria scalded the
teapot and filled it with loose tea and boiling water.

"Let's try not to fight with him," Satoshi said. "The
last fight was kind of hard on us all."

"It was," Victoria said. "I will try."

"You were up early this morning," Satoshi said.

"I went swimming with J.D. and Zev," Victoria said,
grateful for the change of subject. "And if I'd known
how much fun it'd be, I'd've made you get up and come
with us."

"Swimming at dawn in this season doesn't sound fun
to me. It sounds cold."

She brought her teapot over to the table and sat
down to wait for the tea to steep.

"We swam in the gulfstream, and the lagoon. Divers
don't just swim. They play." She rubbed her foot against
his leg, stroking his calf with her instep. "It isn't quite
sex, it's too quick. But it's very sexy."

"Quick?" he said doubtfully.

"Quick touches, over a long time." She touched his
shin with her toe, like brushstrokes. He looked at her
quizzically. "It'd be fun to go swimming with you and
Stephen Thomas and make love in the water."

"I don't know," he said doubtfully. "I tried that
once, back home. Wasn't very successful."

"Why not?"

"Salt water interferes with the natural lubrication.
My partner . . . took exception to continuing."

"Worked for me," she said with a grin.

He put his foot in her lap. She rubbed it, massaging

his sole and stroking her fingertips up the sharp strong tendons. She bent down and nipped his toe gently. Satoshi yelped in surprise.

"I'm starved!" Victoria said. "Is there anything to eat?"

"Not much," Satoshi said. "I made some rice."

Victoria had never warmed to the Hawaiian custom of having white rice with practically every meal.

She jumped up and opened the refrigerator.

"Don't—"

"Wasn't there a tomato in here someplace?" Victoria said. "I could broil it."

She picked it up. It collapsed in her hand.

She made a sound of disgust.

All the vegetables were wilted, the leftovers moldy. The housekeeper had kept the kitchen clean, too, and before Feral came to stay with them they had kept very few perishables around. They never had time to cook, and none of them was very good at it. They had ordered most of their meals from the central cafeteria.

"This is awful," Victoria said.

"I know."

"Why didn't you throw it out?"

"Because I don't know if the recycler's coming. There's a big empty hole in Arachne where the schedule ought to be. I figured the stuff wouldn't smell too bad if we kept it cold."

"Oh," Victoria said. She put the squishy tomato back in the refrigerator. "We've got to do something with it. Do you know how to make a compost heap?"

"In theory."

"Maybe we'd better try it. But I've got to have some breakfast. I'm going over to the cafeteria, want to come?"

"Sure. Shall I get Stephen Thomas?"

"Do you know where he is? All I've seen of him since yesterday is his muddy tracks in the bathtub."

Satoshi hesitated. "He's sleeping in Feral's room."

"In *Feral's* room? Is somebody with him? Why didn't he use his own room?"

"He's alone."

Victoria stared at him in disbelief.

She strode down the hallway to the spare room. The guest room. The room that should have been Merry's, but never was. She could *not* think of it as Feral's. He had been a guest, an acquaintance, a passing fancy for Stephen Thomas. Not a member of the family, not even a friend. Not yet.

I don't make friends in two weeks, Victoria thought. Even Stephen Thomas doesn't make friends in two weeks.

She opened the door without knocking, went to the window and pulled the curtains open, and in the flood of light sat on her heels at the edge of the futon.

When she saw Stephen Thomas she drew away sharply, lost her balance, and sprawled backward. She caught herself and knelt beside him.

He lay with one hand over his face, his fingers spread, the translucent webs spread between them. The webs had grown all the way to the second knuckle on each finger. Even his hands had grown. The fine gold pelt surrounded his arm and shoulder like the auras he claimed to see. He had always been so fair: now his skin was deep amber, far darker than his gold hair.

"Stephen Thomas!"

He drew his hand down from his face, opened his eyes, and looked at her blankly. Concern overcame her moment's incoherent, absurd relief that the color of his eyes had not changed. His blank look scared her.

The changing's gone wrong, she thought in terror. He's changed—

She loved him and she found him exasperating, often both at the same time. If the change were to obliterate his personality . . .

He blinked, and he was suddenly Stephen Thomas again.

"What's the matter?" he asked. "What time is it?"

"It's about eight." She answered the answerable question first. A flare of sheer relief heated her irritation. "What are you *doing* in here?"

"Trying to sleep," he said, and spread his strange, changed, webbed hand over his face again.

"Wake up!" The fear he had given her only made her angrier.

"All *right,* I'm awake."

Satoshi appeared in the doorway, worried.

"Why are you sleeping in here? Why not in your room? Why not with us? Where have you been?"

"Take it easy," Satoshi said. After a moment Victoria realized he was talking to her, not to Stephen Thomas.

"I don't much feel like taking it easy right this second," she said to Satoshi. "I want to know—"

"Which question should I answer first?" Stephen Thomas said.

"I don't care!"

"I'm sleeping here because I wanted to. I never did, you know . . . or maybe you don't know."

"It didn't make any difference to me if you did or didn't," Victoria said, "when Feral was alive. But now . . ."

"Where I've been is in the wild cylinder. In a thunderstorm—"

"A thunderstorm!" That was impossible.

"Digging a grave."

"A grave . . . ?" Victoria said. "You can't mean— You took his body, all by yourself?"

Victoria's distress was as strong as her anger. She could not bear to think of Stephen Thomas all alone with his grief, burying his friend, and she wanted to have been there, so she too could say goodbye to Feral.

"What about the rest of us?" she cried. "What about his friends, what about J.D.?"

"Gerald said forget about a funeral," Stephen Thomas said. "He wanted Feral just to lie there forever in the morgue! I couldn't stand it. Besides, nobody else thought about him."

"Stop it, Stephen Thomas, that isn't fair," Satoshi said.

"But nobody did anything. Nobody else had even

opened his files to see what Feral wanted, if something happened."

He pushed himself up on his elbows. The gold glow covered his chest and belly. His face and his neck remained bare. Victoria wondered where his necklace was; she had seldom seen him without it. At the center of his collarbone, slightly thicker, slightly darker hair formed a thin line that streaked down his body, stopped just above his navel and started against just below it, and disappeared beneath the bedclothes.

Victoria sat on the edge of the futon. Satoshi joined them, sitting crosslegged on the foot of the bed.

"We didn't have *time,*" Victoria said. "When did we have time?"

"Yesterday," Stephen Thomas said. "Last night. And not just us. Anybody could have looked for his will, the whole time we were gone. Nobody did."

"It's awful that he died." Victoria felt unfairly put on the defensive. "It's a tragedy. In the classic sense of the word. If he'd done as I asked—"

"He couldn't! I knew he couldn't. Why didn't you?"

"How could you know? You're trying to beat me up with twenty-twenty hindsight."

"I'm not trying to beat you up at all. I'm trying to tell you where I was and what I was doing and why I was doing it."

"And why I'm responsible for Feral's death."

"No," he said. "No, I'm not blaming you. But I'm not letting you blame him, either. He knew the risks, he chose to take them, he couldn't do anything else."

She said, again, doggedly, "If he'd done as I asked—"

"We'd still be back at Tau Ceti," Satoshi said.

"But we could always take another run at the transition point."

"A hundred light-years behind Europa and Androgeos," Stephen Thomas said. "We never would have caught them. We might even have gotten stranded back there."

"I thought you *wanted* to stay back there," Victoria said. "To try to colonize the planet."

"What if I did? I didn't block consensus. Feral was trying to help *you* do what you wanted. Uphold *Starfarer*'s charter. Catch the alien ship—"

"And a lot of good it did us!"

"Don't try to tell me Feral died for nothing!" Stephen Thomas shouted. "I don't want to hear that Feral died for nothing!"

He threw off the blankets and lunged out of bed, sleek and lithe as an otter. Victoria stood up, unwilling to let him flee the discussion.

"Ow! Shit!" Stephen Thomas yelped in pain and sat down hard.

He grabbed his toes and rocked back and forth, his teeth clenched. Victoria stared at him. Satoshi hurried to his side, reached toward him, hesitated, then put one arm around his shoulders.

"What—?"

"Nothing. Nothing at all," Stephen Thomas said. "It's just that all my fucking toenails are falling out."

His little toenail had disappeared; the next largest hung by a thread of connective tissue. His toes were as bruised as if he had dropped a rock on his feet. He wiggled his big toenail, and the next two in turn, each successively looser. Victoria felt a little sick. Stephen Thomas took the hanging toenail between his thumb and forefinger.

"Don't—" Satoshi said.

Stephen Thomas pulled the toenail off.

Stephen Thomas put the toenail, shiny with the transparent polish he used, on the narrow shelf at the headboard of the futon frame. Then he bent over his bruised toe and poked at it, oblivious to Satoshi, who sat back away from him, and to Victoria. She felt ill and angry at the same time. He was so good at deflecting arguments—not defusing them, as Satoshi did, but deflecting anger away from himself and setting up a situation where anger was no longer appropriate, no longer acceptable, and the argument could never be resolved.

Beneath the toenail, the bruised end of his toe had begun to form a valley, a cavity, where a claw would grow. It would interest her, in an intellectual way, if the foot the claw was growing on belonged to a body with which Victoria was less intimately familiar.

Even angry with Stephen Thomas, Victoria felt the attraction of his powerful sexuality.

"Are you done grieving now?" She forced her voice to remain so neutral that her tone came out cold, and hard.

Stephen Thomas's shoulders stiffened. He stared at his foot, then glanced at Satoshi, then turned to Victoria.

"No," he said. "No, I don't think I am."

"I know you liked him! But you barely knew him. I knew him better than you did—"

"You knew him longer than I did. Not better."

"Next I suppose you'll say the same thing about Merry."

Stephen Thomas looked confused. "What does Merry have to do with this?"

"Nothing. Except that Merry was our partner and Feral was our acquaintance, and it seems to me that you're grieving a lot harder for Feral."

Stephen Thomas stood up slowly, gingerly, balancing precariously on his abused feet, and walked out of the room.

Victoria wanted to scream, or apologize, or cry— what she really wanted was for Stephen Thomas never to have received the changing virus, and for Feral and Merry never to have died.

She followed Stephen Thomas as far as the doorway. He was halfway down the hall to his room. In the dim light the new gold pelt was invisible, but it made his outline fuzzy.

He disappeared into his room.

Victoria glanced back at Satoshi, expecting him to tell her what she deserved to hear: that she had been far too hard on Stephen Thomas.

"I shouldn't criticize him for his feelings," she said,

before Satoshi could speak. "Your feelings are your feelings. He can't help being so open. . . ."

"I hate what's happening to him," Satoshi said abruptly.

"I—what?"

"I loved him the way he was," Satoshi said. "God, I don't want to think of myself as changing my feelings for someone because of the way they look. . . ."

"He hasn't changed that much," Victoria said, because that was how it seemed to her. "Not physically . . ."

"He's changed a *lot,*" Satoshi said. "And he's going to change more. I hardly even know him now. . . . I can't stand to say it."

He folded his arms across his knees and buried his face against them. Victoria sat beside him and hugged him, trying to reassure him, trying to comfort him, not doing a very good job of it. She was used to Stephen Thomas being the most emotionally demonstrative of them all, to Satoshi being the most reserved and calm, to taking the middle ground herself. Satoshi's shoulders began to shake. Victoria could not remember— Yes. At Merry's funeral, Satoshi had cried. So had Victoria. Stephen Thomas, dry eyed, held them both. At the time she had been grateful that one of the partnership could maintain some equilibrium. She had not considered how strange it was that the calm one was Stephen Thomas.

Satoshi straightened up, drawing in a deep, harsh breath. He flung himself back on the rumpled bed and scrubbed his bare arm across his eyes. He tried to smile.

"This is so weird," he said.

"What is?"

"I'm upset with him because he's doing something so different I can't even understand it . . . and you're upset with him because he's behaving exactly the way he always does."

As he dressed, Stephen Thomas gradually dissociated himself from the fight with Victoria, from the aches in his bones and the pain in his feet, from everything he had lost in the last week. In the last year.

He usually wore running shoes to the lab. Shoes, today, would make the pain impossible to ignore. He tried his sandals, but even sandals hurt. He shoved them into his pack. Professor Thanthavong would take off the rest of his toenails one by one if he worked barefoot in the lab—she would do it in private; she would do it metaphorically. But she would do it. So he would have to wear the sandals part of the day.

He did not know what to do about the fight with Victoria. He could not answer any of her questions any better than he already had. She wanted more from him, but he was damned if he knew what. He would give it to her if he could. He had made himself stay in control after the accident that took Merry, because the partnership needed someone who could still function. And right after Feral died . . . Victoria honestly thought she had put Feral in a position where he would be safe. Stephen Thomas smiled, fondly, sadly. Trust a reporter to get out to the front, even if nobody could figure out where the war was being fought or whether there was a war at all.

Walking cautiously—no point to limping, since both feet hurt—he went out through the French windows of his room.

Despite everything, the hour was still early when he got to the lab. Neither Mitch nor Bay had arrived yet, and Lehua Aki sprawled sleeping on the couch in the Biochem lounge. A small image of Nemo's chamber hovered above her.

By the evidence of their work, his students had all stayed very late last night. The isolation chambers held several racks' worth of growing alien cells.

He was proud of them for getting so much accomplished when he had been useless to them for the past day. They were working under another handicap, too, camping out in the Biochem labs while the silver slugs tried to rebuild Genetics Hill.

Worse than losing their lab space, the geneticists had lost their equipment, the probes and genetic subroutines that everyone developed over time. All the work in progress was destroyed. The missile had stolen a year of Stephen Thomas's professional life.

He checked the preparation he had started the day before. At least one thing was going right today. He had plenty of material for another series of experiments.

Ordinarily, this kind of preparation would be safe by this stage. No matter how virulent the original cells, they were now dead, dismembered, each cell separated into parts. Cell walls. Mitochondria. DNA. But these cells were alien; he had no proof—not even any evidence—that they could no longer replicate once he vibrated them apart with ultrasound and centrifuged them into layers.

He was not particularly worried about infecting *Starfarer* with some alien illness that would attack animals or people or plants. It would make more sense to worry that tobacco mosaic virus might infect a human being. Those pathogens were from the same evolutionary scheme. But he had cultured an autotroph, a free-living cell, from Nemo's web. A microbe that could get by on light and water and simple molecular nutrients could grow independently in the starship.

This was something Stephen Thomas preferred to avoid.

He got Arachne to project an image of the squidmoth in its chrysalis.

"Why wouldn't you give me another sample?" he muttered.

He suspected that, eventually, Earth's biosphere would have to co-exist and cope with alien autotrophs, but he did not intend to be responsible for the first uncontrolled contact. Among other things, Professor Thanthavong would not just have his toenails, she would have his lungs as well. In all her decades of research, it had taken a missile attack to contaminate her lab for the first time.

"Damn!" he said suddenly. He had forgotten to set up the DNA sequencing of the soil bacteria from Europa's ship. A complete sequence would give him a detailed picture of the microbe, rather than the more general view of DNA and protein fingerprints. He set up the analysis with a couple of controls and left it running.

"Hi, Stephen Thomas."

Satoshi's young graduate student Fox stood uncertainly in the doorway of the lab. With her forefinger, she nervously twisted a lock of her flyaway black hair into a curl.

"Hello, Fox," Stephen Thomas said.

"Anything I can do?"

"Why? Thinking of changing departments?"

Her expression brightened. "Can I?"

"No."

"Oh."

"Don't you have some geography to do?"

"Yeah," she said. She stepped back into the hall and he thought she had left.

He went back to work, forgetting, after a moment, that she had ever been there. He pressed his hands into the manipulator gloves that gave him access to the isolation chamber and his new preparation.

"I could wash some glassware—"

"Jesus!" Stephen Thomas exclaimed.

"—or something," Fox whispered.

"I nearly dropped this," Stephen Thomas said. "Don't sneak up on people like that."

"I didn't mean to."

"There's nothing you can do here. We don't wash the glassware, we recycle it. Easier to get rid of contaminants. Anyway, you wouldn't want to spend all day up to your elbows in cell guts."

"I wouldn't mind."

"There's still nothing you can do."

"I *can't* go back to geography."

"I keep telling you, Satoshi isn't mad."

"Did you ask him?"

"The subject never came up. But if he were mad, he'd mention it. Fox: Satoshi doesn't get mad. He'll talk to you. It sounds to me like *you* need to talk to *him.*"

"He ought to be mad. So should you."

Watching the holographic image from the safety chamber, Stephen Thomas put the prep carefully back on its stand and disengaged his hands from the manipulator gloves. The swimming webs itched slightly; the gloves had pressed the webs back between his fingers farther than they would ordinarily go.

He crossed his arms and faced Fox, leaning back against the lab table.

"I don't blame you for what happened to me. But if you really want to know, I think you made more trouble for yourself and for us than any of us need. You should have been on the transport."

"A lot of difference that would have made! I'd still be here!"

"It'll make a lot of difference. The folks who were on it will be legally free and clear. Maybe even entitled to reparations. Gerald and the senators and Esther Klein . . . hm, I'm not sure about Esther. Doesn't matter. You and Zev, though—you're in as much trouble as the rest of us. Maybe more."

"I don't care."

"And the president might not be able to—"

"I wouldn't ask him to!"

"You wouldn't have to."

"Stephen Thomas, I just want to be part of the expedition. I just want to help." Her smile strained as she fought tears.

"You are part of it," Stephen Thomas said gently. "And the way to prove you deserved to come with us is to work your ass off. In your own department."

"Are you sure—"

"I don't—" He stopped. There was no reason to involve Fox in the partnership's problems. No reason, and no excuse. What good would it do to tell her that he had not talked to Satoshi about her, or about much of anything else either, for the past several days?

"Satoshi is the most reasonable and sympathetic human being alive. He lives with me, after all." He smiled at her, reassuring. "Okay?"

"Yeah," she said. She smiled back. "Thanks."

"Good. I've got to get back to work."

He unfolded his arms and turned back to the manipulator gloves, spreading his fingers, stretching the webs. He heard Fox's quick intake of breath. Probably she had just realized how much about him had changed, and the changes spooked her. He must look pretty fucking weird from outside, with the webs and the fine gold pelt covering his darkening skin, and his battered toes sticking out of the straps of his sandals.

"I love you," Fox said.

Oh, god, no, not again, Stephen Thomas thought.

For the third time, he faced her. He could not pretend not to have heard or not to understand.

"That's too bad," he said.

She did pretend not to hear or not to understand.

"When Satoshi asked us all over to dinner, the first time I saw you—"

"Fox. No."

"Won't you even consider me? I know you're not monogamous—"

Flabbergasted by the comment, Stephen Thomas laughed.

Fox blushed. "You know what I mean. Whatever the term is when you've got two legal partners and you still get involved with other people. What is it you don't like about me?"

"Nothing to take personally."

She laughed as sharply as he had a moment before. "That's kind of hard."

"I don't get involved with grad students."

"I'm not your grad student."

"Five minute ago you were standing here trying to be."

"I changed my mind, okay?"

"I don't get involved with any grad students."

"Why not?" she asked, honestly perplexed. She grinned. "We're people, too—don't you think? So why not?"

"Why not . . . ?" Stephen Thomas sighed. "Why not is because in school, every instructor I ever had hit on me." Miensaem Thanthavong was the first superior he had ever had who had never tried to take him to bed.

"How could they resist?" she said softly.

"They should have."

"But this is different."

"No, it's not."

"Sure it is. I'm not your student and you're not my instructor."

He could see this deteriorating into "Is not!" "Is so!" He made himself keep a straight face.

"It doesn't matter whether it's the same or not. The answer's no."

"But—"

"Please take the answer gracefully."

She did not take it gracefully, but she neither erupted into anger nor burst into tears. He never knew what to do when either happened in this particular situation. Anger was easier to defuse than tears. When it was someone crying over unrequited love for someone else, it helped to give them a friendly hug, a shoulder to cry on. Touching Fox now would only make things worse. Stephen Thomas found it very difficult not to respond to another person's grief.

"Okay," she said finally. "If you change your mind—"

"That just isn't going to happen."

She went away, then, but as she disappeared down the hallway he heard what she was saying, as if to herself but in truth to Stephen Thomas.

"Maybe I should have gone home after all."

Stephen Thomas let his irritation out in one quick snarl.

"Oh, fuck!"

He returned at last to his work, pushing away the

anger from his past and the guilt Fox had just tried to hand him. She *should* have gone home, or tried to. If he had anything to do with her staying, it was not by design. And then he thought: she grew up around politicians. She knows how to turn coincidence to her own advantage.

Mitch hurried in, his long gangly limbs all angles.

"Is Fox okay? What did she want? She didn't even say hi."

Mitch had been trying to get Fox to say hi to him, even to remember his name, since the first week she came on board *Starfarer*. So far he had had no luck.

Mitch was gawky and shy. Not a bad-looking kid, dark brown hair and eyes, pale intense face, heavy eyebrows over well-defined features, sharp mind and good ideas.

Stephen Thomas, who thought Mitch spent too much time in the lab and not enough with other people, was grateful beyond imagining that Mitch had not heard what Fox had just been saying. If he had, the kid might draw completely into a shell. Bad enough that he could not get Fox to see him. Far worse if he knew she was looking for someone, but the someone was not Mitch.

"She wanted to ask me something about Satoshi," Stephen Thomas said. He finished the 'scope slide, projected the image, and forgot about Fox instantly.

Mitch whistled softly.

Lehua came into the lab, knuckling her eyes, combing her long straight red-gold hair with her fingers. As usual she was dressed better than the grungy-casual popular on campus; her crisp shirt and slacks somehow did not look like they had been slept in. Visitors to the genetics department sometimes mistook her for the professor and Stephen Thomas for a technician. His third student, Bay, followed Lehua in.

Lehua's display of Nemo's chamber drifted in after them, touched the identical display Stephen Thomas had set hovering, and melded with it.

"How come the Biochem couch is so much more

comfortable than the one in Genetics was?" Lehua
asked. She yawned.

"Come look at this," Stephen Thomas said.

Lehua and Bay joined Stephen Thomas and Mitch.
Together, they looked at the holographic projection of
the 'scope field.

"What is it? Is it what I think it is?"

"It could be a lot of things. But what I'm guessing is
3-D genetic information. Dendritic molecules."

"*Dendritic* genes?" Bay said with disbelief. He
leaned toward the display, squinting in concentration;
his crinkly, shiny black hair swung forward along his
smooth chestnut skin, the ends tracing the straight line
of his jaw. "How would they work? I can't figure . . ."

Stephen Thomas let his eyelids flicker; he connected
with Arachne and sent a message to Professor
Thanthavong.

He watched the enormous spherical molecules vi-
brate.

Grief and anger, pain and confusion, had blanketed
his life since Feral died. For the first time since then, a
flicker of joy broke through.

"I can't figure it out either, Bay," Stephen Thomas
said. He knew his expression was a silly smile, and he
did not care. "Isn't it great?"

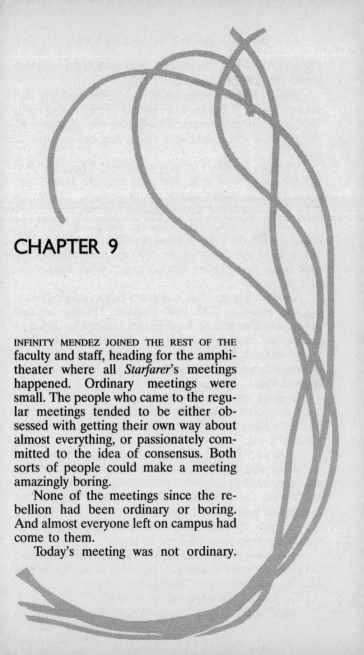

CHAPTER 9

INFINITY MENDEZ JOINED THE REST OF THE faculty and staff, heading for the amphitheater where all *Starfarer*'s meetings happened. Ordinary meetings were small. The people who came to the regular meetings tended to be either obsessed with getting their own way about almost everything, or passionately committed to the idea of consensus. Both sorts of people could make a meeting amazingly boring.

None of the meetings since the rebellion had been ordinary or boring. And almost everyone left on campus had come to them.

Today's meeting was not ordinary.

Jenny Dupre had succeeded in convening a meeting about the fate of Chancellor Blades.

Infinity wished desperately that Jenny had left well enough alone. If Blades was content to stay walled up in his house till they returned to Earth, why change anything? What else could they do to him but put him in jail?

Will they kill him? Infinity wondered. There are people on board who're maybe mad enough. Jenny. Stephen Thomas. And Griffith would probably kill Blades if he even suspected Kolya wanted him dead.

Infinity did not want to believe the faculty and staff could decide on cold-blooded revenge . . . but he did not want to test them, either. He kept remembering the mob Jenny had created with her anger, when Blades was first discovered.

Arachne was another unknown factor. After observing the evidence J.D. and Stephen Thomas tracked down, Arachne had severed Blades's computer link and immunized itself against his neural signature. The slugs had dissolved the hard links into his house. Without electronic communication, he was very little danger to the starship.

Without his link, Blades must be just about going crazy from boredom, Infinity thought. His house must be like a cave, with the windows covered over and the electricity off. . . .

To protect Blades, Infinity had given over control of the silver slug guards to Arachne, so no one could pull academic rank or seniority and call them off. He did not know what the computer web would do if the meeting decided to punish the chancellor.

I'll have to block consensus, Infinity thought. If it comes down to that, I'll have to block.

Esther sat down hard beside him. He was surprised not to have seen her come in, because, as usual, she was wearing her fluorescent lime-green jacket.

"Is this place a community, or not?"

"Yes," Infinity said. "Sure. What's the matter?"

"I put out a call for volunteers. Yesterday! Want to know how many responses I got?"

"Just on a guess . . . not enough."

"Nobody!" She made a sound of disgust. "God forbid that any of these famous scientists muck up their hands with rotten AS brains."

Infinity had never opened an artificial, never had to replace one's neural tissue, but Esther had described the operation in more detail than he wanted to know.

"You should have . . ."

"Called you? I suppose you've been lying around doing nothing?"

"Uh, not exactly."

"I didn't think so. I bet you've been outside since breakfast with nobody to help you."

"Not nobody. A few other folks. And some of the slugs. Kolya, for a while, but I don't know where he went."

Kolya sat on the terrace on Esther's other side.

"Where Kolya went," Kolya said, "was to throw up."

"Kolya, you look awful! What's wrong?" Esther touched his hand. "Your hands are freezing!"

She took off her bright jacket and flung it over his shoulders.

"Stick your arm through here—"

"I had better not, I'll rip it." He was slender, and very tall for a cosmonaut, much taller than Esther: she barely came up to his breastbone. The sleeves of her jacket would hit him around the elbows. Kolya hunched himself inside her jacket. "This is better, this makes a difference, thank you."

"What *happened*?"

He did look pale. Sweat beaded his upper lip and his forehead, and matted his streaky gray hair. And he smelled strange: sharp and acrid, unpleasant.

"Nothing happened, exactly. But I am trying to quit smoking."

"Smoking!"

"Smoking! Smoking what?"

"Tobacco, of course," he said.

Esther wrinkled her nose. "I didn't think . . ."

"That anyone did that anymore? Such an old-fashioned drug. Like snake oil."

The terraces of the outdoor amphitheater were full to halfway up the slope. The meeting would start soon. This time, they could hope that the light would remain constant. The last two meetings, Blades had sent the light level to extremes to try to disrupt the rebellion.

Kolya pulled the edges of Esther's jacket closer together.

"When I was a cosmonaut, I never smoked. But later . . ." He shrugged. "I had no reason not to. It can be . . . quite comforting." He smiled. His front teeth were slightly crooked. "I never expected to live to such an advanced age, or to reach it in a place where tobacco was so difficult to get."

Infinity felt uncomfortable, torn between being glad Kolya was trying to quit and wanting to do something to help. Kolya looked unhappy, tired, and sick.

"Did you run out?" Esther asked sympathetically.

"Abruptly. I kept my stores in one of the genetics department freezers."

"Oh."

The freezers in the genetics department had been destroyed along with the rest of the building.

"Maybe it's for the best," Esther said. "I mean . . . it really isn't good for you, and now you'll have to quit."

"I suppose I will. The designer of *Starfarer*'s ecosystem was far too health-conscious to grow tobacco on campus." He chuckled ruefully. "I went so far as to ask Alzena once. She was horrified."

"When she had a choice, she picked stuff you can eat or make things out of," Infinity said, feeling miserable and guilty about Kolya's distress. "Or flowers."

"Very sensible," Kolya said, with resignation.

His hands trembled; the energy that made him seem . . . not younger, exactly, but vital, had drained away.

"I've tried to quit before," he said. "I never succeeded. I'm one of those unfortunates upon whom nicotine takes a very tight grip." He squeezed Esther's hand in gratitude. "I will be all right."

Conversation ebbed abruptly.

The meeting began.

No one rose to speak. Jenny had not arrived, and Gerald Hemminge was nowhere to be seen.

Motion in one of the dark entry tunnels drew Infinity's gaze. Neither Jenny, nor Gerald, but Stephen Thomas appeared, late, accompanied by his clutch of grad students. He paused and glanced around to find a good seat, unhurried, aware of the attention he had attracted but nonchalant about it. He moved, footsore, to a place near the top of the amphitheater.

The one other person Infinity did not see that he expected was Griffith. Infinity did not like Griffith, though the government agent no longer scared him. Infinity wondered what Kolya thought of Griffith hanging around him all the time. When he was not making himself blend into the background, Griffith allowed his attitude of arrogant superiority to slip out. But he worshiped Kolya.

"Why'd Jenny call this meeting if she isn't even going to come to it?" Esther muttered. She shifted nervously. Infinity knew how she felt. Being asked to sit in judgment of someone was bad enough. Being left in the dark about what was going on made it worse.

He linked into Arachne. The computer web acknowledged him. The silver slugs waited to accompany Chancellor Blades to the meeting, to guard him, to guard Arachne while he was free.

But Chancellor Blades refused to accompany the silver slugs.

Infinity let out a quick, sharp, incredulous laugh.

Jenny Dupre and Gerald Hemminge arrived at the amphitheater. Without the chancellor. Jenny looked furious and embarrassed, Gerald, as usual, carefully neutral and controlled.

Jenny did not even find a seat, nor did she state her name, then pause, as meeting etiquette required.

"He won't come out," she said angrily. "He's too

cowardly to face his own trial." She sat down abruptly, sullenly, and folded her arms.

Gerald remained standing.

"Gerald Hemminge," he said, and waited. The assistant—now acting—chancellor never lost his good manners, even when he was using them to be rude.

No one interrupted or challenged him.

"Chancellor Blades . . ." Gerald said. "The chancellor denies that you have a right to try or judge him. He . . . requests . . . that you return to Earth and hand him over to the authorities."

"The same authorities who sent him in the first place!" Jenny said bitterly.

Infinity wished she would at least follow meeting rules, especially since she was the person who had called it.

"Ruth Orazio."

Across the amphitheater, the senator waited longer than the usual couple of seconds, as if she expected someone to object to her speaking.

"I know you all feel betrayed," she said. "Frankly, I do, too. What's happened is what always happens when decisions get made in back rooms and secrecy. But the justice system of the United States is public and open. If you do return to Earth, the chancellor will get a fair trial—"

"Will *we*?" Jenny said.

The senator continued as if she had not been interrupted.

"—a fair trial, and the powers that controlled him will have to come out in the open and answer for what's happened."

Jenny started to speak again.

"Ms. Dupre," Gerald said.

Annoyed, Jenny rose. "Iphigenie Dupre," she said. "If I may—?"

Infinity did not blame her for being bitter and angry. But it hurt to see the change in her. During the first deployment of *Starfarer*'s solar sail, her creation, she had glowed with joy. Stephen Thomas had broken out a bottle of fancy champagne and let it loose, in the free-fall of the sailhouse. Jenny had drunk one of the fizzing globules with a kiss.

"The U.S. constitution says the accused has a right to face the witnesses against him, and the U.S. insisted that we operate under their constitution. Fine. But we're here. We're willing to face him. *I'm* willing to face him. Nothing says he has to face us. But nothing says we can't make a decision about him even if he isn't here to listen to it. Or to defend himself. If he *could* defend himself."

"He also has a right to legal counsel," Gerald said. "Is anyone willing to defend him?"

"I assumed you had that job reserved for yourself."

"Firstly," Gerald said, "I am not a barrister. Secondly, my defending the chancellor would be an inexcusable conflict of interest."

"J.D. Sauvage." J.D. paused, waiting her turn to speak. "I don't see how we can proceed if Mr. Blades won't come out. Maybe it's legal for us to proceed. But should we? I don't think so."

Infinity felt very grateful to J.D. for saying something that he, too, believed. He knew he was going to have to speak out later, and no one was going to want to listen to what he had to say.

"Do you think he should be allowed to get off free?" Jenny asked, disbelieving. "I thought Feral was your friend!"

"He was," J.D. said. "And I'd like to see justice done for him. *Justice.*"

"Chancellor Blades is innocent," Gerald said.

Jenny laughed. So did Stephen Thomas, and a few other people, coldly and without joy.

"So much for not defending him," Jenny said to Gerald.

"I can't defend him in a court of law," Gerald said. "Which, by the way, this is not. I didn't say I wouldn't speak for him."

"William Derjaguin." The senior senator from New Mexico stood up.

Infinity had powerful feelings about Derjaguin. Powerful, and mixed. Disappointment because of Derjaguin's implacable opposition to the deep space expedition. Admiration, because Derjaguin had been one of the few people to oppose the weapons testing scheme that ended in disaster for the southwest, one of the few to stand up for land others called beautiful and valueless.

No one objected to letting him speak.

"I've talked to the chancellor, too," he said. "Not that it's easy, with a couple of lithoblasts threatening to dissolve me with acid if I go one step closer."

He had it wrong. The lithoblasts would block his way. They could physically restrain him. They might even put up a barrier of rock foam if he was persistent enough. But they would not dissolve him with acid. Only lithoclasts could produce acids and solvents. All the lithoclasts were outside working. People always thought of repair as building, but clearing away was at least as important.

Outside is where I ought to be, Infinity thought.

"The chancellor told me he was innocent," Senator Derjaguin said. "I have a great deal of experience at judging character. I believe him."

"What a load of bullshit," Stephen Thomas said.

"He doesn't believe he can get a fair hearing, on this ship with this crew."

Infinity hated to hear *Starfarer* referred to—especially by politicians—as if it were a military vessel and the people on board, its recruits. *Starfarer* was not a warship, and he was not a soldier.

"If he's innocent, he ought to be willing to stand up in front of us and say so," Jenny said.

Both Gerald and the senator reacted with indignation.

"You incited the mob that went after him!" Gerald said. "Who knows what might have occurred, had he not fled—!"

"I had to get him out of the web!" Jenny cried. "Do you blame me? Has anyone ever tried to kill *you*?"

Derjaguin moved, a quick, repressed reliving of the shock of an assassin's bullet.

"Yes," Derjaguin said.

Jenny had no reason to know the personal, even the public, history of a U.S. senator. He surprised her with his reply, but she continued.

"And how do you feel about the person who tried to kill you?"

"That person . . . is still at large," Derjaguin said. "I've reserved judgment."

"Noble of you," Jenny said.

"Jag," Ruth Orazio said, "you *must* understand how she feels."

"I do." He turned his presence and his considerable charisma back toward Jenny. "And I can understand your desire for revenge. I hope I never have the person who shot me at my mercy. That's what the judicial system is for. To dispense justice. To prevent revenge."

He must be used to seeing people blossom into eagerness, or wilt into compliance, under the light of his attention. But Jenny was immune. The solar sail designer was at least as renowned as he, and probably richer. She did not fawn over celebrities. They fawned over her.

"I'm not convinced you've caught the right entity," Derjaguin said. "The crash could have been programmed in from the start. A Trojan horse."

Jenny challenged him.

"Have you *looked* at the evidence J.D. and Stephen Thomas found? Even looked at it? If you had, you wouldn't think Arachne crashed because of a horse!"

J.D. rose again.

"Jenny . . . Infinity's isolated Blades from Arachne. Isn't that enough punishment, for now? If Blades doesn't want to object to his exile, maybe we shouldn't insist on something worse. The way things are, if he's guilty we're all safe. If he's not, we haven't done anything irrevocable."

"How do you know we're safe from him?"

"He's cut off from the web—"

"How do you *know* we're safe from him?"

J.D. regarded Jenny with sympathy.

"I spend a lot of time in the web. I'm enhancing my link. If there's danger, I'm vulnerable. I think the risk is small enough to take."

Jenny stared at J.D. for several seconds; it felt like a very long time. She turned completely around, raking all her colleagues with her gaze. She faced J.D. again, having seen that even the people who had joined her mob —maybe those people in particular—would not side with her now. She could produce no consensus for the chancellor's guilt, or for his punishment.

"I think you're wrong," she said. "And I think you'll find it out the next time we go into transition. I'm not touching the web. If we miss the insertion point, that's too damned bad." She straightened her shoulders and flung her head back; the iridescent beads on the ends of her braids clinked together loudly, decisively.

She strode from the amphitheater.

As people rose to leave, relieved to think the meeting was over, Infinity stood up and spoke his name. No one, except Esther and Kolya, heard him.

He raised his voice. "Infinity Kenjiro Yanagihara y Mendoza."

Intense meetings drained everyone. His colleagues, realizing he wanted the gathering to continue, sank back in their seats with resignation.

"There's some other things we have to talk about," he said.

"Without doubt they can wait," Gerald asked. "A few days—? The other side of transition, at least, when we might know more about our situation?"

"I don't think so," Infinity said. "We have some problems. The first is the weather."

"But the weather has been exceptionally fair," Gerald said.

"It's *too* fair," Infinity said. "It's too hot for the season. First everything got blasted during the last meeting—"

"But that was an anomaly," Gerald said. "A malfunction of the web while it was regrowing—"

"Or sabotage," Stephen Thomas said. "Let Infinity finish."

Gerald subsided.

"And now this heat wave. Arachne's trying to fix it. Maybe it'll even work out for the best. We don't have the supplies we expected to bring. Maybe this will give us a longer growing season. But . . . *Starfarer* wasn't designed to spend time around a star like Sirius. It was designed to visit sun-type stars." Infinity glanced over at Victoria. "Next time through transition . . . where will we end up?"

Uncharacteristically, Victoria hesitated.

"I'm not entirely sure yet," she said.

"Good lord!" Gerald exclaimed.

The amphitheater reverberated with tension like a bell.

Collecting herself, Victoria rose. "Calm down, eh? It's not exactly a secret." Her tone was annoyed. "The algorithm's working in plain sight. Anybody can look at the results."

Infinity waited, rather than vanishing into a communications fugue like some of the folks around him.

"We assumed Europa headed for a system that's full of cosmic string," Victoria said. "Pretty safe assumption, eh? She wouldn't want to go somewhere she couldn't leave again. The algorithm's first solution proves it. The second solution indicates there'll be a star nearby."

"And that's *all* you know?" Senator Derjaguin leaned toward her, angrily. "You don't know where we're going, how far, how long it will take?"

"The third solution will tell us where," Victoria said. "How long—that's always an indefinite number. A range."

"As for getting back—" Avvaiyar rose at Victoria's side. "That's the point of being sure we come out in a full system—a place with more cosmic string."

"When will we have all the answers?" Gerald asked.

"I don't know," Victoria said. "Along about the next millennium?"

Gerald took a moment to realize he was being twitted.

"The answers to your bloody *algorithm,*" he snarled.

"I have no idea," Victoria said. "Before we hit transition . . . I think."

"So we're stuck," Esther said under her breath.

She was right. Infinity saw the situation before Victoria described it. They could pull back and wait for solutions to the current algorithm, to be sure they were heading for a suitable star. They could test other transition points till they found one that would lead them to a sun-type star. But no one could say how long that would take. Arachne was solving the current problem as fast as it could. Giving the computer another could only slow everything down.

"And if we change course," Victoria said, "not only will we be here longer, inflicting Sirius on our ecosystem, but we'll lose any chance we might have of catching up to Europa." She glanced over at Infinity. "I didn't realize the environment was so delicate," she said. "I wish you'd—"

"I didn't know, either!" Infinity said. "It's Alzena who knows all this stuff."

"Why in heaven's name did you let Europa take her?" Gerald said to J.D.

"I was afraid Alzena would kill herself otherwise," J.D. said.

As much as Infinity wished the starship still had an environmental designer, an ecologist, on board, he had to agree with J.D. Europa had taken Alzena with her to save her life.

"Alzena is gone," Victoria said, "and I think J.D. was right to let her go. Maybe we can persuade her to come back—"

"But we have to find Europa to find Alzena," Gerald said sarcastically.

"Yes."

"How convenient."

"It's what we agreed to do anyway!"

"Not I," Gerald said. "I blocked the decision—and you chose to break your own rules."

Victoria grabbed her hair with both hands and cried out with frustration.

"Gerald—!"

Professor Thanthavong rose.

The amphitheater fell silent.

"Miensaem Thanthavong." She waited through the customary pause. "I cede my time to Infinity."

Surprised, Infinity collected himself and continued.

"The bees are dying," he said.

A few people laughed. A few understood the problem. Most looked perplexed by his comment.

"They're *important*," he said. "Directly, to the plants. Indirectly, they represent the ecosystem's health. We'll probably be okay if we're headed for a star that's like the sun," Infinity said. "If we're not . . ." He shrugged unhappily.

"All we can do is wait and see," Thanthavong said, as if that ended it.

"I'm sorry, that still isn't all. We've got to plan some harvests and some planting. There's a bunch of stuff ripe. We should salvage the spinach. We could pick some of the oranges."

"Volunteers?" Thanthavong said.

One of Stephen Thomas's grad students jumped to her feet and tossed her long straight red-gold hair back over her shoulder.

"I can just see Lehua picking oranges," Esther said softly. "Probably break a fingernail."

"There's never anything in the cafeteria. The ASes are supposed to cook and maintain the gardens. Not to mention do the housework. So—where are they?" Lehua turned toward Gerald, her dark eyes angry. "When are you letting them loose again?"

Esther jumped to her feet. "Esther Klein." She barely paused. "Doesn't *anybody* around here ever read their bulletins?"

Infinity sat down, grateful that Esther had the energy to take on the problem of the ASes. Infinity hated speaking in public. He watched his lover with absolute awe. Soon she had faculty members apologizing and embarrassed and anxious to help her fix the artificials, to harvest, even to dig in the dirt that worried Gerald so much. Gerald took on the job—the desk job—of coordination.

"And Lehua's right about the cafeteria," Esther said. "The prepared stuff is pretty much gone. Does anybody know how to cook?"

In the front circle, Florrie Brown rose to her feet. "I'll need help, of course," she said.

"Florrie, are you sure—?"

"I *told* you I used to live in a commune," she said, as prickly as always.

She also told us it flopped miserably, Infinity thought. But maybe—I hope—not because of the cooking.

J.D. lugged a bag of oranges to the storage box. The strap cut into her aching shoulders. She eased the bag to the ground, wiped the sweat from her face, and tried to stretch the cramps from the middle of her back. It was hot out in the orchard. The heat intensified the cloying sweetness of the orange blossoms. J.D. had never lived around orange trees before; strange to see a tree with fruit and blossoms in the same season. And the ripe oranges were not orange, but still green. According to Arachne all that was normal, except that everything had happened too soon, too early in the spring, and the trees had produced an abnormal number of flowers.

At a time when the earth should be damp with spring rain, the ground was dry. Too few bees buzzed in the fragrant orange blossoms. Now that Infinity had mentioned the bees, J.D. kept seeing their small striped yellow and black corpses on the ground.

J.D. poured the oranges carefully into the storage box. She allowed herself a brief glance at the transmission from Nemo's chamber.

Nothing had changed.

Satoshi joined her, watched the transmission with her for a moment, then upended his sling full of oranges into the storage box. J.D. grabbed the sling's bottom and tipped out the last few pieces of fruit.

"I'm glad to have something to do," J.D. said. "Something physical. To keep me from worrying." She gestured toward the display.

"I keep remembering what Stephen Thomas saw," Satoshi said.

"Yes. . . . I wish we had an LTM down at the pool. . . . I wonder if those creatures are metamorphosing, too?"

"Or if they're eating each other up."

They climbed ladders on opposite sides of the same tree. The display shrank to the size of an orange and followed. J.D. moved cautiously, but she felt much better, much steadier, than yesterday. The link was still growing, but her body had accommodated itself to the change.

All in all, though, she thought, I'd rather be swimming with Zev and Victoria. . . .

Her thoughts kept returning to the morning; she found herself staring into space thinking about the flow of Zev's hair against her hand, the taste of Victoria's lips.

Enough woolgathering! she told herself sternly.

Leaves tickled J.D.'s face. She stood in the midst of the overpowering, intoxicating orange smell, blossoms and fruit, ripe and overripe and fermented.

The ladder was not designed to be used outdoors. It wobbled. Everything about this harvesting party was makeshift, from ladders borrowed from household tool storage to the bedsheet carrying bags.

For the first hour or so, everyone had regarded the work as an adventure, an entertaining physical break in days—lives—devoted to intellectual pursuits. After two hours, it was no fun anymore.

People used to do this for a living, J.D. thought. All day, every day. She had never considered what that meant. If she had thought about it, she would have imagined the experience wrong without knowing it. Now she *knew* she would get it wrong; she had only a taste of the work.

On the other side of a heavily laden branch, Satoshi worked steadily. He picked each orange with a sharp snap of his wrist.

"How—" J.D. started to ask about Stephen Thomas, but changed her mind. "How are you doing?"

Satoshi glanced up. His thoughts, too, had been somewhere else.

"Victoria and I decided to have our regular potluck tonight," he said. "Try to get back to normal for a change." He laughed, quick and sharp. "Whatever normal is, these days. We haven't had one since . . . since before you arrived, I guess. Would you like to come? Zev too, of course."

"I'd like to," J.D. said. "What should I bring?"

Satoshi grinned.

"Oranges," he said. "What else?"

Shouting erupted from the next row of trees. J.D. turned—she grabbed a branch to keep from overbalancing. An argument—? A fight?

Zev ran past, laughing and shouting, pursued by Chandra. In the gold and green orchard, drenched in white light, they were like fauns. Zev slipped on a rotting orange, caught himself as he fell, turned, scooped up the fermenting pulp and moldy rind, and flung it at Chandra. It caught her full on the chest, spattering her with slimy orange goo.

Chandra stopped short. J.D. had no idea what she would do: she never had *any* idea what Chandra would do.

Chandra burst out laughing and barreled toward Zev, scooping up another fallen orange and throwing it at him point blank. He was already running; the orange spattered across his back, staining his sleeveless shirt.

In a moment, the harvesting party had exploded into a full-fledged food fight, fallen oranges zinging past and hitting people, trees, the ground, with a liquid *sploosh*.

Everybody joined in, the older adults as well as the younger people, everyone but J.D. J.D. observed it from her perch on the ladder high in the tree.

Zev definitely had the advantage, shoveling up the worst of the squashed oranges in his webbed hands, flinging them through the air as if he were playing jai alai.

He looked up at her, laughing.

"Come down!"

She laughed, too. "Don't hold your breath!"

He stopped, and thought about that, an idea that never would have occurred to him back home. In the sea, most of the time, he *did* hold his breath.

"I mean—look out!"

Chandra snuck up behind him and stuffed a handful of slimy orange pulp down the back of his shirt. He yelped and jumped away, spun around and chased after her. She had a good head start.

She almost ran into Gerald Hemminge. He stopped; she stopped; Zev stopped behind her. They looked like a couple of guilty schoolchildren, and Gerald looked like an irritated schoolmarm.

"I thought I could trust you to apply yourselves," he said. "I'm glad I came out to supervise."

"For heaven's sakes, relax," J.D. said. "Nobody was hurting anything."

"We hardly have resources to waste!" Gerald said.

Zev hefted a squashed, reeking orange. J.D. flinched, expecting him to fling it at the acting chancellor. Instead, Zev extended his hand.

"I didn't mean to waste anything," he said. "I didn't throw this one—you can have it if you want."

"How extremely amusing," Gerald said coldly.

J.D. giggled, and had to grab a tree branch to keep from falling. Satoshi started to laugh. Soon everyone was laughing except Zev. He watched Gerald with a completely straight face. J.D. suspected he got the joke perfectly well, but was still pulling Gerald's leg.

Gerald got the joke, and did not appreciate it.

"I see," Gerald said when the laughter finally died

down. "It's terribly funny that the harvest will rot on the trees and we'll all starve. Terribly funny. I see." He glared at J.D., having picked her as the ringleader. "I don't know why I waste my time."

Infinity Mendez came into the clearing where the storage boxes lay. He glanced into one and frowned slightly. J.D. figured he thought the harvesters were pathetic, taking all afternoon to accomplish so little.

"That's probably enough," he said.

"On the contrary," Gerald said. "I expect the entire orchard to be picked by tomorrow at the latest."

"Why?" Infinity said.

Gerald stared at Infinity. So did everyone else.

"They store better on the trees." Infinity hesitated. "You never did this before, did you?"

"Certainly not," Gerald said.

"You can pick oranges as you need them," Infinity said. "As long as we aren't planning another frost."

"You said they needed to be picked!" Gerald said.

"I said we needed to plan harvests so we'd have something to eat."

"Thank you for being so articulate," Gerald said. He turned his back on Infinity and the harvesting crew and stalked away into the trees.

"Oh, dear," J.D. said.

Satoshi sighed. "I'll talk to him."

Satoshi grabbed a branch, swung to the ground, and followed Gerald out of the grove.

J.D. glanced toward Infinity. He looked embarrassed. She had thought Satoshi meant to talk to him, not Gerald.

She climbed down the ladder.

"I'm sorry," she said awkwardly to Infinity.

"You didn't do anything," he muttered.

"I didn't listen very well, I think. I remember what you said, and it wasn't 'Let's go pick all the oranges.' "

"I put a note in his mailbox," Infinity said. "Scheduling and stuff . . . I guess he had too much else to do, I should have talked to him."

J.D. thought it more likely that Gerald had either

ignored Infinity's message or deliberately discounted it.
But she was not about to say so to Infinity.

Satoshi knew Gerald heard him, but the acting chancellor stalked through the trees, slapping every branch that
got in his way.

"Gerald!"

Satoshi caught up to him.

"Come on," Satoshi said. "This isn't doing anybody
any good."

Gerald plowed on, a few more strides, then stopped
and glared at Satoshi.

"No, apparently nothing I do does anybody any
good."

"That isn't what I meant."

"It *is* what everybody else means."

"Gerald . . ." Satoshi tried to think of something
soothing to say, but the truth was that a lot of people
found Gerald abrasive. When he supported the proposal to decommission *Starfarer,* he won himself no
friends; when Arachne crashed, he made enemies.
Satoshi believed him when he said he had nothing to do
with it, but other members of the expedition did not.

"What *are* you trying to do?" Satoshi asked. "It's too
late to stop the expedition."

"I'm trying to make sure we all survive it!" Gerald
exclaimed. He caught his error and looked away. "All
the rest of us, I mean, of course." He met Satoshi's gaze
again. "I'm certain—*certain*—no one was meant to be
killed in the system crash."

"Is that what the chancellor said?"

"I . . . haven't put it to him directly. But I'm certain nonetheless. I very much regret the journalist's
death. By all reports he was a talented young man."

"Yes. And a nice guy. He was closest to J.D. and to
Stephen Thomas."

Satoshi was not about to tell Gerald that Stephen
Thomas had buried Feral's body on the wild side.

"You could probably make them both feel better," Satoshi said, "if you told them what you just told me."

"Oh, indeed," Gerald said, disgusted. "And have your partner attempt to knock out all my teeth again. No thank you."

"When you say stuff like that," Satoshi said mildly, "I can kind of understand his urge."

"What would you have me do?" Gerald shouted. "I'm responsible for *Starfarer,* for all of you—"

"Bullshit," Satoshi said.

"—and I'm completely losing control. . . . I beg your pardon?"

"You're not Sir Francis Drake, for god's sake. You don't have life and death responsibility and you don't have life and death power. You aren't losing control."

"Perhaps I've maintained that appearance."

"You never had control of the expedition," Satoshi said gently. "How could you lose it?"

Gerald opened his mouth, then closed it again. His shoulders stiffened.

"I had to take over the chancellor's duties. I had no choice."

"That isn't the point. You *can't* control the expedition. There are a couple of people who could, if they wanted."

"Such as who?" Gerald asked belligerently. "Do you mean the spy? I suppose he could, with enough blackmail and extortion."

"Griffith? No."

It surprised Satoshi that Gerald confabulated power with force. Satoshi had been thinking of ethical power, a quality Griffith lacked almost entirely. Professor Thanthavong possessed it, and so did Kolya Cherenkov. Either one could take over the expedition in a second. Satoshi thought they had that power because they did not want it.

"You're trying to get people to do what you think they should be doing," Satoshi said. "Then you want us all to do it the way you think it ought to be done. Why's that important to you?"

"Someone has to be sure the work gets done."

"But the work is getting done."

"It isn't getting done right."

Satoshi did not say anything about Gerald's current score at getting work done right; he did not want to rub the assistant chancellor's nose in what Infinity had just pointed out.

To his credit, Gerald got the idea.

"I'm doing my best," he said, stiff but sincere. "If you have suggestions, I'd be most happy to hear them."

"Okay. People think you're conspiring with Blades. That isn't doing you any good."

"Conspiring!"

"You, and Derjaguin, and even Orazio."

"Just because we're the only ones who'll *speak* to the man? I still consider him my superior."

"That's not likely to win you any points," Satoshi said dryly.

"And I have the same sympathy I'd have for any other victim of unjust political imprisonment."

"Unjust—!"

"And don't cite your partner's spurious evidence anymore! He found it in Arachne, and Arachne was severely damaged. Besides, Stephen Thomas had a motive to find the chancellor guilty."

"Stephen Thomas liked Blades," Satoshi said.

"He liked Feral better."

Satoshi had to concede that point. "The chancellor's safe, thanks to Infinity."

"Safe? He's in solitary confinement! I have no intention of abandoning him to go mad in that cave."

Nemo's ship continued to pace *Starfarer,* but Nemo remained silent. The LTMs watched the squidmoth, and J.D. watched the LTM transmissions. Beneath the mother of pearl chrysalis, the structure of Nemo's body dissolved. Only the single exposed tentacle remained.

Every so often, one of the attendants crawled in, staggering, burrowed into the chrysalis, and disappeared. Luminous white pearl closed the burrows, sealing the attendants inside. Once they touched Nemo's amorphous shape, their forms, too, dissolved.

In the window seat of her house, J.D. sat back from the holographic projection of Nemo's central chamber. Her back twinged and her shoulders ached fiercely. She tried to massage her trapezius muscles, but aside from the difficulty of giving oneself a massage, her bicepses and tricepses hurt as well.

Zev looked up from the book he was reading.

"Is it time to go to Victoria's house?"

"Just about," J.D. said. "If I can get up."

"What's wrong?" He jumped to his feet and came over to her, leaving the book open and face-down on the floor. J.D. was glad she collected books for the words and not their physical value.

"I didn't realize picking oranges was such hard work," J.D. said ruefully. She did not think she could jump to her feet if her life depended on it. She reminded herself that she was more than twice Zev's age. "I thought I was in pretty good condition, but I hurt all over."

"I thought it was fun," Zev said. "Easier than picking mussels."

He urged her forward, knelt behind her, and rubbed her shoulders. She leaned back against his hands with a groan of pleasure and relief.

"That feels so good, Zev."

He moved his hands down her spine, and massaged low in the small of her back.

"You picked more oranges than I did," he said.

She chuckled.

"I guess I did. But you moved them farther than I did."

"Faster, anyway."

The fragrance of oranges and the faint sick-sweet scent of fermented juice still embraced him. He put his arms around her. J.D. stroked his arms, the softness of his fine pelt, the hardness of his muscles.

"You like Victoria, don't you?"

"Yes," he said. "This morning was fun."

"It was."

"Almost like being back home."

He bent down to nuzzle her neck, to rub his cheek against her short brown hair, still damp from the shower.

"You like her, too."

"Very much."

"Will she go swimming with us again?"

"I think so. She might even come over and spend the night."

He sat back on his heels away from her.

J.D. turned around. "Wouldn't you like that?"

"I don't know," Zev said slowly, sounding surprised by his own reaction. "Would she come to stay with you?"

"With both of us."

"I like . . . sleeping just with you. Making love just with you. At first it was strange. All land manners are strange at first. But I like being able to think just about you. About what you want. What you need."

She kissed him. His lips parted over his sharp, dangerous teeth. She wondered if he felt jealous, but dismissed the absurd idea of a jealous diver.

"I like that, too," she said to Zev. "We won't give it up. But we can include Victoria sometimes, too."

"Okay."

He bit her earlobe gently. "I'm hungry!"

She laughed. "Me too."

"But I don't want to eat oranges!"

In the main room of the partnership's house, Stephen Thomas slouched on one chair with his feet up on another. He had thrown a towel over his toes to hide the bruises, the loose nails. The bento box containing his half-eaten dinner sat open on his lap.

Victoria wanted things back to normal. Stephen Thomas could not blame her. Tonight was the normal night for the regular potluck for their grad students.

Stephen Thomas wished she and Satoshi had asked him before they scheduled the dinner. He was trying to make the best of it.

As usual, other people came besides the students. Stephen Thomas had invited Florrie Brown, without considering his motives for doing so. He liked her. Unfortunately, Victoria did not, and the feeling was mutual. Florrie thought Victoria was stuck up, and Victoria thought Florrie was condescending. Both of them were right. Victoria could be stuck up, and Florrie could be condescending. But Stephen Thomas thought they would like each other if they could ever get over their first encounters. That did not look like it would happen tonight.

He shrugged. Give them time.

Nearby, Lehua and Bay bent over a display of the new cells. Mitch, on the other hand, stood in the shadows gazing mournfully at Fox.

Even Fox had come to dinner. Stephen Thomas was glad; it must mean she had no hard feelings because he had turned her down. He was glad she accepted his point of view. She had not talked to him, but that was understandable. She stayed on the opposite side of the room; about all he had seen of her tonight was her back. Sometimes he had the feeling she had just turned away.

Stephen Thomas poked through the remains of his dinner with a pair of chopsticks, searching each small compartment of the bento box for something he felt like eating.

Maybe I ought to try catching a fish and eating it raw, like Zev, he thought.

J.D. had brought him an orange. "The great hunter offers you the spoils of her kill," she said when she handed it to him.

And we thought we'd opted for the intellectual life when we came up here, he thought.

She had not mentioned Gerald's altercation with Infinity, but Stephen Thomas knew about it. Everyone on campus knew about it. Infinity had not come to the potluck.

Did we ever invite him? Stephen Thomas asked himself with a shock. To any of them? Fuck, I don't think we did. Stephen Thomas made a note to himself to ask Infinity to the next one.

All that was left of his orange was torn rind. He could get himself another piece of fruit, but his feet hurt.

He hoped the potluck would not last too long. If it did go on forever, that would be partly his fault. He had stayed up talking till all hours with almost every guest here, often after Victoria and Satoshi had given up and gone to bed.

It was already getting on toward midnight, and nobody showed any sign of leaving. Most of the kids clustered around J.D. and Zev, asking questions about Nemo, like children anxious to hear an old story told again. The room glimmered with multiple copies of the LTM transmissions, floating like bubbles in free-fall, all different sizes.

On the other side of the room, Florrie Brown and Fox sat with their heads together, talking seriously. Stephen Thomas pushed away a twinge of discomfort. He had no reason but egotism to assume they were talking about him. They spent a lot of time together. Fox had been at Florrie's almost every time Stephen Thomas had stopped by to see if Florrie needed anything.

Fox gave Florrie a quick hug and a grateful smile. She went over to the table and poured a couple of glasses of beer.

Great, Stephen Thomas thought. With everything else that's happened, now somebody will tell our honorable senators that we're giving drugs to the President's underage niece, and *that's* what we'll get thrown in jail for when we get home.

Oh, fuck it, he thought. A little beer won't hurt her. Didn't hurt me when I was her age, swilling home brew in the basement of the biology department.

On the porch just outside, Victoria and Satoshi stood face to face, framed by the open French window, talking and laughing softly. Just watching them together shot a ray of happiness through his depression, like light probing a thick curtain that cut Stephen Thomas off from the world. Victoria stroked the back of her hand down Satoshi's cheek, a gesture so loving, so erotic, that Stephen Thomas's eyes filled with tears.

His body responded to his sexual impulse with a stab of pain so sharp he nearly fainted. He caught his breath and froze. His left hand clenched. The chopsticks snapped, ramming splinters into the new web between his thumb and forefinger. His right hand gripped the arm of the bamboo chair, his nails bending against the hard wood.

He breathed cautiously and shallowly for several minutes. When he finally chanced a deeper breath, the pain had faded. He sighed shakily, with relief, put the broken chopsticks into the bento box, and released his death grip on the chair arm. As far as he could tell, no one had noticed his distress, no one knew or cared that he felt disoriented and dizzy. He picked chopstick splinters from his hand.

"I'm disappointed in you, Stephen Thomas."

He looked up.

Florrie Brown glared at him. Her feathery voice had an edge like a paper cut, invisible and shocking.

"Disappointed?"

"I didn't think you were a tease," she said.

Oh, fuck, he thought. What did Fox tell her?

He decided to take no chances on his answer.

"Florrie, what are you talking about?"

"I think you know."

Up till now, he had found her coquettish way of dancing around a subject to be old-fashioned and charming. Up till now.

"No."

"You make promises, but you never intend to keep them."

"Promises?" What *had* Fox told her. "What promises?"

"For one thing, you promised me a tea ceremony."

Thank god, they weren't talking about Fox after all.

"Jesus, the tea ceremony? Florrie, that takes a whole day. You can't just do it, you have to prepare for it. When have I had a whole day free since your welcome party?" Her welcome party seemed like months ago. He *had* promised her a tea ceremony, and the truth was he had not thought about it since. He still intended to do it, but he still had to finish learning the damned thing. Not that he was about to admit it to Florrie.

She pressed on, insistent. "You shouldn't make a promise you don't intend to keep."

"I *do* intend to keep it," he said. "I just haven't kept it *yet*. There was this rebellion, remember? And then some aliens—it complicated my schedule."

"And you flirt with people without any intention of carrying through."

He laughed. He could not help it. Victoria and Satoshi teased him—even Merry had teased him, and Merry was hardly one to talk—about carrying through all too often.

Florrie brought her hand down fast and slapped his forearm, surprisingly hard.

"Ow—!"

"Don't you laugh at me!"

"What'd you do that for? And I wasn't laughing at you, I was just—"

"Don't change the subject!"

"What *is* the subject?"

"You toyed with Fox's affections and then you broke her heart."

"Now wait a minute—"

"You counseled her—"

"*Counseled* her! Christ on a couch, I listened to her bitch about her family!"

"And you let her sit in on your seminars—"

Stephen Thomas tried to think of a seminar Fox had sat in on. The impromptu discussion on the hillside? Not that it made any difference.

"I let *anybody* sit in on my seminars. That's what seminars are for. *You* sit in on my seminars."

"Don't patronize me!"

She raised her hand.

Stephen Thomas lifted both arms to ward off the blow he expected.

"Don't hit me again!"

"Why shouldn't I?" Florrie clenched her fragile fist. "Because you're too good for anybody to touch you?"

"Because it hurts!"

The rest of the company had tried hard to pretend nothing unpleasant was going on. This was too much; they had to notice. When the hush fell, Victoria glanced inside. A moment later she and Satoshi were hurrying across the room.

"Florrie, stop it!" Satoshi said. He got between her and Stephen Thomas without actually shouldering the old woman aside.

"Aunt Florrie, what are you *doing*?" Fox was still carrying the two glasses of beer, but her hands shook. Foam dribbled down the sides of the glasses and splatted on the floor.

"I'm giving Mister Stephen Thomas Gregory a piece of my mind, that's what."

"You're making a spectacle of yourself, Ms. Brown." Victoria's calm voice held the coolness that meant fury.

"Florrie, how could you?" Fox cried. "I told you what I told you because . . . because . . ."

"I thought you wanted my help!"

"I only wanted you to listen. What could you do to help? He already said no!"

"Sometimes . . ." Florrie's voice faltered for the first time. "Sometimes people say it and don't mean it."

"I don't say it unless I do mean it," Stephen Thomas said. "Fox, I thought you understood that you shouldn't take it personally—"

"Personally? Why should I take it personally? All you did was tell me to fuck off and die!"

"I told you I don't sleep with graduate students."

"And now I'm being humiliated in public—"

"Not by me!"

Tears streamed down her face. She looked around, distraught, at her fellow students, and her major professor, and her professor's partners, one of whom she loved.

Lehua tried to change the subject. "About time to pack this party in," she said. People began to edge toward the door.

"Don't anybody leave on my account," Fox said.

As Fox turned to flee, Florrie snatched at her arm.

"Fox, my dear, let me—"

Fox turned back angrily, trying to speak. The beer sloshed out of the glass in her free hand and splashed down the front of Florrie's black tunic. Florrie gasped and stepped away. The glass slipped out of Fox's hand and shattered on the floor, gouging the smooth rock foam. Droplets spattered on Stephen Thomas's bare calf.

Fox looked at Florrie, looked at the broken glass, looked at the full glass in her other hand. It was as if nothing she could do could possibly make things any worse. Stephen Thomas saw it coming, and did not move.

Fox splashed the second glass of beer in his face, flung the mug on the floor, and fled to the explosion of shattering glass.

"Are just going to let her run out of here?"

Florrie sounded so mad that Stephen Thomas had no idea whether she meant someone should go after Fox to comfort her, or go after her to berate her for bad manners.

Stephen Thomas started to rise, painfully. Cold beer dripped down his front and plastered his silk T-shirt and his running shorts to his body.

"I guess—"

"Don't, you're barefoot!" Satoshi said. "There's glass all over."

"I don't think it's a good idea for you to go," Victoria said.

"So you'll just let the child run all alone into the dark—"

"Ms. Brown," Victoria said patiently, "there aren't any wolves out there."

"This is no time for humor. You're a very cruel young woman."

Victoria turned her back on Florrie Brown. "Satoshi?"

Satoshi had already started for the door. "I'll try to find her. I wish I knew if she's even speaking to me. . . ."

"I'll go with you," J.D. said.

"Thanks."

Stephen Thomas sagged gratefully back into the squeaky bamboo chair, surrounded by shards of broken glass. What he would have said to Fox, if he found her, he had no idea. He was damned if he would apologize for doing what he thought was right.

J.D. and Satoshi and Zev crossed the yard. *Starfarer*'s bright night turned the blossoms in the grass and on the banks to pale shadows on dark shadows.

J.D. hesitated at the break in the garden wall. Satoshi stopped beside her.

"Any idea where she might've gone?"

"Home, I guess," Satoshi said. "I don't know." He sounded resigned. "She didn't exactly tell me her secrets. She kind of gave up on me when I couldn't get her a waiver to come on the expedition."

"I didn't think anybody under age got one."

"Nobody did."

"I did," Zev said.

"Chandra invented you a new name and a new occupation and a new family, and changed your subspecies!" Satoshi said. "If she didn't add five years to your age, too, she's not as smart as I thought she was."

"Oh," Zev said. "Yes. She probably did that too."

"Fox's family's so wealthy," J.D. said. "And so powerful . . . She's probably used to getting her own way. Except about the expedition."

"And Stephen Thomas."

"And Stephen Thomas." J.D. knew more or less

how Fox felt, though she had not compounded her
problem by telling Stephen Thomas. Or Florrie Brown.

"We'd better try her house—"

"She's over there," Zev said. He pointed.

"Are you sure?"

"I can hear her."

They went with him down the path.

"She's crying," Zev said.

"Fox?" J.D. called softly.

She heard no answer, but a moment later someone
came toward them through the darkness.

One of Stephen Thomas's grad students—J.D. tried
in vain to remember his name—appeared from between
the small young trees. J.D. had met him at the party, but
she had not seen him follow Fox.

"She doesn't much want to see anybody," he said
apologetically.

"I'm worried about her, Mitch," Satoshi said.

"Yeah, she's pretty upset. Embarrassed, mostly."

Satoshi hesitated. "I'd better talk to her."

"I'll stay with her. She'll be okay, honest. I promise."

"I'm sure that's true," Satoshi said, "but I still have
to talk to her."

Satoshi stepped around Mitch and entered the deep
shadow of the tree. Fox sat against its spindly roots, her
head buried against her folded arms.

"Fox." Satoshi knelt beside her.

She raised her head. Her face was blotched and tear-
streaked.

"You're not speaking to me," she said.

"Of course I am. You haven't made it easy, though,
the last few days."

"I didn't want her to do anything!" Fox exclaimed.
"I just wanted to . . . to tell somebody how I felt."

"I know."

"I really do love him." She stopped, as if she had just
realized who she had said that to. "I'm sorry, but I do."

"I know you do," he said. "It's . . . hard not to."

She smiled, shakily. "You're so lucky. You and Victoria."

Satoshi turned the conversation away from the partnership, back to Fox.

"Please try to understand how he feels about what you offered him. He won't—he *can't*—accept."

"He told me why, but it doesn't make sense. He didn't ask me—and there weren't any conditions!"

"No. But . . . things can change."

Satoshi started to tell her that Stephen Thomas's decision was for Fox's own protection; but that would insult her, to have the decision so one-sided, so out of her hands. He almost told her that the situation had nothing to do with her directly, and decided she would be even more insulted.

She hid her face against her arms again; her voice was muffled. "It hurts so bad," she said. Her shoulders shook.

"I know," he said. "I know."

He waited till she had stopped crying.

"I think you should go home," he said, when her breathing eased.

"No! I don't want to talk to my housemates tonight. I don't want to talk to *anybody.*"

"And I don't want to leave you out here all by yourself."

She pushed herself back against the tree, glaring at him.

"What could *happen*?" she shouted. "I want to be outside, okay?"

The tall shadow that was Mitch moved from the reflected starlight into the darkness nearby.

"I couldn't help hearing what you just said." Mitch hesitated. "Nothing before, but, when you yelled . . ." His voice trailed off. "What if I hung around? For company, I mean."

Fox took a deep breath and let it out slowly, steadying her voice.

"That'd be okay," she said. "I'd . . . I'd like that. I'll be all right, Satoshi. Hey. It isn't like Stephen Thomas is the first person to ever turn me down. And . . . I'm glad you're still talking to me, anyway."

He suspected that Stephen Thomas was, in fact, the first person to ever turn her down, but he appreciated what she was saying to him.

"Everybody's talking to you," he said. "It's just—Everything will be all right."

"Yeah," she said. "Okay. Sure. I don't want to talk anymore." She turned away, huddling against the tree. It should have been a thousand-year-old oak, with great gnarly roots reaching out around her.

"Okay," Satoshi said. He rose. Mitch passed him and hunkered down near Fox.

Stephen Thomas has a high opinion of Mitch, Satoshi thought. He's a good kid, and he'll keep Fox company as well as anybody can. Lord knows, better than I can, all things considered.

Mitch glanced up at him and raised one hand in a gesture of acknowledgment and farewell.

Satoshi returned the gesture, and joined J.D. and Zev.

"Is she all right?" J.D. asked.

"I think so," Satoshi said. "I hope so."

They returned, in silence, to the partnership's house.

Coldly courteous, Victoria mopped the worst of the beer off Florrie's dress. The antipathy between them had reached a new peak.

Victoria delegated Lehua and Bay to see Florrie home. Finally the main room of the partnership's house was empty except for Stephen Thomas and Victoria; the garden was deserted.

"That horrible woman," Victoria said.

Stephen Thomas covered his face with his hands, then pushed his fingers up through his hair.

Victoria tried to grin. "What did her aura look like tonight?"

"I don't know," Stephen Thomas said. "There's no such thing. You were right all along. Auras are bullshit."

Victoria looked at him curiously, but let the comment pass.

She cleared up the glass; it made a wet, scraping noise when she scooped it into an empty bento box. The house did not even have a broom and dustpan; cleaning the floor was the housekeeper's job.

When she was done, she sat on her heels beside Stephen Thomas and stroked his arm, moving her fingers along the growth pattern of the fine gold hair. He tensed at the trickle of pain that crept along his bones. Victoria took her hand away.

"What a fucking nightmare," Stephen Thomas said.

"I don't suppose," Victoria said hesitantly, "that you could have let her down a little easier?"

"Oh, shit, Victoria!" Stephen Thomas exclaimed. "How could I let her down, when I never picked her up? One minute I was telling her that no, Satoshi wasn't mad at her because the genetics building fell on top of us while we were trying to talk some sense into her—"

"Very convincing," Victoria said dryly.

"—and the next she was telling me she was in love with me. And I told her what I *always* tell grad students—"

"Okay, I'm sorry, never mind," Victoria said. "Into the shower with you."

Stephen Thomas levered himself up. The towel slid off his toes. He yelped in pain. His right big toenail had gotten caught in the terrycloth loops. Only the nail of the left big toe remained. He could barely put his feet on the floor.

"I feel like my toe bones are coming out the ends of my feet."

Victoria grimaced in sympathy tinged with disgust. She slid her arm around his waist. His cold wet shirt warmed, where her body pressed against his.

Stephen Thomas laughed suddenly.

"What?" Victoria said.

"My bones sort of *are* coming out the ends of my toes."

"Stop," Victoria said, her tone unsure. "Please stop."

"All right." They reached the bathroom. "I'll be okay now. I just want to slop off the worst of the beer."

"Will you come to bed?"

"I don't . . ."

"I only want to know you're there!" Victoria took his hand and held it between her own. "It feels like forever since I've touched you!"

Stephen Thomas drew his hand away. "This'll all be over soon," he said. "Soon. Then everything will be back to normal."

Victoria let her hands fall to her sides.

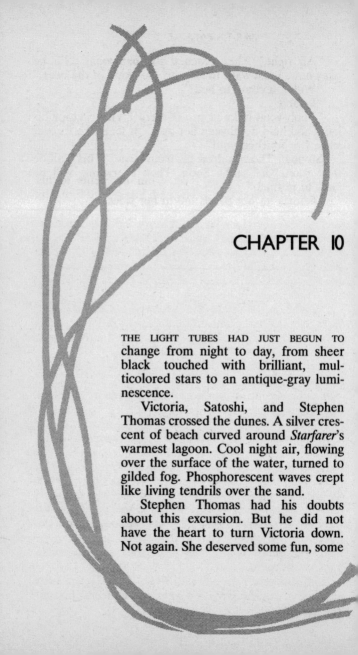

CHAPTER 10

THE LIGHT TUBES HAD JUST BEGUN TO
change from night to day, from sheer
black touched with brilliant, multicolored stars to an antique-gray lumi-
nescence.

Victoria, Satoshi, and Stephen
Thomas crossed the dunes. A silver crescent of beach curved around *Starfarer*'s
warmest lagoon. Cool night air, flowing
over the surface of the water, turned to
gilded fog. Phosphorescent waves crept
like living tendrils over the sand.

Stephen Thomas had his doubts
about this excursion. But he did not
have the heart to turn Victoria down.
Not again. She deserved some fun, some

play. She had even persuaded Satoshi to get up early
and come along.

Maybe it would work out all right. Stephen Thomas
felt pretty good, especially compared to the way he had
felt yesterday. His last toenail had fallen off, and his feet
did not hurt quite so badly. He suspected they would
hurt worse later; he could already feel the small sharp
lumps of claws developing where his nails had been.

Last night's stabbing pain, from his penis to his
spine, had not reoccurred. The pain had scared him. His
bruises should be healed by now. Maybe the slugs had
hurt him worse than he thought. A hairline fracture,
something the health center could miss?

Victoria stood on the beach, up to her knees in
dense fog, kicking off her jeans and stripping her shirt
off over her head. Satoshi undressed beside her, slowly
and deliberately.

"Come on," Victoria called, her voice low and eager.
Water condensed in her hair and caught the light, shin-
ing soft as transparent pearls. She splashed into the sea.
The fog closed over her, muting sounds.

Naked, Satoshi folded his pants and laid them on a
twist of driftwood.

"Reminds me of the genetics department . . ." he
said. "During the attack. The fog . . ."

"I don't—" But Stephen Thomas *did* remember—

The missile struck. The building quivered and fell
around Stephen Thomas and Satoshi and Fox. It
crushed the freezer. Liquid nitrogen flowed out in a
thick, unbreathable fog. A shard of rock foam struck
Stephen Thomas across the forehead, and blood flowed
into his eyes. Everything he saw after that, he saw
through a red haze. When he saw his own blood, he
fainted.

—The flash of memory disappeared. Stephen
Thomas shivered.

Satoshi drew a deep breath. "Oh, hell!" He sprinted
across the wet sand. With a yelp, he launched himself
and belly-flopped into the waves.

Stephen Thomas took off his shorts and shirt and kicked away his sandals.

The new diver walked into the sea for the first time.

The warm water slid up his body, raising the fine new hair away from his skin. Air bubbles caught and sparkled beneath his pelt. Stephen Thomas stroked forward into the sea. The bubbles escaped, swirled away, spiraled to the surface, and burst with a velvety pop. The warm water soothed and relaxed his body. He wished the water were cold and exhilarating.

He opened his eyes.

He could see perfectly. The water was very clear, the bare white sand arrayed in ripples. His hair tendrilled in front of his face. He pulled forward with a long breaststroke, and the motion pushed his hair out of his eyes.

Victoria swam toward him, her stroke smooth and strong. Satoshi slid beneath him, nearly silent. Satoshi was close enough to touch Stephen Thomas, but he kept his arms close to his sides, streamlining his body.

Victoria did touch Stephen Thomas, swimming past on the surface, stretching out her arm, stroking him against the direction of his fur from the back of his knee, up his thigh, across his buttocks, along his spine. He tensed, shuddered, relaxed. He kicked forward, rising beneath Victoria's hand, letting her fingers and the pressure of the water smooth his delicate pelt back into place.

When she swam beside him, he turned to face her. They sidestroked, slowed, and he caressed her. He wondered where Satoshi was. With the thought, Stephen Thomas found his partner treading water behind him in the faint, fuzzy sound picture of his surroundings.

Exhaling explosively as he surfaced, Stephen Thomas gasped in a deep breath and dove beneath Victoria. He touched and teased her, all over, with his fingers and his tongue. He slid his hands, his swimming webs, over her breasts. Her nipples hardened, their heat glowing. He could smell and taste her excitement, familiar, comforting, arousing, intensified by his changing senses. He listened for Satoshi; he opened his mouth

and let the sea water flow over his tongue. Satoshi
hovered, near, yet out of reach, and the taste of his body
in the water was cool, uninterested.

Stephen Thomas blew his breath out in a stream of
bubbles. Victoria touched his hand, then swam toward
Satoshi. Stephen Thomas followed, kicking along easily
beside her. He touched her breasts again, stroked his
fingertips down her body, and slid his hand between her
legs. He let the rhythm of her kicking rub the swimming
web against her clitoris. She gasped and pressed her legs
together and lost her momentum. Stephen Thomas
jerked his hand away, afraid he had hurt her with the
strong, resilient edge of the web. But Victoria grabbed
his wrist.

"Yes," she said. "That's just right—it's like . . . like
being made love to by a silk scarf."

They trod water together, face to face in the warm
sea. Victoria embraced both men, drawing them to her
and against each other, clasping Stephen Thomas's
hand between her thighs. She kissed Satoshi, then Stephen Thomas, her tongue quick against his lips, sliding
between his teeth, hesitating as if she had never kissed
him before. Stephen Thomas tasted her, with new intensity.

The triad sank. Breath bubbled from Victoria's
mouth, from her nose, tickling Stephen Thomas's lips
and face. She pulled back and kicked to the surface.

"Let's go where it's shallower," she said. "*I* can't
breathe underwater!" She grinned and plunged toward
shore, diving between Stephen Thomas and Satoshi.

Stephen Thomas followed her, pressing himself past
Satoshi, letting the whole length of his body stroke his
partner's belly. Stephen Thomas felt no arousal in him,
no excitement.

Victoria stood chest-deep in the water. The fog was
dissipating; it swirled around her like a wraith. Gentle
waves covered her breasts, then exposed her again. She
hugged Stephen Thomas and wrapped one leg around
his hips. Satoshi swam up behind him and touched him,
tentatively, sliding his fingertips over his shoulders.

Stephen Thomas gave himself to the seduction of the water and his lovers' desires and his own.

Suddenly Victoria cried out. She pulled away. Off balance, Stephen Thomas and Satoshi both splashed forward, submerged, and tumbled apart. Stephen Thomas gulped a mouthful of salt water and struggled to his feet, gasping and coughing.

"Stephen Thomas, oh, I'm sorry, I thought—"

She stopped and patted his back gently till he got his breath again.

"I can't breathe underwater, either," Stephen Thomas said. "Yet. What . . . are you okay? Did I hurt you?"

"Oh—not really. Not exactly. When we started, it was wonderful, but then—" She glanced ruefully at Satoshi. "I guess you were right."

"Yeah," he said. "I guess so. Sorry."

They stood together, closer to shore, waist-deep in the water and nearly in full daylight. The fog had vanished with the breeze that chilled the air. Chagrined, Stephen Thomas shivered.

"Yeah," Victoria said. "It *is* cold." She sounded disappointed, but also amused. "Maybe we should go back home . . . back to bed."

"I just can't," Stephen Thomas said. "I've *got* to get to the lab." The last thing he felt like, right now, was sex. His penis hurt, and it had begun to itch and sting.

Great, he thought. Just fucking great. I can't do anything for the people I love, and now I've got a case of jock itch, too.

"Yesterday, with Zev and J.D.," Victoria said. "It was awfully nice."

"Maybe divers have secret sex techniques," Stephen Thomas said, trying to joke. "Maybe I don't get to find them out till I'm completely changed. Maybe they're hard-wired."

"Maybe," Satoshi said dryly to Stephen Thomas, "Zev is smaller than you." He glanced at Victoria. "Is he?"

"I didn't notice," Victoria said lightly, and then, in

response to the skeptical glances of both her partners, she protested. "No, really. J.D. wanted to talk and Zev went on ahead. Then we were in the water. He liked . . . being touched quickly. You couldn't hold him, he'd slip away." She paused, thinking. "I never got a good look at him, eh? I certainly didn't say, 'Stand there while I look at you, Zev, and see how you measure up to my partners.' "

They waded toward shore. Stephen Thomas was anxious to get out of the salt water. He hoped that then the stinging would stop.

"Good lord!" Satoshi exclaimed. "What happened—did you go face forward in the sand? You're all scraped—"

"No, I never hit bottom." Stephen Thomas looked down.

The blood drained out of his face.

The darkening skin on his penis had sloughed off, fading from its new deep tan to a sickly gray, hanging in flimsy strips, leaving the shaft angry-red, ugly.

Stephen Thomas knocked hard on J.D.'s door. No one answered. He banged his fist on the dense rock foam.

"Hey! Zev!"

He was about to be very rude and look through the open French windows when Zev opened the door. He saw Stephen Thomas and grinned.

"Hi—"

"Why didn't you reply to my message?"

"I'm sorry, I was busy."

"Busy!"

"Yes, J.D. and I were making love." Zev joined Stephen Thomas on the porch and closed the door. "Don't shout, she's sleeping."

"I need to talk to you!"

"Shh. Let's go for a walk."

He led Stephen Thomas through the wild garden, away from the house and the open windows of J.D.'s bedroom.

"Are your claws growing yet?" Zev looked at Stephen Thomas's feet. Because of the bruising, it was hard to see what was happening to his toes.

"Yes, and they hurt like hell."

"I'm sorry."

"Stop apologizing! You're always apologizing to me."

"But what's happening to you, it's my fault."

"It's done. Stop feeling guilty, and tell me what I should expect."

Zev glanced over at him, curious, troubled.

"But you know what. You're turning into a diver."

"I want to know what's normal and what isn't." He turned to Zev, shouting again. "Is it supposed to hurt this bad? Is my *skin* supposed to peel off?"

Zev took a step away from him. "I'm sorry—"

Stephen Thomas flung up his hands in exasperation.

"—but I don't know all those answers," Zev said. "Your . . . your skin is peeling? That doesn't sound right. Did you get sunburned?"

Zev's distress scared Stephen Thomas.

"You *don't know*?"

"If J.D. had accepted our invitation and come to live with the divers, Lykos would have been with her. My mother knows all about how the changes happen. But I don't. I was born this way."

"Great," Stephen Thomas said, disgusted.

"I'm . . . never mind."

"Victoria and Satoshi and I went swimming this morning. We tried to make love in the water. But we couldn't because it hurt her. It didn't with you. Why not?"

Zev thought for a moment. "Maybe ordinary human men are bigger than diver men?" he asked.

"I'll show you mine if you'll show me yours," Stephen Thomas muttered.

"What?"

Stephen Thomas shrugged. "Nothing. Forget it."

He strode angrily along the path beside the river. A ghost of pain grew behind his pelvic bone, as if a knife were tickling him, teasing him with the threat of the fatal stab. He slowed down and tried to stay calm, hoping to stave off the pain with caution. Zev caught up to him.

"Can I look at you, Zev? I don't even know what I'm going to look like when this is over."

"You'll look like Stephen Thomas, you won't look like me."

"I mean naked."

"You can look at me if you want. Can I look at you? I never saw—"

The pain hit Stephen Thomas. For no reason, and with too much warning, the pain flamed through his pelvis, along his backbone.

He gave up. He sank to the path, drawing his knees to his chest and wrapping himself in his arms. The hair stood out straight all over his body. He shivered, and groaned.

"Dammit, Zev, what's *happening* to me?"

Zev sat on his heels beside him, upset and helpless. "I don't know."

"I wish you'd quit saying that!"

"I better call Victoria."

"No!" He grabbed Zev's arm. Moving made the pain shoot through him again; his fingers clenched harder than he meant them to.

The young diver flinched but stayed where he was, balancing on his toes, scared for Stephen Thomas but not scared of him. Stephen Thomas had the feeling that Zev could break his hold in a second if he chose. He let go.

"Please don't call Victoria, or Satoshi, or anybody. Just give me a minute."

"You'll feel better in the water. Can you stand up?"

"Yeah." The stabbing pain diminished to a throbbing ache. He stayed where he was. "But I can't walk all the way to the other end of campus. Not right now."

"You don't have to. Come swim in the river."

"Is that all you ever—" Stephen Thomas heard himself complaining to Zev about Zev's obsession with wa-

ter the way Victoria complained to him about his being
able to see auras. It did not matter that he no longer
saw them. Now he knew how Victoria felt.

Except that it *would* feel good to be in the water. A
warm bath, a cold swim—anything to ease the throbbing
ache in the center of his pelvic girdle, and the itch that
was turning sore and hot.

He lurched to his feet. "Okay."

They tramped through a meadow of wildflowers, a
carpet of color like the pastel reflection of a rainbow.
Stephen Thomas followed Zev down the riverbank to a
beach of small rounded rocks, designed to look water-
worn, ancient. They were of course no such thing. They
were moon rock, reshaped and carefully placed during
Starfarer's construction.

The river curved, cutting into the stratified bank, exposing one of Crimson's fossil beds. The water rippled
and softly splashed. Downstream, the channel narrowed; the river roughened and raced with a hollow
roar.

Stephen Thomas took off his shirt, hesitated, and
slipped out of his shorts. He moved gingerly.

Zev watched him, worried that he might collapse
again.

"Is it swollen?" he said, when he saw Stephen
Thomas naked. "Does it hurt?"

"It isn't swollen. It's sore."

"Then I don't blame you for leaving it out." The
river rocks rattled hollowly as Zev crossed them. He
tossed off his clothes and picked his way over the
treacherous footing to the river. Stephen Thomas followed slowly.

Zev threw himself into the midstream current, let
himself be carried fifty meters through the rapids, then
vanished beneath roiling white water.

"Zev!"

Upstream from the rapids, halfway back to Stephen
Thomas, Zev reappeared. He waved and beckoned.

It looked like fun, but Stephen Thomas lowered

himself into the cold eddy near shore. Today, a sitz-bath was about his speed.

The water did feel good, easing the soreness, massaging away bits of dead skin.

Zev splashed toward him.

Stephen Thomas got a close look at an adult male diver for the first time.

Struggling to stay calm, he patted the water. He slapped harder than he meant to, sending an angry splash toward Zev.

"Sit down."

"Does your penis hang out like that all the time?" Zev asked suddenly.

Stephen Thomas shifted on the uncomfortable rocks. He was trembling.

Instead of replying, instead of asking all his own questions, Stephen Thomas started to laugh. Hysteria tinged his laughter, but this really was funny. He thought Zev looked strange, and Zev thought Stephen Thomas looked just as alien.

Zev smiled uncertainly.

"Yeah," Stephen Thomas said. "It hangs out like that all the time. But I guess . . . it won't for long. Does it . . . ?" He took a deep breath. "I guess you don't know if it falls off, or withers away, or . . ." He stopped, confused. "But Victoria said—"

"It won't do either," Zev said. "I don't think it will. It will just go inside."

Though Zev had no idea what stages Stephen Thomas would have to go through to become a diver, he knew—he was an example of—the result. He explained to Stephen Thomas about internal genitals, and then he showed him.

"It's more streamlined," he said. "All aquatic mammals are like this."

"So are a lot of terrestrial mammals," Stephen Thomas said. "But not ordinary humans. It never occurred to me. . . ."

Now, at least, some of the pain made sense. If his body was creating a place for internal genitals . . .

238 VONDA N. McINTYRE

"You're a lot different than I thought," Zev said. "I knew you kept your scrotum outside—that's so silly, you have to work so hard not to be fertile—but I didn't know you kept *everything* outside." He shrugged cheerfully. "I didn't know men humans looked so different from women humans. Divers don't."

Stephen Thomas let himself slide into the water until it covered him completely. He wondered how long he could stay submerged. He wondered if he could breathe underwater yet. He tried to take a breath.

He jerked upright, choking and coughing and gasping for air, just like last time.

Zev watched him, bemused.

"What are you doing?"

Stephen Thomas flung his wet hair out of his face. "Trying to breathe underwater."

"Why?"

"To see if I could. Maybe I don't want to come up."

"You shouldn't breathe underwater unless you have to," Zev said.

"Why not?"

"Your lungs get full of water. It's hard work, and it isn't very good for you. It's just to save your life if you get stuck. You get enough oxygen to keep your brain from dying till somebody finds you. You can get pneumonia if you're not careful."

"Great." He coughed and snorted and got rid of the rest of the water.

"Anyway," Zev said, "you should stick your penis out when you want to pee. Especially if you're living on land, otherwise you'll get all itchy."

"What about sex?"

"Then it sticks out by itself," Zev said solemnly. "Of course."

"Right. Of course." God, Stephen Thomas thought, I'm blushing. "Why did it hurt Victoria when we tried to make love in the water?"

"I don't—" Zev cut off what he was going to say, and thought for a minute instead. "Did you try too soon? Were you ready?"

"Of course she was ready," Stephen Thomas said, irritated. "What kind of a jerk do you think I am?" It annoyed him to have to ask for advice in the first place, but to have Zev act like a teenage sex therapist—

"Were *you* ready?"

"Obviously," Stephen Thomas said sarcastically. But then he went back in his mind and listened to what Zev had just said. "What do you mean by 'ready'?"

"She—"

"Not for Victoria. For me. How would you know if you were ready?"

"I'd be slick, of course," Zev said.

"Oh," Stephen Thomas said. *"Oh."*

"That doesn't happen to men humans?"

"No."

"And it didn't happen for you?"

"Not as of this morning."

"You're still changing," Zev said. He patted Stephen Thomas on the arm. "It'll be better when you're done." He cocked his head, thoughtfully. "You'll have to learn how to retract and extend. I never thought of that." He jumped up and stood knee-deep in the water. "Come on. Come swimming."

Stephen Thomas pushed himself to his feet. "I can't right now, Zev."

Zev glanced over his shoulder, wistfully, down the river. "Are you okay? Can you get where you're going by yourself?"

"Sure."

Zev grinned and waved and pushed off backwards. The current caught him. He vanished into the tumble of white water.

Stephen Thomas waded out onto the dry rocks. They were uncomfortably hot. He slid his feet quickly into his sandals and shook himself off. Droplets scattered from his body. In the bright light, his pelt was white-gold against his darkening skin.

He eased into his shorts, tempted to return to the cool solace of the river. He needed time to think and reflect . . . or he needed to be distracted from too much thinking and reflecting.

As he climbed the path, Crimson Ng strode down it, pulling a wheelbarrow.

"Hi," she said.

"Hi. Current project?"

"A new one." Crimson let him look into the wheelbarrow. He expected to see the bones of one of her heavy-boned, long-fanged predators.

The rough slab of stone contained alien shapes, the fossilized soft bodies of creatures never in any vertebrate line. Tentacles writhed and tangled. Eons ago, some violent accident had crushed the feathered legs.

"It looks like—"

"I devolved Nemo," she said. "And invented the rest of the ecosystem." She gazed past Stephen Thomas to the riverbank, barely aware of his presence. "It's ready to go in the ground. Want to help?"

"No," he said, aware that she was offering him a courtesy. "Thanks. I have to stop by the lab, and then I promised Esther a stint with the ASes."

"Yeah," Crimson said. "Right. I should do that, too." She grabbed the handles of the wheelbarrow and hurried past, instantly oblivious to everything but her work.

The cells from Nemo's ship thrived in growth medium. Stephen Thomas set to work parceling cultures out for the other departments.

Stephen Thomas tried not to worry about the weird changes in his body; he tried not to dwell on them. It was hard, when what felt like the world's worst sunburn was peeling and itching in his crotch. He could not forget the raw red flesh. Zev's explanation helped, but not much.

He kept imagining that his genitals had drawn up inside his body.

Imagining, hell! he thought.

He knew if he scratched himself, it would just start hurting.

I'd rather have the pain than the damned itching, he thought. But when he remembered the pain, he changed his mind.

He surrounded himself with images: Nemo's chamber, a recording of the cell growth, a micrograph of the huge dendritic molecules. He brought the cell growth image closer, and speeded up its replay.

The cells grew in a snowflake-shaped colony, stretched out in a network of interconnecting processes. The pattern was clearer in two dimensions than in three. In three, the concentric layers obscured and confused the lacy structure.

He let the cell colony recede and studied the strange three-dimensional polymers that he suspected of being the alien cell's genetic material.

He could not figure them out. The magical beauty of DNA was that its structure implied its means of replication: simple, elegant, self-evident. The double-stranded molecule split; the dividing cell recreated the missing half of each strand, using the strand itself as a map for its mirror image.

Dendritic molecules, though, were both more complicated and, ordinarily, simpler: structurally more complicated, but with less room for variation within the structure. He could figure out how they could form. But he could *not* figure out how they replicated. If they replicated. And he could not yet see a straightforward way of getting genetic information into or out of them.

You have plenty of time, he said to himself. What do you have to show for visits to two alien ships? One ordinary bit of living bunch-grass, and a couple of species of alien bacteria. Shit, all you *have* is time. You can afford to dissect a sample atom by atom, if that looks promising.

Stephen Thomas composed a note telling his colleagues that their alien cells were ready. He closed his eyes and linked with Arachne.

The computer opened up to him, serene and limitless, apparently unscarred and undaunted by the system crashes that had crippled it. Arachne's confidence could mislead him into believing nothing had changed. The truth was that the crashes had left invisible pockets of emptiness, as undetectable and as treacherous as snow-covered crevasses in a glacier.

Stephen Thomas sent out his message, then, on impulse, asked Arachne to show him Feral's files.

Feral had specialized in reporting on the space program. Both Victoria and Satoshi held him in high regard as a writer, but Stephen Thomas had read few of his articles. Stephen Thomas had liked Feral for himself.

Feral had left a lot of work on the system. A collection of his finished pieces, written back on Earth. Some slice of life reportage. A long series he called "Life Log." The last installment reported Feral's trip from Earth to the transport to *Starfarer*. It ended with the communications cutoff before the missile attack. After that, his work lay unfinished, stored in private files.

Someone should put it together and publish it for him, Stephen Thomas thought. *If we can get to it.*

The names of the files were intriguing. His final "Life Log." "Resonances: *Starfarer*." "Stephen Thomas."

Stephen Thomas asked Arachne to let him into the files. Receiving a polite refusal, he shrugged. He had not expected it to be that easy.

Feral had recorded no will, no next of kin, which could mean that the files were locked forever. But Stephen Thomas was not ready to give up.

He tried the obvious sorts of passwords: Feral's name, his birthdate. Stephen Thomas even tried his own name.

Nothing worked.

I'll figure it out, Feral, Stephen Thomas thought.

Reluctantly, he put the locked files away and withdrew from Arachne. He had promised some time to Esther Klein and the artificials. He had better get going.

Mitch sauntered in, looking ridiculously happy.

"Sorry I'm late," he said cheerfully and without a

shred of regret. He dragged a chair up beside Stephen
Thomas and straddled it.

Stephen Thomas thought, this does not sound like
unrequited love anymore. I wonder . . . ?

"Listen, Mitch—" Stephen Thomas said. "Yesterday. When Fox was here. It all came right out of thin
air."

"I know. She told me. And at your house last night,
she just wanted to talk to somebody. She sure picked
the wrong person." Mitch chuckled. "Boy, is she mad at
Florrie."

"That's probably the only thing Fox and I agree on
right now," Stephen Thomas said. It hurt that Florrie
had junked the connection they had made—that he
thought they had made—so readily.

"She's pretty embarrassed, too. I think she's afraid
everybody will take your side."

"There aren't any sides! Shit, people aren't taking
sides! Are they?"

"I don't know. I don't think so. Maybe a little bit."

"Thank you for your incisive analysis. Is Fox okay?
Are you?"

"Yeah. She was upset last night, but . . ." He
shrugged, and grinned, awkward, pleased with himself.
"I just sort of patted her till she fell asleep. I sat up with
her all night. It was kind of . . ."

"Romantic?"

Mitch started to answer. He stopped. He laughed
with a high, delighted, nasal bark.

"It was cold, is what it was, and along around dawn
it got kind of damp. How come it's so cold at night and
so hot during the day? I kept thinking I should wake her
up and get her home. And then I wondered how come
she could sleep and I couldn't."

"Maybe you should've waked her up long enough to
ask to share her jacket." Stephen Thomas thought, It's
still unrequited, but at least this is a little more promising for Mitch than it was before.

"I just hope . . ." Mitch's voice trailed off.

"That you won't get pneumonia?"

Mitch laughed again. "That from now on, she won't forget my name every time she sees me."

"I don't think you have to worry about that anymore," Stephen Thomas said.

Victoria jammed her shovel deep in the heavy, clayey dirt. *Starfarer* had not been in existence long enough to develop much good topsoil. Spring rain saturated the ground, and the abnormal heat of the day supersaturated the air with humidity. She turned over a spade full of dirt and broke it up into clumps.

She had promised to spend the morning working in one of the garden plots. Esther could give no estimate of how long it would take the field tiller to regrow its brain. For the last half hour, Gerald and Avvaiyar had been arguing the possibility of building a plow.

"There's nothing simpler than building a plow," Gerald said. "Then the only difficulty is figuring out how to hitch it to one of the silver slugs."

Victoria leaned on her shovel. "Infinity said we should quit calling them in for anything that wasn't an emergency."

"I see," Gerald said. "Perhaps I should turn over coordination to our Mr. Mendez."

Victoria thought that might be a good idea, but Gerald was in such a foul mood, and so obviously irritated at Infinity, that she decided not to say so.

"I think we should catch some of the horses and get them to earn their keep for a change," Avvaiyar said.

"They're *pets*," Victoria said. "Could they even pull a plow?"

"Why not? We could hitch them up in series like a dog team."

"I think you'd have better luck with a dog team."

"If we had any dogs."

"Clearly the silver slugs are the best choice," Gerald said. "Unless we propose to pull the plow ourselves."

"Forget it!" Victoria snapped. She jammed the shovel into the ground.

I'll dig up every square meter of *Starfarer* with a shovel, Victoria thought angrily. I'll catch fish to put in with the corn seeds. I'll stand up to my knees in water to set out rice plants. But I will *not* pull a plow!

Infinity headed for an access tunnel to the surface of *Starfarer*. He needed to get outside for a while. At least out in space he would be safe from more of Gerald Hemminge's cold messages, like the one Arachne handed over this morning:

"Do not ever contradict my orders again."

So much for government by consensus.

The nearest hatch lay beyond a patch of temperate forest. The shade of the fast-growing trees and the green-gold coolness made Infinity happy.

A small creature squawked in terror. It struggled and fluttered, pummeling the ground.

Infinity sprinted toward the sound. Last year's fallen leaves deadened the thud of his boots.

He stopped.

A bird lay on the ground, a sparrow, its brown feathers blending in against the forest colors. Infinity knelt and touched it. The heat of its body radiated through its soft ruffled feathers, but it was dead. He turned it over. Its blood dripped to the ground, bright red, wet.

Whatever had killed it had disappeared. It left no footprints, only disturbed ground.

Infinity picked up the bird and took it off the path. He left it where *Starfarer*'s scavengers would find it.

But what had killed it? Falcons and a pair of eagles lived on the wild side, but Alzena had not, as far as he knew, introduced predators into *Starfarer*'s campus cylinder.

Maybe Alzena had let loose some small carnivore. She might even have reported it in the daily news. If she had, Arachne's crash had lost it.

Curious, Infinity followed the scuffed-up leaves. He wondered if he was seeing a real trail, or a path his eyes and mind were making up. The dead leaves glistened, black from winter, damp and rotting into the soil. Here and there the leaves rumpled, like a carpet pushed into folds by a scampering child.

Each step released the fertile, musty smell of leaf mould. The young forest basked in the hot spring sun, green and gold, the new leaves nearly full. A life cycle began above Infinity's head and circled beneath his feet.

Alzena had planned the ecosystem carefully. First she had prepared the soil and the free-living microbes. Then she had established the plants and the pollinating insects, the invertebrates, the scavengers. Then she added the smaller herbivores, the songbirds, the bats. When each branch of the environmental network made its connections, she added to its complexity.

She might have released a mammalian predator, a badger, a ferret, a fox. The time was right. Otherwise the forest's life cycle would overbalance. Had she had time to complete the network? Infinity did not know.

He reached the edge of the forest. The trees gave way to a meadow. Infinity blinked in the sudden brightness of hot sun. The stream's reflection dazzled him; water brushed past him with a musical sigh.

A piercing whistle cut the air.

Infinity barely caught the quick motion at the top of a tumble of stones. The black tail of a small furry animal vanished behind the rocks.

Infinity sprinted for the bank. He clambered up the slope, pebbles sliding beneath his feet.

When he reached the top, only the stream's humming disturbed the silence. A dragonfly hovered, vibrated the air, vanished, and reappeared five meters away as if it had teleported.

Infinity sank down, lying flat on the slope. The stones pressed the heat through his jeans and into his skin. He was glad of his leather vest.

For a long time, nothing moved.

Whatever it was, I lost it, Infinity thought. It ran off into the bushes, or along the stream bank out of sight. . . . And maybe it didn't have anything to do with the dead bird. Maybe it was just minding its own business when I jumped out and scared it. But what *was* it? The tail was wrong for a squirrel or a chipmunk, but it wasn't naked enough for a rat. I hope. We're in trouble if the campus has rats.

The rocks beneath him had not had time to weather. They were sharp and raw.

Enough of this great native hunter business, he thought. I'll get Arachne to keep watch on the spot. . . .

Just before he moved, a creature scampered to the highest point of the bank. It moved with a smooth canny pacing gait. It rose on its hind legs, its back to him, counterbalanced by its tail. It gazed upward, watching for predators. Paws crossed on its belly, it turned to survey the land.

It saw Infinity. They stared at each other for a split second, each as surprised as the other, the creature peering with shiny black eyes through a black mask of fur.

It cried out in warning; it dropped to all fours and fled, pacing quick-footed down the slope and between some rocks.

It was one of Europa's meerkats.

"Damn!" Infinity said softly. He rose from the sharp-edged stones, no longer trying to hide.

He supposed he should trap it, or even shoot it. It had no business here. It did not fit this environment. It was a creature of heat and deserts.

Why'd Europa leave it here? he wondered. Or did she leave it? Maybe she just forgot how many she brought with her. Maybe this one got lost.

The arrival and departure of the alien humans had been abrupt and confused enough for the disappearance of one small critter to attract no notice.

I wish we had noticed, Infinity thought. If Alzena knew a weasel was running lose in her ecosystem, I bet she'd have snapped out of her funk. I bet she'd've stayed.

In response to Infinity's request, Arachne set a watch on the mouth of the den, and began a simulation of what effect the meerkat could have. Infinity decided not to do anything until the simulation produced results, not even to tell anyone he had seen the creature. Someone might panic and come out hunting it. Infinity felt sorry for the meerkat, stranded in an inhospitable environment, a communal being left all alone.

J.D. descended into the basement of the administration building. Her hands and her hair reeked with fragrant citrus oil. She had spent the morning helping sort and store yesterday's oversupply of oranges. Ordinarily J.D. liked the smell of oranges. After two days of it, though, it was the last thing she wanted to smell.

That was what she thought until she entered the basement.

She nearly gagged. The stench of rotting AS brains filled the cavernous room, intensified rather than attenuated by the flow of air pushing past her. Esther must have turned the ventilation up to maximum, and still the sick-sweet odor overwhelmed everything. Including the scent of oranges.

A few ASes stood on one side of the room, hooked up to nutrient feeders. A larger group stood in ranks, carapaces open but empty. The majority of the mobile artificials remained in a large ragged crowd that stretched into the darkness.

Esther glanced up from an open AS.

"Hi, J.D. What's up?"

"Can I help?" She took a long breath through her mouth.

Esther smiled wryly. "It is pretty awful, isn't it? We're trying to get the bad part done before it gets worse. Still game?"

"I guess so."

Esther took her to the clump of ASes where her volunteers were working.

"It's not that complicated," she said. "Just nasty."

Stephen Thomas looked up from the AS that had spattered him with grayish slime.

"And if you need advice," he said, "I consider myself an expert. Hours of technical experience."

Esther chuckled. She opened the carapace of the housekeeper in front of them and cleaned out the broken brain. J.D. watched, fighting nausea.

"This is disgusting," J.D. said. "And I have a strong stomach. It doesn't bother me to eat raw clams. It didn't even bother me to eat sea urchins or beche de mer."

"Not to mention those things with the legs," Esther said.

"Those were pretty good, honestly," J.D. said. "I don't know about this, though."

Stephen Thomas shuddered theatrically. "*Eating* doesn't come into the equation," he said.

J.D. grimaced. "Sorry. I should have thought how that would sound."

Esther finished cleaning the carapace. "Then you just wash the remains down the waste digester—" She stopped. "I *wish* that wasn't what it was called," she said.

They all laughed, if shakily. J.D. mastered her nausea, took a long breath, let it out, and snapped open the seal on the next AS. Spores puffed up from a drying mass of mold mycelia, another strand of smell added to the tapestry: dry, musty, lingering.

"I'll do my best," J.D. said. She sneezed.

Esther patted her arm and went away. J.D. picked up the vacuum nozzle and set to work. The vacuum whispered as soft as the mold spores, sucking out the dead tissue.

Stephen Thomas straightened up and stretched his back. The swimming webs on his hands had completed themselves. His skin had darkened past gold to bronze.

"How are you?" she asked. She felt awkward making small talk with him, especially after last night.

"Running on empty," he said.

"Oh . . . I thought the party broke up right after . . ."

"We got up kind of early," he said. He hesitated, then continued with the first real excitement she had heard in his voice since Feral died. "I found some stuff of Feral's. Some stuff in Arachne, I mean."

"His stories on the space program?" J.D. said. "Yes. I read them—" Thinking of Feral made her sad. She had liked him. He had been both sweet-natured and intense. She had not even minded, too much, when he teased her about her attraction to Stephen Thomas. She had not even been jealous when she realized it was Feral's attraction Stephen Thomas would respond to.

Not jealous, but a little envious, she thought wistfully. I have to admit I was envious.

"Not just his stories. He had another project going. He collected a lot of research. J.D.—Feral logged his life."

"What do you mean?"

"Not like Chandra. He wasn't built for that. But he kept up a running dialogue with the computer web. Notes on what he was doing, his observations, his conversations—"

J.D. remembered some of the things she and Feral had discussed. She felt herself blushing, the heat rising up her cheeks, uncontrollable. Her skin was so fair that when she blushed it was painfully obvious.

If I were turning into a diver, she thought, I wouldn't have this problem anymore.

"What's the matter?" Stephen Thomas asked.

"Nothing!" she said, too quickly. "I mean . . . Feral and I talked about some personal subjects. I hadn't intended . . . it wouldn't be interesting to anyone else. I'm sure he didn't bother to record that," she said hopefully.

"He was a journalist," Stephen Thomas said. "You should have known he was taking notes on everything."

"I suppose . . ." She felt embarrassed. Feral's notes could reveal her with naked transparency to Stephen Thomas. Not that her embarrassment would make much difference in the scheme of the world. Stephen Thomas was used to handling people he wasn't interested in. Last night proved that. But she would prefer not to put herself in the same situation as Fox.

"You better know this, too," Stephen Thomas said. His manner had changed. He sounded cold. "If I can, I'm going to edit what he collected and publish it for him."

Both his words and his tone hurt her. She could think of no explanation for his sudden change of attitude. Unless, of course, he had already seen her conversations with Feral and was giving her fair warning, both of his publishing plans and of his lack of interest in her.

"I'm sure he'd like that," J.D. said, forcing her voice to stay steady.

Stephen Thomas replied belligerently. "But?"

"But nothing. He loved you. He'd trust you to handle his work."

Stephen Thomas glared at her, inexplicably. He was angry and yet his eyes were full of tears.

He threw down the cleaning tools, left the AS half enervated, and stalked out of the basement without another word to anyone.

It would be pointless to follow him; obviously he did not want to talk to her. And if she begged him not to embarrass her in public, that would be even worse. So what if everybody knew she thought he was the most beautiful human being she had ever met? She had a lot of company in that thought, and she had avoided making a fool of herself to him directly.

I would have thought he'd just laugh, she thought. Say to himself, Oh, fuck, *another* one. Or even say to me, J.D., what the hell made you think I'd even be interested? And maybe I'd say, I didn't think you'd be interested, that's why I never said anything to you. If you were a gentleman, you never would have said anything to me.

She stamped her foot angrily at herself, pushing away her anxiety.

She hoped Stephen Thomas would cool off; she hoped he would eventually be able to be friends with her again. She hoped he was not so irritated that this would damage her friendship with his whole family, with Victoria.

•   •   •

Stephen Thomas ran home through the hot afternoon.

He entered the garden, soaked with sweat, reeking of rotten AS brains. He went straight to the bathroom, stripped, and flung his clothes into the sink. While the sink filled with warm water and soap, he grabbed a clean towel off the shelf and wrapped it around his hips.

Ordinarily he would not bother, but he could not stand to look at himself. When the change was over, delicate thin skin would cover his penis. Not quite a mucous membrane, but skin at least as sensitive as his lips. So far, though, the skin still peeled like sunburn, and his penis and scrotum had begun to withdraw into his body. He felt squeezed.

He did not yet have voluntary control of his genitals. As Zev said, he would have to learn. They were new muscles, or muscles he never knew he had. They ached with tension.

The soft cotton towel rubbed the fine gold hair on his hip, pushing it upward. He pulled off the towel and smoothed his pelt. He slid the towel downward before wrapping it again, so his fur would stay sleek. Now he understood why Zev wore as few clothes as possible.

He washed his T-shirt, swished it around in the sink, squeezed out the water, and held it up.

The stains from the AS bioelectronic guts marred the turquoise silk.

"God *dammit*!" he shouted. The shirt was ruined. He flung it across the bathroom. It slapped against the glass tiles and lay in a puddle.

It was his favorite shirt. Victoria had brought it back with her on her last trip to Earth. He should have packed it away with his other silk shirts, to save for special occasions. But he could not bear to give it up so soon.

"Dammit, dammit, dammit," he muttered.

He snatched the shirt from the floor, wrung soap and water out of his shorts, and slapped both pieces of clothing over a towel rack to dry. By the time *Starfarer* got back to Earth—if *Starfarer* got back to Earth—he would probably be grateful for anything to wear. Whether it was stained and ruined or not.

He dropped his towel on the floor and got into the shower.

Admit it, he said to himself as water streamed down his body. You aren't mad about the shirt. Yes, I am, said another part of himself. All right. But what you're really mad about is that J.D. got to sleep with Feral and you didn't.

It was so obvious. When J.D. heard that Feral had recorded their conversations, she had blushed from the curve of her breasts to the roots of her hair. Though she was unusually shy about discussing personal subjects, she was transparent, emotionally and physically.

Stephen Thomas felt completely opaque, even to himself. What difference did it make? Why shouldn't they get together? They had spent the whole trip from Earth to *Starfarer* on the same transport. Feral was alone and J.D. had thought she might never see Zev again. They had spent a lot of time together, tracking down the system crash. If they had found some pleasure in each other, he could only be happy for them both.

Would you regret Feral's death any more, he asked himself, if you and he had made love? Would you regret it less?

He answered himself, in his weird monologous dialogue: If I regretted Feral's death any more, I think I'd go nuts. It doesn't make sense to be mad at J.D., to be jealous of her.

As he had when Feral died, when Merry died, he pulled himself away from his anger and his grief. Both were pointless, and he could not afford to let himself fall apart.

Kolya was miserable. Coffee did nothing to ease nicotine withdrawal; neither did beer. Both made him need to pee more often. So now he was sweating an ill-smelling sweat and having to pee all the time. He had drunk enough beer to disorient himself, to make his balance chancy. He had drunk enough coffee to make him jumpy. He had thrown away the usual easy relaxation and cheer of Gerald Hemminge's best English stout.

He lay folded up in the window seat, the curtains pulled aside, a chill breeze blowing through the open windows. He sought the cold so he would have a sensation to concentrate on besides the need to smoke a cigarette.

Someone knocked on his door. He frowned. He had not heard anyone approach. He was not *that* drunk. . . .

Another knock. Kolya stayed silent, stayed still. Soon they would go away.

The door opened a crack. Kolya tensed.

This was ridiculous. There were no spies for the Mideast Sweep on board *Starfarer*. If there were, they would have sought him out months ago. Either he would be dead, a victim of the Sweep's death sentence, or he would have killed them in self-defense.

And it would be doubly ridiculous to be stalked by the Sweep during the only time he had been really drunk in the last twenty years.

"Kolya?"

Kolya's body sagged with relief, his reaction magnified by intoxication. Then, angry, he pushed himself to his feet and jerked the door open.

Griffith started. For an instant he looked as dangerous as he was.

"I might have known," Kolya said.

Griffith was the only person on campus foolish enough and self-confident enough to enter Kolya's house, or rude enough to enter anyone's house, uninvited.

"What *is* it?" Kolya snarled.

Taken aback, Griffith hesitated.

"Do you *want* something?"

"I can't figure you out," Griffith said.

"That suits me well," Kolya said.

"One time I see you, you're friendly. The next time

you threaten to kill me. Then you apologize. Then you bite my head off."

"And you suppose," Kolya said irritably, "that your actions have nothing to do with my reactions?"

"I was worried about you. You look like shit, since you ran out of cigarettes."

"Thank you, Marion. I'm grateful for your opinion."

Griffith glowered at him, as he always did when Kolya used his given name. Kolya sometimes could not resist, though he knew he should have more self-discipline. Today, though, getting a rise out of Griffith gave him no satisfaction.

Kolya sighed and stepped back from the door.

"You may as well come in." He did not particularly want to talk to Griffith. But he had neither the energy to make him leave nor the strength to remain standing.

He folded himself back into the window seat. He had never gotten around to getting a chair, for he seldom had visitors. Griffith sat crosslegged on the floor without comment or complaint.

Griffith had changed his clothes. When he came on board he wore the attire of a General Accounting Office middle manager, slacks and shirt and jacket. Now that he had given up pretending to be a GAO accountant, he wore *Starfarer* regulation pants, cotton canvas in a rather military green with an EarthSpace logo on the thigh, and a similar sweatshirt. If he was trying to fit in, he had, for once, guessed wrong. No one on campus wore regulation clothes without altering them.

The strangest thing about Griffith's clothes was that they were grubby. Griffith looked rumpled, not his usual neat and unnoticeable self. Kolya tried to recall seeing him unkempt before, even after an hour in a survival pouch.

"Where have you been?"

"Camping," Griffith said. "In the wild cylinder. I needed . . . to get away for a while. To survive on my own."

An overnight on the wild side, which—as far as Kolya knew—hosted no large predators and few pests, did not sound very challenging. But, then, Griffith came from the city.

Kolya's lips twitched up in an involuntary smile that Griffith saw before Kolya could repress it.

"What's so funny?"

"Marion Griffith, guerrilla accountant."

Kolya thought he had gone too far, as he often did with Griffith. Sometimes he went too far deliberately; this time, he had spoken without thinking because he was past rational thought. He shivered, and wished again for a cigarette.

Griffith opened his mouth to retort, then stopped. He shrugged, and his lips quirked in a smile.

"More or less accurate," he said.

He always had maintained that he really was an accountant. But he usually did not admit that he was anything more.

"Do you want a cup of tea or something?" Griffith said. "When's the last time you ate?"

"Who knows? It isn't tea I want. It's nicotine." He shivered, imagining one long drag on a cigarette. Then he could not stop shivering.

Griffith went to the kitchen nook, heated water, made two cups of strong tea, brought them back, and insisted that Kolya drink some. It did help. He still felt dreadful, but his shivering stopped.

"What is your father's name?" Kolya asked.

"Peter," Griffith replied. Then his usual suspicion kicked in. "Why?"

"Your patronymic is Petrovich. The same as mine."

"I guess. So?"

"Your given name doesn't form a diminutive that you'd like any better than you like Marion. Masha, perhaps."

"You're right. I don't like it any better."

"It's a custom for friends to call each other by their patronymics. I'm going to call you Petrovich."

"What should I call you?"

"Petrovich."

"Uh . . . okay."

No one had called Kolya "Petrovich" in many years. In decades. He had persuaded his colleagues on *Starfarer* to call him Kolya, or Nikolai Petrovich, instead of General Cherenkov. But he had never before developed a relationship of the right sort, respect and friendship combined, to ask anyone to call him simply Petrovich.

"And I am all right, Petrovich," Kolya said. "Thank you for your worry. Every minute, I think, I cannot survive this, and every other minute I remind myself I have no choice."

"What if you did?"

"But I don't! It's pointless to speculate."

"But what if?"

Kolya slid down in the window seat till he was lying flat on his back, with his feet up against the wall. His thigh muscles twitched and trembled. He flung one arm over his face. The unpleasant cold sweat soaked into his sleeve.

"I would probably kill for a bit of tobacco."

"You don't have to. Here."

Kolya looked out from beneath his arm. Griffith held a fistful of large crumpled green-brown leaves.

"What—!"

"If I remember right, and if Arachne's refs are right, that's what this is."

Kolya scrambled to his feet. He grabbed the leaves, rudely, crushed them under his nose, breathed deeply. They smelled like tobacco. Green, wet tobacco. The smell of it made his whole body thrill.

"Alzena said there was no such thing."

"Maybe Alzena wasn't the most reliable witness in the world. Or maybe," he said quickly, "somebody else planted it. Or maybe I'm wrong and Arachne's wrong and it isn't—"

"It is."

Now that Kolya had it, he had no idea what to do with it. He peeled off a shred of the leaf, put it in his mouth, and chewed. The green tobacco released the worst taste he had ever experienced, sour, bitter, potent.

Saliva spurted from every salivary gland, as if he were about to vomit. His mouth filled with revolting liquid. He gagged. He pushed past Griffith, hurried out onto his porch, and spat violently over the rail. The green blob of chewed tobacco plopped in the dirt.

He hung over the porch rail, panting and sweating. His mouth tasted vile.

"God, I'm sorry," Griffith said.

"Don't be," Kolya said.

It astonished him, how much better he felt, and how quickly, as if the nicotine had diffused straight into his brain. He fingered the leathery leaf, and pulled off another shred of tobacco.

Victoria entered the physics building gratefully, glad of the cool constant underground temperature. She wiped the sweat off her face with her soaked sleeve. She felt dirty and sticky. Her shoes were muddy from the garden; so were her pants, from the knees down. She flung herself gratefully into the deep, soft chair.

The maintenance work on *Starfarer* was important, of course, but she *had* to get some of her own work done. If she could spend some concentrated time on the algorithm, she knew she could speed it up. *Starfarer* was less than a day away from transition, and she still could not tell where they were going.

I keep reassuring people about it, she thought, but I'm nervous, too. What if Europa suspected we might follow, what if she led us somewhere she can survive, but we can't? Would she do that? Are we such a threat that she'd be willing to wipe us out?

Starfarer ought to be more resistant than Europa's ship to difficult conditions. *Starfarer* enclosed its ecosystem. But Victoria had no way of knowing what hidden abilities Europa's strange ship might have, and Infinity had brought home to her the essential fragility of *Starfarer*.

No, she thought. Fragility's the wrong word. But resilience has limits.

She gave herself a moment to appreciate the tight-knit, symmetrical form of the three-dimensional representation of her multi-dimensional algorithm. It hovered, complex and colorful, forming itself in the corner of her office.

It stopped.

Victoria jumped up, her sore shoulders and sweaty clothes forgotten. She queried Arachne, expecting to be told No, be patient, it just *looks* finished, it's still working, inside where you can't see.

Arachne presented her with the algorithm's solutions.

Starfarer was about to set out for 61 Cygni.

Victoria whistled softly. 61 Cygni was a long, long way away: completely on the other side of Earth from Tau Ceti. And yet the transition duration had a lower maximum than the range from Tau Ceti to Sirius.

"Curiouser and curiouser," she said softly.

She checked the spectral signature. 61 Cygni A was a K5 star on the main sequence, not too different from the sun. She hoped that would reassure Infinity; she hoped the change toward terrestrial conditions would stabilize *Starfarer*'s environment. She put a message into Arachne for everyone to see.

She hurried next door to J.D.'s office and found her colleague curled up in the deep fabric-sculpture chair, writing in her notebook. The holographic image of Nemo's chamber hovered over her desk.

"J.D.! The algorithm's done!"

"It is? Victoria, that's wonderful!"

J.D. tried to jump up out of the chair, but it was so low and so soft that it made her struggle. She made a sound of disgust. J.D. hated her office furnishings. They were left over from her predecessor in the alien contact department, and she had had no opportunity to replace them.

Victoria hugged J.D., joyful. J.D. embraced her gently, and let her go with regret.

Arachne presented a star map, and a copy of the algorithm.

"It's beautiful," J.D. said. "Beautiful results. It's different from the others."

"They're all different," Victoria said. "But . . . you're right. The other solutions had some visual similarities. This one's completely changed."

"61 Cygni," J.D. said softly. "Will we find our neighbors?"

"Could be."

They knew they had neighbors: Europa had referred to them. Unfortunately, she had not been willing to reveal anything about them, including where they lived or how to make contact with them.

J.D. sat on the edge of her desk and stared at the solution, the star chart, the time range.

"What is it?" Victoria asked.

"Nemo."

Victoria sat beside her. "There's still time. We don't hit transition till tomorrow afternoon. Nemo knows what we're doing. If he—she—?"

"I don't think our pronouns fit Nemo," J.D. said.

"One wouldn't have started metamorphosis and invited you back if one knew there wasn't going to be time."

"I hope not. Only what if Nemo didn't have any choice about when it began? We pretend we know all about our own physiology. But we still can't predict exactly when somebody will be born . . . or die."

"Nemo will follow us through transition. We can meet on the other side."

"If Nemo's still alive." J.D. gestured to the time range. "Using Civilization's algorithm, the trip will take a lot longer."

Victoria hesitated. "Do you want me to give . . ."

"I . . ." J.D. leaned back, gripping the edge of the desk. "You have to make that decision."

They sat together in silence. The algorithm was an example of natural beauty, like a waterfall, a mountain view.

Victoria laid her hand over J.D.'s.

"Yesterday was fun," she said softly.

"Yes."

J.D. brought Victoria's hand to her lips. She kissed her palm, her fingertips.

"Come stay overnight with me and Zev," she said. "Would you?"

"I'd like that," Victoria said. "Satoshi and Stephen Thomas and I have some things to work out, first. But soon."

"Is everything okay?"

Victoria shrugged, and smiled as well as she could manage. "Changing into a diver is more disorienting than Stephen Thomas expected. Not just for him."

Stephen Thomas started dinner. He was a lousy cook, but he needed to pretend everything was normal. He boiled water and stirred in the rice. At that point, both his imagination and the household's supplies failed him.

He could go over to the central cafeteria and get bento boxes . . . except if he did, he would have to face Florrie Brown.

Outside, Victoria and Satoshi crossed the garden, laughing. Stephen Thomas opened the door.

"Stephen Thomas! The algorithm's finished!"

Victoria fairly glowed with the success of her work. She showed off the algorithm's new pattern.

Stephen Thomas was glad to see her happy, after so much stress and despair, after this morning's fiasco in the ocean. Satoshi acted more content, too, though Stephen Thomas felt an inexplicable distance separating him from his partner.

Inexplicable? he thought. How would you like it, if Satoshi's skin started peeling off?

He could not answer the question. He wanted to think he would take the changes in stride, if they were happening to Satoshi, or if something comparable were happening to Victoria. But he distressed himself, with his battered toes, his raw penis, the swollen flesh redesigning itself to hold his genitals within his body. At the moment he did not want anyone to look at him, much less touch him. How could he be sure he would accept it any better if it were happening to one of his partners?

Victoria came up behind him, slid her hands around his waist, and leaned her cheek against his shoulder. His body balanced on a narrow line between pleasure and pain. One step farther would take Stephen Thomas wholly into one or the other, but he could not tell which. He wanted to fling himself around and take her in his arms and never let go. But he was afraid. Afraid of the pain, afraid of losing someone else he loved. He put his hands over hers, stilled her.

"I talked to Zev," he said. "When the changes are done . . ." He felt awkward, discussing what had happened. He had never felt awkward discussing sex. He had never hurt anyone during sex, either. Not until today. "I won't hurt you again," he said.

"It didn't exactly *hurt,*" Victoria said.

He laughed, harsh and skeptical.

"A little," she admitted. "I was more surprised—"

"It won't happen again," he said, with more intensity than he intended. He pushed her hands away. She stepped back.

"People weren't built to screw in the ocean," Satoshi said.

"Human people," Stephen Thomas said, his voice sharp. "It'll work after—"

"Maybe for you. Where does that leave me?"

Victoria glanced uncomfortably from Stephen Thomas to Satoshi.

"I didn't intend to make a big deal out of this, eh?" she said. "I thought it would be fun."

"Yeah," Stephen Thomas said. "I know."

He and Satoshi gazed at each other. Stephen Thomas looked away.

"I'd better drop by the lab. Don't worry if you don't see me till late."

"It's *already* late," Victoria said.

"Are you coming back?" Satoshi asked.

"What?"

"Are you coming back?" Satoshi repeated himself, emphasizing each word.

"What kind of a question is that?" Victoria cried.

Satoshi did not answer her. He glanced down, then stared at Stephen Thomas, into his eyes. Stephen Thomas wondered if he could get out the door before Satoshi said anything else.

Satoshi kept his expression neutral.

"Are you going to tell us . . ."

He stopped. The careful, neutral tone caught in his throat. When he spoke again, his voice shook.

"Are you leaving us? If you are, do you plan to tell us?"

Hurt by Satoshi's unfairness, shocked into anger, Stephen Thomas replied without thinking.

"I don't know."

He fled.

CHAPTER II

STEPHEN THOMAS PLUNGED DOWN THE dark curved stripe of path, through the pale glow of flowers and the carnation-spiced air. He stopped at the garden gate, his breathing hard and shaky.

He had nowhere to go. He did not want to spend the night in the lab. He was too tired to get any work done. He was damned if he would sleep on the couch in the student lounge, in public; he had no idea how his body would betray him next. His makeshift office was too small to sleep in.

He should turn around, go back inside, and tell Victoria and Satoshi he wanted to go to bed and go to sleep alone. But nothing would be that easy, not after what he and Satoshi had said to each other. Satoshi's question had struck painfully at what Stephen Thomas feared might be the truth.

Is he right? Stephen Thomas wondered. He leaned against the steep bank that formed the garden wall. It was cool and damp. Ivy crinkled against his hands.

What would it be like to live apart from Victoria and Satoshi? A couple of weeks ago the idea would have been unimaginable. Now, strain showed between them all. Stephen Thomas had said things to Victoria that he regretted; and he had felt so disconnected from Satoshi since the changes began that he hardly felt like they were living together at all.

. He glanced back at the house. In the main room, Victoria and Satoshi held each other. Stephen Thomas felt excluded and exhausted, unable to face talking to his partners, or anyone else, tonight.

Lots of people on campus would give him a place to sleep. Some of them would not even ask why he needed somewhere to stay. But *Starfarer* had many of the attributes, positive and negative, of a small town. Including the gossip.

What about the guest house? Stephen Thomas thought.

It was where Feral had been planning to stay, till Stephen Thomas invited him to use Merry's room. As far as Stephen Thomas knew, no one was staying there at all. A solitary retreat where he could get his bearings was exactly what he needed.

A vile smell rolled out of Kolya's oven. Not the odor of tobacco smoke, but the poisonous scent of crushed nightshade leaves: Nicotine, nicotinic acid, tobacco boiled and abused into a useless mush.

Griffith recoiled and hurried to open the front door.

"Don't do that!" Kolya said.

"But—"

"Someone might smell it."

Griffith bolted outside and slammed the door behind him.

Kolya glanced regretfully into the dish. One of the tobacco leaves lay steaming in its own juice.

"This is not a success," Kolya said.

He joined Griffith on the front porch.

"Petrovich, you look positively green."

"I feel negatively green."

Kolya chuckled.

"I tried smoking once," Griffith said. "I didn't like it."

"The leaves need preparation. That green tobacco was not tasty."

"I know," Griffith said.

Kolya gave him a questioning glance. Griffith shrugged.

"I've tried a lot of things . . . at least once. I didn't like chewing tobacco any more than I liked smoking."

"It smells better when it's cured," Kolya said.

"You need to dry the stuff. And ferment it."

"Ferment it? Like beer?"

Griffith shrugged. "The refs say you ferment it. They don't say how."

"I was trying to dry it, I thought that would be adequate."

"You don't cook much, do you?" Griffith asked.

"Rarely. Why? Do you?"

"Yeah. Some. A little. I don't think microwaving is a good way to dry something out."

"Why didn't you say so before?"

"I didn't want . . . I don't know."

Kolya smiled wryly. "I'm not always right," he said. "Haven't you learned that yet, Petrovich?"

"I guess not."

"What would you suggest we try?"

Griffith glanced toward Kolya's front door, and his color grayed. "What do you mean, 'we'?"

"You shouldn't have—" Kolya stopped. If he embarrassed Griffith about finding the tobacco for him, Griffith would likely decline to get more when Kolya ran out.

"Maybe toasting it would work," Griffith said. "Toasting it *gently*."

Stephen Thomas entered the lobby of the guest house.

None of the people in charge of it remained on board *Starfarer*. With the cleaning ASes out of commission as well, dust had begun to collect in corners and on the windowpanes.

Stephen Thomas climbed to the second floor. Since he was the only guest, he supposed he could have any of its dozen rooms.

He opened the door to the room Feral had been planning to use.

Stephen Thomas had shown Feral to the guest house—

Feral had just arrived on the same transport that brought J.D. to *Starfarer* and returned Victoria from her trip to British Columbia. Stephen Thomas and Feral had barely met. But Stephen Thomas liked him from the start.

He and Feral had stood in the doorway. The room was comfortable and attractive. It had better furniture than Merry's room, the unused room, back at the partnership's house. But Stephen Thomas did not want to leave Feral here all alone.

"You don't have to stay here," Stephen Thomas said. "Come home with me. We have a spare room."

"That would be great." Feral smiled. He had a great smile. "It's tough to get involved in a community when you're staying in a hotel. Thanks."

—Stephen Thomas still wondered if, somehow, Feral's association with the alien contact department—or with Stephen Thomas and his family—had contributed to his death.

Someone had used the room since Stephen Thomas was here last. The bed had not been slept in, but scraps of paper lay on the desk in the bay window. Arachne maintained a small display nearby. Bright sunlight washed out the display's colors; Stephen Thomas could not decipher it from here.

He crossed to the window, sat at the desk, and glanced up at the display. It contained a copy of the alien maze that had—they thought—been humanity's welcome into the interstellar civilization.

Stephen Thomas smiled sadly. Lots of people had kept a copy of that maze around, trying to decipher it. Until *Starfarer* encountered Europa and Androgeos, and discovered that their welcome had been withdrawn. The maze was just a maze.

Arachne informed Stephen Thomas that Feral had set the maze image in the window.

Feral used this room as an office, Stephen Thomas thought.

That made sense; all the members of the partnership had offices outside the house. A separate office made it easier to concentrate on work, and to get away from work at home.

Stephen Thomas wished he had known about this place. He had no particular reason to know; Feral had no particular reason to tell him or not to tell him. He just wished he had known.

Stephen Thomas picked up the scraps of paper. They contained a couple of handwritten scribbles.

"Family."

"Maze."

Passwords, Stephen Thomas thought. Feral wrote down passwords till he was sure he had memorized them.

He asked Arachne for Feral's locked files.

He tried the word "Maze" as a password.

It was a public key. Not the key itself, of course, which was too long to remember, but a vector to the key.

Arachne responded with a message from Feral.

Please record your observations about the deep space expedition. I'll use your replies in the book I'm

writing. I hope everyone will choose to sign their comments, but you *can* remain anonymous . . .

. . . but if you want to remain anonymous . . .

. . . but if you insist on . . .

Stephen Thomas frowned. This was getting him nowhere. He could send a message, but it would go one-way into Feral's file, encrypted through the public key, and only Feral would be able to get it out. He wondered why he had not known about it.

You don't know about it because it isn't finished! he thought. What else could those last lines be? Feral was tinkering with his announcement, trying to balance his preference for signed contributions with his willingness to respect privacy. He never had a chance to release his project. He set it up, but he never polished it, never told anyone that it existed, never released the public key.

"Shit," Stephen Thomas muttered. "Oh, shit, what a goddamned waste. . . ."

A public key implied a private key. Stephen Thomas fingered the second scrap of paper. "Family."

He was afraid to try it. "Maze" had given him a tantalizing glimpse. "Family" might give him Feral's private key. Or it might give him nothing.

Stephen Thomas turned the soft ragged scrap of paper over and over in his fingers, afraid to speak the word to Arachne, afraid to encounter the same bleak emptiness that had surrounded him when he first learned of Feral's death.

He rubbed his eyes; he spread his fingers across his face and looked at the world distorted by his amber swimming webs.

Closing his eyes again, he spoke to Arachne.

" 'Family' is the private key," he said.

Arachne opened a hidden room to him, a room filled with Feral's log files.

Stephen Thomas stretched out on the bed, and went exploring.

Feral kept lists. A list of places he had been. A list of his articles, of course. A list of the pieces he wanted to write, the places he wanted to go, the people he wanted to interview.

A collection of references he planned to look up: Technical reports on *Starfarer,* on Arachne. The thesis Stephen Thomas had defended in order to earn his Ph.D.

Stephen Thomas smiled sadly. No wonder it was on the "to be read" list. It was technical and specialized, tough going for a member of the field, much less a lay person.

We're even, Stephen Thomas thought. I haven't read much of his stuff and he hadn't read any of mine.

He moved on through the reference list.

Professor Thanthavong's acceptance speech for the Nobel Prize for medicine, for creating viral depolymerase. That one was an important, touching historical document, written years before Feral was born. Before Stephen Thomas was born. It was a shame Feral had never gotten to it. Maybe he had heard it, on one of the documentaries made about the professor. He had known a lot about her; he had admired and respected her.

J.D.'s first novel. Stephen Thomas felt an embarrassing flash of satisfaction that Feral had not read it. It was neither dry nor technical, but it was hard going: obscure and unbalancing, disturbing. As hard to read in its own way as the Ph.D. thesis. When Stephen Thomas had tackled it, he had given up halfway through.

He left the list of work Feral would never see, and glanced into the file of work that Feral had read. It extended back to Feral's early teens. It ranged far and wide over subjects and technical level. Right at the top, most recent, was a book on braiding hair. That struck Stephen Thomas as strange. Feral's chestnut hair had been medium length and curly. Not as curly as Victoria's, but tight enough to keep it out of his face.

He left that file and explored farther, deeper.

He could hear Feral's voice in every sentence. Stephen Thomas forced himself to listen, to stay calm. He could not manage to remain unmoved.

Fantasies made him ache with regret and physical pain; observations made him laugh, and wince, in the darkness. He saw himself through Feral's eyes.

Arrogant and charming, physically compelling, his sexuality insistent and innocent . . .

Stephen Thomas resisted "innocent." Insistent, maybe, though he hoped he was civilized about his affairs. He thought he was. He was capable of backing off, of taking no for an answer, though hardly anyone ever said no to him.

Stephen Thomas is vulnerable . . .

Vulnerable? Stephen Thomas thought. What the fuck did I ever say to Feral, to anybody, that made him think I was vulnerable? Vulnerable about *what*? Bullshit.

He saw a couple of files that referred to J.D. He skipped them. He could not bear to look at them right now.

And then he came upon a picture of himself, a picture altered by Arachne to show his long hair loosely French braided, the light, sun-bleached strands on top crossing the darker blond hair underneath.

He leaned forward in the dark, staring at the picture of himself. In his imagination, Feral separated strands of his hair, smoothed them, plaited them. Stephen Thomas tried to comb his hair with his fingers, tried to loop the strands together the way they were in the picture, but his hair slipped from his grasp when he held it loosely, or cut against the swimming webs when he held it tight.

He felt in danger of breaking down. He let his hair fall; he buried his face against his knees and crossed his arms around his head and curled himself up.

• • • •

J.D. cuddled with Zev, gazing out across the open field.
The river in whose banks Crimson buried her fossils
rushed and gurgled in the quiet night.

Zev sighed and nestled closer. He had begun to
breathe constantly while sleeping on land, instead of in-
termittently as he did in the water. He had begun to
sleep soundly instead of napping like an aquatic mammal.

J.D. wished she could sleep so soundly. But Nemo's
long silence troubled her. If *Starfarer* entered transition
before Nemo called her, would she ever see the
squidmoth again? If *Starfarer* left Nemo behind in the
star system of Sirius, J.D. would not have to witness
Nemo's death. But Nemo would die alone.

She touched Arachne, looking for messages. Silly;
unnecessary. When Nemo called, J.D. would know.

A breeze sprang up. It flowed past the open French
windows, bringing the scent of spring flowers, new grass,
even a hint of the sea. Strange: shouldn't the breeze
flow toward the sea, this time of night?

The night grew darker as clouds collected. The
breeze, gusting faster, chilled the air.

J.D. snuggled deeper in the comforter. Zev made a
questioning sound in his sleep, and rubbed his cheek
against her breast. She stroked his fine pale hair. His
body felt hot against her.

Outside, the breeze evolved into a wind; it rushed
across the field and into the house, rattling the windows.
It touched her face with icy fingers, ruffling her hair and
Zev's.

I should get up and close the windows, she thought.
But she did not want to disturb Zev, and the cold had
not yet penetrated the comforter. There was no hint of
rain, only the insistent wind. It whistled and hummed; it
rattled in a nearby stand of bamboo.

J.D. thought the first white flakes were flower petals,
whipped and scattered from a cherry tree. Some of

them landed on the comforter at her feet. They disappeared, leaving a dark, wet patch.

Snow.

The snow surprised her, but a quick touch to Arachne assured her that it did, on occasion, snow on board *Starfarer*.

Within a few minutes the snow was falling fast and hard, huge wet flakes driven horizontal by the wind. J.D. slid from beneath Zev's warm arm and went to the windows. The wintry air exhilarated her, roused her, almost as much as diving into the sea. Before she started to shiver, her metabolic enhancer kicked in.

Zev joined her by the window, sliding his arm around her waist. She hugged his shoulders. They stood together, in silence, watching the late spring blizzard, thinking how beautiful it was.

A spot of warmth blossomed at the back of J.D.'s mind.

With a start of excitement, J.D. closed her eyes and accepted the message.

"J.D.," Nemo said, "it is time to come and witness my metamorphosis."

"I'll get my colleagues," J.D. replied. "We'll be there in—"

"Come in your ship alone," Nemo said.

"Alone?"

She did not think of danger, but of disappointment. Victoria and Satoshi and Stephen Thomas—how could she tell them they could not come? And Zev—? He stood beside her, watching her expectantly, made aware by her physical reaction that something was happening.

"Nemo, please—they'll be so sad. . . ."

"You are frightened."

"No!"

"I will transmit instead. You need not come."

She was sure she heard regret in Nemo's voice, and she knew she had to go. By herself. How could she let Nemo change and die, all alone?

"I will," J.D. replied. "I'll be there soon."

. . .

Stephen Thomas fell into an exhausted sleep. Maybe
the sleep did him some good. Near dawn he woke,
moved cautiously, stretched, and discovered that he no
longer itched and ached. Tentatively, he slid his hand
between his legs.

He bolted up, snatching away the bedclothes and
dragging down his shorts.

His genitals had pulled themselves nearly inside him.

Though he knew what to expect, he still felt shocked
and scared and sick. He tried to control the new muscles, the changed muscles, to extend or retract. Nothing
happened. He was stuck three quarters of the way between ordinary human and diver. Stephen Thomas
shifted uncomfortably. He felt no pain, only a tense discomfort. But he sure looked weird.

What the hell am I going to do, Stephen Thomas
thought, if I *can't* learn the control?

The skin of his penis was soft and new and very
sensitive, so sensitive that touching it brought back the
threat of pain.

"Fuck it," he muttered. "Or don't." He lay down
and flung himself over, twisting himself in the blankets.

When Arachne signaled an urgent message, he
wanted to ignore it, he wanted to refuse it. Instead, he
struggled up again and accepted it.

"What?"

J.D.'s image appeared in his room.

"Victoria, Satoshi, Stephen Thomas," she said. Was
it only his imagination, or had she hesitated before saying his name?

As she spoke, holograms of Victoria and Satoshi appeared nearby. Arachne oriented their images as if they
were all in the observers' circle. Stephen Thomas could
project his image and join them. He remained invisible.

"Nemo's called me."

"We'll be right there!" Victoria said, excited.

"There's something else," J.D. said.

"What is it?" Satoshi asked.

"Nemo asked me . . . to come alone. Alone on the *Chi*, I mean."

Stephen Thomas flopped back on the bed in disbelief.

"I'm sorry," J.D. said. "I tried to . . . I'm sorry."

Zev's image appeared, too, in his usual place to J.D.'s left.

"I can't go, either," he said sadly. "Nemo won't let me."

"How can it stop us?" Stephen Thomas asked angrily.

J.D. glanced toward the place Stephen Thomas would be if he were sending his image. From her point of view, his voice would emanate from an empty spot in the air. From his point of view, she looked straight at him.

"I don't know," she said mildly. "But I also don't know that I want to find out."

Victoria, too, glanced toward Stephen Thomas's invisible presence.

"It isn't something we're going to test," she said. "It would be . . . bad manners."

"What the hell difference does it make?" Stephen Thomas said. "No matter what we do, we don't measure up to what Civilization expects of us. We might as well behave badly and get some benefit out of their shitty opinion."

"No." Victoria turned away from him. "And if you insist on being invisible, you can be invisible." She spoke to J.D. "Get ready. We'll be over to see you off. To help if we can."

"Oh, Victoria," J.D. said. "Why come all that way in this weather?"

"Nonsense. We'll see you in a few minutes."

"All right." J.D. smiled, gratefully. "Thanks."

Her image faded out, and so did Victoria's.

What weather? Stephen Thomas wondered. A storm, like wild side's, on campus? Was I sleeping so hard I didn't even hear it? What the hell is going on?

Stephen Thomas went to the balcony door and

cupped his hands around his face to look outside. The night was bright with a layer of shining snow, and flakes drifted from the sky. He cracked the door open. Cold air washed over him. It felt alive, it felt like the bubbles in champagne. The snowflakes landed with a faint, musical, crinkling sound.

"Stephen Thomas?"

Stephen Thomas turned quickly. Satoshi's image remained in the middle of the room. Satoshi gazed into thin air like a blind man.

"Are you still there? Are you all right? Where are you?"

"I'm all right."

"Will you project, dammit?"

"I don't have any clothes on."

Satoshi hesitated. "I don't care. I want to see you."

"What are you so mad about?" Stephen Thomas asked.

"Mad? Why should I be mad? You withdraw, you disappear—"

"You can find me if you want me!"

"I started to. But you acted like you wanted time alone. I can't read your mind, I—"

He stopped, upset and confused.

"I can't read yours, either, Satoshi," Stephen Thomas said quietly.

"No," Satoshi said. "I know you can't. Look, I'm sorry about— We have to talk. I'm afraid you—" He glanced away, to reply to Victoria, outside the area of his image. "Be right there," he said over his shoulder. "Will you meet us at the dock?" he asked Stephen Thomas.

Stephen Thomas had no idea how he would react when he saw J.D. again. One temper tantrum was plenty for any twenty-four hour stretch.

It's not her fault, he told himself. None of this is her fault. Or Victoria's, or Satoshi's.

"Come on," Satoshi said, his tone uncharacteristically edgy. "The weather's not *that* bad."

"Okay," Stephen Thomas said quickly. "I'm on my way."

J.D. asked Arachne to notify the rest of the faculty and staff of Nemo's message, but she put no emergency flag on her communication. There was no point to rousing people out of their warm beds, just to sit around waiting till she reached the planetoid. In an hour or two they would wake up, admire the snow, drink their morning coffee, and watch whatever she was able to send back.

J.D. waded through the drifts. Zev leaped along beside her. She smiled. She loved to watch him. He scooped up a loose handful of snow and threw it, the way he had flung the oranges. It scattered into J.D.'s hair. She decided not to show him how to make a snowball. She was sure he would figure it out for himself soon enough.

"It snowed once when I was a kid," he said. "But not very much."

He was wearing his suit and his shoes. Divers enjoyed cold water, but Zev was neither acclimated nor adapted to arctic conditions. The snow caught in the cuffs of his pants, forming icy pellets.

J.D. looked up, hoping for a break in the clouds, a glimpse of the other side of *Starfarer*. All she could see was snow falling from the luminous grayness of the night sky.

Arachne guided J.D. to an access hatch. Knee-deep snow covered it, pressing it down so it could not open automatically. J.D. kicked the snow away. The hatch buzzed and groaned, trying to rise.

"Help me, Zev." She groped for the emergency handle, grasped it, and pulled. Zev hunkered down, grabbed the edge, and pushed.

The hatch popped open. Wet clumps of snow avalanched into the entrance. J.D. and Zev climbed into the warm service tunnels of the starship, the veins in its skin that led to its underground organs, and all the way to the outside. More snow fell in with them and around them and on top of them. J.D. brushed it from her shoulders and hair, and did the same for Zev. She stamped her feet, leaving a patch of slush on the rock-foam floor.

J.D. continued toward the docking end of campus. She squelched along in snow-soaked shoes that grew wetter, but no less cold, as the snow melted. She hurried, anxious to reach Nemo before the squidmoth emerged from the chrysalis.

We should have stayed, she thought. If we'd stayed, the whole alien contact department would be there. Not just me.

She and Zev met no one. Hardly anyone ever had the need to come down here. Infinity did, J.D. knew, and Kolya, when they went out on the skin. Even if people did often use the access tunnels, anyone with any sense would be asleep. She hoped everyone would wake up in time to see the snow, because it was beautiful. She also hoped it would be melted by the time she returned.

"You can tell me what *Starfarer* looks like," she said to Zev, "when the clouds have snowed themselves out, but before the snow melts. It will be pretty, with everything covered in white."

"I'd rather come with you."

"I know. I'm sorry."

"Squids *never* do what you tell them," Zev said.

"They don't?"

"No. They make terrible pets." He considered for a moment. "I guess it's because they're always afraid you'll eat them."

When J.D. and Zev floated into the waiting room at the *Chi*'s dock, Victoria and Satoshi had already arrived. There was no sign of Stephen Thomas. J.D. wondered if he was still trying to avoid her.

Victoria kicked off from the handhold, brushed against J.D., and hugged her. As they spun slowly across the waiting room, J.D. held Victoria, bending to rest her head on her shoulder. When she finally drew back from their embrace, she kissed Victoria's cheek, her lips. Victoria laid her hand along the side of J.D.'s face and looked into her eyes.

"Good luck," she said. "I hope . . . I don't know. Just good luck."

"I want you all with me," J.D. said. "I don't understand . . ."

"I wouldn't want a lot of people hanging around staring at me if I were changing my shape," Satoshi said, just as Stephen Thomas arrowed in through the doorway.

"I don't know," Stephen Thomas said, his tone careful, brittle, and offhand, his sapphire eyes shocking and intense against the new bronze of his skin. "As a life experience, it's got its points."

"I didn't mean—" Satoshi said, flustered. "I was talking about Nemo."

Stephen Thomas shrugged and touched the far wall, bringing himself to a stop. His thin damp clothes clung to his body. He ran his hands along the sides of his head, slicking the curling tendrils of his wet hair. He separated two thick strands from the temples and twisted them at the nape of his neck to hold back the rest of his hair.

"You must be freezing!" Victoria said.

Stephen Thomas glanced at Satoshi. "What do you mean, the weather isn't *that* bad? How bad does it have to get?"

"If you dressed in something more than underwear—"

"You used to like my clothes."

"J.D.," Nemo said in J.D.'s mind.

Nemo's voice slid smoothly along J.D.'s enhanced link, following the surface of a four-dimensional melody onto a fifth dimension.

"It is time."

"I have to go." Still caught in Nemo's melody, J.D. could barely whisper. "I'm sorry. . . ."

"How long will you be gone?" Victoria asked.

"I have no idea."

"We're going into transition in a few hours! You've got to come back before then."

"But . . ." Her voice trailed off. She glanced around, from Victoria, to Satoshi, to Stephen Thomas and quickly away, finally to Zev. "I have to . . ."

"Nemo must understand the problem," Stephen Thomas said. "Maybe it'll hurry up—"

J.D. glared at him angrily. "Hurry up and die?"

He shut up. J.D. wished she had overlooked his careless comment; surely he had not meant to sound so inconsiderate.

"I'm sorry—" J.D. said.

"Never mind." His voice was hard; he sounded the way he had yesterday, just before he stalked away from the AS repair. "You're right. Of course."

"I'm going," J.D. said. "I only wish you were all coming with me. You know that, I hope."

"Of course we do," Victoria said, worried. She kicked off gently toward her and embraced her again. They parted reluctantly. Satoshi's hug was friendly, Stephen Thomas's brief and cool. Zev hugged her and kissed her cheek, her lips, the base of her throat.

And then the hatch was closing behind her and she was alone in the *Chi*.

J.D. hurried to the observation circle and strapped herself into her couch.

The hatch access retracted with a loud, mechanical *clang*. Arachne finished the launching check and gave over control to the onboard computer, an expert system that would ferry her to Nemo's ship, and back, without her intervention. She had not given it a second thought when she was on board the *Chi* with her colleagues; now, alone, she was worried.

How silly, she thought. No one in alien contact is a pilot. If the computer failed we'd all have been in trouble.

As far as she knew, Esther Klein was the only person on *Starfarer* who knew how to fly spaceships. Every time someone proposed to save money by eliminating human pilots from the transport runs, the proposal failed. Now J.D. understood why.

The edge of the dock slid past the transparent surface of the observers' circle.

J.D. was free in space.

Starfarer loomed, first a rock face, turning, beyond its support structure, then resolving into a pair of huge rock cylinders that faced her end-on, one spinning clockwise, the other counter-clockwise. Off to one side, the stellar sail gleamed in the sunlight. The sail powered *Starfarer*'s headlong flight from Sirius, toward the cosmic string, toward its plunge into transition.

The *Chi*'s engines vibrated. Their subsonic moan surrounded her. The acceleration pressed her gently toward the straps of her couch. The *Chi* spun so the observers' circle faced forward, away from *Starfarer*. The effect was of the acceleration moving around her, pushing her first from the back, then from the side, finally settling her into the cushions. The couch folded at her hips and knees, moving halfway to its chair configuration.

Starfarer fell behind her.

She could not yet pick Nemo's dark little planetoid from the starfield. She felt alone, and isolated.

During her two previous trips on the explorer, she had often come to the circle and sat alone in the transparent chamber to watch the stars. The darkness and the beauty had been soothing. Now, riding the deserted ship away from *Starfarer* and her colleagues, she felt alone and apprehensive. Her veneer of confidence dissolved, revealing the bravado behind it.

She could feel the presence of her colleagues, watching her, as the public access transmitted her image back to the starship. Instructing the computer to focus the exterior camera on Nemo's ship, J.D. transferred the image to the public access transmission. Once she herself no longer occupied the center of public attention, she felt easier.

The PA channel reproduced Nemo's planetoid in the center of the observers' circle. Stark white light gleamed from the silk-filled craters and threw the rocky surface into deep relief.

Victoria's image appeared before J.D. The Milky Way shone faintly through the translucent image. The effect intensified J.D.'s impression that she was riding in a ghost ship.

"Want some company?" Victoria said.

"Yes."

"About Stephen Thomas . . ." Victoria said. "I'm sorry. There's no excuse for his behavior."

J.D. could think of lots of excuses, or at least lots of reasons, and it surprised her that Victoria apologized for him instead of defending him. But, of course, Victoria did not even know the real reason. J.D. supposed she should tell her, but she could not bring herself to do so.

"He's under a lot of stress." Trying to be tactful, J.D. ended up feeling evasive.

Victoria laughed. "But he thrives on stress. If he doesn't have enough in his life, he does something to stir more up."

J.D. smiled. "A useful trait, thriving on stress. I wish I had a touch of it myself."

"Everything will be all right," Victoria said. "I trust your instincts about Nemo. You were right about Europa and Androgeos."

"I guess I was," J.D. said. "I wish I'd been wrong."

J.D. was the one who had realized how desperately Europa wanted Victoria's transition algorithm: so desperately that she was willing, in effect, to steal it.

"Would you do me a favor?" J.D. asked.

"Of course."

"Ask Zev to stay with you while I'm gone? Divers don't spend much time away from their families."

She remembered how desperately lonely she had been on *Starfarer* at first, before Zev arrived, before Victoria first kissed her. She had felt like she was starving to death through her skin.

"As good as done," Victoria said.

"Thanks."

"J.D . . ." Victoria said.

"Hmm?"

"Please come back before *Starfarer* goes into transition."

"I will if I can."

"You *have* to! It's too risky otherwise. Something might go wrong. You might end up anywhere."

"Victoria, you're scaring me. I'll do my best. I promise."

"I know you will."

Victoria looked like she was about to burst into tears. The change was so sudden and so unexpected that J.D. involuntarily reached toward her. Toward her image. Feeling foolish, J.D. pulled back. It would not have surprised J.D. to be having this conversation with Zev; it did surprise her to be having it with Victoria.

Victoria wiped her eyes. Her chin stopped quivering.

"Sorry," she said, trying to smile. "I didn't mean to do that. I miss you already. I can't imagine . . ." She stopped.

"Then don't," J.D. said, chiding her gently. "Imagine me coming home."

Infinity opened the access tunnel, expecting night, and emerged into a white-out.

Thick sloppy clumps of snow slid through the opening onto his face. He was so surprised that he ducked back into the tunnel and let the hatch *thunk* shut over him.

Snow? It was far too late in the year for snow on *Starfarer*. When it did snow, it frosted the ground with a light sugar-coating of small, dry, sparkling flakes that sublimed at the first touch of the sun.

Infinity brushed away the clusters of heavy wet snow melting on his shoulders. He touched Arachne, asking for a way to change the weather, demanding an explanation.

What a mess, he thought, when he saw the reply. Arachne tried to cool things down—but now the weather's oscillating between extremes. We're in trouble. If we don't get to 61 Cygni soon, and *stay* there for a while . . . we're dead.

Arachne could open the sun tubes early and pour heat into campus. The snow would stop . . . and a monsoon would start. Rain and melting snow would saturate the land. The result would be floods, erosion, mudslides.

He could tell Arachne to shut off all heat transfer into the ship, to starve the weather of energy. Then they would get a hard freeze. Probably an ice storm. That would be disastrous for the vegetation and the animals.

As far as Infinity could tell, letting the snow fall till the clouds exhausted themselves would cause the least damage.

He was glad the planting had only just started, that the seeds had not had time to germinate. Some of the crops would survive.

They'll survive if this doesn't happen again later in the spring, he thought. Arachne's got to get a chance to stabilize the weather.

He climbed out of the hatch into the snow.

The oranges, Infinity thought. The damned oranges . . . if they freeze, Gerald will love saying "I told you so."

The snow fell hard and fast. Infinity was only fifty meters from his front door, but he would have been lost without Arachne to guide him home.

He stumbled into his house and closed the door quickly. Esther slept, her snoring a soft buzz. The lights rose.

"Dim!" he whispered.

Esther sat up in bed, blinking in the twilight.

"Hi," she said sleepily. "What happened? You're all wet."

"It's snowing."

He started to shiver. Esther jumped up and hurried to him, pulling the blankets with her. She took off his sodden shirt. He fumbled at the buttons of his jeans. The cold had numbed his fingers, though he had been outside only a few minutes. Esther pushed his hands away, helped him finish undressing, and wrapped the blanket around them both.

"You're so cold!" She rubbed his back, and warmed his hands between his body and her own. "Come to bed and get warm."

"I can't," he said. "We need to call out everybody, and call in all the slugs—"

He paused long enough to tell Arachne to sound the alarm.

"We have to go around and knock the snow off the plants. It's too heavy, it'll break the branches. The citrus trees . . . if we open the access tunnels, and force warm air out around them, maybe we can keep them from freezing."

Esther slumped against him, resting her forehead against his chest. She had spent another whole day in the basement of the administration building.

"Open *all* the access tunnels," she said. "What about the sun tubes? Spotlight the orange grove."

"I wish," he said.

He showed her Arachne's report. Esther took in the risk at one glance and whistled softly. Warming a single spot with the sun tubes in this weather would not start a monsoon. It would start a tornado.

"Damn." She sighed. "I've been lying in bed for the last hour, I kept falling asleep and waking up and thinking how cold it was and how nice it would be when you got home and got in beside me."

His hands felt warm, now, nestled against her belly. He wrapped his arms around her and held her close. His long hair, still wet, swung forward and touched her cheek. A drop of icy water flicked from the end of one lock and dripped on her face.

"When this is done, we can stay in bed all day."

Esther giggled.

"What?"

"I was griping this afternoon that I had to work inside." She quoted an aphorism favored by transport pilots: "Be careful what you wish for, you might get it."

A few minutes later, dressed in dry clothes—the

warmest he had; Esther wearing one of his flannel shirts under her jacket—they hurried out into the deepening snow. Arachne guided them to the access tunnel. The snow formed a curtain, as featureless and impenetrable as full darkness. The flakes turned sharp and hard and dry. If they froze, it might be better to risk rain and floods.

Infinity just did not know.

As they passed through his garden, he wondered, briefly, if his cactus would survive.

Infinity's message spread through *Starfarer*'s night, asking people for help and alerting them to the danger of the snow's beauty.

Stephen Thomas followed a medium-sized silver slug into a young apple orchard. The trees bent beneath the snow. Infinity had recommended knocking away the snow if the tree leaned over, if it looked like it might break.

The slug burrowed through to the ground and pushed itself forward, ploughing the heavy wet snow to either side. Stephen Thomas walked in the cleared path, grateful that he did not have to break trail. He was wearing his warmest clothes, but his warmest clothes did not amount to much.

At least the snow had stopped falling.

Following the slug at a respectful distance, Stephen Thomas used its trail to get to the saplings. If he pulled the outer branches gently, he could knock off the snow without standing beneath an avalanche. He could not tell if the apple blossom buds were damaged.

Being so near the silver slug made Stephen Thomas wary. He knew, intellectually, that this one had no reason to turn on him. The one that had pinned him down had been protecting Chancellor Blades. But if—*if*—the slug did attack, Professor Thanthavong might not come along this time to release him.

In the distance, a tree branch snapped with a violent

crack. Its covering of snow cascaded down to land with a feathery thud.

As Stephen Thomas worked in the orchard, he let his attention drift back into Feral's files. He still avoided the notes on J.D. Stephen Thomas liked J.D.; he did not want to spoil his affection for her by feeding his stupid jealousy.

Feral would still be alive if any one of half a dozen events had occurred only a little differently. If he had been involved in the web more shallowly. If he had heard J.D.'s warning, or Victoria's. If Stephen Thomas had not so easily restored Feral's canceled guest access to Arachne.

Feral had logged the incident in which he had been thrown from the web. It was such an unusual thing to happen that Stephen Thomas set it aside for later, when he could give it his full attention.

The slug crawled through the orchard and headed across a meadow. Stephen Thomas was tempted to call it back, to get it to break a trail through the drooping pear trees a few fields over. Surely Infinity had enough slugs to uncover the access hatches among the orange trees?

Stephen Thomas stamped his cold feet. Infinity had recommended that no one stay out in the snow too long. Stephen Thomas decided to go inside for a while and get warm. When he came back out, maybe he could borrow another silver slug.

The whole world was black and white, silver and gray, motionless. Stephen Thomas stretched. The clouds had snowed themselves out; the sky had cleared except for an icy cloud blanket around the sun tube.

Obliquely overhead, on the far side of *Starfarer*'s interior, black streams meandered through the white landscape. A pinprick of darkness appeared where someone knocked the snowy cover from a sapling.

Zev slogged from one buried sapling to another. J.D.'s transmission of Nemo's planetoid followed him.

Back home, when his family returned from their migration, the sea water was cold with winter. Summer would not touch the sea for a month yet. But he had never felt so cold in the sea as he did now. He was wearing his suit, and a sweater of J.D.'s, but still he shivered.

At the moment, Zev envied Victoria, even though he knew she was risking her life. She had gone out to the sailhouse to help Jenny Dupre align *Starfarer* for transition, doing the same task Feral had been doing when he died. Zev understood that Victoria was in danger. Risk was always more exciting and more fun than discomfort.

His hands were nearly numb. He had no gloves. He had wrapped his hands in clothing, and he carried a bundle of bamboo with which to knock the dense, heavy covering of snow from the collapsing branches. But if he unwrapped his fingers, his swimming webs would be gray with cold.

He banged the bamboo against a drooping, bending evergreen shrub. The sticks hit with a quiet crinkle of wood on ice. The wet snow beneath the new ice let loose with a soft, sliding *thud*. The straining evergreen shrub exploded upward. Zev did not move fast enough when the boughs sprang free. Snow and ice erupted like a geyser, showering his chest and face and hair.

He brushed away the melting clumps and the frozen shards. His wet hair slicked down cold around his ears; ice water dribbled down the back of his neck and under his collar.

Zev found himself staring at a hummock of snow, not only wondering if it was bending or leaning or merely, safely, crouching, but wondering if it were a plant. He was so cold, and none of this was any fun. But almost everyone was outdoors tramping through the snow, making sure the animals had shelter, trying to save young trees from breaking beneath their freezing shrouds.

He worked his way toward Satoshi, on the other side of a line of trees. The snow collapsed and slid, avalanching as Satoshi knocked it free.

Zev joined him and worked alongside him.

"I'm very cold, Satoshi. You look cold too."

"I'm all right," Satoshi said, but his teeth chattered.

"I think we should go inside and warm up."

"In a while," Satoshi said stubbornly. "You go ahead. I want to do a little more."

Zev followed, unwilling to leave Satoshi out alone in the snow. He wondered if hypothermia was less serious on land than in the sea. He doubted it, and he thought Satoshi was right on the edge.

They walked through a stand of young lilac bushes, knocking away the icy blanket to release the bright green leaves, the heavy purple and white blossoms, and the disorienting fragrance of lilacs in the snow.

"Infinity said not to stay out too long." Zev did not like to argue with someone older than himself. Among the divers, it was very bad manners. But this was different. Hypothermia caused confusion in the wisest, most experienced person.

"We haven't been out that long," Satoshi said.

"You're shivering."

"Do you want all the plants to die?" Satoshi spoke more sharply than Zev had ever heard him.

"No, but I don't want you to die either."

"I'm not going to die."

"Do you hear something?" Zev stopped. Before Satoshi could answer, Zev plunged between two bushes that showered him with snow and wilted lilac flowerets.

In a clearing in the middle of the lilac grove, Chandra stood naked, arms spread wide, gazing up into the clouded sky. The chattering of her teeth had attracted Zev's attention. Her clothes lay in a sodden pile, ice crystals forming on the folds.

"Chandra!"

She lowered her head and looked at him with her strange, blank-gray eyes, but she did not answer him. Her fingers were blue with cold. Swollen nerve clusters twisted and bulged all over her body and her face and her hands.

"How long have you been out here?"

Satoshi followed Zev into the clearing.

"What's the matter with her?"

Chandra tried to reply to Zev, but her teeth chattered so hard she could not speak.

"I think she's collecting an experience," Zev said. "But I think we should get her inside."

"What about the trees?" Satoshi looked around at all the lilacs bent over and crushed in the snow. "I feel sorry for the little trees."

Stephen Thomas heard the flutter and snort of horsy breath, and the muffled beat of hooves. The herd of miniature horses broke from the edge of the forest. They plunged through the meadow, spraying snow, lithe animal shapes, brown and chestnut and gold against the stark landscape.

Squealing, they galloped and plunged through snow up to their chests, toward a person standing uncertainly in the meadow.

It was Florrie Brown. Florrie was the last person Stephen Thomas wanted to see, this side of Fox.

Stephen Thomas wished he could vanish into the orchard, but he was taller than most of the young trees.

The herd exploded past Florrie, wheeled around, and galloped toward her again. She never moved, but wrapped her arms around herself, hugging her fringed black poncho tight. She flinched when the horses crowded her.

Stephen Thomas wondered why she was so frightened. She often sat on her front porch, feeding tidbits to the miniature horses. Sometimes they climbed up on the porch beside her.

He crossed the field, kicking away the snow. It caked on the legs of his pants.

"Go on, shoo!" he shouted.

The appaloosa stud flung up his head, nostrils flaring. Stephen Thomas's scent spooked him. He squealed and kicked and plunged away, and the whole herd vanished into the evergreens.

Florrie stood shaking among the hoofprints.

"Did you have to scare them?" she said. "I thought they'd knock me over."

He stopped.

"I thought you wanted them gone," he said.

She looked back across the field, toward her house fifty meters distant.

"It's so slippery out here, I was afraid I'd fall."

"Why'd you come out, then?"

"I'm going to work, of course. To the cafeteria. People still have to eat." She squinted at him, peering up into his face. "Are you Stephen Thomas?"

"Of course I am," he said, startled.

"You look so different. I didn't recognize you."

"I don't look *that* different," he said. Not where she could see him. "Do you need some help, or do you want me to disappear again?"

"I'm afraid to fall," she said.

Stephen Thomas took this as one of her roundabout ways of getting something without coming right out and asking for it. He could hardly leave her out here in the field. He offered her his arm.

"I'll walk over with you," he said.

She hesitated, then grasped his elbow with both hands. They walked in silence for a while.

"You shouldn't have teased us," she said. "Me and Fox."

"Teased you!"

"Flirted with us. Without meaning anything."

"I never flirt unless I mean it. I never flirted with Fox at all. Did she say I did?"

"She said . . . she fell in love with you. But you hurt her feelings, and I thought you planned to hurt mine."

"Thanks a lot." He glanced down at her. "So you decided I'm a malicious shithead."

"What was I supposed to decide?"

"I'm glad to know the depths of our friendship," Stephen Thomas said bitterly.

"I thought you *liked* me!" Florrie said.

"I thought the feeling was mutual," Stephen Thomas said. "Why did you change your mind?"

"I *told* you. I thought you didn't mean any of it."

"Why didn't you ask me, instead of lighting into me like that?"

"Because I was angry. For Fox. But now you're mad at me. And so is she."

Stephen Thomas sighed.

They approached the cafeteria. The silver slugs had partially cleared the path, but had not got all the way down to the rock foam. The beaten snow had turned to ice, with a treacherous texture of frozen ripples. Someone should have scraped the path, but there was probably not a snow shovel to be had on board *Starfarer*.

Stephen Thomas walked carefully. Florrie grabbed tight to his arm. If he slipped and went down, she would fall, too.

"Aren't you?" she said. "Mad at me."

"I wish you'd had enough regard for my friendship to get my side of what happened," he said.

They reached the porch of the cafeteria. Stephen Thomas helped her up the ramp, over the threshold. Here the floor was merely wet and slick, not icy. Warmth and the aroma of herbs and hot pepper, cooking food, surrounded him. His stomach growled. He was famished. He could hardly remember when he had eaten last, and he could not think when he had been so hungry. He could even imagine diving into the lake and coming up with a fish to eat raw, as Zev had done the other day.

Cold as he was, the idea of diving into a chilly lake gave him a thrill of pleasure.

"So that's all it was," Florrie said, her voice cutting and sarcastic. "Just friendship. How very flattering."

Stephen Thomas glanced at her, surprised and confused. Friendship was an important word to him, one he did not take lightly or offer easily. He had had fewer close friends than lovers in his life.

"It could have been friendship," he said.

Florrie drew herself up angrily. "Then you never *were* serious."

When she took on that imperious tone, Stephen Thomas found it even easier than usual to see beyond the changes of age and the papery delicacy of her skin, even past the character time had given her. The stunning beauty of her youth overwhelmed all that. No wonder she expected people to throw themselves at her feet, and no wonder they did. She attracted people, and they wanted to please her.

She glared at him.

"I thought as much."

She let go of his arm and left him, making her way toward her helpers, who greeted her and waved and hurried over to help her out of her layers of dramatic black wraps.

I *told* her how I felt, and she didn't believe me, he thought. Damned if I'll tell her again. Give her another blade, when she's already proved she'd use it to cut out my guts? Fuck it.

His feet were so cold he could barely feel them. It was time to take Infinity's cautions seriously and get warm. Not here, though. The smell of boiled coffee made him feel sick.

He grabbed a couple of hot lunches from the holding table and plunged back out into the cold, heading home.

Maybe Satoshi would be home for a little while, too, and they could eat together and talk while they got warm.

Satoshi was right. They needed to talk.

"Over here!" Zev shouted.

The crunch, crunch, crunch of footsteps on icy snow came closer. Infinity Mendez appeared at the edge of the clearing.

"How are you guys—" He saw Chandra.

"Satoshi doesn't want to go inside," Zev said. "Neither does Chandra, I think."

"The trees—" Satoshi said.

"I'm not done." Chandra's shivering made her words nearly unintelligible. "Am I saving anything? My brain is cold."

"I *told* everybody—!" Infinity cut off his outburst and continued, more quietly. "Come on, Chandra, you've been outside too long. You, too, Satoshi."

He took off his outer coat, started to put it around Chandra's shoulders, but suddenly changed his mind and gave her his heavy inner shirt instead. When he put his coat back on he felt the inside pocket as if he was afraid he had lost something.

"Where does she live?"

"I don't know," Zev said. "But Satoshi's house is over there, and it has a big bathtub."

Infinity looked very worried. "Damn, if people didn't pay attention . . ."

Infinity let his eyelids flicker, going into a communications fugue with Arachne. Zev felt a warm spot at the back of his mind that meant an emergency message. He grabbed at it, hoping it was from J.D. He glanced at the exterior planetoid image, which had followed him obediently into the lilacs.

The emergency message was not from J.D.; it was the message Infinity had just sent to everyone on board, warning them again not to stay out too long.

Chandra had apparently read the message, too.

"You just *told* me that," she said querulously, as Infinity led her across the field. Zev followed, pulling Satoshi along.

With Zev helping Satoshi and Infinity helping Chandra, the cold little group reached the partnership's house. Inside, the warmth of the air closed in around Zev but barely touched him. He wished he were bathing in the hotsprings where the divers lounged and played.

Stephen Thomas sat at the kitchen table, wrapped in a red kimono, drinking hot tea. His wet clothes lay in a pile near the door, soaking one of Satoshi's floormats.

"I was about to come looking for you guys," Stephen Thomas said mildly to Satoshi. Then Infinity came in with Chandra. "Christ on a toboggan, what happened to her?"

"Is there more tea?" Infinity said.

Stephen Thomas had already jumped up to get more mugs.

Satoshi stared at the water dripping from his clothes and hair onto one of the floor mats he had made. He moved off the mat, but stumbled. Stephen Thomas steadied him, wrapped Satoshi's hands around a warm mug, and held them there. With his help, Satoshi sipped the tea.

Zev hurried down the hall to the bathroom, shedding his wet, cold clothing. By the time he reached the blue glass tub, the household controller had already responded to Stephen Thomas's orders. Hot water gushed into the tub, and the rock-foam floor heated itself. He felt much better naked, with warm air folding itself around him, warm stone beneath his feet.

Infinity and Stephen Thomas followed him into the big bathroom, bringing Chandra and Satoshi.

"I got some good stuff." Chandra sounded drowsy. Zev had heard her say the same thing before—when she nearly drowned in the divers' wilderness, before he got her to the artificial lung.

"Don't go to sleep!" Infinity chafed Chandra's hands. "What you almost got is frostbite," he said. "Not quite, but close."

Stephen Thomas helped Satoshi into the big tub. Infinity turned Chandra toward it, too, but she held back.

"I don't *like* water," she said.

Zev jumped into the tub. The hot water stung his chilled feet.

"It's okay, Chandra," he said. "Remember? You were okay when you swam with me."

He took her cold hand and drew her forward. She resisted, then relaxed and came to him and stepped delicately over the rim and into the water.

The tub was more than big enough for three people. Maybe land people liked bathtubs they could nearly swim in. That seemed strange to Zev, to want to be in a place not *quite* big enough for swimming. He gave up trying to figure it out, and let himself sink into the tub beside Chandra. She had stopped shivering. She held her teacup close to her face, breathing the fragrant steam.

Lying between Zev and Chandra, but with his feet pointed the other direction, Satoshi was coming back to himself. Stephen Thomas sat on the edge of the tub, mostly covered by the kimono. Zev wondered how his changes were progressing. Claws had begun to form in the clefts where Stephen Thomas used to have toenails.

"I don't *believe* I said that stuff," Satoshi said. "Sad for the little trees? God."

"You get confused when you get hypothermia," Infinity said. He was the only one of them still fully clothed; he was also the only one of them who had spent time outdoors without getting soaked to the skin. He shrugged inside his heavy jacket.

"Are you okay?" Stephen Thomas asked.

"Yes," Infinity said quickly. "Sure, why?"

"You look uncomfortable."

"It's too hot in here." He let his eyelids flicker. "Esther and Kolya and Griffith are checking on people," he said when he opened his eyes. "I better go help. Will you folks be all right?"

"I think you got to us in time," Satoshi said. "We'll keep an eye on Chandra, though. Thanks."

Infinity left. It seemed to Zev that as well as being uncomfortable he was upset, but no one said anything about that. Stephen Thomas stroked Satoshi's shoulder; Satoshi lay up to his neck in the hot water and stared into the steam; Chandra . . . who could tell, by looking at her, what Chandra thought or felt?

Satoshi had not even noticed when Zev tried to tell him he was getting too cold, and that made Zev feel hurt. He let himself relax, took a deep breath, and submerged completely in the comforting hot water. His breathing automatically ceased.

He was suddenly surrounded by splashes and shouts. He sat up again, spilling water over the side of the tub.

"What's the matter?"

"I was afraid you'd passed out!" Satoshi said. "I thought you were going to drown!"   •

"I won't drown," Zev said. "It's warmer, okay?"

"Okay," Satoshi said doubtfully.

Zev took Satoshi's hand, and submerged again, keeping hold so Satoshi would know he had not died.

J.D. gazed through the *Chi*'s transparent wall. Nemo's planetoid had expanded from an obscure point of light to a perceptible disk. The stars spread out beyond it, a field of colorful, dimensionless points. The starship was a shape of variegated light and darkness, approaching fast. It looked different from when she had left.

J.D. glanced toward its image; she asked the *Chi* for magnification.

"Omigosh!"

The surface of each silvered crater no longer lay concave within the rock, but had swelled into a hemispherical bulge. Only the one J.D. had entered remained in its original shape.

· Messages flew back and forth and around *Starfarer,* within Arachne, an excited whisper in the background of J.D.'s mind, as her colleagues discussed the planetoid's changes, noticed new ones, and speculated.

"Nemo!" She sent the communication direct, without thinking or worrying about it, without the usual hesitation of direct contact with another being.

"I am here, J.D."

"Your ship—your body . . . it's changing."

"My body is changing," Nemo agreed.

"I'll be there soon."

"I am anxious to see you."

The *Chi* closed in on the worldlet, spurred by J.D.'s anxiety, edging close to the safety limit of its fuel supply.

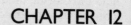

CHAPTER 12

THE *CHI* LANDED NEAR NEMO'S CRATER. The tunnel extension remained, lying relaxed on the ground. It rose like a snake and fastened itself around the airlock. J.D. waited impatiently for the lock to cycle. As soon as it opened, she hurried into Nemo's warm, caustic air, plunged down the slope, and followed the intricate path by memory and scraps of the lifeline.

Eagerly, she anticipated the touch of Nemo's speech through her new link. She could almost, but not quite, recreate the multidimensional spaces Nemo had shown her. She reached for them, tantalized; they remained just beyond her grasp.

"Nemo, I'm coming."

"I am anxious to see you," Nemo said again.

She burst into Nemo's chamber, into warm bright light. Her throat burned.

Everything was silent, motionless. The silken sacs bulged, waiting. J.D.'s LTMs perched halfway up the surrounding curtains, watching, recording, electronically probing the plump and iridescent chrysalis.

J.D. moved cautiously toward Nemo's shell. The single free tentacle twitched, its fur standing out, ruffling, smoothing itself.

"I'm here," J.D. said. Her comment spun off into a sleek new surface.

Instead of words in Nemo's reply, she discerned a feeling of welcome and gratitude. She sank down next to the chrysalis.

She waited.

The chrysalis began to shift and churn. At first random, the motion evolved into a regular wave of contraction from back to front. A second wave began, opposing the first. The waves canceled each other, separated.

The chrysalis alternated between stillness and slow rippling, like the tides, like birth contractions.

The welcoming surface in J.D.'s mind quivered and fragmented, leaving emptiness.

"Nemo?"

Silence.

One of the mother of pearl circles along Nemo's flank dissolved. Iridescent liquid splashed out like blood. Tiny fringed appendages probed through the new hole. A small new creature pulled itself free. One after another, the pearl disks melted and dripped away. The creatures dragged their amorphous bodies from Nemo's chrysalis, fell into the mother of pearl puddles, and writhed, splashing and squeaking.

J.D. watched, amazed, frightened, wishing she could do something to help, wishing she knew the normal progress of the change so she could be sure that what was happening was right. Were the new creatures attendants, or were they parasites, feeding on Nemo's flesh?

The new creatures washed themselves in the liquid pearl; their bodies condensed and hardened like organic precious stones. They pulled themselves beneath Nemo's twisting chrysalis.

J.D. reached out spontaneously to grasp Nemo's uncovered tentacle, but stopped with her hand just short of it, taking in its warmth. She was reluctant to cross the last millimeter, afraid her touch might disrupt the change.

The opposing waves of contraction strengthened and met, meshed and augmented. Nemo's chrysalis writhed violently.

The shell burst with the high, tense scream of ripping silk. J.D. held herself motionless by force of will. Her heart pounded.

The edges of the shell pulled apart, shredding and tearing, falling to the floor in ribbons of color. The opening exposed a dark, crumpled, angular mass.

The single tentacle writhed and convulsed and lashed around J.D.'s wrist. It was as hot as an electrical wire with too much current flowing through it. J.D. gripped the tentacle and held it. She thought of comfort, reassurance. She had never borne a child herself, or attended a human childbirth, but she had witnessed an orca bearing her young one. The divers and the orcas had given her the privilege of sharing their joy. She hoped Nemo was doing the same.

The angular mass moved. A bundle of sticks rose from the destruction of the chrysalis, drawing with them a fine film like a veined soap bubble, like the swimming webs of a diver's hands. The sticks resolved into fan-shaped frameworks, several pairs emerging from the length of the broken chrysalis. The veins engorged; the skin lost its transparency, but its iridescence increased. Delicate scales of color formed a pattern as complex and seductive as the alien maze. The new wings were as thin as gauze, yet J.D. could stare into their depths forever.

She broke her gaze and squeezed her eyes shut, disoriented.

She was scared.

If my instincts about Nemo were wrong, she thought, it's too late now.

She shivered, and repeated to herself: It's my job.

It *was* her job, and she could not change the way she approached it. Maybe eventually—maybe inevitably—she would regret leaving herself open. But for now she would expose herself to whatever Nemo chose to offer.

The head of the new being emerged last, rising from the tangle of shredded skin. Iridescent facets of chitin interlocked to form its surface, glistening like the carapace of a beetle.

But the eyes were Nemo's, a ring of compound lenses protected by a mobile lid that opened, blinked, and closed halfway, languorous.

Nemo's wings stretched high above her, ten meters, fifteen, reaching to the roof of the chamber, brushing it with their tips. Five sets of wings, and at least one more trapped closed where Nemo's body disappeared into the floor of the chamber.

The wings fluttered. Dry now, they rustled like moths, and J.D. understood the name of Nemo's species. Europa had thought the name an insult, but she had never known its meaning. Embraced and dazzled by the fluttering wings, J.D. felt sorry for the alien humans. They had accepted the judgment of Civilization. They had never given Nemo's people a second thought.

The knowledge both depressed and encouraged her. She had come into space hoping, perhaps, to find a utopian system that would magically rescue Earth from all its problems. At the same time, she feared perfection. She distrusted easy answers.

There are no easy answers, J.D. said to herself. And Civilization isn't the perfect organism Europa represented it to be. They may have the right to judge us. But they don't have the right to judge us without appeal!

"Nemo?"

"I am here, J.D."

"I'm glad to have you back," J.D. said.

"I'm glad to be done with the change."

J.D. did not know what to say, because the change meant Nemo soon would die.

The pearl creatures crawled out from beneath Nemo's body, pulling with them shreds of Nemo's shell. One snatched up a bit of the shredded chrysalis and shoved it into its mouth. The iridescent fragment crinkled like paper and disappeared.

Like a horde of fuzzy ants, the tiniest animals swarmed up Nemo's wings and groomed them.

"I thought you were beautiful before your metamorphosis," J.D. said. "And I think you're beautiful now."

Nemo's wings swept down, brushing J.D.'s face, and up again. They quivered, and the quaking sound filled the chamber with the sound of leaves in the wind. The wings were much more mobile than the wings of moths or butterflies; the articulated framework moved the surfaces like bird wings.

The tentacle around J.D.'s wrist relaxed and drew away. She had almost forgotten it; she flexed her fingers and shook her hand to get the blood flowing again. Nemo brushed her cheek, her shoulder, with the tip of the tentacle.

Creatures crept from folds in the floor, from pores in the curtains, creatures different from the attendants of Nemo's previous form.

A whole group of larger attendants, nearly the size of housecats, bumbled out. They looked like giant sowbugs with a mass of small, slender hind legs and a cluster of thick, pudgy-toed front legs. Each time one bumped into another they slowed, till they all coalesced into a pile.

J.D. turned some of the LTMs toward the new attendants. She let her eyelids flutter, tapping into the transmission, hoping for more information than her own senses could supply.

Her connection to the LTM link exploded, leaving her stunned and confused and frightened.

The attendants scuttled around, multiple feet scrabbling and scratching on the floor in frenzied motion.

They scrambled toward the LTMs and engulfed them, climbing over them, tumbling recklessly.

Nemo's pleading voice penetrated her disturbed link. "J.D., stop, stop."

All J.D. could think of to do was shut down the LTMs. They folded beneath the attendants, and cut off their sensors.

The attendants fell away from the LTMs. From giant sowbugs to tentacled shrimp, they withdrew and returned to Nemo's side.

"Nemo, what happened?" J.D. was shaking. The dissolution of the link was too much like what had happened to Feral. "That's how I watched your metamorphosis—I thought it would be safe for you!"

"But, J.D., I am different now," Nemo said, "and my attendants are different."

"I'm so sorry."

She did not know what else to say. She locked all the LTMs—her attendants—on passive systems only, and set them to record.

"What about my link to *Starfarer*?"

Nemo hesitated. "It's very strong, and very near. . . ."

J.D. got the hint. She sent a quick message back to *Starfarer*: I'm okay. But I'd better shut down communication for a while.

With a word of understanding and regret from Victoria, a yelp of protest from Zev, and a curse of apprehension from Stephen Thomas, J.D.'s perception of her link to *Starfarer* vanished into silence.

"Did I cause you harm?" J.D. asked Nemo. "Are you hurt?"

"I'm unhurt. But there's not much time."

Nemo's tentacle stretched out, wrapped itself around one of the silken sacs, and drew it in, slowly, painfully.

"What should I do? Can I help?"

"You may help," Nemo said.

J.D. hoped the obvious thing to her was the obvious thing to the squidmoth. She picked up the sac in both hands and presented it in front of Nemo. It was astonishingly heavy.

"What happens now?"

"I combine my genetic material with the genetic material of the juvenile parents of my offspring."

The single tentacle curled around the sac. Nemo's head reared up, exposing a gaping, toothless mouth. Like a frog's tongue, the tentacle drew the sac inside.

"Nemo, what—?"

"I cannot speak with you now, J.D."

Nemo's adult body was slender and mobile, unlike the ponderous squidlike juvenile body. The legs and the feather-gills and the rippling horizontal fin had vanished —transformed into wings? Or was that too simple an analysis?

Nemo's wings began to beat, in a wave from front to back. The motion of the wings eased the bulge of the sac through Nemo's new form, expanding the translucent, peacock-hued skin before the sac, contracting behind it. The colors changed over the bulge of the egg sac, flowing from iridescent red through orange, yellow, green, blue, purple.

The egg case hesitated at a second, smaller bulge in Nemo's body, beneath the last free pair of wings. The two shapes touched, merged, engulfed each other; and then the egg case continued to move.

Nemo's wings fluttered faster, harder, creating a low, trilling whirr that filled the air. The giant sowbugs streamed from their congregation and surrounded Nemo's body where it entered the floor. Using their front appendages, they massaged the egg sac and pushed it along. It disappeared beneath the level of the floor. The whirring wings relaxed, and drooped. The attendants fell away and crawled blindly around, undirected, slowing as they touched, till they lay again in a compact, pulsating mass.

"You may help," Nemo said again.

J.D. hurried to the pile of satchels and brought another. Again, Nemo engulfed it. The wings stretched, pulsed, and resumed their flowing, steady beat, pumping the sac on its long traverse.

J.D. fetched another egg case.

"Not yet, not yet," Nemo said.

She stopped.

Maybe it's a reflex, engulfing the egg sac, J.D. thought. Maybe that's why the tentacle is so slow. Maybe the timing is critical.

Another bulge began to form beneath Nemo's posterior full wings. By the time the second sac reached it, it had stopped growing. Again the bulges merged, again the sowbugs pressed the egg bulge out of sight.

Time passed.

J.D. continued to bring the egg sacs to Nemo's mouth, leaving the tentacle to conserve its strength for the engulfing. Nemo remained silent, eyes closed, body and wings pulsing with exertion.

J.D. was in awe of the effort Nemo expended. Of course the squidmoth could not talk to her now. But the silence of J.D.'s enhanced link felt huge and empty. She wondered if the change had been futile, just enough to give her a glimpse of Nemo's complete communication.

With each egg sac, the traverse through Nemo's body occurred more slowly. The secondary bulge, the egg, took longer to form.

J.D. helped, and waited, for several hours. Her friends back home would be worried by her silence.

After the fifth egg sac, Nemo's wings drooped. J.D. stroked the heavy, chitinous head. Nemo's tentacle curled; the wings rose, and stretched.

J.D. picked up another egg sac and brought it to the tentacle.

I must be getting tired, too, she thought. These things are beginning to feel heavier and heavier.

Nemo's tentacle wrapped around the egg case, dragging it weakly in. J.D. stood anxiously by while Nemo's mouth worked around it. The iridescent wings sagged nearly to the floor, and their colors had begun to dull. Right after the metamorphosis, Nemo's body had looked sleek and well-fed. Now it had begun to shrivel.

Nemo's sunken flanks defined the egg case in more detail. The long wings labored to continue their beat. Even
the attendants moved slowly, tentatively.

The egg case merged with the egg bulge, and disappeared, and the giant sowbugs tumbled away from each
other in response to the renewed throbbing of the
wings.

The tentacle sagged out of Nemo's mouth, twitching
and searching. J.D. hurried to bring the seventh sac.
Nemo engulfed it, and the first set of wings moved it
with agonizing slowness.

Six more egg cases remained in the pile. J.D. felt
frightened, because Nemo could never ingest them all
before *Starfarer* hit transition. She should give herself at
least an hour to get back.

Nemo quivered, exhausted. J.D. stroked Nemo's
tentacle, the pulsing flanks.

Nemo's wings swept down, trembled against the
floor, and lifted themselves slowly, painfully.

The passage is going to take at least an hour, J.D.
thought. If I'm quick—

She touched her link to Nemo. "I'll be right back."
She gently squeezed the furred tip of Nemo's tentacle.
Hoping the squidmoth could hear her, could still under-
stand her, she rushed back to the *Chi*.

On board *Starfarer,* the sun tubes brightened with morning. The temperature rose slowly. All over campus, the
snow began to melt. Icy drips collected at the ends of
branches and splashed to the ground; rivulets rushed
down hillsides, formed tiny new streams, flowed into the
rivers.

Infinity's boots squished in mud and crunched the
ice crystals that remained beneath the surface.

He reached the dripping orange grove, stopped, and
looked around.

The emergency measures had saved most of the
trees. The fruit was another story. About half the ripe

oranges had fallen, and the blossoms for the next crop
had wilted and died.

Infinity sighed.

Guessed real wrong on this one, he thought.

His inside coat pocket scrabbled against his chest.

He opened the coat and slid his hand into the
pocket.

"Ow!" He jerked back his hand and inspected his
nipped finger.

"Is that the thanks I get for saving you from freezing?" Infinity said aloud.

The meerkat burrowed deeper, her claws catching
on the material of his coat.

"What is it you want?" He had tried to let the meerkat loose near her burrow, but she would not go.

I bet this critter is Europa's house pet, Infinity
thought. And I'll bet she wants to live in a nice warm
house.

Especially since she's about to have kittens.

Someone squelched through the deep mud toward
him. Infinity caught a glimpse of Gerald Hemminge on
the other side of the orange grove.

Listening to Gerald say "I told you so" was the last
thing Infinity needed. The last thing, except maybe having Gerald find out about the meerkat.

J.D. rushed back to the *Chi*. The *Chi*'s transmission to
Starfarer had not troubled Nemo, so J.D. could safely
open her link.

Zev's image popped into being before her.

"J.D.! We thought—I was afraid—"

"I'm fine, Zev. How much got through before I
pulled the plug?"

J.D. grabbed sandwich makings out of the cupboard
and started some coffee.

Victoria's image appeared near Zev.

"Just enough to scare us. We've been so worried
about you!" Victoria floated in the sailhouse, helping
Jenny position *Starfarer* for transition. Jenny still did

not, could not, trust Arachne. That left Victoria to buffer her, in the same position Feral was in when he died.

"*You're* worried about *me*?" J.D. asked. She slapped a sandwich together and wolfed down a bite.

"At least everybody knows where I am." Victoria smiled wryly.

"I'm right here," J.D. said. "I'm going back inside in a minute."

Satoshi appeared, surrounded by the complex equipment of the observatory. "How mad is Nemo?"

J.D. swallowed another bite of sandwich.

"Nemo's not mad at all, as far as I can tell." She glanced at the image Arachne created of Nemo's planetoid. Several of the craters bulged with distended silk.

"You aren't in any danger?" Victoria asked.

"I'm sure not."

Esther Klein's image appeared. "I can bring help with the transport. It's ready."

"Thanks, Esther. But it isn't necessary. Really. I better get back."

"How much longer?" Victoria asked.

"I just can't say."

"You're cutting it awfully close!"

"I can't help it."

"But what are you *doing*?" Zev asked.

"I guess . . . I'm acting as midwife. I have to go, Zev, I love you. Keep an eye on those other craters. I think . . ." She smiled. "I don't know for sure. But I think you should watch them."

She rushed back through the tortuous silken path. The curtains continued to deteriorate. J.D. followed a trail of her own footprints, bruises in the silk, back to Nemo's chamber.

Infinity patted the nest of towels on the floor of the closet. In the corner, the meerkat stood in sentry position, her paws crossed on her rounded belly. She fixed him with a suspicious gaze through her mask of black fur.

"Oh, my god," Esther said behind him.

"Don't scare her," Infinity said.

"I can't believe Europa left her behind! What a rotten thing to do." She knelt beside Infinity and tried to pet the meerkat. The meerkat snapped at her. Esther snatched back her hand.

"I think we better leave her alone."

Infinity sat back on his heels. The meerkat walked a few steps on her hind feet, then dropped to all fours and jumped into the center of the towels.

Someone knocked on the front door. "Are you ready?" Kolya asked.

Infinity quickly slid the closet door most of the way shut, hiding the meerkat.

"We're ready."

He and Esther joined Kolya on the front porch.

"This is getting to be a tradition," Esther said, "watching transition from outside—" She cut herself off when she saw Griffith. "Oh . . . are you coming?"

"I'm checked out on the suits," Griffith said, defensive.

"I invited him to come with us," Kolya said. "He's allied himself with the expedition. We should accept that."

Infinity shrugged. "Whatever you want."

"Do you feel better today?" Esther said to Kolya. "You look better." She hugged him, then drew back, startled.

Kolya reeked with the smell of tobacco. Not the sour smell of his sweat, when the nicotine fits had hit him, but the fresh sharp smell of smoke.

"You said you ran out of cigarettes," Infinity said.

"I did," Kolya said, embarrassed. "But . . . I found another source. Tobacco grows wild. My friend Petrovich discovered it." He gestured toward Griffith.

"But you'd almost quit!" Infinity glared at Griffith. "Some friend *you* are!"

"Mind your own damn business," Griffith said.

"It *is* my—"

"No, it isn't," Kolya said gently. "I appreciate your concern, my friend. And you're right, I'd be better off if I'd quit. But I was miserable and sick, and now I'm not miserable and sick. Let's leave it at that."

He set off across Infinity's garden, heading for the access hatch on the other side of the field. Griffith followed him, hurrying to keep up.

Infinity glared after them. Esther took his hand. "Come on," she said. "He's right. It isn't any of our business."

Without replying, Infinity walked with her through the garden. They avoided the corner where his cactus grew. He was afraid the floods had drowned it.

The path was full of water. A nearby stream had escaped its banks and turned the meadow around it into a pond. The access hatch was underwater. Kolya and Griffith hesitated at the pond's edge.

"We'll have to find a hatch on higher ground," Kolya said.

"Can't you make the water level go down?" Griffith said to Infinity.

"No."

"But—"

"I *can't*," Infinity said. "There was too much snow. It melted too fast. There's no place else for the water to go. It's flooded the rivers, too."

"You should evacuate some of the water into space."

"We already lost some when your damned missile hit!"

"It wasn't *my* missile!"

"*Starfarer*'s a closed ecosystem. If we lose much water, it'll turn into a desert."

"Okay, but doesn't this place have reservoirs? Can't you fill them? Or let the ocean get deeper?"

"All of that's happening," Infinity gave up trying to keep the note of irritation from his voice. "What do you want me to do, bail?"

"Petrovich," Kolya said to Griffith, "the rivers drain

into reservoirs and the ocean. As you can see, they're working as fast as they can."

Griffith shrugged. "Lousy planning, then."

"I'm going over to the wild side," Infinity said. "The rest of you can do what you want."

He walked away with his hands shoved into his pockets, his shoulders hunched. After a moment, Esther caught up to him.

"That Griffith can be a pain," she said.

Infinity did not reply.

"Okay, what's wrong?" She splashed through a puddle. "It *is* Kolya's business whether he smokes."

"I planted it," Infinity said.

"Huh?"

"I planted the tobacco!"

He stopped. Esther stopped, astonished.

"I planted it. There's not that much. I never thought anybody'd use it—I never thought anybody'd find it."

"Why?"

"Because . . . it *ought* to be there. It belonged in the ecosystem, and it wasn't there. And it was part of the tradition—I know this doesn't make any sense. . . ."

Esther slipped her arm around his waist and hugged him.

"Sure it does," she said.

When J.D. reached Nemo's chamber, the squidmoth was wrestling weakly with another egg case, drawing it slowly inward. J.D. hurried to Nemo's side and helped position the egg case for its journey through Nemo's body.

With each new egg case, Nemo's deterioration continued. The edges of the wings shredded iridescent scales throughout the chamber. They swirled like the snow back on *Starfarer,* but in drifts of color. Nemo's tentacle twitched spasmodically. The squidmoth's whole body was shrinking in on itself, collapsing in folds of skin and scales. The articulation of the wings, where they joined the body, stood out in sharp relief.

J.D. picked up the last egg case. She took it to Nemo, but hesitated before setting it down.

"Enough, Nemo," she whispered, not using her link. "Isn't it enough?"

She drew a deep breath and knelt down to present the egg case.

Nemo did not respond.

"Nemo—!" she cried, afraid Nemo had died without saying goodbye.

"It is done," the squidmoth said. "The last must go to waste. I have nothing left to give it."

Weak with relief, J.D. looked blankly at the egg case. She was exhausted, too, not from work but from worry. Her mind moved, slowly understanding what Nemo had said.

She put the egg case out of reach of the tentacle, and returned to Nemo's side. The squidmoth's eyes opened and blinked. Instead of their usual faceted glitter, they were dull and dry.

"What happens now?" J.D. said.

"Your help has left us time to talk."

If I leave here this instant, J.D. thought, I can still get back before *Starfarer* enters transition.

If I go back . . .

As soon as she realized she would have to decide, she knew she had already made the decision. Nemo had asked her to stay; she would stay.

She sat on the ragged silken floor.

She wondered how long she would be here all alone.

Nemo's wings folded in on themselves, a controlled collapse of the long articulations. The membranes covered Nemo's wrinkled, shriveled body like a shroud.

"I enhanced my link," J.D. said. "Maybe I can communicate the way you do, now. Will you try again? Can you?"

"I can," Nemo said.

Faint patterns appeared in J.D.'s mind.

Nemo poured information into her brain.

The world disappeared.

J.D. gasped. She knew she had not shut her eyes—but she could not see, and she could not feel whether her eyes were open or closed. She could not smell the caustic air of Nemo's nest, and she could not hear the glide and scratch of Nemo's attendants. She was blind, and deaf, and her senses of smell and taste and touch and proprioception vanished.

Before she could panic, a point appeared. The simplest geometric shape. She rotated around it.

It turned into a line. She had been looking at it from its end, no, from within it, an infinite line made of infinite points, each one discrete. A fractal line of fractional dimension, neither the dimensionless shape of a pure point nor the one-dimensional unity of a perfect line.

She rotated around the line, and the shape metamorphosed again. It twisted and moved, all in the same plane, filling up more and more space despite having no width, existing in the conceptual realm between a one-dimensional line and a two-dimensional plane.

Nemo rotated her around the plane. She found herself in a landscape of jagged peaks and valleys as the plane torsioned itself into three dimensions, no longer two-dimensional, not yet a solid, but somewhere in between.

Space rotated again. J.D. caught her breath with delight and anticipation. She plunged toward the shape Nemo had created.

Now she knew how her mathematician friend had rotated a sphere around a plane.

It was easy. Nemo led her through the dimensions in imperceptible steps. Sometimes she could not see the differences, but could hear or smell or feel them. Nemo gave her a shape that tasted of citrus in a snowstorm beside a crashing sea.

J.D. lost count of the dimensions, the sensations. She needed more senses than a human being possessed. She disappeared into the maze of the squidmoth's communication.

She disappeared, but she did not feel lost. The

mazes of Europa and Androgeos had confused her. In Nemo's maze, she found herself: the place that represented her in Nemo's universe. She found Nemo. She found the bright new edges—she wondered if a shape of infinite dimension *had* edges—that represented Nemo's highest art form, the extension of knowledge and understanding.

As it had appeared, the communication faded with inexorable serenity. Her sight and sound returned; her body came back to her.

Nemo lay before J.D., trembling wings bound in a cocoon of dappled silk. A few attendants fell in a scatter around the motionless body, their gill-legs contracted against their undersides, each trailing a loose silk thread.

"Nemo—?"

She received no answer. She reached out, carefully, tentatively—the world disappeared again—through her link and through her memory of Nemo's communication, but the squidmoth remained silent, draped in the new cocoon.

J.D. felt as if her brain had been taken out through her ears, whirled around her head a few times, and reinserted. She waited for the dizziness to subside. As it faded, she expected her new ability to think multidimensionally to fade as well.

To her astonishment, the memories remained clear.

"I wish to give you a gift," Nemo said.

"A gift—!"

She almost demurred; she almost told Nemo that the gift of knowledge exceeded any physical gift the squidmoth might offer.

And then she thought, J.D., are you nuts?

She stroked Nemo's long tentacle. The wings' quivering eased.

"I'll accept your gift with great pleasure," she said.

"You aren't curious about the nature of my gift."

"I'm extremely curious."

"You aren't afraid of the nature of my gift."

"No. I'm not afraid. I trust you."

"You're not concerned that my gift will change you."

She hesitated. She wanted to say that if she were afraid of change, she would never have come to space. But . . . if she were not afraid, she would have accepted the divers' offer regardless of the other consequences. She still wished she *had* accepted.

I won't make the same mistake twice, she said to herself.

"I'm not so frightened that I'll turn it down."

"I give you myself," Nemo said.

"I . . . I don't understand." Then, with joy, she said, "Do you mean you're going to live—? Nemo, that's wonderful!"

"No, I'll die."

"Then . . . I really don't understand."

"I give you the inorganic parts of myself that I leave behind."

What Nemo was trying to tell her came clear.

"The part of you that I called your ship," she said softly.

"I give you my ship," Nemo replied.

She tried to speak, but she was too stunned. She could hardly breathe. Nemo's ship—!

The tentacle writhed weakly from her limp hands, touched its way up her body, and brushed her face, her hand, with its furred tip. It left a trace of iridescent dust.

"You say nothing."

"Because I'm speechless," J.D. said. "It's a response humans have to being this surprised."

"You accept my gift."

"Yes, Nemo. Oh, yes, I accept. Thank you." Her hands were trembling. "But—how will I fly it? Do I have time to learn before . . . before . . ."

"Before I die."

"Yes," she whispered.

"My life has been long and full, and I don't regret its passing," Nemo said.

"But I'll grieve for you," J.D. said. "I'll wish I'd had more time to know you."

"My offspring will know all that I know."

"They'll be just like you?"

"Each will develop separately, and each will possess my knowledge and the juvenile parent's knowledge."

"But they won't be you."

"Each will be unique," Nemo said.

"I'll look forward to meeting your children," J.D. said. "But I'll still miss you." She hardly had time to consider the idea that Nemo's children would be born with all the knowledge a squidmoth could collect in a long, dedicated life. Nemo would have been born already steeped in ancestral knowledge . . . for how many millennia, how many generations?

"Is there anything you don't know?" J.D. asked softly, in awe.

"The shape of my knowledge is so incomplete," Nemo said, "that my children and their children will never finish it."

She let Nemo's communication shape appear in her mind. The squidmoth was right. Now that she looked, now that she knew what she was looking for, she could see where it ought to extend a great distance in many dimensions. She could see where it fell short. How strange: the first time she looked at it, entered it, she had perceived it as infinite.

"If I only knew the details of the surface . . ."

"You will extend my knowledge, as my offspring will."

J.D. managed to smile. "Does that make me your daughter?"

"I like that idea," Nemo said.

Nemo's tentacle caressed her again: her cheek, her hair. It quivered and collapsed, sliding down her arm to coil unevenly on the floor.

The wings shed more of their iridescent scales. Small creatures like ants crossed with periwinkles, like minuscule hermit crabs, carried the scales away. Their paths formed lines of iridescent, unreadable hieroglyphics.

J.D. shivered suddenly. If the new generation of attendants was going to dismember Nemo . . . she could not watch it. Yet she could not leave Nemo to die alone, either.

"Nemo, what's going to happen?" she asked again. "How will I learn to fly your ship? What about your real children? Shouldn't you leave it to one of them?"

"My children can't make use of what I'll leave behind."

"How will I make use of it? I should have asked Esther to come over and help, but there's no time now."

The tentacle crept up, slowly, painfully, and grasped her wrist. She fell silent.

"You have the means to learn."

Nemo led her into the internal reality.

J.D. cried out.

She *was* the ship. She *was* Nemo. She felt the weakness in Nemo's organic body, and the unlimited strength and power of the inorganic body that would remain. Nemo led her to the proper set of intersecting surfaces. To move from place to place was as easy as walking, as easy as thought. She could see the path into transition, the long, looping route through it.

"We need to go *there*," she said, pointing.

She could even see a different direction toward transition, toward 61 Cygni, but she was cut off from it by a depthless chasm. She could get no closer. It might be the direction *Starfarer* would take. Though its shapes and curves echoed Victoria's transition algorithm, she could not quite fit the shapes together.

Nemo's path into transition was intricate, convoluted, beautiful.

It was a maze, but Nemo showed her the route that allowed her to pass.

They returned to the real world.

"It's a long distance," Nemo said, "and I fear you will be lonely."

"I've never minded being lonely," J.D. said. "Not too much, anyway. But I will mind this time. I'll miss you." She opened her eyes, but shut them quickly. In her mind, Nemo was an ethereal presence. The crumpled, spent body that lay before her, its long eyelid com-

pletely closed, its battered wings shrouded, only
reminded her how little time they had left. She
squeezed her burning eyes shut; her throat ached with
the effort of holding back her tears.

Stephen Thomas tried to ignore the discomfort of the
changes. As long as he stayed still, he could imagine
nothing was wrong. But every motion reminded him of
what was happening to his body.

Starfarer neared transition point. J.D. had checked
in once, then fallen silent again. Victoria and Satoshi
had tasks to perform during the next few hours, but
Stephen Thomas had no official responsibilities.

During *Starfarer*'s first entry into transition, he had
been unconscious in the ruined genetics department. As
the second transition point approached, he had helped
track Arachne's crashes to the neural node of Chancellor Blades.

I want to *see* transition, Stephen Thomas thought. I
want to be where I can experience it.

With the thought, he jumped to his feet.

The constriction of his genitals froze him. Nause-
ated, he sank cautiously into his chair.

"Fucking hell," he muttered. He had no control over
muscles that were, for Zev, completely voluntary; he
could not take the last step that would change him from
ordinary human to diver.

He folded his arms on his desk, put his head down,
closed his eyes, and opened his link to Arachne.

The biofeedback routines reacted as if he had ordered a refresher course in an ordinary subject—beard
repression, fertility control. He told Arachne to help
him learn the use of muscles that an ordinary human
man did not possess.

Having no restrictions against what he asked,
Arachne proceeded. The web sought out new neural
pathways that Stephen Thomas *did* now possess, and
reinforced their connections.

As Arachne worked, Stephen Thomas's perception

of his body grew remote. His conscious mind stayed free and alert. Both bored and apprehensive, he sought something to occupy his attention.

J.D. remained isolated. Stephen Thomas almost sent a message to his partners, then reconsidered. They were busy, and he did not know what to say to them. Nor did he know if they wanted to speak to him.

He tapped into Arachne's reports on transition approach, surrounding himself with a holographic representation and using his link to listen in on the telemetry.

Nemo's ship followed *Starfarer,* silent; the cosmic string coiled invisibly before the starship. Arachne felt solid and steady.

This is what Feral was doing in the last few minutes of his life, Stephen Thomas thought.

He backed away from Arachne, spoke Feral's passwords, and re-entered his communications fugue under Feral's guest account.

An unusual resonance probed toward him. It snatched itself back. He grabbed for it, but it eluded him so swiftly that it left him doubting its existence.

Suspicious and disturbed, he watched, and listened, and waited for transition.

Victoria linked easily with Arachne. Her view of *Starfarer* from the transparent sailhouse merged with Arachne's view of the state of the starship. For once, finally, all the systems hovered within reasonable ranges and the sail aligned the cylinders with transition point. No military vessels chased them, firing orders and nuclear missiles; no saboteur—Victoria believed—hovered in the background waiting to crash Arachne at the worst possible moment; and the cosmic string, though it was withdrawing from Sirius, moved without twisting, and at a constant acceleration. The starship had nearly caught up to it.

Jenny glanced up from the hard link, then down again. She typed something, hunt-and-peck. Nobody ever typed anything; the keyboard was an anachronism, a third-backup redundancy.

Arachne formed a display in the air above the keyboard, mirroring the report in the back of Victoria's mind.

Avvaiyar's image appeared between Victoria and Jenny. She had been participating in *Starfarer*'s transition approach, but physically she was in her observatory.

"You know what I wish?" she asked.

"What's that?"

"That we'd find a nexus. A crossroads. The real freeway interchange, the one we *thought* we'd found at Tau Ceti. An intersection too important to disrupt just because troublesome human beings are using it. They would never blow up a major transportation system because of a couple of infidel joy-riders."

Victoria chuckled, but the image was apt.

"That's all right with me," she said. "If I could jump from freeway interchange to freeway interchange, shouting at Civilization at the top of my lungs till they listened—that's what I'd do."

She turned her attention to the image of Nemo's ship. The rock sphere had budded out a dozen silken bubbles.

"Hadn't you better try to call J.D.?" Jenny asked.

"I don't think so. She's very even-tempered, eh? But if you interfere with her job she can get quite sharp about it."

"She's cutting it too close."

"I know it," Victoria said, trying to keep her voice steady.

She yearned to call out to J.D. and persuade her, command her, to come back to safety. It took all her strength to keep her silence.

"She isn't coming back," Victoria said. "Jenny, she won't leave Nemo. If that means going into transition on an alien ship . . . that's what J.D. will do."

"How far behind us will she be?"

"I don't know!" Victoria lowered her voice. "She might be gone . . . a long time."

"You know, Victoria . . ." Avvaiyar's image hung rock solid in the air; Jenny and Victoria, in zero g, hovered and drifted. "You could—"

"I know!" Victoria exclaimed. "Don't think I haven't considered it. But . . . if I send J.D. the algorithm, it'll be in Nemo's memory. In whatever Nemo's ship uses for a computer web. That would be like turning it over to Civilization."

"No strings attached," Avvaiyar said wryly.

What would J.D. want her to do?

Victoria had only a few minutes left. She had no time to call a meeting to discuss the question with *Starfarer*'s faculty and staff. She hardly had time even to confer with any of her colleagues.

Admit it, she said to herself. You're afraid to ask for advice; you're afraid someone will close off your options. Satoshi would say you must send it; Gerald and the senators would say you must not. And Stephen Thomas . . . it shocked her to realize she had no idea what Stephen Thomas would say.

Victoria took a long, deep breath and let it out slowly. Arachne lay calm around her. *Starfarer* fell toward its transition point. The stellar sail began to furl.

"Avvaiyar," she said. "Jenny . . ."

"Yes," Avvaiyar said gravely.

"I agree," Jenny said. "I thought you'd come to that decision."

J.D. felt the quiet power of Nemo's body. She could see, and sense, how to move it, how to guide it, as easy and as natural as walking. She had no more idea of how it powered itself than a child would have of the intricate energy cycle within her own body. J.D.'s adult mind wondered about gravity waves or mass exchanges of subatomic particles. But Nemo's method of propulsion remained speculation, a mystery.

She could reach out through Nemo's senses and re-create the shape of the universe around her. The surface of the planetoid formed her skin; the egg sacs pressed against her, laden with potential.

In the distance, perilously close to the loop of cosmic string, *Starfarer* plunged toward transition. The last silver flicker of its sail furled and darkened.

"Goodbye!" J.D. cried.

Starfarer disappeared.

J.D. squeezed her eyes shut, reflexively, as the bright transition spectrum flooded through the system. The starship left nothing else behind.

She opened her eyes, breaking her connection with the world outside Nemo's chamber. The silken curtains drooped and shredded like old cobwebs. The whisper and crunch of the symbionts' mouths and mandibles surrounded her.

"They're gone, Nemo," she whispered.

"Look," Nemo said, "my offspring are free."

Together, J.D. and Nemo watched the surface of the planetoid.

The bulge of one of the silken craters had grown spherical. It expanded, huge and taut, like a quivering soap bubble. Its diameter was much larger than the crater, but it clung to the crater's mouth as if it were being blown up like a balloon.

It detached.

It sank: the planetoid had too little atmosphere to buoy it. But then, as it bounced once, the small opening left in its bottom fluttered. A spurt of glowing gas propelled it from the surface of the worldlet.

J.D. laughed with delight.

The balloon rocketed, silent and free, into space.

In quick succession, Nemo's planetoid released half a dozen of the translucent powered balloons. Malleable surfaces covered obscure, tantalizing shapes. They shrank to blips of light. She—Nemo—had done everything for them that she could. They were on their own. She wished them well, but she would never—

J.D. brought herself abruptly back to herself. She *might* see them someday in the future. She was *not* Nemo. She was *not* preparing to die.

J.D. reached out to Nemo to offer her congratulations.

She encountered emptiness.

She reached desperately toward the squidmoth's mind. She found a small dim spark in blackness. It flared, welcoming her, and Nemo's soft tentacle twitched feebly in her hand.

Everything grew still around her.

The spark moved. It expanded, spreading itself over the surface of the shape of Nemo's knowledge. But as it expanded, it faded, too. The tenuous light vanished so gradually that J.D. could not be certain of the moment of its disappearance.

"Oh, Nemo . . . Goodbye."

The knowledge surface changed. It grew cold, and solidified. As Nemo's personality dissolved, the surface lost an uncountable number of its infinite dimensions. J.D. reached out as if to stop it, and then drew back, knowing she could have no effect.

Nemo was gone.

J.D. felt more alone than she had ever felt before, in a largely solitary life. She *was* alone, more alone than any human being ever had been. Nemo's children, for all their potential, were no more than a few cells each, zygotes clinging to great yolk sacs of knowledge, not even embryos.

J.D. was the only sentient creature in the star system.

She shivered.

All around her, the tattered silk came alive with scavengers. The sound of destruction filled the chamber with a soft, inescapable vibration of rending threads. A new sound added itself to the tapestry: the viscous slide of dissolving support cables. Beneath her, the floor sagged.

Nemo's tentacle twitched. J.D. flinched in surprise, in a brief flash of joy as quickly wiped out by shock. She dropped Nemo's tentacle.

Two of the symbionts struggled with each other, vying for possession of Nemo's tentacle by lashing at each other with the clusters of scorpion-tails that projected from their armored shells.

The leftover egg case, the one that remained unfertilized, writhed against the floor. Unseen creatures moved within it. The silk tore, with a long, ripping scream: claws on prehensile limbs thrust out, snapping.

The fate of Nemo's organic body was the same as what would happen to her own body when she died and was buried in the earth or allowed to sink into the sea. It was all perfectly natural.

But she could not watch it.

J.D. stroked her hand once across Nemo's long eyelid, pressing the squidmoth's eyes closed. She rose to her feet. Shaky and stiff, she fled Nemo's ruined web.

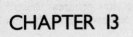

CHAPTER 13

J.D. CLIMBED FAST, NO LONGER CAREFUL about damage. The nest was coming apart around her. Panic chased her. She *had* to get back to the *Chi*. How stupid to leave her space suit behind, how complacent—!

The web tunnels shivered as J.D. ascended. More unfamiliar creatures, symbionts and attendants and scavengers, worked and worried at the silk and at each other. Optical fibers hung loose along the walls, some broken and dimmed, some still glowing, their ends bright as white flame.

No longer would Nemo convert the light of Sirius to useful energy, process rock and extract nutrients, and create the webbing that nurtured the ecosystem. The symbionts would deplete the webbing, the attendants would feed on the symbionts, and the scavengers would feed on the leftovers, till nothing remained of the squidmoth but inorganic matter, dust, a few desiccated bacteria.

Nemo's body was dying.

The tunnel to the *Chi* billowed down against J.D.'s face. The weight of the heavy sides counteracted the air pressure, collapsing the tube.

The air escaped, osmosing silently through failing walls. Panting for breath, J.D. fought her way past the folds of the silken shroud, making slow progress toward the explorer. If the tube's mouth fell away from the airlock . . .

Remember those stories where somebody had to cross ten or twenty meters of hard vacuum without a suit . . . ? she thought. Maybe you'll find out if it's possible. . . .

Not an experiment she wanted to try.

Blinded by the collapsing tunnel, she ran into the side of the *Chi* and bumped her knee and her nose. She yelped in pain and flung the silk upward, trying to get beneath it to reach the tunnel's opening.

Several of Nemo's creatures hugged the seam between the tunnel and the *Chi*. They extruded a gluey, fibrous substance that stuck the organic fabric to the inorganic hull. But the creatures had exhausted themselves. Escaping air hissed around a broken seal.

J.D. held her breath and plunged into the airlock.

"Seal!" She spoke through her link, conserving her air.

The *Chi* obeyed. The hatch slid, but caught on a swath of silk that tangled around J.D.'s foot. She grabbed the fabric, ripped it, freed the opening. The webbing parted in her hands like old cobwebs.

The hatch closed in silence, its motion barely vibrating the deck. The air was too thin to carry sound. As the hatch sealed, J.D. thought she saw a patch of black space and bright stars, unshielded by silk or air or glass.

A heavy warm draft from the *Chi* poured in around her. Tired in every way a person could be tired, J.D. lay on the floor. She breathed long and slow and deep. Once more she thanked good fortune and habit that she had not allowed her metabolic enhancer to atrophy.

The inner hatch slid open. J.D. stayed where she was, resting, gathering her energy.

She had no vital tasks. Nemo's shell was headed for Europa's transition point. J.D. could control the shell, but she feared interfering with Nemo's navigation till she had caught up to *Starfarer*. She wondered how long that would take.

Claws scuttled on metal.

J.D. bolted upright.

Several of Nemo's symbionts scuttled across the floor, scrabbling at the hatch with clawed, feathery legs.

J.D. gazed at them fondly.

Rising to her knees, she gathered up the creatures in the scrap of soft frail webbing.

Flecks of iridescence covered J.D.'s hands. The tiny scales from Nemo's wings gilded her, and when she rose, a scatter of the glitter shimmered to the floor.

Transition surrounded *Starfarer*.

Arachne continued, strong and steady, indifferent to the border *Starfarer* had crossed, leaving normal space behind. Victoria let out her breath and unclenched her teeth.

"The web's intact," she said.

Jenny stared out into transition. Tears pooled in her eyes, collected at her upper and lower eyelids, and drifted into the air in droplets when she blinked.

"It's over," she said softly. "It's finally done. We're safe."

"I hope so," Victoria said.

And then they smiled at each other, and Jenny laughed, her laughter warring with her tears. She sniffled and coughed and pulled a handkerchief out of her pocket and waved it over the floating teardrops to catch them, and blew her nose.

"Safe!" Jenny said. "Halfway through transition and going where we've been told not to. For all we know they'll blast us out of the sky when we get there."

"That's not allowed," Victoria said. "Their only weapon is coercion."

"Unless they get desperate enough to break the rules to stop us. *I* think Civilization works by peer pressure."

"You don't mean that as a compliment, do you?"

"I do not. There's nothing more brutal. People will do anything to get other people to do what they think is allowed. Or right. Or holy. Especially holy. The end always justifies the means."

Victoria said nothing. She did not want to think about ends justifying the means; the charge hit too close to her own doubts and fears.

This was the third time *Starfarer* had crossed into transition, the first time Arachne had been able to record, and the first time Victoria had been able to watch. On the journey from Earth to Tau Ceti, she had been helping Satoshi drag Stephen Thomas out of the genetics building. On the journey from Tau Ceti to Sirius, she had been trying, and failing, to save Feral's life.

The recordings did not do transition justice. They showed nothing but a formless gray fog. Transition was much more than that.

Victoria wondered if she would be able to describe it afterward. She wondered if Arachne would be able to reproduce a view of it.

The sailhouse hung suspended and isolated in a silver flurry of sparks. Now and then a streak of color or a shape coalesced from the storm, then disappeared. Victoria could not tell whether she was seeing something real, or if her mind was creating pictures from random intersections of the matrix around her.

"It's like the maze," she said. "We kept thinking we saw a pattern in it, but there wasn't any. Just a maze."

She felt isolated, alone out here with Jenny. They

could not even see *Starfarer*'s main cylinder through the silver storm.

The isolation J.D. must be feeling struck Victoria hard.

"Goodbye," J.D. had said, and nothing else, in that last second before *Starfarer* disappeared.

It sounded so final.

In the *Chi*'s small bio lab, J.D. placed the creatures in sample cases, one to an aquarium so they would not eat each other. She divided the shred of webbing among them.

They probably would not survive. They had not evolved to survive Nemo's death for long; they were part of the body that was dying. Maybe Stephen Thomas or Professor Thanthavong could figure out how to keep them alive. If she could save the symbionts until she caught up to *Starfarer*.

I wonder how long that will be? J.D. wondered. How long will I be here alone?

Nemo must have been able to calculate transition duration—or would the time even matter to someone who lived for millennia, who lived a life almost entirely of the mind?

J.D. reached for the knowledge surface of Nemo's shell. She found it—and again her expanded link took over all her senses, disorienting her, leaving her suspended in nothingness—and cast around for the answer she needed.

It overwhelmed her. She skittered along the surface, unable to penetrate its depths, distracted on every side by hints and shadows of Nemo's experience.

She came back to herself, still with no idea how long it would take her to reach the 61 Cygni system. Worse, she had no idea how to find the information in the maze of the knowledge surface.

Maybe Nemo didn't care how long it took, she thought. Besides . . . is it an answer I want to know?

The *Chi* was well-stocked, but its stores were finite.

If transition duration lasted weeks, or months, she could find herself in a lot of trouble. The *Chi* possessed a few organic systems, but it had never been designed to support a human being during a long separation from *Starfarer.*

She chuckled ruefully. If she had let Victoria give Androgeos the new transition algorithm, no doubt Nemo would have snagged the information, too.

"Outsmarted yourself this time, didn't you?" she said softly, trying not to feel how scared she was.

She wished she had sent a better, more comforting farewell to her friends. "Goodbye"? That told them nothing; it might even frighten them. They had no idea how long it would take her to traverse the space between Sirius and 61 Cygni, either. Only that it would take her longer than it took *Starfarer.*

Leaving Nemo's symbionts to explore the hard edges of their new homes, J.D. headed for the observers' circle.

She caught her breath in surprise and apprehension.

The sinuous, beautiful shape of Victoria's algorithm twisted itself into being in the center of the circle.

J.D. took her place in the circle. The transition algorithm hovered at the focus, Victoria's final message, her final gift.

Nemo's shell plunged toward transition point. J.D. had only a few minutes to decide what to do.

With apprehension, she closed her eyes and opened her link completely, sliding onto the knowledge surface, stretching to connect it with the *Chi*'s onboard computer. The real world vanished as J.D. approached the chasm in the knowledge surface and compared it to the algorithm.

They *do* match, she thought. Not a perfect fit . . .

She asked herself a question: What happens if the fit isn't good enough? Do I end up on the other side of the galaxy?

Gently she moved the algorithm, rotated it, and translated it into the chasm.

The algorithm joined the knowledge surface, rough,

raw beauty touching elegance refined and polished by time. The algorithm was a crystalline chunk of ice on the cracked surface of an ancient, flowing glacier. The crystal's edges melted; it sank in; the points of attachment melded. The surface and the algorithm remained distinct.

If Nemo were still alive, the fit would have been precise. So much detail was lost when Nemo's personality slipped away. J.D. withdrew from the surface. Now all she could do was wait.

When her senses returned to her, she gazed through the wall of the observers' circle, toward Nemo's crater. The flattened access tunnel lay between the *Chi* and the nest, like a shed and discarded snakeskin.

The wings and sails of Nemo's nest shuddered.

Nemo's convoluted tapestry collapsed, like ice cliffs avalanching. One side tore free of the rock. Limp and silent, it flopped inward. It dragged the access tunnel from the *Chi*'s hatch, to the crater, and over the edge.

The nest vanished into the crater's depths.

Nemo's shell slipped from space into transition. J.D. perceived the change, a change in angle down the knowledge surface, from an oblique traverse to a headlong plunge.

She had to choose *now:* To travel with the ancient glacier along the smooth, long ice slope, or to plunge into the choppy, dangerous terrain of the new algorithm.

She guided Nemo's shell into new territory.

J.D. felt like a chambered nautilus, shelled and tentacled, extending herself far beyond her own body, exquisitely sensitive. The shell found the pathway she sought and fitted itself to the jagged curve.

J.D. felt exhilarated, yet frightened. She believed she was following *Starfarer*'s path . . . but she could not be absolutely certain.

As she thought of the starship, she thought she saw it—or heard it, or felt it, with a sense Nemo had possessed but humans lacked. An anomaly appeared in the part of the knowledge surface that represented transition. The anomaly vanished, then appeared again, like a train chugging down the track into a valley and out of it again.

The anomaly distracted her. She wanted to catch up to it, to be sure it was *Starfarer* and to be sure she kept following it. She knew she *could* make Nemo's shell catch up to the anomaly. That surprised her. *Starfarer* had never tried to change its vectors from the time it achieved transition energy to the time it re-entered normal space.

J.D. restrained herself. One experiment was enough for any trip.

She drew her attention back toward herself, back within Nemo's shell. She was trembling with excitement. She breathed deeply of air tinged with the hydrocarbon-drenched odor of Nemo's ship. She sneezed.

I'll have to do something about the atmosphere, she thought. Nemo isn't creating it anymore. Will I be able to terraform the shell, like Europa's ship? Again she wondered how Europa had acquired her starship, and how she had configured it to her liking. Surely starships were a booming business within Civilization.

Sally's Used Starships, J.D. said to herself. Gort's Starship Redecoration.

J.D. laughed. She laughed, and then she cried for a while.

She extended her attention to the edge of Nemo's shell, and stretched beyond—

She discovered that Nemo's last two egg cases had detached and vanished, leaping off into transition while her thoughts were elsewhere.

Frantically J.D. cast her new senses around her, but caught no glimpse of the egg cases, no hint of them anywhere in transition's many dimensions. The anomaly of *Starfarer* glimmered in the distance, but nothing else marred the knowledge surface.

"Nemo, I'm so sorry. . . ."

She had failed. She should somehow have held on to

the two cases until she reached the new star system and
normal space.

But now they were gone.

Despite being able to look straight into transition, Victoria felt blind. The environment flung *Starfarer*'s radar
back only a few meters from the surface of the cylinder.
They might as well have been traveling through murky
water without sonar. *Starfarer* had no sonar capabilities,
of course, though Victoria would have tried it if it were
available.

I can just imagine what Senator Derjaguin would
have said if we'd outfitted a spaceship with sonar, she
said to herself.

Starfarer was taking samples of the transitional medium, but Victoria did not think the samples would reveal a material medium, an ether, that would respond to
sonar.

The source of the light storm was another mystery
entirely.

Jenny hovered nearby. She had returned to the
sailhouse a few minutes ago, looking refreshed, looking
better than she had since *Starfarer* left the solar system.
A few other people had come out to the sailhouse to
watch what was happening. Victoria wished Satoshi and
Stephen Thomas were with her. But Satoshi was in the
observatory waiting for a first glimpse of the new system, and Stephen Thomas . . . Victoria had no idea
where Stephen Thomas was. That was true more often
than not these days.

As abruptly as a blink, *Starfarer* fell out of transition.

Victoria whooped with triumph and relief. She dove
into Arachne's perceptions. *Starfarer* remained in danger: Europa's ship might be anywhere. Last time
through transition, it had come out immediately on
Starfarer's tail. The sail gave the starship some mobility,
but no description of *Starfarer* would call it agile. It was
Europa's ship that had dodged, turning aside from
Starfarer just as the two spacecraft were about to collide.

Arachne pinpointed a nearby anomaly: a sphere, blue and green and hazed with atmosphere, far too massive for its size, an asteroid biologically and geologically sculpted to house humans comfortably.

Arachne expanded the anomaly: Europa's starship, only a short distance ahead.

We made up a lot of time, Victoria thought. A *lot*.

Starfarer's sail deployed. The metallic film untwisted, then unfolded, then opened into a great sheet of silver.

Jenny was nowhere near the hard link. Her eyelids fluttered open and she glanced at Victoria, and grinned, and shrugged self-deprecatingly, as if to say, "I couldn't resist Arachne anymore," and withdrew again into a communications fugue.

Satoshi's image appeared.

"Can you look at the astronomy report?" His voice radiated excitement.

"Sure." She let Arachne send her the first information from 61 Cygni A and its planets.

The system crackled with electronic communication. When Victoria glanced at the planetary information, she gasped.

61 Cygni A possessed no fewer than four planets within the limits for carbon-based life: two sets of twin worlds, one set at the sunward side of the region, the other just within the farthest, coldest limits.

All four worlds possessed the unmistakable signs of living systems. More than that, all four worlds cradled civilizations.

Victoria's elation and her apprehension fought each other to a draw.

"Wow," she said.

"Don't get carried away with excitement," Avvaiyar said dryly.

Satoshi laughed. "That's pretty excited, for a Canadian."

They grinned at each other. Then Satoshi sobered.

"We can't stay here, you know."

Victoria stared at the system map, wishing she could argue with him, but knowing he was right. If they stayed, the cosmic string would withdraw. *Starfarer* would cause 61 Cygni—and all its inhabitants—to be cut off from the interstellar community. How could they sentence other civilizations to the punishment they were trying to avoid?

"But *Starfarer*'s ecosystem . . ." She stopped. "You're right. I know you're right."

She reluctantly set Arachne to work on a new solution to her transition algorithm.

"We're going to have to change the name of the ship," Satoshi said.

"To *Murphy's Law*," Victoria said, repeating a wisecrack Stephen Thomas had made.

"I was thinking, *Flying Dutchman.*"

"Oh, god. Goddamn! Europa *must* have known the risk! Why did she lead us here?"

"To take advantage of our good natures, so we'd give up and leave?"

"That makes . . . a certain amount of perverted sense." She laughed bitterly. "Does Europa believe we *have* good natures?"

"Maybe she wanted some help driving us away," Jenny said, floating beside her.

That, too, was a possibility, one that sounded rather more like the alien human's style.

Infinity stood on the inspection net below a fissure in the rocky outer surface of *Starfarer*'s wild side. Nearby, clinging to the cylinder—hanging upside down, from Infinity's point of view—a silver slug probed the fissure, touched the strange iridescent mass, and withdrew again. The slug moved back and forth, confused, uncertain.

The stars spun past behind and below Infinity; the surface of the cylinder loomed overhead, marred by the weird growth.

"What do you think?" he asked Esther.

Still bewildered and awestruck by the voyage through transition, Esther stared upward in silence.

Infinity sent his image, and an image of the growth, to Victoria in the sailhouse.

"We picked up something kind of strange, in transition," he said.

There was a long silence.

"It wasn't there before," Infinity said.

"Are you *sure*?" Victoria asked.

"You can look at the scans if you don't believe me!" he snapped.

Esther glanced at him, startled. Infinity looked away, embarrassed by his own outburst.

"I didn't mean . . ." Victoria said. "I'm just surprised."

"Yeah. Join the club."

"Maybe it's interstellar trash," Esther said. "You know . . . Civilization's landfill?"

It was Infinity's turn to give Esther a skeptical glance. She shrugged and grinned.

"Just a suggestion," she said.

She stretched up and laid her gloved hand on the bulging surface.

"Be careful!" Infinity said.

"It's kind of hot," Esther said. "And it's *moving*."

"It's one of Nemo's egg cases!" Zev's voice appeared out of nowhere, followed by his image.

"Oh, nonsense," Victoria said.

"It *is*."

"How could it be, Zev? It resembles one, but Nemo's egg cases are back in the Sirius system."

Griffith's image appeared. He and Kolya perched precariously on the inspection web of *Starfarer*'s campus cylinder.

"I think we should get rid of it," Griffith said. "I'll go over and pry it loose—"

"No!" Victoria said. "Don't do *anything*. Do you hear me? Kolya, tell him—!"

"It might destroy the ship!" Griffith exclaimed. "It's a risk I—"

"Petrovich, Victoria's right."

"If it's one of the egg cases," Zev said, "J.D. will hate us if we kill it."

"We aren't killing anything," Victoria said. "Whatever it is, I think we should watch it for a while before we decide what to do. I wish J.D. . . . " She stopped speaking for a moment. "Infinity, would you set Arachne to watch it? To keep an eye on it? Please don't you and Esther put yourselves in danger!"

"We'll be careful," Infinity said.

Starfarer disappeared from J.D.'s perception.

She gasped, first frightened, then hopeful. *Starfarer* must already have reached normal space on the other side of its flight path.

She waited impatiently to follow it across the border at the edge of transition.

Instead of fleeing, the alien starship decelerated. Soon *Starfarer* was gaining on it. The details of its surface grew clearer. Arachne displayed the pattern of its islands and lakes, confirming Victoria's judgment of its identity.

Unless, Victoria thought dryly, the interstellar community only makes its starships in a few models. . . .

Arachne's warm touch notified her of an emergency message. She accepted it.

The maze of the alien humans formed itself, twisting and complex, as fascinating and beautiful as ever. And as uncommunicative.

I hate that maze, Victoria thought, startling herself with her vehemence.

The maze faded; Europa's image appeared in its place. The Minoan was exquisitely beautiful, her cinnamon-colored skin clear and perfect despite her age, the brightness and blackness of her eyes enhanced by narrow lines stroked onto her eyelids, her graying hair in perfect ringlets, dressed with strands of silver so artfully crafted that they moved like living things.

"It's beginning to look a little crowded in here," Jenny said.

The alien human, survivor of the Minoan civilization, smoothed her homespun skirt and smiled at Victoria as if she were a beloved, errant child.

"Hello, Victoria," Europa said. "I'm very glad to see you."

"Hello, Europa," Victoria said, astonished. "I didn't expect such a warm welcome."

"We have things to talk about."

Androgeos appeared beside her. He was as beautiful as Europa, though he maintained himself at a much younger apparent age. They were both small, about Victoria's height, narrow-waisted, and muscular, especially in the thighs. Victoria always wondered if they practiced bull-leaping.

"Is Alzena all right?" Victoria asked.

"Alzena is no concern of yours anymore," Androgeos said. His tone was nowhere near as friendly as Europa's. "Alzena is gone to you."

"Is she all right?"

"She wants her privacy," Androgeos said. "Can't you understand that?"

"Certainly I can. Thank you for answering my question."

"Now answer mine," Androgeos said. "Do you intend to turn the Four Worlds into an empty system, the same as you've done to Sirius? There are *people* here, not just squidmoths."

Zev arrowed into the sailhouse, missed Jenny by a handsbreadth, passed rudely through the holographic images of the alien humans, touched off from the transparent wall, and came to a graceful, perfect stop beside Victoria.

"What about—" Zev exclaimed.

"Shh!" Victoria said.

Zev grabbed her hand, panicked. Maintaining a calm expression took all Victoria's strength. She squeezed his fingers, trying to comfort him, but she was worried about J.D., too. If what Androgeos said was true, if J.D. had not entered transition before the final withdrawal of the cosmic string, then she was stranded. Without the support of a living ecosystem, without supplies . . . she would die.

"If you're so worried about the Four Worlds," Satoshi asked, "why'd you lead us to them?"

"I'll explain that when I see you," Europa said. "May I visit? I'd like to talk to you face to face."

The terraformed, anomalously massive asteroid approached, changing its course without apparent effort, moving to draw *Starfarer* into orbit around it. Jenny turned the sail edge-on to the star, so the light pressure would not interfere with the gravitational attraction.

"A few days ago you couldn't wait to see the last of us. Why do you want to visit us now?"

"If you plan to chase Andro and me to the end of the universe, we have to come to some arrangement."

"Does anyone have any objections?" Victoria asked. Almost everyone on board would be listening to and watching the conversation.

The silence stretched out.

"I believe," Gerald Hemminge said, "that another conversation would be . . . an excellent idea."

"All right, then." Victoria did not, however, intend to let Gerald take over this encounter the way he had the last one. "Europa, you may bring your boat to *Starfarer.*"

Stephen Thomas struggled from his communications fugue. His brain felt bruised. He withdrew from Feral's temporary guest account, into the safety of his own permanent neural node.

Now he knew for certain that Feral's murder had been deliberate.

He was not certain he could prove it, not without subjecting someone else to the experience he had just been through. But he *was* certain it had happened.

Stephen Thomas was lucky. If he had matched Feral's profile better, if Arachne's unconscious memory of

the search and destroy routine had echoed stronger, he
would be dead.

Expecting pain, constriction, nausea, Stephen
Thomas took a deep breath, hesitated, and pushed himself to his feet.

His body responded. The aches had faded. His new
claws itched with potential. The sharp stab to his pelvis
had subsided and the awkward, embarrassing constric-
tions eased. He felt reborn: comfortable, powerful, exu-
berant.

Gingerly, apprehensively, he unfastened his pants
and let them slide down his hips.

He no longer looked like an ordinary man. Nor did
he look like a woman. His body had formed a neat
pouch enclosing his genitals. He looked like he was
wearing string bathing trunks, without the string. The
line of dark gold hair below his navel widened into a
sleek patch of thicker fur that tapered between his legs.

The new muscles responded to his thought. His penis, pink-gold and sensitive, probed beyond the opening
and slipped through the soft fur.

The pain, even the threat of pain, evaporated.

He was tempted—but he let the extending muscles
relax. When he tightened the retracting muscles, his penis slid back inside the pouch through the tantalizing
texture of his fur.

Stephen Thomas fastened his pants and glanced at
Arachne's display.

Astonished by too much information to take in all at
once, he forgot his own changes. A new star system.
Four inhabited planets. Technological civilizations.
And . . . Europa's boat approaching *Starfarer,* about
to dock. The alien humans had returned, and half the
alien contact department was not even there to meet
them. J.D. had an excuse—he checked quickly; she had
not caught up to *Starfarer.* Nemo's ship was nowhere to
be seen.

Stephen Thomas hurried from his office.

Victoria's going to kill me for being late, he thought.

And if I tell her I was late because I was in the web pretending to be Feral . . . she'll kill me twice.

Out of habit, he glanced at the DNA sequencer as he headed out of the lab. It had finished working. He expected these results to be as confusing as all the others.

He stopped short.

All the conflicting results between the bacteria from alien, human, and alien human environments suddenly came clear to him.

The test samples were normal.

But the recent samples from *Starfarer,* the bacteria Stephen Thomas had used as a control, had changed. They had been contaminated.

Stephen Thomas flung his presence through Arachne and into the waiting room of the boat dock. Arachne created an image of the waiting room around him. He was standing, but everyone else was floating in zero g. Vertigo spun the image before him for a moment: it spun, but it did not move. He felt drunk.

The pressure equalized between *Starfarer* and Europa's boat; the hatch opened.

"Don't let them in!" Stephen Thomas exclaimed.

Europa floated into *Starfarer.* Androgeos followed, his pleated red kilt flowing around his legs. Gerald Hemminge shook their hands in greeting. Europa's meerkats bounced in after her.

"Oh, *shit!*" Stephen Thomas said.

"What a charming welcome, Stephen Thomas," Europa said. "How nice to see you again, too, and when did you get so tan?"

"You contaminated us!" Stephen Thomas said.

Everyone stared at him.

"Contaminated—?" Victoria said. "But we tested—"

Stephen Thomas ran his hands through his hair, pushing it out of his face; it had come loose again. The swimming webs smoothed the strands behind his ears.

"Are you an ichthyocentaur, too?" Europa asked, surprised. "Why didn't I notice before?"

"The *Chi* came back clean," Stephen Thomas said.
"But . . . I'm coming up there." Stephen Thomas
withdrew his image from the waiting room.

Splashing through the muddy spots, wading across a
bridge inundated by an overflowing creek, he strode
down the path that led to *Starfarer*'s end. He started to
run, letting his anger at Europa—and his pleasure in his
body—fuel his speed.

By the time Stephen Thomas reached the waiting room,
floating in to join the visual cacophony of people, real
and virtual, the atmosphere quivered with tension. The
meerkats hovered together, each in sentry position.

"Explain yourself, Stephen Thomas," Professor
Thanthavong said. He had never seen her so distraught.

"The bacteria have changed," Stephen Thomas said.
"The free-living, garden variety soil bacteria. Sometime
between now and the last time we took samples—"

"After the missile attack," Professor Thanthavong
said. "As a precaution. What do you mean, 'changed'?"

"Their DNA fingerprints are the same. That's what
confused me for so long."

Everyone except Professor Thanthavong and Europa looked confused.

"When DNA mutates, the print changes. It's almost
impossible to put in an alteration that *doesn't* change
the print." He glanced at Europa with grudging admiration. "Quite an accomplishment—to make so many
changes without changing the print. Clever. Subtle. Deliberate. Nothing showed up till I did a complete sequence."

"You shouldn't be angry," Europa said mildly. "I
gave you the traditional gift for new members of the
community."

"Some gift!" Stephen Thomas said.

"It protects your ecosystem!"

"It is unforgivable," Miensaem Thanthavong said.

"I would appreciate it," Victoria said, her voice soft

and tight, "if one of you would explain what you're talking about."

"They supercharged our bacteria," Stephen Thomas said.

Everybody looked at him like they thought he was crazy. We have too damn many specialists, he thought. I'll bet J.D. would know what I was talking about.

"So alien bacteria won't survive," he said.

"You should be grateful," Europa said. "You should pour wine to the gods for such a gift. We've solved a serious problem for you."

"You should have *told* us!" Professor Thanthavong said. "Asked us! How dare you introduce biological contaminants—!"

"The changed bacteria won't hurt you! They aren't any different from what you're used to, except that they're stronger. As long as they're in their own environment, alien autotrophs won't grow in their presence."

"Can we stop them?" Thanthavong asked.

"Of course not. That's the point."

"Your anger's normal," Androgeos said. He sounded disappointed in them all. "So *ordinary*. Can't you appreciate what we've done for you?"

"You've fixed it so we can't join the community—"

"You did that yourselves!"

"—and maybe we can't go home, either."

"Wait a minute." Infinity's image appeared, its background stars and the inspection web. "Andro's *right*. I wish Europeans had thought about the problem! Their diseases killed ninety percent of the people in the new world. . . . Europa and Androgeos didn't bring diseases. They brought prevention. Protection."

"I'm glad someone is sensible here," Androgeos said.

"We aren't monsters," Europa said. "We *exist* to help you join the community. Can't you give us a little help?"

"You should have *told* us," Thanthavong said stiffly. "Infinity may be right. *You* may be right. But you should have let us make the choice."

"I'm sorry." Europa sounded sincere.

"J.D.'s going to be really pissed off at you," Stephen Thomas said.

"I think you're all crazy!" Androgeos could restrain himself no longer. "You're objecting to bacteria, when your ship is infested with parasites! I *told* you to avoid the squidmoths."

"Parasites?" Stephen Thomas said. "What parasites?"

"The squidmoth egg," Androgeos said.

Victoria nudged Stephen Thomas and gestured toward the small exterior display.

"Christ in a clutch," Stephen Thomas muttered. The thing bulged, moved, nestled deeper into its rocky cradle.

"The squidmoths don't even bother to raise their children," Europa said. "You'll have a job prying it loose."

"Maybe you'll be lucky," Androgeos said, "and it'll die."

"I don't think so," Infinity said. "It's already changing. It's growing, and it's, I don't know, putting *feelers* down into the rock."

"Oh, great."

"We aren't in any danger yet," Infinity said quickly. "It's only half a meter down, and there's nothing vital anywhere near."

"You should destroy it," Androgeos said confidently.

"No," Victoria said. "Zev was right. J.D. will never forgive us if we destroy it." At least part of her urge to protect it was because Androgeos wanted to be rid of it. "What will happen if we leave it?"

"As you see . . ." Andro gestured toward the image.

In the cross-section, mycelia from the egg case extended another handsbreadth into the substance of the wild side's shell.

"Ultimately, I mean. How big will it get?"

Andro shrugged. "Who knows? We have other things to do than follow the life cycle of a squidmoth."

"I want to talk about this," Europa said.

She reached into a deep pocket in her skirt, and drew out an age-mottled jawbone with unsettling proportions. It had lost all its teeth, except a single sharp fang.

"The art project," Gerald Hemminge said.

Europa gazed at Gerald fondly. "Your intelligence gives me hope for our species. Until I inspected the fossil myself, I was inclined to believe in the art project. Clever of you to disguise it so openly." She smiled at Stephen Thomas. "Rather like the bacteria. But this bone is real, it's very old, and it's of critical importance to Civilization. I must see where it came from."

Gerald started to say something. Stephen Thomas interrupted him.

"Why?"

"I believe you've found a clue to the other ones," Europa said. "The ones who came before us, and disappeared, except for their starships . . . and their control of the cosmic string."

"Good god," Stephen Thomas said, and thought: *Now* what?

"If you'll follow me," Gerald Hemminge said, "I'll take you to the . . . the fossil bed."

On the path to the riverbank, Europa quickened her step. She allowed herself to look like a person well advanced in years, but she had the energy of a teenager. Her meerkats followed her, pacing at her heels or scampering to the top of a hummock to make a quick scan for predators.

Victoria had to lengthen her stride to keep up.

"What do you expect to learn from the fossil bed?" Victoria asked Europa. She chose her words with care.

"I expect nothing," Europa said. "I *hope* . . . for some clue to their origin."

"If we found where they came from," Androgeos said, "we might discover how they control the cosmic string."

Victoria glanced at Stephen Thomas. He rolled his eyes. Victoria was glad the fossil bed *was* a fake; no matter what else happened, it would never lead Andro to a source of great power.

"And we might overcome the effects of the squid-moths' greed," Andro said.

"The squidmoths!" Victoria said. "Why do you hate them so much? They didn't seem greedy to me—quite the opposite."

Victoria found herself on the side of the squidmoths. Europa and Androgeos respected Victoria because they believed she was descended from the Pharaohs, as they claimed to be. But she was descended from escaped slaves, and her family history included stories of abuse and discrimination, not worship and power.

"We don't hate them!" Europa said. "But . . . they're an old species. Just because they've been around longer than the rest of us, they inherited the possessions of the other ones, the earlier star travelers."

Satoshi frowned. "What possessions? The squid-moths aren't dragons, sitting on a pile of gold! We met one of the beings, we talked to it. We saw how it lived. If an earlier culture left it everything they owned . . . they must have been Spartans."

"They left their *starships,*" Europa said. She watched Victoria's reaction, and Satoshi's. "You understand. The squidmoths inhabit the other ones' starships. Civilization is left as scavengers. We're dependent on their cast-offs."

"Some squidmoths never travel to another star," Androgeos said. "They could live on any piece of rock." He flicked his fingers toward the image of *Starfarer's* wild side. "And obviously some of them aren't particular."

"They never use the ships to their potential. And they won't sell! There's nothing they want!"

"Then how do you get any of them?"

"We scavenge."

"*Salvage,*" Androgeos said.

"Sometimes you find the ships abandoned," Europa said. "Maybe the squidmoths die. Who knows?"

"If you're lucky enough to be in the right place at the right time . . ." The face of the beautiful youth took on a predatory look. Androgeos grinned suddenly, showing his teeth. "Every time we returned to Tau Ceti, we hoped that starship might be empty. It would have made our fortunes."

What will this mean for J.D.? Victoria wondered suddenly, worried all over again for her friend. What if someone else was lurking, hoping to steal Nemo's ship . . . and J.D. was in the way?

"You've already got one starship," Satoshi said. "What do you need another for?"

Androgeos glanced at him, annoyed. Satoshi always asked the alien human questions he preferred not to answer.

"It isn't a matter of needing it," Europa said quickly. "As Andro said, a starship is valuable. If the opportunity comes up . . . Why shouldn't we take it?"

Europa glanced at Victoria and chuckled softly.

"Ah, Victoria, my dear, you have such a low opinion of us. We got off to a poor start, and now you wonder if these ancient Minoans don't wait for a ship to be empty. Perhaps we're really pirates."

"The possibility . . . crossed my mind."

"Too bad we can't be," Androgeos said. "We'd be a lot richer."

"Good lord, what else do you need?" Satoshi exclaimed. "You have a starship, a whole world of your own, complete freedom—!"

"One likes to have respect, as well," Europa said. "So far, you haven't helped our position in the community." She glanced at the fossil bone in her hand; she stroked the fang with her index finger.

"*Are* you pirates?" Zev asked curiously.

Europa laughed. "No, young Zev, my ichthyo-centaur. We're civilized people, we don't murder each other for possessions. Besides, the squidmoths are far from defenseless. They want you to think they're harmless voyeurs. But in their own way, they're quite powerful."

"And deceitful and selfish," Androgeos said.

"Look who's talking," Stephen Thomas muttered.

Androgeos glared at Stephen Thomas, but Europa smiled at him benignly. "There are stories, old, old, stories, of people with . . . fewer ethics than our company here, who pursued squidmoths through transition, hunting them for their ships. The squidmoths were seen again. The hunters were not."

They reached the canyon, where the path plunged down to the river bank.

Crimson Ng sat alone on the canyon edge, gazing into the current.

The river had flooded. Dirty brown water rushed and raced past the cliff. It riffled past the rough rock, showering everyone with muddy spray.

On the other side, a section of cliff collapsed into the water. The wild current snatched the shattered stone downstream, then dragged it beneath the surface.

The tremendous sound of floodwater possessed a pressure all its own, a low, dangerous roar with a counterpoint of boulder percussion rising from the bottom of the river.

The current was often strong enough to move the fist-sized rocks that formed its bed and beaches. Walking beside the river, Victoria liked to listen to the click and roll of stones in water. But now the river was changing its contours to the background of a kettledrum symphony.

When the water finally fell, the rapids and the pools would all be changed. And so would the riverbank, where the fossils lay.

Europa stared into the water. Stricken, she glanced at Crimson.

"We've had some bad weather," Crimson said calmly.

"But the fossils—! The other ones—!"

"It all washed downstream," Crimson said. "We'll have to do salvage archaeology."

· · ·

Europa sat disconsolately on the riverbank beside Crimson. Crimson gestured down into the muddy water where the fossils had lain, describing what she had seen but not yet excavated. Androgeos kicked the rocky edge of the cliff, as if he might uncover another fossil bed. Professor Thanthavong spoke quietly and urgently with Stephen Thomas. Satoshi and Victoria stood together, with Zev nearby. Gerald hovered near Crimson and Europa, no longer trying to maintain that the fossils were an art project. The meerkats foraged on the bank, sending up sprays of wet dirt as they dug for insects. One of them climbed to the top of a bush, chittering when a branch sprayed it with collected raindrops.

"I don't believe this," Satoshi said softly.

Victoria covered her face with her hands, afraid she would start laughing.

An image coruscated around them: the rainbow edge of a transition spectrum. When it faded, Arachne projected the sight of Nemo's ship plunging into the star system.

"J.D.!" Zev was the first to welcome her. He whistled softly, a descending cascade of notes. He grimaced. "It doesn't sound right, in the air."

The gravity of Europa's ship had pulled *Starfarer* aside; the starcraft were in no danger of colliding. Victoria felt a rush of joy, unalloyed by fear.

"Are you okay?" Victoria asked. "That *is* you—?"

They waited impatiently through the instant's time-lag.

J.D.'s image appeared

"I'm here, Zev. I understood what you said. Me, too. Hi, Victoria."

"I'm so glad you're all right. What . . . what about Nemo?"

"Nemo's dead."

"J.D. . . . . I'm so sorry." Victoria wished she were near enough to hug her friend.

"It's strange. . . . I'm sad, but I—is that Europa with you?"

"Hello, J.D.," Europa said. "You've lost a friend? I'm sorry."

"Thank you," J.D. said.

"How did you persuade the squidmoth to bring you here?" Europa asked.

"I didn't. The squidmoth—Nemo—died."

Androgeos swung around from the riverbank, his kilt swinging around his powerful legs. His feet were muddy to the ankles.

"I claim salvage!" he shouted.

"Salvage?" J.D. said. "What are you talking about?"

"The ship's abandoned. I claim salvage."

"My *friend* died and left the ship to me," J.D. said coldly. "It is *not* abandoned."

"Don't be selfish!" Androgeos pleaded. "It's useless to you."

His usual tone of disdain vanished in his desperation; he spoke in the same tone as when he begged Victoria to give him her new algorithm.

"I'll come over and pith it, so we can harness it," he said. "Otherwise the Four Worlds will send out a salvage crew. What good can it do you? You have to go back to Earth!"

"If I have to go back to Earth," J.D. said, "I'll take Nemo's ship with me."

"And just how do you propose to do that? Tow it with your pathetic sail?"

The sailhouse trembled. A touch to Arachne showed that Europa's ship was moving again, curving its path in such a way as to fling *Starfarer* none too gently out of orbit.

"Hey, be careful!" Infinity said.

"Why should I?" Androgeos snarled. "You don't care enough about your ship to keep it clean of squidmoth spawn!"

J.D. looked confused. Victoria forwarded the silver slug's transmission to the *Chi,* so J.D. could see it.

"We don't quite know what to do about it."

J.D.'s smile was radiant. "Don't do anything! Victoria, please—Nemo's other children are stranded back at Sirius."

"Don't worry. We won't hurt it."

"Prepare to receive me," Androgeos said to J.D.

"If you try to land here," J.D. said, deadly serious, "I'll spin you off into space, and you can *walk* home!"

Androgeos laughed. "It's easy to make threats. Not so easy to carry them out."

"Andro," Europa said slowly, "you are the one making empty threats. J.D. has learned squidmoth tactics already. Look."

"She can't—" Androgeos fell silent.

Slowly, deliberately, Nemo's starship began to rotate.

J.D. gave Nemo's shell a gentle spin. It was more than a demonstration to Androgeos; it was a first stage in terraforming. Rotation would gradually even out the temperature extremes that Nemo had preferred, frozen darkness giving way abruptly to a star's searing radiation.

J.D. moved the shell gently toward *Starfarer*. The transmission lag shortened to imperceptibility. She stayed distant, to moderate the gravitational stresses. Europa's craft had shaken *Starfarer* more than enough for one day.

Androgeos and Europa remained uncharacteristically silent. J.D. watched their images, amused by their surprise.

So you *can* still be surprised, even after four thousand years, she thought. That's some comfort.

Androgeos composed himself. When he spoke, he replaced his querulous tone with one of friendly, helpful persuasion.

"J.D.," Andro said, "Europa and I know how to refit an abandoned ship so you can navigate it."

"Don't beg, Andro," Europa said.

"But we could be partners—"

"Listen to her! Look at it! She controls it, Andro!"

J.D. turned toward Victoria. "Thank you," she said, without mentioning the transition algorithm aloud. Europa and Androgeos saw Nemo's shell as a valuable prize. No telling what they might do if they knew it possessed Victoria's transition algorithm as well.

"I'm so glad to see you," Zev said. "When can you come home?"

"I don't know," J.D. said. "All things considered . . . I don't think I'd better leave Nemo's ship just yet."

"It's your ship now," Zev said. *"Nautilus."*

Nautilus, J.D. thought. Of course. How could it be anything but *Nautilus*? She grinned at Zev.

"It's a relief to have you back," Victoria said. "I had second thoughts about leaving you behind as soon as it was too late. . . ." She said less than she might have, if Europa were not listening.

They had all become secretive around the alien humans. That troubled J.D., but she refused to let her concern overcome her excitement: Her first successful flight of *Nautilus,* the discovery of the last egg case, and a system of inhabited planets . . .

"I've had a pretty amazing time over here," J.D. said. "I'm looking forward to telling you all about it."

She wondered how long *Starfarer* could safely stay in the system, and whether the cosmic string would flee from her as well. She touched the knowledge surface—

"Victoria . . . the cosmic string is staying stable!"

Twice before, the cosmic string had begun to withdraw as soon as *Starfarer* entered a star system. This time, it remained steady. Excited conversation burst up around her.

"But how do you know?" Victoria asked, amazed. "Arachne's still surveying—"

"From *Nautilus*," J.D. said.

Victoria's eyelids flickered closed, then open, as she touched her link to the computer web. "I think you're right. . . ."

"Are we forgiven?" J.D. asked Europa. "Is this our second chance?"

"I . . . I don't know." Europa sounded shaken and confused. "This is . . . very unusual."

J.D. picked out the two predominant strands of discussion among her colleagues:

We can go home now.

Now we can stay.

"You had better follow us," Europa said. "To meet representatives of the Four Worlds. We have a great deal to talk about."

J.D. smiled, trying not to burst into tears.

"I'm sure that's true," J.D. said. "But you'll have to wait while we all discuss what to do next."

J.D. glanced at the members of the deep space expedition: Victoria and Satoshi and Stephen Thomas, Infinity and Esther, Crimson and Jenny, Chandra and Florrie Brown and Avvaiyar, Professor Thanthavong and Nikolai Petrovich and Griffith, Fox and Mitch and Lehua and Bay, Senator Derjaguin and Senator Orazio and Gerald Hemminge.

And finally, Zev. She ached for him to be with her. Their gazes touched.

"I'm sorry about Nemo," Zev said. "But I want to tell you properly."

"I want that, too," she said.

She imagined an ocean, a small ocean with mysterious depths, a place where she and Zev could talk together in the language of the divers, the language of true speech.

About the Author

VONDA N. MCINTYRE has been writing and publishing science fiction since she was 20. Her novels include **Dreamsnake** (winner of the Hugo Award, presented at the World Science Fiction Convention, and the Nebula Award, presented by the Science Fiction Writers of America), **The Exile Waiting,** and **Superluminal.** She has written one children's book, **Barbary.** Her books and short stories have been translated into more than a dozen languages. The *Starfarers* series includes the national bestsellers **Starfarers, Transition, Metaphase** and **Nautilus,** a series that has the distinction of having had a fan club before the first novel was even written. She is also the author of Bantam's next *Star Wars* novel, **The Crystal Star.**

"The most important series in science fiction"* concludes in the spectacular final chapter of the *Starfarers* saga!

NAUTILUS
by Vonda N. McIntyre

The *Starfarer* had traveled farther than any human expedition in Earth history, only to encounter alien beings and a galactic civilization stranger than they ever could have imagined. Now, as the galactic string that is the ship's only means to travel back to Earth recedes from its reach, the crew must make the choice between withholding the one secret that could ensure its survival and its entrance into Civilization, or turn back before they're trapped forever, far from home in the company of a society ready to turn on them at a moment's notice!

❑ **Nautilus** (56026-3 * $5.99/$7.99 Canada)

Don't miss the first three books in the *Starfarers* saga:
❑ **Starfarers** (56341-6 * $5.99/$7.50 Canada)
❑ **Metaphase** (29223-4 * $5.99/$7.50 Canada)
❑ **Transition** (28850-4 * $5.99/$7.50 Canada)

And be sure to look for Vonda N. McIntyre's Hugo and Nebula Award-winning novel of one young healer's quest to replace the alien snake with healing powers so vital to her life and her people.
❑ **Dreamsnake** (29659-0 * $5.99/$7.50 Canada)

*Ursula K. LeGuin

Look for all of Vonda N. McIntyre's science fiction, on sale now wherever Bantam Spectra Books are sold, or use this page for ordering:

Send to: Bantam Books, Dept. SF 253
            2451 S. Wolf Road
            Des Plaines, IL 60018

Please send me the items I have checked above. I am enclosing $_____ (please add $2.50 to cover postage and handling). Send check or money order, no cash or C.O.D.'s, please.

Mr./Ms._____

Address_____

City/State_____ Zip_____

Please allow four to six weeks for delivery.
Prices and availability subject to change without notice.   SF 253 10/94

Enter the dazzling science fiction worlds of

DAVID BRIN

"The most popular...author of hard SF to appear in the 1980s...David Brin gives joy and imparts a sense of wonder."
—*The Encyclopedia of Science Fiction*

❏ **Otherness** (29528-4 * $5.99/$7.99 Canada) A brand new collection of short fiction and nonfiction of the near and distant future, featuring "Dr. Pak's Preschool," "NatuLife," and "Bubbles."

❏ **Glory Season** (56767-5 * $5.99/$6.99 Canada) The coming-of-age of one young woman as she wanders her distant planet and meets a traveler who threatens the delicate social balance of her homeworld.

❏ **Earth** (29024-X * $5.99/$6.99 Canada) An epic novel of an Earth on the edge of destruction when a black hole falls to the planet's core. "A powerful, cautionary tale."—*San Francisco Chronicle*

❏ **The Postman** (27874-6 * $5.99/$7.99 Canada) The story of a man wandering a post-Holocaust America carrying the dream of reconstruction in the tattered jacket of a long-dead postman.

❏ **Heart of the Comet** (25839-7 * $5.99/$7.99 Canada) A daring expedition to the heart of Halley's Comet, co-written with Nebula Award-winner Gregory Benford.

❏ **The Practice Effect** (26981-X * $5.99/$7.99 Canada) When a scientist steps into an alternate reality where familiar physics no longer apply, he finds himself hailed as a wizard facing a battle with a mysterious warlord.

❏ **The River of Time** (26281-5 * $5.99/$7.99 Canada) Brin's first collection of short fiction, including his Hugo Award-winning "The Crystal Spheres."

❏ **Startide Rising** (27418-X * $5.99/$6.99 Canada) The Hugo and Nebula Award-winning classic of the search for the Progenitors, the First Race who seeded intelligence throughout the stars.

Look for all of these titles, on sale now wherever Bantam Spectra books are sold, or use this page for ordering.

Send to: Bantam Books, Dept. SF 248
2451 S. Wolf Road
Des Plaines, IL 60018

Please send me the items I have checked above. I am enclosing $_____ (please add $2.50 to cover postage and handling). Send check or money order, no cash or C.O.D.'s, please.

Mr./Ms._____

Address_____

City/State_____Zip_____
Please allow four to six weeks for delivery.
Prices and availability subject to change without notice.   SF 248 10/94

ARTHUR C. CLARKE

THE HAMMER
of
GOD

It is the year 2110, and although many of Earth's age-old problems have been addressed, only one now commands the attention of the entire world: the approach of an asteroid that hurtles toward the planet, threatening the end of civilization as we know it. Astronomers and astronauts christen the rock Kali, after the Hindu goddess of death and destruction. As Kali barrels through space, Captain Robert Singh and the crew of the Goliath are charged with turning Kali from her terrible course. From their quiet assignment near Jupiter, they are thrust into the center of a race against time to find a way to save Earth from being smashed by the hammer of God.

The Hammer of God is on sale now in hardcover wherever Bantam Spectra books are sold, or you can use this page for ordering:
❏ The Hammer of God (09557-9 * $19.95/$24.95 Canada)
Send to: Bantam Books, Dept. SF 205
           2451 S. Wolf Road
           Des Plaines, IL 60018
Please send me the items I have checked above. I am enclosing
$_____ (please add $2.50 to cover postage and handling). Send check or money order, no cash or C.O.D.'s, please.

Mr./Ms._____

Address_____

City/State_____Zip_____
Please allow four to six weeks for delivery.
Prices and availability subject to change without notice.   SF 205 9/93